Head Lion

Head Lion

Neil Peter Christy

Head Lion is a work of fiction. Names, characters, places, and incidents are the products of the author's imagination or are used fictitiously. Any resemblance to actual events, locales, or persons, living or dead, is entirely coincidental.

Copyright © 2022 Neil Peter Christy

All rights reserved. No part of this publication may be reproduced, distributed, or transmitted in any form or by any means, including photocopying, recording, digital scanning, or other electronic or mechanical methods, without the prior written permission of the publisher except in the case of brief quotations embodied in critical reviews and certain other noncommercial uses permitted by copyright law. For permission requests, please address Neil Peter Christy.

Published 2022
Print ISBN: 979-8-9863321-0-9
E-ISBN: 979-8-9863321-1-6

For information, visit www.neilpeterchristy.com
All company and/or product names may be trade names, logos, trademarks, and/or registered trademarks and are the property of their respective owners.

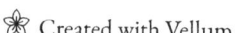 Created with Vellum

To God.
To the shoulders that lift me,
my mother Dulcie, my wife Sabrina, and my
sisters Charmaine and Nina.

To the arms that are my strength,
my children Chanel, Cy, Nia, and Jeremiah.

Head Lion

Red Bull gives you wiiings.

Prologue

Thud! the sound was deafening. It was unlike any she had ever heard before. It was profoundly immoral and unholy. It kept playing in her head over and over again. The sound froze her movement and nestled in her mind as if it had found its home.

She wasn't blinking; she wasn't moving; she wasn't even breathing. She was only trying to make sense of what had just happened. A ghastly sight accompanied the ungodly sound, an unholy pair made for each other. A body had just fallen.

She knew it was from the penthouse forty stories above. She recognized the emblazoned "HR" on the silk slippers that landed a few feet away from her. Even the slippers seemed crouched as if scared of the disfigured body sprawled on the pavement.

A splash of warm blood had hit her face, synchronized with the sound she heard. The blood wasn't just on her face but also the child's face clinging to her waist.

Her firm black hand clasped the child's tiny white hands even more tightly. She immediately covered the eyes of the shocked girl and picked her up in her arms. Her chubby warm palm covered the white girl's entire face, not just the eyes. She hurried inside the building toward the elevator. The personal elevator that opened to their penthouse was just around the corner.

For the last five years, the maid had taken the girl for walks, and for the last five years, she knew where the elevator was when she got back. Not today!

"Ding!" the sound muffled the "Thud" echoing in her mind. It reminded her where the elevator was. The world outside her seemed silent. The screams, the cries, the shrieks were no longer audible, they had become visible, as if someone had muted the sound on the picture. All she could hear was the "Thud" echoing in her mind. The maid rushed inside the elevator and let the girl slide down from her large bulky arms.

She pressed the penthouse button, hoping the elevator would go up as slowly as possible. Ignorance, she felt, was better than confronting the truth. The doors slid shut, and the elevator moved upwards. The maid finally felt safe in the confines of the cubicle and looked at the girl.

The little girl was speechless, and her head was tilted upwards, staring at the maid. She was trying to make sense of everything happening around her. Her blonde hair was drenched in red blood dripping on the shining floor of the elevator. The girl's face was covered in uneven splashes as if someone had splattered red paint across her face.

The little girl stared at her maid like a frightened caged animal looking at the visitors across the glass. The maid looked at her distorted reflection and realized why. The blood also covered her own face. She gazed down and looked at her plain dress that now seemed patterned. Tiny red and white pieces adorned the fresh stains of blood.

The bewildered maid looked down on her dress and picked up a small lump. She managed not to throw up the moment she realized it was her employer scattered across her dark grey dress.

The maid quickly took off her scarf, covering her large frame. She wiped her face, then the girl's face, and then her hair. She kept on repeating the ritual, even though it was hardly making any difference.

"Ding!" slowly the maid stepped out, grasping the girl's hand, which now seemed tinier than before. Sweat poured down her body. She could feel the silence staring at her as she walked in. She hoped to see Mr. Raymond sitting on his favorite club chair, sipping his Martini.

She had planned the entire week to ask for a raise and quit if Mr. Raymond refused. He had hardly paid her salary in the last few months, giving part payments. She knew he was going through a rough patch. She had seen the letters from his creditors and the overdue utility bills. She started to feel guilty. *I can manage for a few weeks,* she thought.

The maid walked slowly toward the door; her feet felt heavier. She was now oblivious to everything except the silence in the hallway. The deafening silence was mocking her. She knocked on the door even though she never did; she had the keys. She was hoping Mr. Raymond would open the door, and everything going through her mind would stop. She would have a glass of water, have a warm shower, and talk to Mr. Raymond about her salary. "I'm just being ungrateful," she said to herself.

She knocked again, a few extra knocks, a little louder than before. Still no answer. She clutched the handle with her left hand and turned it clockwise. She entered the house, tightly grasping the child's tiny hand that was turning blue. She realized that the worst-case scenario was an empty lounge. The best case would be Mr. Raymond scolding her for being late.

It was the first time she was praying for a reprimand. An

apartment with no one inside would validate her worst nightmare. Her eyes had seen everything, but her mind was unwilling to believe. She was holding on to that tiny glimmer of hope that Mr. Raymond was alive, and all this was just a nightmare she was going to wake up from in a few minutes.

The maid entered the luxurious penthouse. Everything seemed normal except for the oval mirror above the console table. The large mirror encased in wrought iron was one of the most insignificant objects in the house. Today she noticed the mirror and the ornate metal that held it on the wall. She recognized the writing as she read the three words written in capital letters. *"I AM SORRY!!!"*

She put her hand across the little girl's shoulder, pulling her closer to her large frame. The girl almost disappeared in her faded cotton dress. The embrace lasted a few seconds as she stared at the writing. She knew what it meant. She finally saw her face as the focus tilted toward what was behind the writing. She could feel the liquid on her face and taste its saltiness in her mouth. She ran and threw up in the kitchen sink.

She needed a shower, and so did the little girl. She led the little girl to the bathroom, took off the girl's clothes, and turned on the hot shower. She decided first to bathe the girl. She soaped and washed the little girl under the hot shower, drenching herself with the splashing water. Her clothes were now soaked in water as she wrapped a large towel around the little girl and brought her out. The tiles were still red as the pressure from the shower pounded on the floor, diluting the color.

She dried the little girl, helped her get into clean clothes, and took her to the living room. She brought a warm glass of milk and finally said her first words.

"Have the milk, watch some TV. I'll shower in five minutes."

She walked toward the phone in the kitchen, turned back, and saw the girl settling in and drinking the milk. She called the police.

She gave her version, not even sure if it was true. Mr. Raymond had jumped from the penthouse. Her mind pictured him falling as she told the police what had happened. She could hear the "Thud" again in her mind, and a cold shiver ran down her spine. The police told her to stay at the apartment as they had a few questions.

The maid took off her clothes; they felt heavy. She turned on the shower, keeping the temperature higher than usual. It was the first time she had showered in Mr. Raymond's house, and it felt strange. The luxurious shower, the bright lights, the tiled floor, and the scent of lavender was a far cry from her small and dingy bathroom. Just the shower cubicle was bigger than her bedroom.

The maid looked down as she vigorously soaped herself. The tiled floor turned red again as the shower scraped off the blood that embraced her. The hot water felt good, like a warm hug, almost telling her that things would be fine. She didn't want to be afraid anymore. After all, she hadn't done anything wrong. She wondered what would happen to the girl. The girl's parents had died a few months after she was born. The girl had no one except her grandfather.

The hot shower enticed her to stay a little longer. Loud banging on the door interrupted her thoughts. The cops were here. She forced herself out of the shower. She was now desperate to get back home and put all this drama behind her. She missed her bed and her two sons. She dried herself and found a dry bathrobe in the closet. The knocking stopped, and the house fell silent again.

She walked out, thinking about what to do next, until she heard the sounds that defied the silence in the apartment. The sounds felt strange and out of place. The peculiar voices echoing from the TV room became recognizable. She picked up her pace, walked into the lounge, and saw the little girl staring at the large TV. An old black and white film was flickering on the screen.

There was no other sound besides a man moaning in pleasure;

the picture was even more distressing. The film seemed to be shot on those vintage cameras and converted to video. She stared at the TV. It took her a few seconds to comprehend what was happening. A young man was having sex with an older man, and there was nothing gentle about it. She panicked, abruptly looking for the remote.

The little girl was tightly holding the remote. The maid sprang toward her and snatched the remote from her hands. She couldn't find the stop button and was pressing all the wrong ones, and the frustration was now making her cry. She froze, screaming in anger. Then she felt the little girl's hand on the remote as she pressed the pause button. She wiped her tears, her eyes focused. It was Mr. Raymond. The little girl's grandfather. She gasped. Her legs weakened, her hands trembled, her fingers loosened up.

The remote slipped out of her grip and fell on the tiled floor with a gentle "Thud!"

Chapter 1

I ♥ NY

(New York State Department of Economic Development, 1977)

Ryan had less than an hour. Fifty-two minutes to be exact, to fix the mediocre pitch that could make or break his life. He shouted in frustration as he stepped out on the sidewalk. Only one pedestrian stared at him. The rest of the thousand behaved as any New Yorker would. They ignored him and kept walking.

The immense frustration was not because the pitch was mediocre or because a lot was riding on it. It was because Ryan couldn't come up with a winning idea, and that had never happened before.

His mind was distracted, swinging between thoughts, from the most banal to the most bizarre, from buying a dishwasher that broke down a day earlier to figuring out a convenient day to kill himself. His mind had declared a coup d'é·tat, and it was a battle he was losing. The autumn in his life was waking up and stretching out. He felt like October. The month that stood alone from the rest of the eleven, especially in New York.

October, and you knew winter was here. You knew life would be slow. The leaves would fall. Scotch would become more tempting, and women would be lonelier than ever before, especially in New

York. The city had a surreal effect on people. It made you invisible. Everyone was oblivious to everyone. *It was me, myself, and I,* he reminded himself, again losing sight of the crucial pitch due in less than an hour.

Walking through the maze of high rises, Ryan Walker smiled, mocking his memories. He swayed through the fast-paced New Yorkers, walking heedlessly like zombies on steroids. He knew he would get into trouble if he bumped into someone. He had no time to apologize. Ryan tugged at his tie almost violently. He hated to dress up formally. He could feel the sweat building up in his armpits, soiling his wrinkle-free new shirt.

Think, think, think he scolded his mind three times, like a teacher reprimanding the class brat three times. Oddly, he lived most of his life in threes. He drank three cups of coffee. He did coke three times in a day and not the drinking kind. He dated three different women every month. The women would always know about each other because he didn't lie. He hated lying, even though he worked in a profession that thrived on lies.

Professionally, he was a terrific liar. He had won many awards for lying, albeit the juries had a fancy name for it. They called it *"Excellence in advertising."* He knew it was lying with a bit of make-up. No, a tire wouldn't make you more lovable, a photocopier couldn't make you more intelligent, and a stapler would never make you sexy, he would tell his interns.

Advertising was like parents telling their kids hard work would solve all their problems. Of course, everyone knew that wasn't true. You needed to throw betrayal, treachery, and pushing someone off the proverbial cliff in the mix, the three secret elements that added to the rise of his spotless career.

Ryan had even thought of three ways not to kill himself. He didn't want to die with a rope hanging around his neck (too much work). He didn't want to jump out through his glamorous penthouse on the 55th floor (too much splatter). He didn't want to poison himself (too much time to change his mind if he panicked). It had to be creative. The news should not be that he killed himself but how he did it.

The only thing that was not in threes were the chapters in his life. He had just two: before and after his wife and two children died in an accident. The accident gnawed at him like a parasite eating him up from the inside. He carried the guilt with him wherever he went. The "What ifs" lurked behind him like his shadow, only disappearing in the night when he was asleep. What if he had missed the meeting and driven his daughter? The routine meeting was avoidable.

Even though Ryan hated his work, the reason why his life shattered into a million pieces, he immersed himself in it. Advertising became the ventilator that kept him alive. It was the only room his mind allowed him to enter to escape the guilt. His life was the only thing that had two chapters. Ryan didn't expect his life to have a third.

The coke helped. Ryan was aware snorting cocaine every day could kill him, and that was the reason he enjoyed it. He had discovered the most pleasurable way to end his life. It didn't affect his work. Since using cocaine, work was all he did, interspersed with sporadic bouts of meaningless affairs. As far as he was concerned, drugs were saving his life.

I need to change, he lied to himself. Every day, he thought of quitting coke. Every night he would give up quitting. Today was another quit-day, *not a good day to quit,* he thought. Even at 59, his willpower had the same schedule. It would wake up every morning with him and fall asleep as soon as he left the office. That was usually around midnight.

Think, think, goddammit think, he tried to compose his thoughts. Miamart was coming at ten. The agenda was the make-or-break pitch for Ryan and also the company he worked for, "Sun

Advertising." Miamart was Sun's biggest client, and was looking for a new agency for their new brand.

Ryan knew if another agency got their foot in the door, it would become easier for them to win the rest of the portfolio. Everyone at Sun jittered at the thought of losing their biggest client. It was not about money; it was about lots and lots of money.

He saw his reflection in the display windows as he walked by the bustling cafes of Manhattan. He noticed his salt and pepper hair becoming saltier. Maybe that was why it took longer for him to come up with a decent idea. He almost bumped into a brunette dressed in a maroon skirt and a low-cut beige top.

"Sorry," he muttered.

She smiled and kept walking in the other direction. Ryan had a feeling she was admiring him. He turned back, and a hard bump made him lose his balance. Almost instantly he fell, his back felt the sidewalk's cold surface, and his front felt the steaming hot coffee spilling on his new shirt. The man who bumped into him thrust a red envelope onto his chest. He was wearing a cheap suit and looked like a pastor of a failing church.

"You need to change. It's all in here." He thumped his heart and pointed toward Ryan's chest and started to walk away. Ryan grabbed his ankle and pulled himself up. Ryan's six feet frame still felt shorter than the tall pastor. He pushed his morning energy into his fist, pulled back his arm like an arrow, and smacked the pastor on his mouth.

"I don't believe in God, and neither should you!" Ryan shouted. He did not wait to see the young pastor react. He had no time to make the pastor apologize to him. Ryan took off his soiled jacket and started walking faster.

Ryan had no time to be nice to the pastor or anyone around him. The only people he was nice to were the ones who were beneficial to his cause. Today, he was thinking about them, even though this was the worst time to reminisce. His mind swung between the distant past and the present, like a teenager pushing the swing farther and farther away. Today, it felt his days as the most wanted creative director in New York were over.

Ryan knew the only person who would have disagreed would be his wife. She always teased him, *I can get bored of your Greek tan and your square jaw, but my love for your storytelling will last forever.*

He inherited the skin tone from his mother, a native American who fell for a white guy. She died the day he was born, and his father ensured he never forgot that. He mocked Ryan for another reason. Ryan was the only Irish in Boston who had black hair and an olive skin. He tried to calm himself and focus on the presentation. He hoped his special skills could save him one more time.

Ryan had a unique talent that separated him from the rest of the world. It was the one ability his peers enjoyed the most: his expertise to read minds. He was great at it. Everyone coaxed him to read someone whenever he was in a crowd. Some thought he was clairvoyant and called him 'Guru,' others called him 'Guru' for his mastery in advertising.

Reading people was the only good thing he'd inherited from his father. He despised that the gift that made him an advertising genius came from his father. The skill that separated him from his peers by getting him into the consumers' minds. Whether a three-month pregnant mom was looking for a cream to soothe her nipples or a metrosexual millennial was looking for the best perfume, he would always nail the unique insight.

Rumors had been rife that he was special. He didn't just let the rumors spread; he fanned them. The only extraordinary power he had was paying extraordinary attention to details.

He never told them that he was listening more intensely to what the body was saying than the words coming out of their mouths. He never revealed that it was the wavering eyes, the twitching fingers, the shifty hands, the toes curling, the itching forehead, and the homework he did earlier that helped him read their minds.

By the age of fifteen, Ryan had started reading people like they were comic books. His father inadvertently taught him the life-changing skill while playing cards. Poker also taught Ryan to pray. He would pray regularly in the mornings, giving God two options. Make his father win the game or make him die. He was fine with either because both ensured him not getting beaten up by his father.

The poker players his father played with gathered in dimly lit rooms behind cheap bars and hidden alleys without streetlights. The dreary rooms stank of tobacco and spit. The pictures of scantily clad women covered the stains on the walls. The music was loud, and so was the swearing.

The free moonshine ensured Ryan's father lost his week's salary in a day's sitting. The players ignored Ryan because that meant someone was there to drag his father home when he passed out. His father was a great player as long as he was sober. Then the drinks would take over the reins, and it got worse with time. Eventually, his father started passing out in the middle of the games.

The games lasted for hours. Ryan killed time by watching the players and learning the game. He had no other choice. He played his own little game in his head, predicting what a player would do next. He would stare at them for hours, watching their moves, their reactions, their expressions, and after some time, he could read what they would do next.

One night his father was breaking tradition and winning. He could barely hold his cards, passing out after every move. No one seemed happy seeing him win, except for Ryan. It meant he would get a hot breakfast with no thrashing on the side. The players would kick his father to wake him up when it was his turn. Ryan watched the players getting frustrated and cursing his father. Finally, the kicks stopped working. His father was not waking up. The players looked around, swearing at him.

"The hand is dealt, asshole." A player shouted in his father's ears while kicking him.

"Wake the motherfucker up!" another player who had lost his entire salary shouted, "Ask his fucking son to finish."

They looked at Ryan. He stared back, got up, and stood next to his father. He picked up his father's hand, awkwardly gathering the cards, and managed to whisper, "He's in!"

He lost the hand and continued to lose till he had a few dollars left. He shut his eyes as if saying a prayer. The players laughed, mocking his meditation. Finally, he opened his eyes and started reading the players while he played. The streak started. By five in the morning, he had cleaned up the table.

His father woke up at home and saw the pile of money on their three-legged dining table. He picked up Ryan in his arms and kissed him on the cheek. It was the first time his father had shown him any affection.

The games and the pattern continued. Reading people became an obsession. Ryan would stare at anyone around him and try to enter their minds. At the age of 13, Ryan was deconstructing everyone he met. The butcher, the waitress that brought him hot breakfast, the women his dad brought home. Everyone was a book he wanted to read. By 15, he would read people in minutes. He could tell their favorite color, the dish they ate yesterday, what they were planning to do next, and if they were lying. At age 17, he got tired of poker and his father. He ran away and never looked back.

Chapter 2

Think Different

(Apple, 1987)

Ryan couldn't stop thinking about his past. The pastor had triggered a nerve in him. He needed his mind-reading skills more than ever today. The same skill opened the doors for Ryan into the advertising industry almost two decades ago.

"You're fucking useless. You don't have any talent for this," the restaurant manager said.

"Well, dishwashing is one talent I'm not keen to be great at," Ryan said to the restaurant manager. It was his third day on the job, night to be exact.

"Then fuck off, do something you're passionate about and let's see if it pays your bills." Ryan stared at the manager's bulging belly, the white circle on his wedding finger that he desperately tried to hide, and the picture of his wife at the beach he discarded from his wallet in the morning.

"You know there are medicines that can spice up your sex life." Ryan teased him with his reading prowess, "The daily arguments would stop. She doesn't have to leave you."

The manager stared in disbelief. Ryan kept his eyes focused on the grimy dishes.

"Mark my words. You're a fucking loser and will always be one." The manager slurred. He had a penchant for late-night drinking.

"You need to cut down on the booze. She hates it when you come home drunk." Ryan teased him again with his reading skills.

"Who the fuck have you been talking to? Are you fucking my wife?"

Ryan was enjoying the torture, increasing the pressure on the tap.

"Well, let's just say the mole on her stomach turns me off."

"How do you know about the mole?" Before Ryan could answer that he saw it in the photograph the manager threw away, he felt the cutting knife blade in his back. His instant reaction was to swing the iron pan he was washing and smack the manager on his face. The manager dropped to the floor.

Being able to read people could sometimes be a curse. A few minutes later, he walked out of the diner, wiping the blood off his hands. The manager was probably dead. Ryan didn't want to be certain. He ran and covered the twenty-minute walk to the train station in seven minutes. A puzzled homeless man took the knife out of Ryan's back and tied a dirty cloth around his back. He jumped a train leaving for New York and picked up a newspaper to hide his face.

A small ad in the classified section of the newspaper caught his eye. Suddenly he knew what he wanted. An agency was looking for a junior copywriter. No experience or degree required.

Ryan had no idea what he wanted to do in his life. He had even dropped out of college because of this uncertainty. He moved from one job to another like a pinball. He tried his luck at everything that came his way. The only thing he liked doing was watching TV and complaining about how bad the advertising was. In his head, he had fixed almost all the ads he saw. This was a sign— Advertising in New York was his calling.

He reached New York early morning, giving him enough time to have a bath at a cheap hotel. Hours later, he walked into the agency carrying confidence on his shoulders instead of a resume in his hand. The creative director Stan Wilson stared at Ryan.

"Why do you want to be in advertising?" Stan asked.

"Because I hate advertising!" Ryan replied.

"Is this a joke?"

"No, I really do hate advertising. I can make it better."

"Let's see you put your ideas where your mouth is, smartass." Stan lashed out at him.

The test was to relaunch the new "Royal Regent Luxury Hotel" and reposition it.

"You can't gain it. You can't lose it," Stan said. "Either you have it in you, or you don't."

Stan had shortlisted five people for the test, all more qualified than him. Ryan tugged at his tie violently as he heard Stan say, "The Royal Regent, previously known as the Grand Hotel, is now—" Ryan zoned out and started reading Stan. Stan was looking for confidence, not talent. He was also extremely insecure and in love with a married woman, not his wife. Ryan suddenly knew what he had to do to get the job.

While others were scribbling notes, Ryan was working on his ideas. Stan finished his brief with an emphatic, "You have until evening." By that time, Ryan had come up with an entire campaign. Like a middle-schooler wishing to be the first to answer, he raised his notepad.

Stan took the pad from Ryan, tossed it across the table, and said the words Ryan never forgot.

"If any of you make it in advertising, which I sincerely doubt, remember one thing. Advertising is all about doing it right, not doing it fast. You get one chance to spend someone else's money. If you want to be a hero, go to Hollywood."

He was drunk when he got home that night. He was certain he had lost the will and the opportunity to make it in the ad industry. He entered his one-room apartment and found the note that someone slid through the door;

Ryan, if you haven't left for Hollywood, see Stan Wilson at ten in the morning.

Think, think, think, he jolted himself back to the present day as he finally reached the familiar sight of the Greek gods standing on marble pillars. The gods carved out of limestone embodied the soul of the 20-year-old Elysium Plaza.

Elysium played a big part in him saying yes to Sun. The brand was his brainchild, and he won his first Clio for Elysium. Ryan nailed his pitch in the first slide; *"In Greek mythology, Elysium is the paradise reserved for the gods, a place where they are conferred immortality."*

The unique campaign for real estate became the talk of the town from the moment the construction started. The massive advertising was based on Greek gods taking over New York. It became the gold standard, and the industry coronated Ryan as the undisputed king of real estate advertising.

"Hey, Good Morning, Mr. Ryan. Everything OK?" said the concerned doorman as Ryan walked inside.

"Good morning Harry. Long story, will tell you in the evening."

He furiously nudged his tie to fix the center of the knot and pressed the elevator button.

Ryan shuddered at the thought of meeting the CEO before the presentation. Gabriel Todd Christopher was a tough boss. Todd was an older man who carried a frail body with the most vigorous mind Ryan had ever seen. The only memorable thing about him was a deep scar shaped like an exclamation mark on his forehead and how he treated the world around him.

Ryan had heard the story behind the scar a million times. "Money is god" was how Todd would always begin telling it. The words his millionaire father, an immigrant from Poland, said to him when he broke an antique vase.

Ryan wished the elevator moved faster as more people walked in on every floor. The headquarter of Sun advertising was on the 40th floor. It included many of the companies owned by the Sun group. But advertising was the founder's first and last love. The founder sat in a corner room on the 40th floor. He watched the world like a hawk from his large window.

The marketing and advertising world loathed the man behind Sun, but they all wanted to work with him. He was like the annual flu shot they could not avoid. His questionable methods and his unending appetite for more business had turned many people against him.

Most of the employees loved Todd. Ironically, he knew the names of less than ten employees. He had one favorite, Ryan. He showered Ryan with love, in cash and kind. Among other perks, he gave Ryan the option to get a new car every year; the agency was paying his mortgage. There was no limit to his vacation days, and Ryan even had unfettered access to Todd's home.

Finally, the elevator bell dinged and broke into Ryan's thoughts.

"Good morning, Guru. What happened to you?" It was Patricia, Todd's secretary. Ryan threw his jacket in the trash bin.

"Long story Patty." Ryan tried to get away.

"The boss is looking for you." Patricia blocked his way.

"I'll be there in a bit."

"That's what you said yesterday. You know he's rude to me when you don't show up. He wants you now!" Ryan reluctantly walked with her toward Todd's room.

Meetings with Todd were usually a waste of time, and he had no time to pretend that he was interested in it. Todd always followed a pattern: updates on work, unnecessary suggestions for improvement, politically incorrect jokes, end of the meeting. Ryan had no time for dumb charades.

"What the fuck happened to you, Guru? Looks like Miamart fucked you before you could fuck them." Todd smiled, which was rare in the mornings. The only thing that made him smile before noon was the smell of fresh business.

"Long story boss." Ryan wanted the meeting to be short. Ryan had a million reasons to hate Todd, but the one reason he loved Todd was his generosity. Over 200 students from Brooklyn were able to afford college because of Todd. Todd donated millions to charities every year. All his philanthropy was kept confidential.

"Tell me who did this to you, and I'll take care of him." Ryan knew he would, and Ryan chose only to see the good Todd. But like anyone else, Todd had a darker side too. He controlled the media industry through the massive budgets he had at his disposal. There was only one thing he couldn't control: his anger. It was ferocious. There were rumors he had paid off many employees and made them sign NDAs after physically abusing them.

"Come sit. I have something important to discuss," Todd said.

"Boss, can we do this later? Miamart is coming in less than an hour and—"

"Fuck Miamart," Todd interrupted in an unusually calm voice, "You need to take a break. Let your fucking minions handle it."

There was one more strange thing about Todd. Ryan could never read his mind. Todd made him nervous. His palms would sweat, and his mouth would become dry whenever Todd was around. All his senses, including his mind, would freeze as if someone had pressed the pause button.

"Boss, are you telling me to forget about the most important pitch for Sun?"

"No! I'm saying fuck it for the next five minutes. Take a break. Stop working like a cheap hooker with a meth addiction."

"Sure!" Ryan knew he had no choice.

"It's not a fucking coincidence that I've called you just before the presentation. Things will change no matter what the outcome of the pitch is. Obviously, it's better if we fucking win."

"You know this winning streak can't go on forever."

"And that's precisely why I've called you an hour before those cunts arrive." Todd paused, lit up a cigar, and pushed a file toward Ryan, "This is your fucking future. It's a partnership offer. Whether we win or lose, you have it. Get it checked by a fucking lawyer and then sign it," Todd took another puff, "This is my way of saying thank you."

Ryan was taken aback. He was never interested in a partnership, but this made him happy. It proved that Todd was not all about money and valued talent.

"Boss, I don't want to get it checked. I'm happy with whatever you decide for me."

"Don't be an asshole, don't ever sign any documents without vetting them."

"I'm overwhelmed. I don't know how to thank you."

"Loyalty. That's the only thing that matters to me. You know I hate getting emotional, so I will only say this once. I've always thought of you as my son. The only time I regret not having a child of my own is when I see you."

"You've always been like a family to me."

"That's one thing both of us have in common. We both have been fucked by fate. I still remember the day I got the news about the accident."

"Todd, you know I'll take a bullet for you any day." Ryan tried to change the topic.

"Yes, I know. But, for now, I want you to win Miamart for me." Ryan stood up.

"You need to change your fucking habits. You know the ones that are fucking you in your ass," Todd said.

"Today is quit day." Ryan nodded and walked out.

Chapter 3

Where's the beef?
(Wendy's, 1984)

If Todd intended to relieve the pressure of the presentation, he had miserably failed. Ryan wanted to win Miamart more than ever now. The thought that he could not come up with a winning idea pinched him more fiercely.

It was 9:25 am. He pulled his tie one more time as he entered the creative department. There to greet him was his squad. Like always, the soldiers were holding the fort in the large hall flooded with sunlight. They were the misfits who fit Ryan like an Ikea piece coming together.

"Hey Guru."

"What happened?"

"Wow!"

Ryan ignored the voices around him and went straight to his office. He came back with a new shirt and an ironed jacket in minutes.

"Long story. Will tell later."

"You need to thank the team," Gina said. She was the associate creative director and the lead copywriter.

Ryan was grateful. When Ryan procrastinated, the team would come up with ideas. Ideas that would turn to gold once Ryan polished them. He was consistently good at turning tap water into aged wine.

"I owe you drinks and dinner, guys."

"And a day off!" Laura pleaded.

She was the youngest member of the team.

"There is no time for your feedback. I hope you know that." Gina said as she brought him coffee.

Gina seemed tense. She was his anchor and his rock. They had become close since last year, but it was completely platonic. The incident that should have torn them apart brought them closer. It was a late night last year, and both were stuck at the office with work. Ryan was high and tried to kiss Gina. She refused and didn't show up to work the next day. Ryan knew he had made a mistake and sent her a rare handwritten apology.

"You're the only creative I can count on, but more than that, you're the only friend I trust. I don't want to lose either. I'm sorry. You will never see that side of me again."

The next day she was at work. Since then, they had become inseparable.

"I think we've done a great job," Gina said.

"Guru, you look like a constipated George Clooney today." Laura giggled as Allen fist-bumped her.

Laura and Allen looked like twins. Both of them were fresh recruits. They were slave-driven by Andy and Fish, mainly with the work they didn't enjoy doing. Andy and Fish were always in their black shorts and plain white T-shirts and looked like nuns in pajamas. Both Andy and Fish appeared utterly drained, walking like they were recovering from a coma. Fish was sprawled on the floor, gulping an energy drink. Andy seemed famished as he swiped for remnants from a huge bag of Doritos.

"Give me the good news first," Ryan said.

"The third idea is a ten, Guru," Fish said.

Gina put the first batch of artworks on the table.

"Guru, hear me out first," she pleaded, "You need to know the strategy to understand the idea."

Ryan rejected the idea in his head before he even saw it. *Rule of thumb*, Ryan always said, *If an idea needs explanation, it needs to be redone.*

Gina walked toward the center as if she was walking on water, expecting everyone to become believers. The campaign showed bold visuals of things that never changed. The first one was a hairpin, the second a stapler pin, and the third a safety pin. The captions read, **"Change is not constant - Improvement is!"** The copy consisted of a single line, **"Introducing the new and improved Miamart."** Ryan could hear Gina talking in the background. He liked the premise of the idea but felt something was missing.

"Great, loving it," said Ryan. *I'm fucked!* he thought.

The squad knew Ryan saying great was not a good sign.

"What about the one Todd came up with?" he asked reluctantly.

"Take a deep breath," said Gina, rolling her eyes.

Andy presented the second idea based on Todd's earlier feedback. It was a safe campaign built around 50 years of Mullens history and included a high-budget TV commercial with a big celebrity. He suggested Anthony Hopkins.

"I guess this is what Todd wanted," Gina muttered.

"Yes, this is a good filler to have in case something goes wrong," Ryan said.

"I'm taking off tomorrow, if it's OK with you, Guru?" She wasn't happy.

"Listen, guys. I'm just nervous. A lot depends on this pitch," Ryan said

"I think we did a decent job, Guru." Gina smiled. It wasn't a pleasant smile. *An angry Gina is the last thing I need*, Ryan thought.

"We followed your usual advice. Now it's time for you to walk the talk." Gina looked at everyone as they all said together, "Get out of your way." It was Ryan's mantra to push his soldiers to think fearlessly.

"Tell you what, take a long weekend, have a blast, or sleep for three days. I'll handle Todd." That was Ryan's way of saying thank you.

"After the meeting, we meet at Harvey's. Drinks on me. Win or lose, both are good reasons to get drunk tonight."

Ryan almost felt guilty as he walked toward his room. He stared at the artworks, blaming himself for the mundane campaigns. The first campaign Ryan worked on was better than this. His mind drifted to that first pitch. He would stare for hours at his notepad, getting up only when Stan would shout, "Coffee!!!"

He reminisced his early days, trying out different lines and doodles until he had his first brainstorm. A spark would light up in his mind turning into an inferno by the time it was complete. The sudden rush was better than sex. The high was the reason he fell in love with advertising. He would always find something that would excite him, and Stan would always find flaws. Predictably, he would remind Ryan of his inexperience and mutter three syllables, "I'll manage," if he liked it. The discouragement was as predictable as the punchlines in James Bond movies. Ryan waited for the day Stan would appreciate his work. It never happened. Later, Stan would unveil the campaigns and get all the accolades. The campaigns were often a medley of the three ideas he had presented to Stan.

He looked at the campaigns one more time. Only a miracle could save the pitch. It was the first time Ryan was unable to develop an idea. He lit up a cigarette and stared at the window. He was no longer wondering if he still had it. He knew the answer. His thoughts were broken by a gentle knock on the door.

"Good morning, Ryan." It was Jeff Barr, the VP for Account Management, the man closer to Todd than his shadow. Ryan knew Jeff was Todd's pet in more ways than one. Todd kept Jeff on a tight leash and treated him like a stray dog, never missing an opportunity to insult him. Ryan had even witnessed Todd hurling ashtrays at him, barely missing his face.

However, everyone knew Todd enjoyed his steadfast loyalty. It was almost as if he tested it every time he got a chance. He was privy to all of Todd's under-the-table deals. Ryan could never understand the dynamics of their relationship.

"Why so stressed out, Guru?" He moved closer to Ryan. He had a strange habit of standing too close to people and would come even closer to whisper the most mundane things that warranted no whispering, like "the weather is great today" or "It's 3 pm."

Jeff tried to compete with Ryan in everything, including creatives. Ryan hated his feedback on campaigns, but that never stopped him. Jeff was not a novice. He had studied in the top schools, moved in the right circles, and was highly ambitious. Things Ryan was not.

"Where are the masterpieces?" Ryan could almost sense a note of sarcasm in Jeff's voice, "Let's see if you were mind-reading the crap out of the client that is about to fire us."

"It's not ready," Ryan said.

"You know you can't mess with Miamart, right?"

It sounded like a threat. Miamart was one of the Big Five. The top five clients, known as the Big Five had been with the agency from year one. They provided the highest revenue and were so secure that none of the top staff at the agency worked on these clients.

Ryan would have loved to work on these brands, provided they were willing to change their archaic strategies. He was only working on Miamart now because there was new management and the blasphemous possibility that Sun would lose one of the Big Five.

"Oh yeah! We have 15 minutes," Jeff replied, "You know I will eventually be selling this. It won't sell on its own no matter how brilliant your work is."

"That's the exact definition of a good campaign, Jeff." Gina walked in. "That's why it has been selling on its own for the past seven years."

"We all know what Ryan has been doing for the past seven years," Jeff said.

"Yes, we do. He has been producing the kind of work no other creative director can dare imagine, let alone execute." Gina snapped at him.

"Oh! Did you forget who won Clio's campaign of the year award last year?"

"Ryan won three Clios last year."

"Not the award that matters. I am just praying she doesn't pitch to Miamart." Jeff smiled and walked away.

"Who is he talking about?" Gina asked Ryan.

"Kate Raymond!"

"His biggest threat and the natural heir to his throne." Jeff walked away.

"Give me ten," Ryan told Gina.

The comfort of silence was what Ryan craved after Jeff and Gina left. He felt the room embracing him as he shut the door. He threw the pitch on the table, opened the small vent next to the window, and lit a cigarette. Manhattan never seemed so quiet, and he never felt so weak. He could hear the blood flowing through his veins. He inhaled and saw Stan staring at him in the distant past.

"Ryan, heard you've applied at Ogilvy & Mather? You thought I would never find out." He remembered Stan saying.

"I would've told you, but nothing has happened." Ryan

panicked, thinking how the fuck did Stan find out? "There was nothing to tell. And as you've always said, I can't get in Ogilvy & Mather; only geniuses do."

"Well, the truth is you're an unlucky bastard. Someone called me to check if you were any good."

Even decades later, Ryan could remember he started sweating. He almost believed his dream of joining Ogilvy & Mather was over that day, and he was stuck with Stan forever.

"My answer was, Ryan isn't good." Stan paused as if enjoying the torture, "He's great and as far as I can tell, has the potential of being a genius, only if he gives his ego a little rest." Stan laughed.

Ryan couldn't believe what he was hearing.

"If you weren't a genius Ryan, you wouldn't be working for me."

"But I always thought you hated my work," said Ryan sheepishly.

"Correction. I hated your narcissism, not your work. I was trying to break a wild horse. I hope there is something wild left in you when you join Ogilvy & Mather."

Finally, a compliment from Stan.

Ryan almost burnt his hand; he butted the cigarette and noticed the butts with lipstick stains. That's when he heard the knock. "They're here."

Jeff led the Miamart team into the boardroom. The cold silence welcomed the visitors. Jeff looked at the gold-plated clock in the center of the room as he seated them. It was almost ten in the morning.

The Sun boardroom was built like the packaging of a Tiffany bridal ring. The purpose of the Sun boardroom, besides business development, was to settle disputes. It was designed not just to dazzle but to intimidate. The tone was set by a large, hand-carved, maroon table and the view of the giant Manhattan skyline staring at the people inside the room. The dark red color reminded Ryan of the dry blood found in old murder scenes. Twenty chairs surrounded the eye-shaped table that depicted an oval sun.

Todd always said that small details made big statements. There was no branding of Sun in the room, no logo, no mission statements. All the colors in the light grey room came from the display of campaigns created by Sun for one most valued client. These campaigns were interchangeable and were replaced depending on which client was coming for a meeting.

Today, right in the center of the room, hung the first Miamart campaign that had won an award. It was made decades ago. The table was set with fresh edibles made at the Miamart Deli. The projector beamed the Miamart logo on the large canvas screen. The room caressed the gigantic egos of the morning guests, screaming, *"You're our most valued client."*

Mullens, the company that owned Miamart, was the agency's first client and the cash cow for Todd's financial woes. The CEO and founder had recently passed away. A sharper, younger Daniel Stewart replaced him.

Daniel was the opposite of Mullen. He was aggressive, conservative, and believed that advertising was an expense, not an investment. He was a bean counter, a wizard from the world of finance. The sudden management change at the company had put Todd in a precarious position. Daniel Stewart was new and challenging the agency on everything.

Only one person was smiling in the room. The perpetual smile Jeff had on his face was annoying Ryan. No one can be this happy all the time, he thought. He knew why Jeff was happy. The loss would allow Jeff to do what he had desperately tried for the last few years. Get Kate Raymond from Madden & Price. A young creative director who became the hottest property in Manhattan since the previous Clio awards. She was also Ryan's biggest rival. They competed with each other behind the scenes and fought ruthlessly at pitches to win clients. Ryan had still not lost a pitch to her but judging from her work Ryan knew that day was not far away. Everyone was raving about her, including Todd. She was young, she was good, and Ryan despised her for that.

Chapter 4

Because you're worth it

(L'Oréal, 1971)

Kate Raymond loved New York but hated the subway. Her obsession with advertising and New York made the commute as bearable as finding a Hermès handbag on sale because one stitch on the side was a little crooked. Advertising to her was the second thing she enjoyed the most. Almost better than sex.

Both New York and advertising came at a high price; she reminded herself once again as she climbed up the subway stairs in her Gucci suit. She was praying that her suit would remain stainless and wrinkle-free till her cameo today in the boardroom.

Today is going to be my day, Kate thought as she scorned the mediocrity in advertising across the subway station. The last time she took the train was a lifetime ago. It was a research assignment for one of her clients. *The alignment is off, too much text here, the caption is flat, bad kerning, no soul.* She was judging all the campaigns that hit her on the subway. She could do better.

Kate knew she wasn't good. She was great. Her rise in the advertising echelons was swift yet organic, which was bad news for the rest of the Madden & Price clan. She was the blue-eyed boy of the management, which generally showed appreciation in more ways than one. She had been winning accolades and awards since the day she joined Madden & Price. She was basking in the spotlight; she was winning it all from the third increment in less than a year to a brand new, fully-loaded Mercedes SLK.

Kate's rise was meteoric, and when a woman at 28 moves upwards at lightning speed, she ruffles a few feathers on the way. *"No self-made person is a saint,"* she reminded herself *"to climb to the top, you have to break a few shoulders with your heels."*

Within two years, she was pitching with the big boys on the 67th-floor. It was blasphemous for the rest of the team. No one under forty had stepped in the big boys' room, let alone led a pitch.

The word around the floors was that her thirty-four C cup size had a lot to do with it. Kate partially agreed. She had no qualms about using all her assets and enjoyed the attention. Her flings, including the recent one with Jonathan, the Director of Business Development, also raised quite a few eyebrows, but she didn't care.

The advertising world had changed since she moved in. It was no longer a "Mad Manish," ass-grabbing, misogynistic cesspool of sexism. In fact, it had flipped, and she believed she was part of the evolution. Women ruled the ad industry now.

Most of the leading ad agencies had women in power positions. It was almost as if the industry was overcompensating. Even the men were feminists or pretended to be if they wanted to survive. It was the first time in the history of 'mankind' that men were scared of grabbing a woman's ass. Women and the new corporate laws had finally reined in their wavering hands and mouths. The playing field was still not level. It had tilted in favor of women, giving Kate another reason to love advertising.

It was a world full of possibilities. Women were now the new "Mad Men" and no longer allowed anyone to judge them for the wrong reasons. They wore their custom-made power suits. They cursed and sometimes grabbed the asses of men just to see what all the fuss was about. They were carrying on the legacy of admen by sleeping around with whomever they wanted to.

The fear of being labeled as sluts was no longer there. There were only two types of women who were not having sex; those who didn't want to and those who didn't have the time for it. They got drunk if they wanted to, they got high if they wanted, and it was OK if they wanted to stay sober. Women were no longer afraid of being branded "loose" just because they had the moral compass of a man.

Kate flaunted her sexuality and carried it like a trophy. She was a great creative and a flamboyant extrovert, the two qualities that guaranteed her success in the advertising world. She had graduated from the shy, introverted, insecure girl to a power player in the top circles of advertising.

Kate considered her relationship with Jonathan a bonus. She made Jonathan's life exciting and sales easy. Her brains, combined with her curvy assets, made Kate a perfect prop for his pitches. Kate knew why Jonathan couldn't keep his hands off her, but that didn't stop Kate from liking him.

It was a win-win scenario for both. The sex was amazing, the conversations were great, and laughing endlessly for hours was a plus. Kate's relationship with him was a practical contract, void of emotions. It filled a gap for both. There was no exclusivity, and there was no jealousy. They didn't have time to fool around with someone else, but they both agreed not to object if an option came along.

Every pitch she had worked on went like a charm; winning seven accounts in her first year was not a bad average for a rookie. Her clients were raking in profits, and her advertising led the trends on social media when it was released. The only win she craved was against Ryan Walker. She knew that time was close.

Today was going to be another win. She had it in the bag, and there was a reason why she was sure about it.

The reason made her weak as she walked past a coffee shop and decided to grab a sandwich. The reason for her confidence was the pitstop with Jacob Morris. Rich, handsome, powerful, and the Marketing Director of Fizzard. The same guy she woke up with last night. The same guy she was meeting before the pitch.

Her affair with Jacob started with an off-the-record meeting with a potential client hunting for an agency. She had asked Jacob to take an early look at the strategy she was working on since Jacob was working in the same industry. For Kate, that was a ploy to make inroads. He was a potential client, and he was good-looking.

Jacob seemed happy when Kate called her. He was looking for an excuse to talk to her. His reply was immediate, and he sounded eager. They met at Starbucks in the afternoon, located in the hotel's lobby where he was staying. The attraction was mutual, and they were in his room in less than thirty minutes. *This was her dream romance,* she told herself. Her reaction to all the men in the first few days was similar till the excitement tapered downwards. *This is it* she thought as she hurried toward him.

Kate had 45 minutes before the pitch. *This better be good,* she thought and knocked on the hotel room door. She had lost her appetite and felt butterflies in her stomach thinking about the next thirty minutes.

Five minutes later, she could feel his tongue inside her. She smiled as she saw him look up and stare into her eyes. She knew how he enjoyed watching her eyes dance, her shuddering synchronized with her moans. She could feel his tongue dancing inside her.

Her mind was wavering between the amazing sex and the pitch due in less than an hour. She needed a few more seconds to come. She didn't want to win the account because Jacob was fucking her. Her creatives should rock his world. *The sex should just be a condiment,* she reminded herself as his wet tongue devoured her insides.

The phone dinged at the wrong time. Jacob pushed the phone away. She moved her hand to the back of her head to reach for the phone. She knew Jacob was busy doing what he did best. There was a message from an unknown number.

Sun is in trouble. You're in. Ryan is out.

The phone slipped from her hand as she shuddered in ecstasy and came.

Chapter 5

Got milk?

(California Milk Processor Board, 1993)

Todd's Jewish parents immigrated to America from Poland and settled in a murky Brooklyn neighborhood. The Brooklyn winter was warmer than the Polish winter; the neighborhood wasn't.

Todd felt the scourge of anti-Semitism on the first day when his father walked into a grocery store and asked for Kosher salt. No one responded. The stares and the sudden silence pushed him to retreat quietly. When Todd's father returned from the grocery store, he had decided on a name that would replace Kreisler. The family changed their surname from Kreisler to Christopher.

Soon Gabriel Christopher became 'Todd' as it sounded more American. He wanted the neighbors to look at them as New Yorkers, not some runaway Jews from Poland. The community was a smorgasbord of skin colors, from white to black and everything in-between.

"We will be welcome here," said his mother, "there are so many kinds of people here. We will gel in like sugar in milk."

His father scoffed, "This will never be our home."

His mother, a teacher in Poland, ensured that he studied every night. She homeschooled him while his father searched for a job. They were finally able to get him into school.

Todd's mother would tell him about the sacrifices his father was making, trying hard to make Todd love his father. His father was an experienced accountant. His father desperately looked for an accountant job as they ran out of savings and anything they could sell. He was visiting offices for jobs during the day, and working nights at construction sites to keep them afloat. He kept telling Todd and his mother the struggle was temporary. With his expertise and experience, it was just a matter of time.

In a city where immigrants were pouring in like mid-summer rain, knowing someone influential was the only way to get work. Todd knew his father could write a book on anti-social skills. He remembered his father losing his sense of humor and the hope that brought him to America within months. His anger and bitterness gradually started seeping into their home and affecting Todd.

There was no escape in the one-room apartment they were renting. Todd would hide under the blankets when his mother's screaming started and would come out when his father left. His father was spending all his money on cheap alcohol. In a few weeks, the whip of his father's worn-out leather belt replaced the sound of slapping. A few months later, the formality of an argument was no longer needed. Todd prayed every night for his father to die.

It was almost midnight when a knock on the door woke them up. A man holding his hat in his hand was standing at the door. He was covered in mud and looked tired. Without any remorse or emotion, he told them that his father had died in an accident at the construction site. His mother crouched on the floor and started sobbing.

Todd kept staring at the nonchalant man, who turned and walked away. Crying endlessly, she huddled on the floor all night while Todd fell asleep in her lap. With no money for a funeral, his mother refused to go to the morgue and left his father there. Todd never saw his father again. Not even at the funeral that never happened.

Life didn't get any better after his father's death. It went from bad to worse. Lunch after school became an occasional treat as his mother tried to manage the expenses. Todd could see her struggling as she tried to find jobs, but the only skill people saw in her was of a vulnerable middle-aged widow.

Todd couldn't remember the exact moment she gave in to the whims of the managers and the construction workers in the neighborhood, but it was a few months after his father's death. She went out for a few hours and earned enough for food and a bottle of moonshine.

Things became easier with the passing days. Todd was happy she was no longer going out to work. Well-wishers were coming home. She had given up and accepted her new reality as her way of life. It seemed that the only ambition she had was to keep them alive and Todd loathed that. He wanted more like the other kids around him.

His mother went from sleeping in bed on his return from school to sprawled on the couch, unconscious and half-naked. Todd could feel his mother's pain and found ways to make her happy. He would cook, clean, and wait for his mother to wake up and smile. Instead, she was hardly ever awake, and she never smiled. She barely spoke to him except for the occasional *"hmm,"* when he would tell her about school.

Finally, the day came when he could not just sit back and watch his mother fade away. He quit school to look after his mother. Todd was excited to tell her that she didn't have to work anymore. Instead, he would find work and support her. A knock on the door woke her up. She tried to walk straight toward the door, spilling what little was left in the bottle from the night before. She was about to open the door when she saw Todd sitting on the broken couch. He smiled and finally heard her speak after months. The words that haunted him for the rest of his life.

"Wait outside!"

Sitting outside, he saw strange men going in and coming out. The men ignored him, knocked, and waited for his mother to say "Yes!" The steady flow continued for three hours. He counted eight men. Most seemed haggard, old, abysmal; a few he recognized from the neighborhood. The last visitor was his landlord. Tired and worn out, she finally walked outside. She smiled and said in a low whispering voice, "You must be hungry. I'm going to get some food for you."

He was still sitting outside when she returned, clenching a crumpled paper bag against her chest. She took out an apple for him and a bottle for herself.

Her drinking got worse. The knocking on the door was no longer waking her up, but it wasn't stopping the visitors. At first, the men would knock loudly and barge in. Finally, the knocking disappeared, and the men would just walk in. Everyone refused to acknowledge Todd's presence, including his mother. Todd gave up on his plan to find work and stayed home to protect his mother. He knew what they were doing. It was his first sex education class. He wanted to run out but hid in the blankets and watched through the torn holes.

They would take off their pants, push his mother's dress up and fuck her while she opened her eyes for a minute. The men ignored the small blanket that barely hid him. He eventually dispensed with the pretense of hiding and just sat there watching the fetid, dirty, older men devouring his mother. After finishing, they left a few coins on the table and disappeared. It was enough for an apple and a bottle of moonshine.

A few months later, a hot midsummer afternoon welcomed a

ferocious downpour of rain. It was a respite for the residents and Todd, who hoped for fewer visitors that day. Hours crawled by and no one came. He was happy that the roaring thunder replaced the noise of the creaking bed.

Finally, there was a knock at the door. The only visitor of the day walked in. He was soaking wet even though he had an umbrella. His white hair and cane reminded him of his grandfather. The visitor threw the half-wet cigarette on the floor, butting it with his patent-leather shoe. He was the owner of a hardware shop in the neighborhood.

Todd was hungry and hoped the sex would end quickly. The man took off his pants and lay on top of his mother. His mother was motionless except for her lifeless eyes that looked at Todd, and then she turned her face away. Unable to get an erection, the man was getting frustrated. He started slapping her, trying to wake her up. She opened her eyes one more time as he slapped her again, blaming her for his flaccid penis.

"Stop!" Todd shouted.

The half-naked men walked up to Todd. "What the fuck did you say?"

"Don't hit her?" Todd whispered. The man stared at Todd for a few moments.

"You want to earn a dollar, boy?"

Todd shook his head in no, too scared to say the words.

"I'll give you two," he counted the coins from his shirt and opened his palm for Todd, "I paid your mama fifty cents. You can earn more."

"No!' Todd watched him turn back. He walked back and picked up his belt.

"Three," Todd whispered.

"Say that again?" He turned back.

"Three dollars."

The man smiled as he came closer to Todd with the belt in his hand. Todd didn't see the buckle flying toward his forehead till he felt the metal scraping his skin. Todd could feel the blood dripping down his forehead. The exclamation-shaped scar was deep, but it didn't hurt him.

"Money is god!" the man said as he took off his shirt, moved his body closer to Todd's face, and dropped three dollars in his lap.

Todd was 15 at that time. It was the first time he bought fried chicken.

In a few weeks, no one was touching his mother, and he was earning more than his mother ever did. There was enough money to buy warm food, candies, and alcohol for his mother. He even bought clothes from thrift stores. The word among the visitors spread fast, and so did his earnings. He did whatever they wanted him to do as long as they left his mother alone. He hated every second of it, washing and gargling vigorously after every episode.

Todd aged fast and was happy to see traces of a mustache sprouting over his upper lip. He enjoyed walking through the neighborhood in the suits he bought at thrift stores. Todd's mother was hardly ever awake to see what he had become. She chose to ignore what was happening as long as she got her bottle every day. Finally, an undercooked moonshine hurled her to the hospital. Her liver was no longer functioning. She died within hours. Todd wasn't happy, but he wasn't sad either. He felt nothing.

He sat there, guarding his mother after washing the body. He wanted his mother to have the best funeral. He bought another suit, fresh flowers, and a cheap perfume bottle. The rabbi refused to perform the rituals. Instead, Todd whispered the only words he knew in Hebrew, "Baruch Dayan Emet," and he had no idea it meant *"Blessed be the one true Judge."*

Todd wore his favorite suit to the Beit Chayim located on the city's outskirts. There were only three people at the funeral, the gravediggers and Todd. He was glad the ceremony lasted only a few minutes. He placed a stone on her grave and walked away.

The evening sun spread a golden vignette of gloom around the neighborhood as Todd walked back home. The reality hit him for the first time as he watched kids his age playing in the streets. The world was changing, and new technology was reshaping America. Rich folks could now afford a television set, and those who couldn't afford it would visit neighbors and relatives that had them. He wanted to escape his putrid life and work in the glitzy world of the new media.

Finally, a sign on a printing press pulled him back to reality. The press bore a depleted and depressing structure. A faded sign painted in what used to be blue read *"Coral Printers and Publishers."* That wasn't the sign that got Todd's attention. The *"Help Wanted"* sign on the washed-out grey wooden door did. Todd knew he was too young to apply, but the sign beckoned him to try. He walked toward the press, imagining what he would buy if he got the job. A new shirt, winter socks, a girly magazine, tickets to the movies, and a shiny television set he'd seen were on top of his wish list.

He quickly crossed the road dodging a carriage loaded with supplies. He knocked and walked in without waiting for an answer. The chaos inside was a far cry from the calmness outside. The screaming and cursing men muffled the loud clanking sounds of the printing machines. The most clamorous man sounded the most important. It was coming from a room with a sign that said "Manager." He knocked a couple of times and walked in without an invitation. A man holding a bunch of papers stopped shouting.

"Who the fuck are you?" He seemed like he was in his late seventies.

Todd could smell the stench of a thousand cigarettes in the room. The cluttered room housed various shades of brown. The boxes were brown, the furniture was brown, and so was the color of the undersized suit the man was wearing. There was nothing noticeable in the room except a cheap print of an oil painting in an oversized golden frame. A huge sunset covered a single boat floating in the sea. It reminded Todd of his life.

"'I'm the new guy." Todd tried to charm his way through the awkward discussion. He pointed toward the sign outside. "Help Wanted," he said, enunciating the words. The man was slouching in a chair that was half his size, trying to light another cigarette. The oversized frame on the sunset painting somehow made the manager look smaller.

"How old are you, boy?"

"I'm almost sixteen."

"Well, Mr. Almost Sixteen, I'm General Patton, and I don't have time for babysitting. Fuck off!"

"Mr. Patton, I need two minutes. Just hear me out." Todd pleaded.

"My name is Will," the man clarified. "I'm the captain of this Titanic, and you have time till I finish my smoke." He inhaled almost half the cigarette, and before Todd could say anything, he started talking again. "But let me tell you this. You're a size small to clean the machines and help the boys around here!"

Todd panicked, waiting for the manager to stop talking before his cigarette ended, along with his chance to work at the press. "Mr. Will, firstly, I want you to stop speaking and start enjoying your smoke. You deserve it after all the chaos I saw here."

Before the shocked manager could swear at Todd and tell him to get out, he continued.

"Size doesn't matter in a printing press. You're the captain of the ship, and you're not huge." Todd knew he was getting his attention. He had no choice and about sixty seconds left.

"You don't have to be old to prove you're strong." He finally took a breath, "If I fail, I don't deserve the job, and I'll walk out myself."

A man burst in the door, almost weeping, "We're out of black ink. We'll be late for the afternoon print."

"Fuck." The manager waved his hand toward Todd, gesturing him to get out.

"I can get the ink in thirty minutes," Todd said.

"That's impossible," Will said.

"We buy ink on credit, moron," said the guy who burst in, "and that too from New Jersey. No one gives credit here." Will stared at Todd and raised his eyebrows.

"How much do y'all need?" Todd smiled.

He rushed out and knew where he was heading. One of his 'visitors' owned a store in Brooklyn.

He went inside and recognized the 'visitor,' who ignored him and continued talking to the customer.

"I need five gallons of black ink."

"Fuck off!"

"I will, straight to your wife, who teaches History at the school. I think she'll be interested to know how you spend your afternoons."

In less than thirty minutes, Todd was back at Coral. He loved the feeling of confidence, knowing he had them by the balls.

"Great fucking news. You have seven days of credit, and it's seven dollars for five gallons," Todd said, hoping General Patton would be impressed.

"We can only pay three," said one of the guys.

"I can return the ink and enjoy you getting fucked. Also, I know you've been paying eight dollars for the same quantity." Todd felt like an adult every time he said Fuck. He was a grown-up now.. He pretended to turn around.

"Wait," Will yelled as he lit up his cigarette. "I'll give you five dollars, and—" he paused, "you can have the job too."

Todd waited for a few seconds. He wasn't paying a dime to the visitor, so this was a sweet deal.

"Aww fuck it, but cash. You can pay the rest later," Todd smiled. He earned a dollar that night, and the manager owed him five. That was enough for a movie, candies, and a hot meal. He had finally figured out his calling. The manager needed the ink and hired him, thinking he would let go of Todd later. He didn't.

Todd was hardworking and funny. He quickly became popular, telling everyone the dirty jokes he read in shady magazines he would buy every morning. He made everyone laugh as he did the chores no one wanted and cleaned the machines for the evening run. *This is going to be good*, Todd thought.

Chapter 6

There are some things money can't buy - For everything else, there's MasterCard.
(MasterCard, 1997)

Todd was erasing the memory of his murky past by spending more time at the press. He diverted all his energy to learning the business, ravishing every piece of information he could get. He was becoming smarter than all the men around him. He was also earning more than he could've imagined.

The unmindful investment in the *"visitors"* was paying off. The meat at the butcher was free. The tailor didn't charge him for the suits. The ink and supplies for the printing press were free, and the landlord stopped asking for rent. It was now time for the *"visitors"* to get fucked.

At seventeen, he convinced Will to make him an advertising salesman. Todd knew Will admired his drive. Todd never said no to a job, and did jobs others refused. Will agreed and eventually gave Todd the keys to the press as Todd was usually the first to arrive and the last to leave. His job included opening the press, cleaning everything, selling ads, and turning off the lights before locking the gates. There were times Todd slept at the press, especially the days he missed having a family.

Todd picked up fast using his 'visitors' network, and in a few months, he was selling more ads than anyone at Coral. He saved most of his earnings because there was hardly anything to pay for, except for the shiny television set he wanted.

Todd worked hard to find shortcuts. His entire social life was composed of clients. He would go out of the way to keep them happy. While the rest of the salesmen were visiting numerous advertisers in a day, he would be chatting with one client for hours.

Soon Todd knew their wives' names, their children's names, their dog's favorite food, and how much mustard they liked on their hotdogs. He even unearthed if they preferred blondes or brunettes. He soon discovered that a scantily clad photograph as a gift made a compelling case for advertising.

Getting nude photographs in the 1940s was not easy, but Todd found an easier way. The solution emerged in the printing press. A desperate model looking for a career jumpstart came directly to the press instead of mailing her portfolios. Late at night, he was cleaning up Will's room when he heard the knock on the door.

"Hi, are you Will?" said the forty-something brunette. She was tall, a little old to be a model but had a great body. She was wearing a thin red blouse and a wrinkled black skirt that seemed older than her. He could see the outline of her black bra through her blouse.

"Depends," Todd said.

A woman walking inside the printing press was as rare as tourists in Harlem. He adjusted the "sunset" painting behind Will's desk and sat on the manager's chair.

"Well, I saw the ad for the models. It said not older than 21, which I thought was unfair." She slightly bent down to show her cleavage, "Everyone tells me I'm pretty, and I should be a model."

"I agree you should be a fucking model. Can you do a twirl for me?" Todd leaned back to test the waters.

"Twirl?" She batted her eyebrows.

"Ya, you know, just turn around so I can see the fucking goods."

She batted her fake eyelashes nervously and stepped back, not expecting to strut for the owner. Instead, she turned around in an awkward circle and tripped on her high heels.

Todd was a heterosexual virgin and had never seen a naked woman. His erection reminded him why he hated having sex with the *"visitors."*

"You could be a model. You've got a nice, umm .chest, but how do I know you're not fucking with me and haven't stuffed tissues in your bra," he whispered hoarsely. He was too nervous to say boobs.

"You know most of our clients sell swimwear," he said. "We have to travel to Florida and Miami and, sometimes, even internationally, like to Japan. Have you ever been to Tokyo? It's fucking beautiful there this time of the year."

"Oh! Wow, Mr. Will, I love to travel. I've been to Virginia and —"

Todd was getting impatient. He decided it was either now or never.

"Listen, sweetheart. I have 20 minutes for you to convince me if I should hire you. One of my models got a role in a movie, and I have to go and sign the fucking contract." He got up, turned, picked up his jacket, and pretended to look for his keys. Then, he looked up and saw her. No blouse, no bra, no skirt, no undies. She was standing naked. They both had seventeen minutes. The sex lasted three. Todd used the next ten minutes to find Coral's camera reserved for official use and took some pictures.

Todd soon discovered advertising was going to change his life. The models were usually older but pretty and very willing. They were no longer allowed to mail their portfolios. They had to come to the office if they wanted a job. He even got better at sex and convincing them. He stuck to his most effective line after the initial introductions, "You have ten minutes to convince me if I should hire you."

Most of the time, it worked. And when it didn't work, Todd didn't waste time being disappointed. He would call the model next in line. It was the easiest, cheapest, fastest way to get sex and a few photographs for his clients. Word spread quickly, and clients insisted on doing business with Todd. Almost eighty percent of Coral's ad revenue was coming from him.

The success also meant Todd was losing his popularity at Coral and making a few enemies. Todd didn't like brandishing power, but he never shied away from it when needed. If someone messed with him, he would get Will to fire the person by the end of the evening. He became ruthless. He had no time for distractions.

His last commission came to $865 and twenty-five cents, to be exact. This commission was unheard of at Coral, and he knew it. Todd was doing great from a business perspective, and no one dared to ring the alarm bells. Instead, the other salesmen waited for Todd to make a mistake. They knew it was inevitable. He had no social life, which became the most significant advantage of working at Coral.

The business Todd was generating for Coral was working on autopilot. The clients were calling him instead of the other way around. Soon, he started getting calls from other publishers for advertising, offering him a higher commission and better perks. Todd was getting business for seven publishers and media houses by the end of summer. Will ignored his side-hustle as long as he got enough business for his company.

A month later, Todd rented a room across Coral and hired a team of assistants to keep up with the growing business. The assistants mainly were overaged models who couldn't work but were pretty enough to turn heads when he walked into a client's office. He was no longer cleaning the machines but didn't want to quit Coral.

He also nurtured a beard to make himself look mature and

refined. He bought his first suit from a designer shop in Manhattan to celebrate his first year as a salesman. He looked around the rising structures and decided this was where he would rent his own office.

After meeting his monthly target, Todd's favorite stop was *"Brooklyn's Fresh World,"* a grocery store in Brooklyn that sold the best sundaes in the city. The place was famous for its hand-churned vanilla and caramel sundaes and was one of the few places Todd actually paid to buy things. It was like a trophy he gave himself for outstanding performance. The owner was fond of him.

"Todd, so what was the number today?"

"Eleven hundred and twenty in commission. Not bad for a Tuesday, Mr. Mullen. Praise the Lord," said Todd knowing Mullen was a devout Catholic. Todd controlled his choice of vocabulary with him.

"Not bad at all," Mullen said as he scooped up a large vanilla ball and placed it on the cone, drizzling extra caramel chunks on it, just the way Todd liked it. Todd didn't just stop here for sundaes; there was another reason.

"I keep telling you," he said as he wiped his face, "you need to advertise and expand. Let New York know what they're missing."

"Can't. I'm selling out every day; can't make more," Mullen said with an emphatic tone.

Todd had a gut feeling that Brooklyn's favorite ice cream had the potential to become America's favorite. The only thing missing was Mullen's drive and ambition. Todd didn't want to sell ad space for the rest of his life, and "Brooklyn's Fresh World" could be his ticket to Manhattan.

He knew the store was a goldmine and felt Mullen was colorblind. The timing was just right. America was entering the age of prosperity as President Roosevelt offered attractive incentives to local businesses. Todd thought there were only two kinds of people, the people jumping on the boom bandwagon and the people standing in the way.

Mullen was standing in the way. No matter what logic Todd offered, Mullen didn't budge. Mullen also didn't seem interested in the models Todd offered him. The only time Mullen showed some reaction to any photograph was when Todd showed him a naked picture of the model, only this picture included Todd—*naked*.

"You need to stop showing me these photos Todd." Mullen turned red. Todd noticed that reaction. Alarm bells rang in his mind, but the bells weren't scaring him. It was the theory that he wanted to test out that frightened him. Sporadically, Todd started showing Mullen his pictures. The more photographs Todd showed, the more interested Mullen seemed. Finally, on a hot, humid afternoon, Todd decided to test his theory.

"Mr. Mullen, how about changing the name Brooklyn's Fresh World?"

"Why would I do that?" Mullen asked.

"Well, for starters, you can expand. You can spread across the state, the East Coast maybe, hell even America if we play it right."

"We?"

"Well, I will handle your advertising, of course."

"Of course." Mullen smiled.

"I don't need anything from the company. It's yours. You will own every brick of the new factory."

"And how do you suppose we get money for a factory?"

"Have dinner with me. I have a plan and a new name for your company," Todd said with a smile. "What have you got to lose?"

"Hmm, and I figure you'll tell me the new name at dinner?" Mullen said sarcastically.

"Nope. I'll tell you right now," said Todd as he stepped back and revealed an imaginary sign with his hands, "Miamart!"

Mia was the name of Mullen's mother. Todd had done his

homework. It would be America's favorite grocery store, Todd believed.

Todd got his new leads from the patent and office of registration. He was paying a hefty fee for potential clients, both cash and in-kind. He was well connected in the office and discovered that a new name was registered, "Miamart." He figured out what Mullen was planning. He had to act soon. That evening, Todd showed up at the store again. He wore his best suit, put on his best cologne, and shaved his stubble.

"I wanted to invite you, Mr. Mullen. I'm starting my advertising firm," Todd said.

"Wow! Congrats, Todd, you deserve it. But you know me, I hate crowds."

"There is no crowd, Mr. Mullen, just you and me." Todd noticed the change in Mullen's attitude.

"Just you and me?"

Todd gave Mullen Coral's address.

Later that night, Mullen walked into the Coral office.

"Is this your new office, Todd?" He asked.

"Well yeah! I'm partnering with Coral, and that's why I have the key," he replied and passed him the glass. He was saving the imported scotch for a big celebration. Todd took off his jacket and turned on the hidden camera.

"Do you have a name for your advertising firm ?" Mullen asked.

Todd saw the hideous sunset painting hanging behind Will's chair.

"Yes. Sun Advertising!"

Chapter 7

I'm Lovin' it

(McDonald's, 2003)

Ryan and Gina walked into the boardroom a few minutes after everyone was seated. Todd insisted on Gina being there for optics. She added glamor, diversity, and calm to the stressful environment.

Ryan couldn't remember the last time he was this nervous. His neck was hurting, and he could hear his blood pressure rising. The stakes were high, and he had a feeling it was a lost battle. The retail giant was fishing for a reason to fire Sun, and their weak pitch was like a toss to a seasoned batter. Jeff introduced the Sun team to Miamart's new management.

"Looking forward to your presentation, Ryan. I've heard so much about you." Daniel stared at Ryan.

Jeff jumped in, "Yes, we always hire the best talent in New York."

"Then tell me, how come the best talent has never worked on our account?" Daniel stared at Jeff.

Ryan broke the awkward silence. "Well, I'm here now promising you my utmost attention."

"If we get a chance to work together," Daniel added the caveat, "Mr. Mullen would've enjoyed working with you, Ryan. He was fond of you. He had heard good things about you."

"Ah! Mr. Mullen, may his soul rest in peace," Todd intervened, "Great friend. I always enjoyed his company."

"Strange! He mentioned that the last time you met him was decades ago," Daniel said calmly and leaned back against the chair. It took Ryan less than two minutes to read Daniel. He had no interest in the presentation. Daniel wanted the meeting to be short, and he was here to fire Sun.

Daniel said, "I also wanted to let you know that Mr. Mullen left behind a letter in his will. It is for Ryan, but it comes with a caveat. Ryan gets the letter if Sun wins the pitch." He paused. "For some reason, he didn't want to change the agency, but I'm under no such obligation."

"So it has been decided that we're out?" Jeff asked.

"Certainly not. As I said, if you win, Ryan gets the letter."

"Wow! That's fucking amazing. Out of curiosity, what's in the letter?" Todd asked.

"No idea. He wanted to keep it confidential."

Ryan was less interested in Mullen's letter and more interested in reading the new CEO. Daniel seemed to be enjoying the bluff he was playing, but Ryan couldn't read what cards he was holding. A knock on the door interrupted the tense conversation. Todd's secretary Patricia peeped in.

"Sorry for the intrusion Todd, but there is a delivery outside for Ryan."

"Oh, for fuck sake, Patty, you know better. Just take the damn thing," Todd shouted.

"It's not the regular guy. This one insists he needs Ryan's signature," Patty replied nervously, walking away before Todd could say something nasty.

"Don't look at me. I have no idea what's happening," Ryan shrugged.

"We've waited ten minutes. A few more won't matter." Daniel smiled.

Ryan apologized and left the boardroom.

"I have a TV appearance at noon, just letting you guys know I can't be late for that," Daniel added.

The interruption gave Ryan time to think. He was desperately groping for ideas to rescue the mediocre pitch. Ryan recognized the man at the reception.

"Hey man!" It was the pastor in the cheap suit. The only difference was his swollen, bleeding lip. "I need to deliver this to you, face to face," he said. He seemed to be in his mid-20s, well-groomed. *Not a pastor*, Ryan thought, probably a rookie media executive.

"Seriously, what the fuck do you want? I have 30 seconds."

"Dude, I'm being paid to make sure you get this package. I can walk away if you tell me you don't want it. I really don't care."

Ryan was running out of time and patience, but the delivery guy was obviously given very specific instructions. Ryan snatched the envelope and rushed to the elevator. His middle finger in the air signaled the end of the conversation. As he got in the elevator, the blood-red color of the envelope stood out. He wondered about the delivery guy and the million questions he should've asked him. The writing on the envelope caught his eye.

"OPEN BEFORE THE PITCH!"

The elevator dinged. Ryan slowed down as he contemplated whether to open and delay the presentation or open later and regret it. He remembered he had stashed a few grams of coke in his office. They were already waiting; a few more minutes won't matter. He decided to sprint to his office to check the envelope. He walked to the exit door leading to the stairs and got to his office. He quickly took out the coke and snorted a line. It made him feel better.

Sometimes clarity can be bad, he told himself as he got high. The envelope intrigued him. He wiped his nose and took out the printouts. The title made him shudder in disbelief.

"The demise of brick and mortar retail by Daniel Stewart."

He checked the date. The announcement was due today. His heart began beating faster as he skimmed through the speech. It outlined the future roadmap for Miamart. It was the opposite of what Sun was presenting. He could feel his heart pump faster. The sound of blood rushing through his veins became louder. His legs felt weak. They were walking into a trap.

The entire presentation they made was a bomb ready to blow up Sun. It would ensure Daniel fired the agency. The brief Miamart gave them was a setup to make the agency admit its incompetency. The roadmap was buried deep in unusable and irrelevant data. The future was indeed changing, and Sun advertising was not a part of it.

Instantly he sensed his legs moving forward. He resisted the urge for another blow. Miamart was on the threshold of becoming the most lucrative client in America. He didn't have a choice but to pull the plug on the existing presentation and minutes to develop a winning idea. He needed a way to align the new idea with Daniel's announcement.

Suddenly it hit him like a wrecking ball. He thrived on this rush. Nothing compared to the pleasure that came with the idea that could change how people behaved. He threw out the rest of the coke through the window, convincing himself he would never do coke again.

Ryan rushed to the boardroom. He took out his phone and started typing ferociously. The message began with two words.

Drop everything!!!

He pressed send as he reached the boardroom, praying someone would read the long message. He took off his tie, smiled, and winked at Patty as he entered the room.

Ryan was back. An awkward silence welcomed him. He could feel the stares piercing through his body as he sat down.

"Can we begin?" Jeff asked with a hint of sarcasm.

"Yes, but," he ignored Jeff, "I would like to begin by showcasing our latest work."

"We know your capabilities," Daniel snapped.

"I agree, but our strategy for Miamart is related to some of the work we've done recently," Ryan smiled and said with an equal assertiveness.

"Ryan, you're aware that our work showreel is almost an hour," Jeff said. "You've already wasted ten minutes with your delivery guy." He smiled as though enjoying Ryan's crisis.

"Oh, shut the fuck up! Ryan knows what's at stake," Todd snapped at Jeff.

Ryan's phone was constantly buzzing. He desperately wanted to pick it up but didn't want to push his luck.

"Ryan, can you please turn your phone off? It's more annoying than your sense of timing," Daniel said.

Ryan reluctantly turned off his phone, praying that the squad understood what was needed. It seemed like a tornado was tearing through his brain, and in a masochistic way, he was enjoying the pain. However, he had one advantage over the others sitting in the room. He knew if the plan was to burn him, he would rather set the fire himself.

The lights dimmed. The video began with an award-winning ad from Ryan's treasured client, an elite, upmarket retirement club called Head Lion. Located in Scarsdale, Head Lion was a unique idea of a permanent club for the retired crème de la crème. The elite gated community was home to billionaires, entrepreneurs, politicians, and celebrities.

Most of the residents were victims of hostile takeovers by the shareholders or their families. The rest were the ones who were unwilling to let go of the power they had enjoyed most of their lives. Alone they were powerless. Head Lion provided them the power that came with unity. The power to change government policies, rattle stock markets, and get the head of the government elected. The power that made them more potent than before.

It was also a wall that held back their ungrateful families and unhinged colleagues. It was their island where they could relish the remnants of power with the peace of mind that their cause of death would never be a stab wound in the back.

Head Lion was in Scarsdale, a suburb thirty minutes away from New York. It was the wealthiest town on the East Coast for the second year in a row, with an average household income of $452,000. Ryan loved working for Head Lion. It was his brainchild. The Head Lion team also loved Ryan and preferred dealing with him directly. Unlike other clients, the Head Lion brief was a brainstorming session with Ryan.

Todd detested smaller clients and considered them a waste of company time. He reined in the account management team, letting the creatives handle smaller accounts directly. Head Lion preferred it that way too. It cut the unnecessary red tape and kept the billing low.

Every year Ryan presented them with one idea, which was approved because their CEO trusted his judgment. Head Lion met its targets. Ryan won awards. The CEO was never disappointed.

The presentation opened with a shot of the CEO.

Maxwell William, the CEO of Head Lion, fell in love with Ryan seven years ago when Sun pitched for the account. Ryan presented a complete overhaul of the previously known brand 'Serenity.'

"If you want to target the rich and the powerful, the name shouldn't sound like the community was made for the senile." Ryan was blunt, "Change the positioning from a retirement home to a permanent club."

"What's a permanent club?" Max asked, sounding intrigued.

"The last waiting lounge. A place where power and pleasure meet the powerful."

"But why would the rich want to live in a community? They can live anywhere."

"Not a community. It's a club. It will have personalized mansions for the forgotten mavens. Head Lion will help them find what they've lost—Power. They have money but are sidelined by the ones close to them, and they hate it. They are addicted to power and will never come to terms with the sad reality that their reign has ended. We flip the narrative. We tell them alone it's over, but together in a powerful elite community gives them the power to topple governments, influence stock markets, nudge the economy in any direction they want."

"But why the name Head Lion?"

"Lions are known for their courage. Not their intelligence. Our community is for people who are not just brave; they are also smart."

"Ryan, I love the strategy. We will move forward with everything except for the name." Max gave his verdict.

"I will not move forward unless the name is approved. You either trust my judgment, or you don't. You can't partially rely on me."

Max stared at him with shock as Ryan picked up his laptop.

"Do you drink cognac?" Max finally spoke.

In a few years, Head Lion was charging residents $100,000 per month, offering personalized mansions for the forgotten mavens. It had a waiting period of months, and one could only get in through member referrals. Head Lion gave Ryan the freedom to develop ideas no other client would risk. It also guaranteed a few awards for him every year.

The second frame forced Daniel to put his phone down as the shot opened with a baby's birth. The baby wasn't crying; it was roaring. The roars of the baby shattered the silence in the boardroom. It was the shock and awe Ryan needed to shut everyone up. The ad showed powerful men and women from all industries endorsing Head Lion, but the roar of lions replaced their speech.

The ad ended with the current CEO Maxwell William. The 80-year-old known as Max beckoned the powerful residents to Head Lion with a roar. Max and his symmetrically-shaped, white beard often reminded Ryan of an older lion. Ryan admired his tenacity. Their shared respect laid the foundation of a friendship that crossed the barrier of age. The mutual love for fine cognac added the cherry on top. Ryan was the only one Max shared his LOUIS XIII cognac with.

Ryan could feel Max's fondness grow after every quarterly report. Ryan's mind-reading skills came in handy. He would say things bluntly to Max, knowing Max enjoyed the rare company of someone who questioned his judgment. Every time Max resisted an idea, Ryan would remind him, *"Get out of your way!"*

The lights in the boardroom suddenly turned on and broke into Ryan's thoughts. The video was over. Ryan was stranded. It was showtime.

There was an eerie silence as everyone waited for Ryan to speak. He wasn't sure if his squad read the messages he sent. Ryan stayed silent. It was the longest thirty seconds of his life. Suddenly there was a knock at the door. The reinforcement Ryan was waiting for had arrived.

Ryan rushed toward his squad as they entered the boardroom carrying posters, banners, packaging. The spectacle was unplanned.

The team looked nervous. Ryan was finally smiling. *I still have it,* he thought. He was the only one in the boardroom who seemed happy because he was the only one who knew what was going on.

The squad started moving chairs around to set the creatives at strategic locations, shattering the awkward silence in the boardroom. It became noisier than a downtown construction site.

Thin white sheets of paper covered the creatives. The loud colors and bold visuals were seeping out of the sheets. Enough to show something was interesting behind those sheets, not enough to show what it was. The perplexed audience tilted their heads, trying to peek through the sheets.

Ryan noticed that the only person not interested in the visuals was Daniel. He was on his phone texting. Ryan started to sweat profusely, knowing well that this would be the make-or-break presentation of his career. Today was his Ragnarök, the doom of the gods.

"Did I make the right choice? What if the red envelope was a trap?" He felt Gina grasping his hand. He looked at his squad, who smiled and nodded.

"You've got this Guru!" Gina whispered.

"Gentleman, this is our entire presentation, and this is our way forward for Miamart," Ryan said in a calm but authoritative voice, flipping his MacBook open. There was pin-drop silence as everyone stared at the first and only slide.

"The demise of brick and mortar retail."

Ryan's mantra was if you don't get the attention in the first slide, you've probably lost the pitch. He focused on Daniel and started reading him. He had Daniel's full attention. He also had the audience mystified as they saw the first pitch in their lives with only one slide.

The silence was sullen and ominous.

"Daniel, if you're shocked, we have another option we will share after this." Jeff finally broke the sound barrier.

"Actually, we don't, Daniel," Ryan smiled, "this is it."

"For the record," Jeff continued looking at Todd. "I do not agree with this strategy, and I would like to present a few ideas separately."

"Will you shut the fuck up and let the man speak." Todd roared at him. Even the sound of breathing died down in the room.

"This is not my strategy, Jeff. It's Daniel's." Ryan was now enjoying the drama he had created.

"Wait, how did you get that?" Daniel's calm persona had withered like the age of a catwalk model.

"Does it matter?" Ryan replied, knowing the answer.

"Gentlemen, I love this quote because it sums up the positioning, strategy, and the campaign we're proposing for Miamart."

As Gina revealed the large poster that displayed the big idea, Daniel moved forward to see what was on it. The minimalistic concept had a single word ***"Homecoming!"*** The visual showed a Miamart branded cart with a short and simple copy: ***"Because we know you better."***

"The future of Miamart is online retail. Miamart is going Digital. What we are proposing is a head-on competition with Amazon." Ryan looked at his watch; he had eleven minutes before the time was over.

He spoke for around ten. The Mullen team was speechless at the amount of work the agency had produced on a brief that they almost never gave. Ryan could tell Todd wasn't surprised. He recognized the recycling from a previous pitch. It was a presentation Ryan had given last year to Amazon. The team had just changed the logos and a bit of copy.

"Here's the crescendo. The entire campaign will be digital, saving you at least 50% of ad spend from traditional media. Which means over $100 million in savings."

Daniel looked at his watch. Their time was up. He didn't seem amused.

"Gentlemen, I'm afraid I have to rush to another meeting." Daniel was the first to leave, followed by his team exiting in perfect sync like an army of well-dressed ants.

Chapter 8

A Great Way to Fly!
(Singapore Airlines, 1993)

The Mullen team walked out of the boardroom, leaving everyone dumbfounded.

"Ryan, stay. Everyone else, fuck off," Todd said.

Ryan was dying for a smoke. *Fuck it,* he thought and lit up a cigarette.

"You can't smoke in here. Remember you won't survive another stroke." Jeff stayed back.

Ryan was surprised that Jeff knew about his stroke. It happened last year. He'd survived as he got to the hospital in time. Only Todd knew that the excessive use of coke was the reason behind the stroke. Todd arranged for Ryan's doctor and ensured no one found out about his addiction. The doctor had warned Ryan that, if he continued, the best-case scenario would be he would die a painless death in a year. Ryan ignored Jeff and took another drag. He was now second-guessing if he had made the right choice. The envelope could be a ploy from a rival agency.

"Ryan, you really embarrassed us and—" Jeff said.

Todd interrupted Jeff with a glare before he could complete his sentence. The only thing that kept Ryan calm was that Todd couldn't afford to fire him.

"Ryan, you fucked up," he finally said, "I'm tired of you fucking us in the ass. We hardly ever know what the fuck we're presenting, sitting like dicks in front of the client."

"Boss—" Ryan tried to interrupt, but Todd raised his hand.

"Don't fucking surprise me. Stop assuming you're the one who decides what happens at Sun. You don't. I fucking do."

Ryan was not surprised by Todd's sudden change in temperature. He was known for his mood swings and would go from warm to cold faster than a teen finishes a sundae. He wondered if the partnership was still on the table if they lost Miamart. He wasn't feeling good. He tried to divert his attention from Todd to what he was going to do next. The craving for a chilled beer and another smoke was dissipating. He could feel a heaviness in his chest. He felt numbness climbing in on one side of his body. He tried moving his left arm and felt the familiar numbing pain. He needed some air. He got up as he heard Todd continue with his monologue.

"Ryan, I'm not fucking done," said Todd. And that was the last thing he heard as he zoned out and walked out.

Ryan felt miserable as he stepped out of the building. He let the cool breeze caress his face. This could be a precursor for another stroke. *I need to see a doctor*, he reminded himself. His phone rang. It was Todd. He decided to ignore his tirade. The phone started buzzing again. It was Jeff now. He disconnected the phone.

He walked to the subway and noticed someone familiar sitting in a black Range Rover across the street. It was Daniel Stewart. He walked toward him. Daniel invited him inside the SUV.

"I hope you could read my mind saying I hate you." Daniel smiled at him.

"Actually, my reading tells me that's untrue!" Ryan smiled.

"So, it's true? You can read minds." They laughed, "I have no idea how you did it, but you won. You got the account." He took out the envelope left by Mullen and gave it to him.

"I have no idea what's in this, but I am certain it's important. Take this very seriously, Ryan."

Ryan couldn't believe it, "Can I announce we won?"

"Yes, I'm about to send an email to Todd. I don't like him, and I don't like you, but I loved your wild pitch, and that's what the brand needs."

When Daniel's car pulled away, Ryan was on the curb, bewildered and smiling. Ryan messaged his squad, *Where are you guys?*

Harvey's. Waiting for you to spill the tea! Gina replied.

Ryan turned around and briskly walked to Harvey's. He was finally feeling great.

He walked in, trying hard not to smile, failing miserably. His team greeted him with loud whistles and applause. He felt like a rock star, uncontrollably smiling, gesturing his squad to calm down. He finally reached the table knowing he was blushing like a carrot.

"I'm assuming you guys know about it?"

"Yes, Jeff texted me just now." Gina smiled.

Fish pushed a chilled beer toward him. "I ordered this for you. Now tell us what happened with Todd? He seemed furious."

Ryan took a sip of the beer and started talking. He gave them all the juicy details, adding a little spice here and there. His squad was mesmerized by his story listening to him like kids listening to a fairytale. By the time they walked out of Harvey's, it was almost five pm.

"I knew you would do something amazing. I'm coming over tomorrow." Gina kissed him on the cheek and left. Within seconds his phone buzzed. It was a text from Todd.

My place, 9 pm.

Ryan smiled. The late-night invitation to Todd's house meant only one thing. He knew winning Miamart was a big win for Sun. And it was all because of the big red envelope. The partnership would give him time to travel, visiting Sun's global offices. *I can spend a year in the Tokyo office,* he thought. It would also shut Jeff up permanently and maybe cure his smile.

He reached his apartment, poured a drink, and headed to the balcony to smoke. The balcony had a majestic view overlooking Central Park. He enjoyed his treat, thinking how far he had come from playing poker games in dingy alleys. He thought about what his father would say to him if he saw him today. He felt lonely. It would've been great to celebrate the victory with someone beside him. He spent almost an hour there, came out, and decided to take a nap.

Ryan woke up with a start to the sound of the alarm. He felt tired, his body ached, and his head felt like it was about to explode. The familiar numbness bothered him. He reminded himself to get an appointment with the doctor. He showered to feel better. The excitement to see Todd and discuss the win pushed Ryan to keep moving forward. He wore his jeans and a white hoodie to stay warm and walked out.

Todd's house was a 20,000-square-foot mansion located in Tribeca, a trendy neighborhood in downtown Manhattan. Besides the eleven luxurious bedrooms, the mansion had a panic room, a Versailles-inspired dining room, and an award-winning greenhouse. Rumors were that Todd bartered the residence away from the senior Mullen. However, no one had a clue what Todd gave in return. Very few employees had the privilege of being invited to the CEO's house.

Ryan was the only creative worthy of walking in unannounced. The management made pivotal decisions and whispered well-kept secrets here. Pitches and big presentations were finalized at his house, usually during late nights. Todd's approval was mandatory even though it was typically too late to incorporate his suggestions.

Ryan had convinced himself that the unannounced access privileges were because Todd loved him. He was always overwhelmed with the entrance and the extravagant art flaunted around the living room. Ryan considered Todd a poseur; if it was expensive, it was good art for Todd. Ryan parked the car and hurried toward the entrance. He was thirty minutes late, but he could get away with it today. The door opened before he could ring the bell. It was Jeff.

Bumping into him was not something Ryan expected. Jeff looked at Ryan with the same plastered smile, trying hard to hide his surprised look. Ryan couldn't wait to see Jeff's expression after the news of the partnership breaks. He walked in through the ajar door without acknowledging Jeff's presence.

The sound of classical music coming from Todd's study beckoned Ryan. The study was on the first floor and had a walk-out balcony. He could tell Todd's mood by the genre of music playing in the background. He climbed the stairs that led to the study.

The door was open, and Todd was on his phone. Todd gestured for Ryan to come in and lowered his voice. Ryan knew this was a conversation his boss didn't want him to listen to, so he walked around the room admiring the vintage advertising posters. Todd's inaudible conversation had now turned into "hmm" and "ahh." He finally got off the phone.

"Congratulations. You're the man, the fucking guru. We've got a lot to celebrate." Todd pushed a small gold-plated box toward Ryan. Ryan knew what it was without opening the lid.

"Boss, I decided to quit."

"Fuck off," Todd laughed, "You were high when you walked in today." Todd pushed it further toward him, "I don't want to talk till I know you're in a good mood."

"But I thought you wanted me to quit?" Ryan was getting uncomfortable thinking about where the conversation was heading.

"Don't be a pussy. A little sniff here and there is fine. Just don't overdo it." Todd smiled and sat back. Ryan picked up and snorted a line to avoid the confrontation. He knew Todd would keep on insisting.

"I heard you got the fucking prized letter." Todd smiled.

"Yes, I can't wait to read it." Ryan lied.

"May I see it?"

"I didn't bring it, boss." Ryan was confused.

"Don't fuck with me. You're telling me you didn't read it?" The frown on Todd's face was getting deeper.

"No, I didn't. What's in the letter?"

"If I knew, why the fuck would I ask you for it. Stop fucking with me. I'm pretty sure you were as intrigued as I am."

"I swear, boss, I didn't read it."

"Are you fucking kidding me, Ryan? It's not something that happens often. How the fuck could you not be curious?" Todd's pitch was getting higher. Ryan's confusion was turning into bewilderment.

"Trust me. I didn't read it."

"I don't trust anyone. I want to see the fucking letter."

"Fine, you'll have it tomorrow, jeez."

Ryan welcomed the short bout of silence.

"Fuck off and get it now."

"Todd, you can't be serious."

"I am." Todd stared back.

Ryan was less concerned about the letter and more about Todd's unexpected behavior.

"OK, but at least let me finish the drink." He poured himself another, "Now, can we talk about something else? Tell me how great the presentation was today?" Ryan smiled, "If only you would stop doubting my skills."

"When have I doubted your work?" Todd said, still with a frown on his face.

"Your team will never let you down, boss."

"Yes, I agree. Running an agency is all about getting the right ingredients together, including a great team."

Ryan gulped the drink, waiting for a natural segue to talk about the partnership.

"Fuck the letter. Let's have another drink." Todd poured Ryan another Chivas, almost filling the glass to the brim.

"Are you sure? I don't mind getting it now." Ryan lied.

"Let me get to the point," he said, passing the drink to Ryan. "The pitch today was a much-needed win, but it was to an existing client. It was like getting a blowjob from your ex. It's good but not great. You don't applaud the cops when they catch criminals, right?"

"No, but if they get an Al Capone, you would surely want to reward them."

He found the segue. It was time to talk partnership.

"Miamart had almost slipped away. We won new business from them. I got them back in." Ryan felt his nerves kicking in. Todd would always make him anxious. The numbness was spreading in his left side.

"Yes, and as you said, it was a fucking team effort, but that's not even my fucking point."

"What's your point, boss?" Ryan felt the pain in his body coming back as he gulped his drink.

"You know I love you, Ryan, as a son. That's why I ignored most of your flaws."

"It was also because of all the business I was getting for Sun. No?" Ryan smiled.

"No." Todd picked up a file and threw it towards Ryan, "You

know we never hire anyone without a thorough background check." The documents inside made Ryan cramp with fear. He suppressed the cold shivers that ran inside him. The documents were about a murder that happened decades ago. Ryan recognized his manager as panic surged through him.

"Let's move to the balcony. It's a beautiful night." Todd nudged the coke toward Ryan, "Here, have another hit. I bought this, especially for you." Ryan sniffed another line hoping the panic would go away. He could feel the weight of the unspoken threat hurled at him. Todd picked up a shining cane. The top had an intricately carved lion's bust in gold. Ryan tried to change the topic.

"That's beautiful!" They moved out to the balcony.

"It's solid gold. It was custom-made for me by the ruler of Dubai. Do you want it?" The bright moon and the stars in the clear sky lit up the city.

"Oh, I doubt I'll ever need it,"

"Never rule out the possibility of needing support." The threat was no longer veiled. It was cold, but the fire pit made it bearable. Todd moved to the ledge and lit up another cigar.

"You've done some great work for us. I consider you one of the best in Manhattan, but advertising is like alcohol, age matters. The difference is that in advertising, with age, you become less valuable." Todd's lengthiest monologue without swearing sounded suspicious.

"You think I'm less valuable now?" He could feel the veins bulging in his forehead.

"Ryan, it's a tough decision, but if you look at it from my perspective, you'll understand it someday." Todd paused as Ryan tried hard to read him but couldn't. His mind felt numb, as if frozen.

"What decision, boss?"

"I'm sorry, but I'll have to let you go Ryan."

Ryan could feel the floor spinning underneath his feet. He could barely hear himself think. His muscles tightened as he rummaged for saliva in his mouth.

Todd looked at him and said calmly, "I need you to resign tonight."

Ryan didn't know how to react. His face felt cold. Tiny droplets appeared on his forehead. The October breeze brushed across his sweaty back. The dizziness spread from the floor to the entire room. He was trying his best to stay calm and not give Todd the satisfaction of seeing him panic. It was getting increasingly difficult for him to hide the obvious. His jaw felt numb, and he could feel the pinching pain in his entire body. He moved to the ledge, gripping the surface as his legs felt weaker than ever before.

"Why? Why tonight?" Ryan slurred.

"Not my choice, Ryan. Daniel specifically asked for it. He doesn't want a fucking junkie working on his account." Todd took another sip from his drink. "You know how it is. It was either the account or you."

Ryan was sweating profusely. He could sense the numbness on one side of the body. Todd smiled at him as if enjoying Ryan's pain like a sadist.

"Daniel is a pussy. He was already giving us the account. The presentation was just a fucking formality. You fucking ignored me, refused to share the fucking presentation with me." Todd turned around and stared at the fire pit, "You fucked yourself. You pissed off the client with your risqué pitch, getting high in the office. I fucking salvaged the deal." Todd's trembling voice couldn't hide the anger and the hatred.

"Plllease call 911." Ryan slurred, looking for his phone, realizing he had left it inside.

"This is not fucking easy for me. You were like a fucking son to me. I loved you; I still do. What I'm about to do is good for you." Todd smiled.

"Cccall 911!!" Ryan whispered as his trembling hands gripped the ledge. They both knew Ryan would not survive the second stroke. He could hardly hear what Todd was saying. He wanted to get out and run, but he felt paralyzed.

Todd turned around and looked at him, "You're not the first asshole in advertising to think they are irreplaceable. Every cunt who comes to Manhattan thinks he is immortal." Todd was not smiling anymore; he leaned toward him and stared at him. "We already have a fucking replacement, someone who makes you look like fucking Gandalf."

The pain became unbearable as he tried to wrap his arms around himself. Everything around him was spinning. He could hear his heart pounding like a jackhammer. His vision was getting impaired. Finally, his dry mouth managed to whisper, "Wwho?" he slurred with a distorted jaw.

Inches away from his face, Todd moved forward and said, "Kate."

Ryan tried to balance himself as he felt he was about to fall. His left side was completely numb, and sweat rolled down his forehead into his eyes. The starry night became blurred. He moved his hand forward as he felt his legs surrendering. He wanted Todd to grab his hand, fearing he might trip over the ledge. Todd raised his hand, and everything turned black before Ryan realized he was falling from the first floor of Todd's mansion.

Chapter 9

What Happens in Vegas, Stays in Vegas!
(Las Vegas Convention and Visitors Authority, 2003)

She was tired, awake for over thirty hours. The pain was like fire spreading across her body as if someone was igniting her nerves. The dreary office didn't help either. It seemed someone moved in and lost interest in life. If a room could be suicidal, this was it.

She had been here for over five hours. Besides the RA from her college dorm, two other women and a man in the room stared at the 21-year-old. She felt like sitting in the middle of an inquisition.

"Let's go over the story one more time, Kate?" said a woman who reminded her of a Russian KGB agent from a low-budget thriller.

"It's not a fucking story." She kept staring at the table in front of her, too tired to move her head and look at them. "I was raped while his friends watched and cheered." Kate almost whispered. She had lost the will to shout at them.

Kate hated the oversized college hoodie that said, "Go Greenwich!" She tucked her hands in the long sleeves of it. She had bought a size larger than her usual fit, but today, it felt tight. The jeans were also bothering her; she should've worn something more comfortable. She shivered and seemed as vulnerable as the last leaf fluttering in the autumn breeze. She took off the band that tied her hair in a pony.

"You've told me and the RA. But Simon just joined us, and he must hear it from you. Let's talk about the specifics one last time," Anna said.

Anna was the campus advisor and had worked at the campus all her life. Kate could tell the room was hers. Anna acted like she had seen everything, and Kate could feel being stereotyped.

Kate could tell they didn't believe her. She blamed her best friend for convincing her to report the rape. No one was going to believe a student who couldn't afford her tuition fees accusing three college football stars of rape. The stars' parents donated millions to the college. There was no way they would listen to her, especially when she was drunk when it happened.

"Miss Kate, I'm sorry that you went through this, and I'll do everything in my power to find whoever is guilty," Simon said. He was from the campus police.

"Whoever is guilty? I'm telling you it was Josh-Joshua Webber. You have a fucking witness, Me! It's not like he was wearing a mask." Kate shouted.

"We still need all the facts to file a report," Simon said. "A couple of months ago, he was your boyfriend. You even refused to report it to the police."

Simon seemed nervous. He was sweating through his maroon polo, and his khaki trousers made him look like he was working for the postal service, not the campus police. He kept pushing his brown hair away from his forehead. The third woman sat quietly, observing Kate.

"Correction, I did not refuse. I still have time to turn in my rape kit. I'm not ready to go to the cops - yet," Kate emphasized.

"Miss Kate, for us to take any legal action, we have to get all the facts cross-checked so there are no loopholes," Simon said.

Kate was making Simon nervous. She could sense Simon being extra nice to her. She pushed back her dark brown hair falling on her forehead and noticed Simon staring at the tattoo on her neck. He quickly looked away as Kate caught his glance. *All men are the same*, she thought.

"You mentioned you were dating Joshua, and you've had," Simon stuttered, "sssex with him on numerous occasions."

There was an awkward pause.

"Is that a statement or a question?" Kate was on the verge of giving up.

"Question," Simon replied, looking away when Kate spoke.

"Yes, I was in a relationship with Josh...Joshua," she corrected herself one more time. "I broke up with him last month. Yes, like any normal couple, we had sex."

"How many drinks did you have that day?" Simon asked.

"A beer, a few shots of tequila. Three, four, maybe six, I don't remember. But I wasn't drunk; I didn't pass out. I remember everything."

"And you didn't put up a fight," Simon said, staring at his notebook.

"I said 'No,' maybe a hundred times. I didn't kick or punch him if that's what you're asking. I couldn't move, and even if I could, they were holding me down."

"So, no physical marks of abuse on your body, like on the wrists or legs?" Simon asked.

"Have you seen how big these guys are? Why the fuck would I lie about being assaulted?" Kate wanted to storm out of the room, "Why does it feel like I'm the one who committed a crime?"

"I think you're tired. Let's take a break," the quiet woman finally spoke, "We can get the facts from Anna here. And if we need anything, we can call you."

"I'm sorry, who are you?" Kate looked at her.

"Sara Jacob, I'm the Marketing and PR Director at Greenwich. I'm on the committee that oversees campus assault cases."

"Do you think I'm lying?" Kate looked at her.

"If it helps, I know what you're going through, Kate."

"No, that doesn't help."

"Why don't we all take a break?" She stood up and walked over to Kate, "Here is my card. It has my cell number." Kate took the card and walked out, screaming in her mind.

She got out of the building. The cool autumn breeze embraced her.

"I'm so glad you did it." Maya was waiting outside for Kate.

"I'm so angry I listened to you. Fuck Greenwich. I should've just stayed in bed," Kate replied.

Her voice was muted, devoid of any pitch or tone. She didn't have the energy to shout at her closest friend. Maya was from Pakistan and came to America through a scholarship program. She tugged at her scarf to straighten it. Her choice of hijab was a stark contrast to what girls her age were wearing, especially in a place where what you wore mattered more than who you were—which made Kate respect Maya even more.

"You can't let them get away with it," said Maya.

"Can't? They've gotten away with it. They are out there probably smoking a joint, talking about me." Kate burst into tears, "The college doesn't care because I don't have any fucking proof. I should've held a camera up, smiled, and recorded everything."

Tears rolled down Maya's cheeks as she hugged Kate.

"Why me, Maya? I didn't do anything wrong." Kate was sobbing.

"I'm sorry, I can't even imagine what you're going through."

"No one can. No one knows what's going inside my head, inside my body. I feel so humiliated, so filthy."

Kate sensed someone standing behind them.

"Err, Miss Kate." It was Simon.

"What do you want?" Maya said to him.

"I just want to talk to Kate." He seemed more nervous than before as he looked at Kate.

"It's not a good time."

"I just wanted to say I agree with her. Greenwich doesn't care. No one does, to be honest."

Kate turned toward him, wiping her tears off. "What do you mean?"

"I can't repeat what I'm saying. The fact is you're in this fight alone," Simon said, looking back at the admin office nervously.

Kate couldn't figure out if he was trying to make her feel better or worse. Simon looked different outside, taller. He was probably in his 30s and came across as genuine and kinder in the sunlight. Kate tried to brush off the thought that he was cute.

"Please stop calling me, miss," said Kate.

"I can't talk to you here. I'm sure Anna is watching."

"What are you proposing?"

"Bluntly put, with your version of the events, you won't even get a hearing, let alone a conviction."

She was perplexed, waiting for Simon to get to the point.

"You've been in a sexual relationship with this guy for the past year. There is no physical evidence. There are no witnesses. It's your word against all the top lawyers of the state who are on retainers with his father."

"Let me get this straight. You wanted to meet so you can tell me I can't do anything."

"No, I wanted to tell you to be creative. Get your revenge, punish them. Just don't do it the traditional way."

"What do you mean by creative?" A part of her was nagging her to forget everything and just walk away. She had her exams in a week and the final project due in two weeks.

"I'm not sure what you're suggesting," Kate said.

"I feel the best move forward is to hurt the Webbers. Get an enormous amount of money from them. It's a lose-lose scenario no matter what you do. Getting some money guarantees you a better life."

"And that, in your opinion, will fix everything?" Maya smiled at him sarcastically.

"Nothing will fix everything. Even if you send them to jail, it won't erase what has happened."

"What about justice?" Maya said.

He ignored Maya, "Do you think five years in jail will be justice for what they did? That is IF they are convicted. Meanwhile, they will splatter you on every newspaper and TV channel in the city."

"So, I take money in return for rough sex. Maybe I should quit college and start doing that." Kate smiled.

Simon's phone started buzzing. He ignored it.

"Remember, you have two options. Have a difficult life, relive the trauma, and maybe get these guys to jail, or punish them financially and live a comfortable life." Simon started to get up, "I have to leave."

This wasn't a solution Kate was expecting. She felt worse.

"Thanks for the help."

"Let's be clear; I didn't help you. I just wanted to give you a reality check. It's your life. It's your battle, and you'll be fighting it alone."

He started walking away, then turned back. "You can't tell anyone that a college employee is telling you that the college is too scared to do anything. This remains between us. Here is my card." Simon gave Kate his card.

"Call me if you think I am making sense." Simon walked away.

Maya looked at Kate, "Why do I get the feeling that he has a crush on you?"

"He seems weird," Kate replied.

Maya picked up her backpack and adjusted her scarf.

"Let's go back to the dorm and figure out what to do next. I don't think you should meet Simon," Maya said.

"I think it's important to meet him. He said one thing that made sense."

"What?"

"That I have to fight this alone."

The dorm was located inside the campus. Kate shared a small room with Maya, but it was their happy place. The interior design drew a clear distinction between the two roommates. One side was embellished. It had fairy lights above the bed, a mirror with lots of makeup, the walls covered with boy-band posters. Maya's side was unadorned except for an Arabic verse hanging on the wall and a family portrait on the side of the table. The portrait was of her disabled father and elder brother, who came from a remote village in Pakistan. She had lost her mother and two elder brothers in the Afghan war. The only thing untidy about the room was the scattered books and assignments.

"Don't forget the meeting with the college board tomorrow. You can't be late."

"Yeah, I know," Kate got into her old high school T-shirt and a loose pair of shorts.

"You're in no shape for the finals. The final project is due in two weeks. Call the teacher and let her know."

"No, I want to get it over with," Kate replied.

. . .

It was four am, and Kate was wide awake. The streetlight streaking through the window was bothering her. She had avoided going on social media for a whole week, a record for her. She knew she would find something terrible. Her timeline was usually Joshua's posts. She lay in bed, overwhelmed with the darkness surrounding her future, hoping to see the light sooner than her sleep. Her sleep was in a constant battle with her thoughts. Her thoughts were winning.

Sleep was sneaking in sporadically, especially when she tried studying for her finals. Sleep was not something she craved. Instead, she had discovered a new pastime; her fantasies of revenge drowning her assailants' laughter. It would start with all three laughing at her, tearing her apart, but the fantasies would lead to her taking control. She imagined numerous scenarios, from the three begging her to forgive to slicing their penises into small pieces. The fantasies ranged from the most bizarre to the most realistic. The only common string was they all had the three vehemently apologizing. Her eyes became heavier, imagining her assailants begging for mercy.

The loud banging on the door woke Kate up. Her room was as bright as an airport lounge in the summer. She scanned the room to catch her bearings and checked her phone. It was three pm. There were 17 missed calls and five new texts. Three calls from the University office and 14 from Maya. None from Simon. *Fuck!* She had missed the meeting with the board and possibly sealed any chance of the college helping her.

The knocking got louder. "Your friend is calling you. She's worried. Is everything OK?" Someone shouted from behind her room's door.

"Everything is fine," she shouted back. "I'll call her back." She got up and called Maya.

"Are you up? Is everything OK?"

"Yes, super."

"You missed the meeting!"

"Yeah, I overslept." There was silence on the other side. "Maya, I'm fine. I'll tell you when we meet." Kate hung up.

She didn't want to have the conversation over the phone. She felt terrible. She took two painkillers and checked the refrigerator. Finally, she forced herself to eat a leftover sandwich from last night. The shower made her feel better. Her thoughts returned, but daytime fantasies for her were always pragmatic.

She knew her exams were coming, and her final project was due. After that, she could finish her communications degree this semester, move to New York and get an internship in an ad agency. Advertising was her passion, and a 4.0 GPA testified to it.

She poured shampoo on her palms and started massaging her hair, soon realizing she had already done this more than once. She got out, dressed up, and decided to go to the library to study for her exams. She was feeling better, stronger, clearer. She would rather chase her dreams than the assailants. After missing the meeting today, it was going to be futile. Going to the library meant she was taking steps toward closure. Erasing the memory and moving forward was the best option.

The newly constructed college library was about a few minutes from the dorm. As Kate got closer, she wondered if it was the right time. She wanted to turn back. But instead, decided to put on some lipstick to look less like a victim. She rummaged through her bag like a dryer spinning clothes, panicked she had left her lipstick in the room. Finally, her fingers felt the familiar shape and took out the lipstick. She looked up, and there he was.

Joshua walked out of the library with two girls. They were laughing. Kate froze, panic spreading across her body. She felt the whizzing sound of blood rushing through her body. She couldn't move, her lipstick still in her hand as she saw him walking to her. She started sweating profusely, tiny droplets appeared on her forehead and the back of her neck. The metal shell of the lipstick felt cold, but she couldn't feel her hands or any part of her body.

Everything around her seemed to move in slow motion. She wanted to run, shout, cry but couldn't even blink. She stood like a mannequin as Joshua smiled at her, nodded, and passed by her. She could hear a constant ringing in her ears. Her legs caved as she started falling. Suddenly, she felt a hug.

It was Maya. Kate dropped all her weight into Maya's embrace. The lipstick slipped from her hand to the ground. She felt her weak legs giving way to her weight, but Maya held on to her. They both were trying to pretend nothing had happened as students and teachers walked by.

"Breathe!" Maya whispered, rubbing Kate's back.

"It was—" She tried to speak.

"Ssshh! I know. I saw them. Just breathe."

Maya took her back to the dorm.

"You need to see a doctor," Maya said, then gave Kate the herbal tea her mother had left her. It was supposed to be a miracle drink from India that would cure everything. It was also the only Indian item her Pakistani patriotism allowed her to keep.

"Do you have anything stronger?" Kate smiled as she took a sip.

"Maybe when I marry a rich white guy!"

"You know there is help on campus too."

"I know." She snubbed Maya's suggestion.

"You can say what you want. I'll keep telling you to do what's good for you." Maya was a good distraction. She was her remedy to get Joshua's image out of her head.

"I hate leaving you. I have an evening class, but I'll leave my phone on in case you need anything."

I need you to stay, Kate thought.

"I'll be fine. Will catch up on my studies."

Maya left. Kate curled up in the bed. She kept staring at the ceiling, thinking about what to do next. The sunlight faded as it began to rain. She loved the sound of the rain. It was calming. She got up and opened the window. The cool breeze and tiny droplets hit her face. The scent of the wet soil was therapeutic. She wanted to talk to someone, and the only person she could think of was Simon.

Chapter 10

We try harder!

(Avis, 1963)

Since the incident, no one from the college had called or spoken to Kate, and she knew why. Everyone blamed her. Joshua knew almost everyone in the class, but she had no friends other than Maya. Her entire social circle was Joshua.

He was popular for many reasons; of course, being rich and powerful helped. The only person she was close to was her roommate. She decided not to go out again. The dorm was her sanctuary. *I can hide in my room for the rest of my life,* she thought in self-mockery. The phone buzzed once, probably a text from Simon. It wasn't. It was Joshua.

Great to see you today!

She held on tightly to the phone. Then, after a long agonizing pause, the phone buzzed again. Her hands started trembling.

I miss you, sweetheart!!! There was a sad emoji at the end.

I know you're angry. I get that.

She didn't respond.

Sorry, it got out of hand that day, honey. I thought we were having fun.

I miss you, babe. I wanna see you!!

She was too numb to reply. The assault, the laughter, the pain was playing in her head like a slideshow. The phone buzzed again like a surge of electricity.

Planning a trip to Virginia Beach. We have a beachfront villa there. Wanna come along? Pleaaaasee!

Kate sulked, thinking about the lack of empathy. To Josh this was just another message on just another day.

Anyway. Thanks for not going to the meeting today. Owe you big time.

She threw her phone as if it were a dead spider she'd squashed. She clenched her trembling fingers to stabilize her hands and herself. It was a strange feeling, a combination of intense fear and anger. Kate stood up and walked to the window, praying for this feeling to end. She was not religious, but she believed in God, and she believed in signs. She didn't care if the signs were her mind connecting the dots or some divine intervention. They usually pointed her in the right direction.

Joshua calling her was a sign. It seemed like a peace offering. Was he too naive or too smart? Each word made her hate him even more. There was no remorse, no empathy, and no signs of a moral compass in his texts.

He still expected her to behave as if nothing had happened. *Am I giving out the wrong signals? Does he think I am weak?* She asked herself. She went to the mirror and stared at herself as tears brimmed in her eyes. *He can't get away with this. He shouldn't.*

It was getting dark, the rain had stopped, and the only sound she could hear was the wind brushing against the trees. Even though the anger was there, this was the best she had felt since the incident. She was energized as if someone had given her a shot of steroids. She started thinking of the options she had. She was not a victim, she told herself. She had just lost one battle; the war was about to begin. She decided to send the text that could change her life.

Can we meet? Kate texted.

Sure! When? Where? Simon replied almost immediately.

Someplace private. No college crowd. She texted back.

Grotto outside St. Bernadette? 30 mins? Simon replied instantly.

St. Bernadette was an old Catholic church about half a mile outside the campus. *Good, no one from the college would be there, especially on a Wednesday evening,* she thought.

Perfect! she replied.

She wore her favorite jeans and a beige top. She didn't tie her hair, and the light lipstick and mascara helped her look less like a victim. The plan was to let Simon know she wasn't looking for a savior; she was looking for an ally. She got there ten minutes late. Simon was sitting on a stone bench across from the sacred Grotto.

The Grotto dedicated to Our Lady of Lourdes was a Catholic place of prayer devoted to the Blessed Mother, Mary. The oldest American replicas of the Lourdes Grotto in France, built about five decades after the apparition of Mary at Lourdes, adorned the beautiful mountainside shrine.

Surrounded by melted candles and exotic flowers, it was used for ornamental and devotional purposes by the church and the congregation. A well-maintained garden surrounded it. There was a fountain nearby, but it was not operational. Simon stood up as she saw Kate walking toward him.

"Hi!" he said nervously.

"Sorry, I'm a bit late. I didn't feel like running." Kate sat down next to him on the cold stone bench. It wasn't comfortable.

"I brought us some coffee!" Simon smiled. "What's the tattoo?" he asked sheepishly.

"It's a phoenix. It's a mythical totem."

"Does it mean anything?"

"It's a magical creature that sets itself on fire every night and then rises from the ashes every day."

"Why?"

"To relive." Kate didn't have time for games.

"You didn't show up at the board meeting!"

"Joshua contacted me." She didn't want to give an excuse, and she didn't want to beat around the bush. She was running out of time and patience. Kate wanted to be sure if Simon was an ally she could trust.

"Oh! That's surprising," Simon said.

Kate passed the phone to Simon to read the entire conversation. She waited for a reaction. There was none.

"Do you think we can use this as evidence?"

"No, nothing is incriminating here. It sounds more like a caring boyfriend who misses you and wants to patch things up."

Kate was about to curse when she realized where she was. "But isn't it obvious what he is saying?"

"To you, yes, not to a jury. Look, if you want me to sugarcoat stuff, you're with the wrong person."

"OK, forget the texts. You know what I want; how do I get it?"

"I don't know what you want," Simon said. It was more of a question than a statement.

"I want him to suffer. I want him to realize what he's done, what they have done is wrong, and it wasn't a mistake you forget and go to the beach," Kate said.

"In my opinion, Kate, you have three options. First, you can go to the cops. Second, you can again file a report with the college, and third, you could settle and get enough money to jumpstart your life."

"What do you recommend?"

"You won't like my recommendation."

"Try me." She knew what he was going to propose.

"Going to the police is the most obvious, but it will take a few years for you to find closure, and that is if they are convicted, which I doubt. Plus, the scandal follows you; you will be scrutinized on social media and not in a good way. You know the drill." He paused. "Option two, the college will be diplomatic. They'll make you believe you're being helped but will protect their interests, in other words, Joshua."

Simon was trying to build a case, she thought.

"Tell me about option three. How does it work?" She wanted him to get to the point.

"We can start by asking half a million and hope to get a hundred thousand, two hundred if we are lucky because there is no guarantee they'll agree." There was a pause. Simon looked at her and then stared at the statues of angels around the Grotto.

"And what would they expect in return?" Kate was calculating the pros and cons in her head.

"Obviously, not reporting the incident would be one. We can also throw in your entire college debt so that when you walk out of college with a degree, you're debt-free."

She took a sip of the hot coffee. "And that you think, is my best option?" Kate wanted him to make the decision. She knew she would not feel good about it, but there was no guarantee that the other two options would make her feel good either. After graduation, she could settle in New York and forget all about Greenwich if she got the money.

"It's not the best solution, but it's the smartest. Look, it's your life. You need to decide because you will be carrying this cross, not me." She was frustrated that he recommended one route but was unwilling to own it.

"And do you think they'll be interested in a settlement when they know I didn't file a report?" She took another sip; it made her feel better.

"They will be interested in it for the next ten years. That's the statute of limitations for rape in New York," he said while getting up.

Their meeting was short, the coffee was finished, and the sun had set. Simon offered to walk with Kate, but she wanted to stay back.

"I'll be fine. I need some time to think. It's just a five-minute walk from here."

She didn't want the conversation to go beyond what they were discussing. She was thinking of an excuse.

"I want to spend some time in the church," she said.

The church was open, the yellowish lights beaming from the entrance and the windows almost beckoning her. It had been nearly ten years since she had walked into a church. She decided it was time. She didn't want to pray; she just wanted to feel at peace. She tried to drown the constant noise in her head.

Kate was still confused even though Simon was making sense. She didn't want to do something that she would regret later. She walked in. The church was almost empty except for an old couple praying together near the altar. The scent of burning candles and flickering light bouncing off stained glass created a mystical backdrop.

Kate sat at the farthest pew from the alter. She felt the peace suffusing in her body. Moments later, she looked at her phone and realized she had been sitting there for thirty minutes. She lit a candle and left some change. She didn't pray; it just felt good, and she needed to feel good.

As she walked out of the church, her eyes caught the sign on the noticeboard *"Fear not, for I am with you!"* The text was a sign, the spark she needed to light the flame. *This is the turning point,* she thought. She felt she was ready to set the world on fire. The phoenix is awakening. She smiled and started walking briskly to the dorm.

Maya was asleep when Kate got there. She trudged across the dim room, trying not to make noise, and finally found the edge of her bed. She couldn't sleep. The loud buzzing on her phone broke the silence in the room. She scrambled to get the phone out of her pocket, accepting the call before it buzzed again. She was wondering who was calling her this late. It was Simon.

"You up?"

She gently turned and stepped outside. She walked along the quiet hallway as she whispered. Most of the girls were either out or headed home for the long weekend.

"No, I'm sleeping." She smiled.

"Oh, sorry, I was just thinking about you. I mean the talk we had." He sounded his usual nervous self.

"Me too," she replied, happy he'd called.

"Just wanted to say hang in there, everything will be fine. I'm with you all the way."

"Thanks. Means a lot."

"Let me know if you need anything." He sounded like he genuinely meant it.

Kate returned to the room. She was happy, and she was beginning to like Simon. Not as a potential boyfriend but as a sincere friend. She needed one.

"Why are you smiling?" Maya was up when she walked in. "Anything I should know about?"

"Oh, sorry, I tried not to wake you up. Simon called." Maya switched on the lamp.

"OK, now I'm up." Maya sat up cross-legged in her bed, wide awake.

Kate told her about Simon.

"Church? Well played, Simon!" Maya smiled, "Now what?"

"No, it's nothing like that. I just needed some advice. I'll probably never see him again."

"I wasn't talking about Simon; I was talking about your next move. But I'll come back to Simon in a bit," she said mischievously.

"Well, Simon makes sense. If I settle, I get something out of it. I get more stress, more pain, and nothing else with the other two options. What do you think?"

"For them, money is the easiest way out. My preference was reporting to the cops, but then I know you're in this alone, and it will be a long and tiring battle, so let the college handle it."

"Maya, I don't want to be the victim. I want to be in control. Make them suffer on my terms; the college will do nothing."

"Do you trust Simon?"

"I don't trust anyone." Kate sighed and quickly added, "except you!"

"So tell me about Simon."

Kate switched off the lamp. "There's nothing to tell." She rolled over to the other side. "I need some sleep. I have to work on my project tomorrow." There was a glimpse of a smile that she didn't want Maya to see.

It was a bright sunny Thursday morning, and Kate was up after finally getting some sleep. She had to finish a media plan for her final college assignment, which was the most challenging part of her advertising project. The campaign itself she could wrap up in one night. The media plan would include talking to the region's top digital, print, and electronic media agencies. She had to get rates and spread the plan out on an excel sheet with other details.

Kate hated this part because this required a lot of precise calculations. She was working on a hypothetical budget of $1 Million. Contacting different ad agencies was at least three weeks of work. She had no idea where to start. Then she remembered Sara

Jacobs, the marketing head she met while filing the report at the Campus office.

Sara Jacobs was the easiest way out of this mess. Kate decided to meet with her. She had to get out; the hushed room was driving her insane. She didn't have time to follow the protocol and make an appointment; after all, Sara told her she would be available night and day. She changed, picked up her bag, and headed for the admin building.

"Sara Jacobs, Director Marketing," she read the sign as she knocked on the door. The office was cheerful. A Marge Simpson doll was on her table and colorful posters on the wall. Sara looked like an executive from a high-end New York ad agency, dressed in a grey skirt with a pink top. She was sitting with her stilettos off. Kate recognized her favorite perfume, the one she couldn't afford. It filled the air. The sensual scent made her room seem more luxurious.

"Hey, I'm so glad you came. Is everything OK? You missed the board meeting?" Kate wasn't sure if it was a question, a statement, or a reprimand.

"Yes, thank you for seeing me. Everything is fine. No, this is not about the report." Kate paused, "You mentioned that day that if I needed help, I could reach out to you." Kate didn't want to talk about the case.

"Sure," Sara replied with a curious frown on her face.

"I need help with my final project. Because of," she said, groping for words, "you know what happened, I'm far behind, and I would never have come if—"

"Kate!" Sara interrupted her, "just tell me what you need. I'm more than willing to help you."

"I need to make a media plan that is part of my final project. That's the only part I don't feel confident about, and since I don't know anyone in the industry, I don't know where to start."

"Well, you started at the right place." Sara picked up her phone and spoke to someone.

"I'm going to give you Mark's number and email. He handles our media and works at a leading media house in New York. Be nice to him if you plan to have a career in advertising. He's very well connected."

I'll be his slave for the rest of my life if he gets me a job in Manhattan, she thought.

"Also, off the record, don't tell him it's a college assignment. Let him think he is getting real business. You'll get the plan faster."

She called Mark the moment she left Sara's office. She didn't disclose the help was for a college assignment. He was more than interested when she told him the total budget was a million dollars she managed to get for a startup. He was charming, and he flirted a little. He was saving her from a lot of work, and he could be her ticket to Manhattan.

Kate went to the library to work, which was bustling with students. The noise of the photocopiers, keys clicking on the laptops, and the loud whispers made it sound like a Ford factory getting ready for the Black Friday sales. Ironically the noise helped her focus more on her work and less on Joshua. She briskly moved to an empty cubicle. She saw a few familiar faces, smiled, and nodded at them. She noticed them whispering and felt they were talking about her.

After a while, Kate looked at the watch. She had spent five hours at the library and had almost finished. She logged in to check her emails. There was one. It was an email with an attachment from Mark. Kate was excited. The subject line read, *SEE YOU IN NEW YORK!*

Mark had pulled off a miracle. She downloaded the attachment and scanned through the excel sheet. She breathed a sigh of relief. The difficult part of her final paper was complete. Now she had time to handle Joshua and had the peace of mind to make calculated decisions. It was time to call Simon. He didn't pick up, so she texted him.

Hi! I've decided. When do we begin?

He didn't reply.

The campus cafe was crowded, so she bought a salad and returned to the dorm. Maya was still in her class. She finished her salad. Simon still hadn't replied. She resisted the urge to call him. Instead, she grabbed her phone, turned on the music, and went for a run. Even the loud music could not silence a million thoughts going through her mind. *Why didn't he reply? Was he upset? Did the college find out about Simon? Did Joshua get to him?*

It was almost 9 pm, and the darkness outside added to her anxiety. She was getting restless and angry. She stopped running, took out her phone, and dialed Simon's number. Almost immediately, Simon picked up.

"Sorry, I was tied up at work."

"That's fine." She was upset. "Did you get my message?"

"Yes, I got it, and I'm happy you've made a decision."

"Well, how do we begin? What do I do?"

"Nothing. I've started the ball rolling. We are meeting Joshua tomorrow."

"We?"

"I can meet him alone, or if you feel comfortable, you can come along. I'm fine with either."

"No," she said, "I'm not ready. I don't want to see him."

"That's fine. It's an initial meeting. We just want to know if Joshua is interested in a settlement."

"If?" Kate was surprised.

"He will be. Just get a good night's sleep. Your life is changing tomorrow."

Chapter 11

Go further

(Ford, 2012)

Waiting was nerve-wracking. Kate desperately needed a distraction. She headed back to the dorm and decided to work on her final project. She spent almost an hour on the campaign while thinking about her escape plan. Finally, the sound of the doorknob turning broke her chain of thought. Maya was back, the interruption she needed.

"You look different," Maya said.

"I feel different. I'm glad you're here. I need your advice."

Maya looked at her as she took off her hijab and settled down.

"You mean the advice that you're not going to take." Maya slumped and sat cross-legged on the bed.

"You're the only one I trust." She didn't want Maya to know that she had already decided. "Well, you're not going to like it."

"And you want me to endorse what you've already decided?" Maya smiled.

"I'm asking for damages." Kate ignored her quip.

"You're settling."

"I hate the term, but that seems to be the best option."

"According to Simon, right?"

"Yes, but that is the option with the minimum pain, Maya. I'm going crazy thinking about it." Kate couldn't stop her tears.

"Once you make the decision, I'm behind you." Maya hugged her.

"Simon is meeting Joshua tomorrow."

"What about you?" Maya said.

"Not me, just Simon. I can't face him." Kate replied.

"Can I give you some advice?" Maya asked. "Control the conversation."

"I am controlling the conversation."

"No, you're not. You're letting Simon do the talking for you. You should be meeting Joshua, not just Simon. Don't let someone else talk on your behalf. Record everything he says and no matter what and always be the first to leave in a negotiation."

Maya made sense.

"I'm scared to meet him."

"You not facing Joshua is exactly what he'll be expecting. Catch him off guard. Do things he will least expect you to do. Be the first one to walk out. Take the money, but don't take it as a handout. Look him in the eye and pull it out from his fucking throat." Maya finally cursed.

"Fuck yeah." Kate smiled, "It makes more sense when you curse." They both laughed. Before she had any second thoughts, Kate picked up the phone and texted Simon. *I'll come along.*

The phone buzzed after a couple of minutes. *Not a good idea, are you sure?* Simon messaged.

Fuck yeah! I'm sure! 9 am at the library. Kate replied.

Kate drafted the text in a way that didn't warrant any replies. *This is it!* Was the message she wanted to send Simon. She chose the library because it was less crowded in the mornings.

Kate tossed and turned the entire night. Her insomnia had

become a beast fed by her fantasies. She spent her night imagining different scenarios of what to say and expect. Maya was right about one thing, catching Joshua off guard was the best strategy. It was the right plan to get under his skin.

Their relationship had been about what Joshua wanted. The clothes she wore, the friends she made, the places they went to; Joshua controlled everything. It didn't bother her at the time, but thinking about it was bothering her now. She knew Joshua was impulsive, and if things weren't going his way, he would lose control.

Finally, things were making sense to her. The soft sunlight started dripping through the curtains. Kate picked up the phone and saw it was almost seven. *It will be a disaster to fall asleep*, she thought. Running seemed like a good way to start the most ominous day of her life.

She loved the morning scent. If hope had a fragrance, this was it. Kate's mind was preoccupied with her meeting with Joshua. Knowing him, he would never take the deal. Simon was the heuristic way out. The run helped clear her mind. She decided to say what he would least expect, close the deal, and walk out. She looked at the time; it was almost 9 am. No time to change. She convinced herself that her running outfit drenched in her sweat was the power statement she needed.

Kate walked into the library and saw Joshua and Simon sitting on leather couches next to a corner table. She took off her headphones and placed her phone and headphones in the front pocket of her hoodie. They both smiled and waved at her. She sat on the empty couch between them.

"Hi!" Joshua said in a friendly tone.

"How was your run?" Simon asked.

"Have you decided yet?" She looked at Joshua. It was all coming back. She could feel the pain sprouting in her neck. The scenario of that night started playing in her head. The guys were laughing, screaming, tugging at her.

"Woah! Slow down. Take a deep breath." Joshua smiled and pushed a cup of coffee to her, "Here I got you your favorite mocha latte, babe."

"I need to work on my final project." She ignored the coffee and turned toward Simon. "Can we please skip the drama?"

It wasn't a request. She was nervous; her voice was shaky. Her hands were trembling feverishly. She slid her hands into the pockets of the green college hoodie she was wearing and tugged on her phone.

"Before we start." Simon put his coffee down on the table, "I just want both of you to know that my participation is unofficial. Whatever happens between us has to remain confidential."

Kate nodded.

"Babe," Joshua ignored him, "I don't even want to see what amount you want. You know I love you. Whatever you want, just say it. I want us back to be the way we were." He smiled.

Her mind exploded with the memories of the assault. Everything was vivid, what he was wearing, what he was saying, the way he pushed her, the stench of alcohol on his breath.

"Can you go to jail?" she replied. Joshua was not smiling anymore.

"Well, you want money, and I'm willing to do whatever you want." Joshua seemed to be in control, and she despised that. She hated that she was asking for money. She hated that he was sitting there calm, composed, and in control.

"Kate, Joshua has agreed to the settlement. He wants this to end. He has already spoken to his dad, and they have agreed to give one hundred thousand," Simon said.

"Listen, Simon." Joshua leaned forward. "I don't want to negotiate. She knows what she means to me. She asked for two hundred. I'm willing to do that. I'll convince my dad. I want this to end so both of us can move on and maybe just maybe get back together." He leaned back.

He was smiling with confidence as if the negotiation was over and the meeting was coming to an end. It wasn't; she had just arrived.

"One million!" Kate didn't recognize the voice that came out of her mouth. There was a pause. The silence was getting uncomfortable by the second. Everyone seemed to be shocked as she said it, including Kate.

"Kate, we've had this conversation. Let's think it through." Simon pleaded as he looked at her.

"That's not all. One million, and all the college debt," Kate said.

"What the fuck!" Joshua squirmed on his sofa.

"One million, and you cover all the college costs, or I go to the cops." Kate looked straight at Joshua.

"Listen bitch!" Joshua leaned forward in anger, "I don't know what games you're playing. I can destroy you. I can fuck you up so bad you would think the rape was a trip to Disneyland." Joshua was fuming, "You think you can mess with me? Do you know who I am?".

He was no longer in control. She was.

"You have 48 hours before I go to the cops." She smiled, composed outside. Inside, she was trembling. She felt her feet sinking into the wooden floor of the library as she stood up. *Always be the first to leave in a negotiation,* she remembered Maya's advice. She got up without blinking once and walked away.

"You're fucked, you fucking whore! I'm not paying you a single dime. I'm going to rape you with thirty guys now, you piece of shit."

She didn't look back. She knew he was out of control. She sensed Simon trying to calm Joshua down as he spewed more filth.

The silenced library echoed with his voice as everyone stared at Joshua screaming at her. She could hear Joshua shouting, his voice gradually fading. The further she walked, the wider she smiled. By the time she walked out of the library, her feet felt as strong as wings in a clear blue sky.

"I need your full attention," she said to Maya as she walked inside. She was trembling, laughing, pacing up and down the room. Kate picked up a bottle of water and gulped it down in ten seconds.

"I have a class in fifteen minutes," Maya said.

"Fuck the class. You have to hear this." Kate reenacted an entire sketch of what happened at the library. She was Joshua one minute and then the next minute herself. She fumed, almost dripping saliva like Joshua, as she told Maya how he reacted.

"Well, say something!" Kate nudged her to break her silence.

"Sorry, do you have any idea what you're doing?" Maya said.

Kate wasn't expecting this response.

"I thought you would be proud of me. I was in control. I handled it like a pro, just the way you told me to."

"I never told you to demand a million dollars and piss off the most powerful guy in the college."

"What more can he do to me than what he has already done?"

"A lot. You're underestimating him," Maya said.

There was silence as the tension between the two grew.

"Tell me you know that I care about you." Maya tried to calm things down, "All I'm saying is prepare for retaliation. He is not the sort who will sit back and enjoy the show. Do you think he will pay you a million dollars?"

"Maya, it was never about the money. I don't want him to pay. I'm going to the cops but on my terms. I want him to stop underestimating me."

"Aren't you scared of how he may react now?"

"I wasn't. I was just happy, but thanks to you, I'm scared now."

"Being afraid is not a bad thing. It means you'll prepare and be ready for Joshua's next move," Maya said as she left for her class.

Kate's phone buzzed.

"Hi, you OK?" It was Simon.

"Yes!" She needed Simon's approval. He had to be on her side.

"Can we talk?" Simon asked.

"About what?" Kate said.

"Kate, you have no idea who you're messing with."

"So, let me get this straight, you met Joshua today, and you know more about him than I?"

"Yes, you were dating him. You've not seen his dark side."

"Yup, you're right. I haven't seen his dark side."

"Did you know he has videos of you having sex?" Simon said.

She sat down on her bed. Yes, he does, she remembered. She hated it, but he insisted and said he would delete them later.

"He plans to upload the videos on revenge porn sites unless you stop pursuing the case." Simon continued, "No money, no cops, no report. That's Joshua's final offer."

Kate was silent. She needed time to decide.

"Tell me now if you need me or do you want to fight alone because you're in deep shit now."

"I need you, Simon. I can't do this alone." She hated feeling weak.

"I will only be involved if you listen to me. I can't guarantee things will work out, but I guarantee that I will try my best."

"So, what happens now?" Kate said.

"Your life will be ruined if this tape gets out. No one will hire you. You need to end this fast and move on. I need an answer now."

Kate kept staring at the wall, thinking about the pros and cons.

"Kate?" Simon said.

"No. He is not getting away with it," Kate said.

"There is no way you can win this, Kate."

"So I get raped twice? I know he'll never pay me a million dollars, but I want him to know this is not going to be a walk in the park."

"Fine, don't listen to me. Do what you want."

She was relieved when Simon disconnected his phone. She was now with the one person she could rely on. Herself.

The plan was to focus on one battle at a time. There was nothing she could do about Joshua, so she decided to go to the library and work on her final project. The media plan was complete; all she needed was the campaign. Her project was a public service campaign, and Kate had to pick the cause.

She was waiting for an epiphany, a unique idea. She now had the clarity she needed on how to move forward. Joshua's father would never agree to a million dollars. She would go to the cops and be done with her degree by the time she got a hearing. It would be easier to figure out what to do once she had a job. She smiled, knowing she had an ace up her sleeve.

Kate walked into the library and checked the noticeboard. There was a plethora of offers spread across the board. Basements for rent, discount deals from diners in the neighborhood, a dinner and dance coming up on the weekend, job opportunities; it was almost like a local newspaper, with only a front page. Finally, her eyes zeroed in on one flyer that stood out. A sign. A window of opportunity she was looking for seemed to be ajar.

"Get Internships Before You Graduate!"

Ogilvy & Mather, Bates, and Sun, three leading ad agencies, were looking for interns. This was a sign. She took out her phone and took a picture of the flyer. Sun was her first choice, and Ogilvy & Mather was a close second. DDB was a safety net if Ogilvy & Mather and Sun didn't call her. An internship at any three of these giants would jumpstart her advertising career.

Kate found a quiet place in the library and started to work on her application. She spent a few hours on it and was happy with the result. She ignored the emails on the flyer and googled the contact details of the creative directors working at the three ad agencies. After the email, she grabbed a sandwich and decided to work on her project. She could almost taste the Manhattan breeze.

She took out her headphones, turned on the music, and switched her brain off. By the time Kate walked out, she had worked nonstop for three hours and finished most of her project. It was almost 9 pm when she got to the dorm.

"Where have you been?" Maya said.

"At the library, calm down. You're scaring me."

"So, you haven't seen anything?"

"Seen what? What the fuck is going on Maya?".

"Kate, no matter what happens, I'm with you."

"Maya, tell me what the fuck is going on."

Maya trudged toward the table and turned the laptop on. She handed the laptop to Kate. Kate waited for the screen to light up, dreading the unthinkable. She sank to the floor as she recognized the tattoo on her neck.

It was a clip of her having sex with Joshua. Her body felt heavy like someone had tied her to a boulder rolling downhill. She could barely move. Her head was throbbing; her heart was ready to explode. She could hardly breathe. She gasped for air and managed to whisper, "I want to die."

Maya hugged her, trying to control her tears. She stayed silent. Suddenly there was a knock at the door. They looked at each other.

"Hi, it's me, Simon."

Maya wiped her tears and walked over to let him in. She stared at his swollen lip and the bruised eye.

"I'm guessing you've seen what's happening on the internet." No one replied. "I've asked one of my friends who is into cybersecurity to trace the source."

"Thank you, but we know who the source is. You know who the source is. So why don't you arrest the fucking source?" Maya hissed.

"We can't. These clips make Kate look bad, not Joshua." He was calm. "He will deny sending these."

"So nothing can be done? This is a crime." Maya screamed.

"Keep in mind he has more; 29 to be precise. He will keep making Kate's life a living hell unless—" Simon paused.

"Unless what?" Maya asked.

Kate was motionless, sitting cross-legged on the floor, staring at the laptop, saying nothing.

"I think Kate knows what I'm saying," Simon replied.

"He wants an apology," Kate whispered.

"From you? No way. She's not doing that." Maya looked at Kate.

"If you're her friend, you need to help her get out of this storm. This ends today, or this will keep on happening," Simon said.

"So, you think the best thing for her is to apologize?" Maya said.

"Not the best, the smartest," he said emphatically, "If she wants this to end, she has to leave this behind like a bad memory and move on."

"Are you crazy?" Maya shouted.

"Yes!" Kate broke the argument between the two as they stared at her. Then, she slowly picked herself up. "Yes, I will talk to him." She looked into Simon's eyes, letting him know how serious she was.

"Once my bank confirms he has deposited the one million."

"And the college debt," Maya added.

"Are you insane?" Simon asked, sounding flustered.

"She's right, and the college debt. I want the money by tomorrow."

Kate got up and opened the door for Simon. "He has left me no option. He has damaged me in a way that it can't be repaired.

Five minutes ago, I was thinking about ways to kill myself. I've finally realized this is the worst I'll feel. He can upload more videos. Now, it really doesn't make a difference. Nothing he can do will make me feel worse than I already feel. I want the money by tomorrow. The ball is in his court. He decides if I'll go to the cops or not."

"Kate, let me help you fix this." Maya nudged Simon toward the door before he could finish the sentence.

"Do you remember what I told you about the Phoenix, Simon? I am setting myself on fire." She closed the door once Simon was outside of her room.

The night was as silent as darkness after Simon left. They were both pensively quiet. Maya managed to get a couple of Valiums from a girl in the dorm. She gave one to Kate and asked for one more. She needed the sleep.

The constant buzzing of the phone woke Kate up from her recurring nightmares. It was one pm. She didn't recognize the number. She picked it up.

"Hello! Is this Kate?"

"Yes."

"My name is Anthony Guerra." The voice seemed excited, "I'm the Manager at One Trust Bank. There has been some unusual activity with your account, and I wanted to confirm the identity before proceeding further."

He proceeded to ask her the usual questions to establish her identity. She was perturbed; her bank had never called her.

"What's this about?" She was getting concerned.

"Oh! It's some great news, nothing to worry about. I'm sitting with a lawyer from the Webb Foundation. I've been told that the foundation looks after students who are doing well and need some financial help. Apparently, they want to take care of your college debt and offer you a scholarship."

There was a pause.

"Scholarship? How much?" She knew the answer.

"A million dollars." He waited for a response, "Kindly come to the bank. Their lawyer wants to meet you. There are a few documents you need to sign."

"I can be there by three pm."

"Since this is an unusual transaction, we prefer you come over after bank hours, say six pm? You know there is paperwork, and I don't want to be distracted by some customer complaining about the service." He chuckled.

"Do I need a lawyer?"

"Only if you want to fight them giving you the million dollars." He fake-laughed again, "No need for a lawyer. You're one of our preferred customers, and I'll personally take care of you."

Kate agreed. She was still not sure what was happening. The only way to know for sure was to go there and see everything in writing. Not in her wildest dreams had she imagined that they would agree to pay her a million. Kate gently nudged Maya to wake her up. She was as motionless as a corpse. She dialed Simon's number and asked if she could come over.

She reached Simon's apartment in less than 20 minutes. He buzzed her in. The small apartment on the first floor was as bland as Simon. There were hardly any furnishings, just a sofa in the living room staring at an old TV. A single-door fridge in the corner, a cycle with a flat tire rested against the wall, and a few Chinese takeaway boxes adorned the apartment.

There were no pictures, no paintings, no ornaments, and no life. Simon was all dressed up, wearing black trousers and a light pink button-down shirt. Kate suddenly realized she hadn't changed, bathed, or eaten since yesterday. She felt miserable.

"Hi! Is everything OK?"

She sat on the sofa as Simon quickly tried to clean up. She felt cold and started shivering. Simon sat next to her and wrapped his arms around her. She melted in his warm hug, tears falling. No one spoke. Simon held her gently and let her cry till she got tired. His ironed pink shirt was soaking with her tears, but he didn't seem to care.

"I'm so sorry; I ruined your shirt." She tried to brush off her tears. He held her hands and looked at her.

"Kate, it's fine; you've done it. It's all over now."

"You know?" She was trying to control the tears spilling out of her eyes. She was failing.

"Yes. I got the call in the morning. I told them not to mess with you."

"This seems too easy."

"It isn't. They can't afford any bad publicity right now. They're coming up with an IPO. Let's get the settlement closed tonight. You're set for life."

"I can't face them alone."

"I'm with you all the way, no matter what happens."

"Simon, I'm really scared."

"Look at me. I will not let anyone hurt you." Kate moved closer and hugged him. He moved his face forward to kiss her.

"I think you need to change your shirt." She smiled

"Sorry," he unbuttoned his shirt awkwardly, "It's been a long time since I let a girl into my apartment."

Simon looked vulnerable without his shirt, almost as vulnerable as when she'd met him. They had come a long way in a few days, she thought. She felt lucky to have him in her life. She couldn't have done this without him, and she wanted him to know that. She moved forward and hugged him again. His hands slowly leaned in as she rested her cheeks on his bare chest. She lay on his chest for a while, savoring the silent moment as he caressed her hair.

Simon moved his hand under her chin and lifted her face. He leaned forward and gently kissed her on her lips. She needed the kiss. She felt warm; she felt safe, and she felt she was not alone after a very long time.

Even though she wasn't ready for a new relationship, she didn't stop him. She was afraid she might lose him and feel unsafe again. She trusted Simon. He had done so much for her without any incentive. He deserved her affection, so she parted her lips and let him taste her. He slid his tongue inside her mouth and grabbed her breasts.

"Slow," she whispered, "I'm not ready for this." She gently pushed him back. He stopped and withdrew his hand.

"Sorry, I'm not used to this." He pulled back.

She could see he desperately wanted her, and she desperately needed someone. She leaned forward, held his hand, and placed it gently on her breast. She kissed him, leading the dance, guiding him. She felt better in control. She wanted to stop, but she owed this to him. It was a distraction she needed. She can't afford to lose the only ally, she told herself as she took off her top.

The kissing became intense; his mouth tasted sweet. She unbuckled his pants and took off her clothes. She held his hand and moved to the bedroom. They made love, and she controlled every move. She was enjoying the power more than the sex. Control was her thing now. He was happy when he came, laughing hysterically. The laugh didn't bother her, neither did the fact that she didn't come. His warm body against hers was what she enjoyed. It made her feel secure and powerful. They embraced each other in silence for over an hour.

"Are you hungry?" He finally spoke.

"Famished!" she replied. They ordered a pizza.

It was almost five pm, and she needed to shower, change, and not look like a homeless person. She went to the dorm, hoping to see Maya. Instead, she saw a note on her laptop.

MISS YOU. Text me if everything is OK! Leaving for class.

She desperately wanted to tell Maya what was happening but not through text. *Everything is OK,* she replied. Kate changed into her favorite jeans and a plain white T-shirt. She tied her hair back and hoped the conversation with Joshua would be as minimal as possible. Sign the damn documents, get in, get out.

She kept thinking about what she would say to Joshua before she walked out of the bank. She wanted to have the last word. Her phone buzzed. Simon was waiting for her outside. He suggested they reach the bank earlier and go over their strategy in the parking lot.

"Let me do the talking," he said as Kate and Simon reached the parking lot, "If they ask you anything, just give a one-word reply."

"I have a bad feeling about this." Her phone was constantly buzzing. It was Maya.

"Just remember, this is your win. This is your revenge."

"Then why don't I feel good?"

"It may not be perfect, but a million dollars can change your life. They want this to end almost as much as you."

"And then?" Kate looked at him.

"And then you can get out of this shitty town and never look back."

"And you? Should I forget about you too?"

"No, you'll always have me." Simon leaned forward and kissed her.

It was six pm when they walked into the branch. Simon held her hand as if her life depended on it. She didn't pull back. It made her feel stronger and a good visual for Joshua. She was surprised when she walked into the bank. Joshua wasn't there.

Chapter 12

Maybe she's born with it. Maybe it's Maybelline.

(Maybelline, 1991)

The large bank looked crowded even though there were just three people inside. Two were sitting together, and one was smoking a cigar, looking out the window. He ignored them when they walked in.

"Hi, Miss Kate." Anthony, the bank manager, greeted her as if she was a childhood best friend reuniting with him.

"I'm Anthony. We spoke earlier in the day. I'm the branch manager and, from now on, your personal banker. Would you like something to drink?"

His obnoxious smile bothered Kate.

He didn't wait for her answer. "This is Mr. Enzo Bianchi. He is the lawyer for the Webber foundation."

He was still smiling. Enzo was not. Anthony ignored introducing the silent man smoking the cigar. The grey hair complimented his grim look, and his tanned complexion and custom-made navy-blue suit gave the impression that he knew what he was talking about. The softness of the light pink tie contradicted his stern demeanor. Enzo Bianchi seemed more like a refined gangster than a lawyer.

"Miss Kate, I'm sure you want to get this over with. You need to sign a few documents, and if there are any questions, I'm happy to answer." His Italian accent complimented his persona. His tone and manner demanded compliance, and it seemed he was used to it.

Enzo leaned forward and gave Kate a stack of freshly printed papers. There were two copies, and she passed one to Simon. She tried going through the documents. There was a lot to read. She began reading but switched gradually to glancing. She hardly understood the jargon. It seemed like the terms and conditions printed for an app download; the only difference was the font size. She glanced at Simon to see if he could make sense of it. He was also scanning the pages but seemed lost.

"Simon?" She looked at him and whispered.

"Mr. Bianchi," Simon looked up, "I'm assuming these include the usual things we discussed earlier."

"Yes, when Miss Kate signs these documents, she acknowledges that she will not pursue the case and not discuss the case at any forum public."

"This seems like an awful waste of paper if it's just saying that," Kate spoke softly to hide her nervous indecisiveness.

"Miss Kate, no one is forcing you to sign these." Enzo crossed his arms, "You can walk out whenever you want."

It felt like a dare.

"The document mainly gives a roadmap of your future behavior regarding the allegations. I'm sure you'll agree we can't afford to be ambiguous. The numerous pages spell out all the areas where you're forbidden to talk, so you don't find a loophole and write a bestselling tell-all." Enzo paused. "In case you feel adventurous and you as much as whisper it in someone's ear, you agree to pay damages worth ten million dollars." He looked her straight in the eye.

The bank manager was still smiling as if he was getting paid for the damages.

"And in return for my ten years of silence, you pay a million dollars."

"Exactly. You're a smart girl." Enzo said as if mocking her.

"Simon?" She turned toward him.

"It's your decision, Kate; this's why we are here. In case you sign this, there is no turning back."

A knock at the door broke the tension in the room. Anthony stood up and brought another man in. He looked at everyone and nodded. The silent man with the cigar kept staring at the window outside. Everyone ignored him except Kate. His presence bothered her.

"Miss Kate, this is Sheriff Ramsey," Anthony was still smiling as he introduced the man who had just walked in.

"Sheriff Ramsey is here to sign as a witness. Anthony is the second witness, and Simon can sign as your witness." Enzo seemed too calm.

Kate shook his hand. The sheriff was tall, wearing dark blue jeans, a suede jacket, and a Stetson cowboy hat. His huge silver buckle on his belt seemed small compared to his large frame. He had a bored expression on his face. Kate felt better knowing someone impartial, who represented the law, was there if things got nasty. Enzo leaned back in the chair as if his work was complete.

Anthony gave Kate a pen. She looked at Simon, and he nodded. She began signing the papers. The intermittent sound of pen scratching on paper filled the tension in the room. She felt better after signing. *Finally, the ordeal is ending,* she thought.

Simon, Anthony, and Sheriff Ramsey signed the papers after Kate. Enzo checked all the documents, and with the same stone-cold expression on his face, he got up, turned to the silent man smoking the cigar, and said, "It's done."

The man turned toward everyone sitting at the table and walked to them. He looked for an ashtray on the table and butted his cigar in

Anthony's half-filled coffee mug lying right next to an ashtray. Everyone turned their attention to him as if he commanded them all. He seemed to know the drama he was creating and was relishing it. Old acne scars covered his rugged face. Kate felt his eyes piercing into her soul. Anthony got up, making way for him to sit in his chair.

"Do you know who I am?" he asked Kate as if no one else was in the room.

Kate noticed the orange in his white hair and the freckled white skin and realized who he was, "Should I?"

"I'm Leon Webber." He had Joshua's looks and his demeanor too.

"I'm assuming you've heard Joshua's version of the story. And you believe he is innocent, right?" Kate said.

"One thing he is guilty of is stupidity. But let's forget about his version of the story. I have mine."

"And what's your version?" she said, pretending to be calm.

The bleakness of his gaze unnerved her. Simon slid his hand under the table, squeezing her hand as if letting her know that she needed to let this one slide away.

Simon interrupted, "It's getting late, and we need to proceed." He slowly stood up.

"Sit the fuck down! You're done when I say you're done."

Quickly, Simon obeyed.

Webber took time to light up another cigar. He seemed to be enjoying the uneasiness he had created in the room.

"My version of the story is pretty simple," he finally spoke, "My son, who is young, good looking, and rich, fucked a girl. The girl put a price tag on her pussy, only she figured her pussy was worth a million dollars," he paused. "That's some expensive pussy."

"Mr. Webber, I need to be somewhere." The sheriff shifted in his seat.

"Stay where you are, Ramsey."

Kate felt a cloud of fear engulfing everyone in the room. She felt sweat trickle down through her armpits in the cold room. Her phone buzzed, and she looked at her hands holding the phone under the table; it was Maya. She barely managed to read her messages. She grabbed her phone, her mind in overdrive, thinking of ways to get out. She was staring at her hands under the table, wishing she was in her bed, regretting coming here without a lawyer or someone who could say something back to this lunatic. Simon sat there like a sheep facing a rabid dog.

"I told Joshua I've had pussy. I've even paid for some. The best I had cost me ten thousand. So I need to see the one costing me a million dollars, and the funny part is I don't even get to fuck her."

Kate wanted to run, but her body was frozen. The only thing working was her brain. She was angry, scared, and panicking. "Enjoy the journey, especially if the destination is not worth it," Webber said.

"Mr. Webber, nothing you say can be worse than what your son did to me."

"Oh, yes, I can. My son raped you once. I'm going to rape you for the rest of your life for messing with me. You signed a contract that gives you a million dollars, but you can't touch it for the next ten years." He paused and stood up.

"I know what you're thinking; you'll break the contract, say you were coerced or run to media or the police. Well, the good news is the witnesses you see here, all will testify against you, including your best friend here." He pointed to Simon. "I own half the media in this state, and the other half runs on my advertising dollars, so the media will fuck you up if you even whisper anything about my son." He stood up, casually walked behind the sheriff, and put his hands on Ramsey's shoulders.

"As for the police in this town, I've kept them on a tight leash."

He squeezed Ramsey's shoulders hard. "Ramsey, I want to hear you bark."

"Mr. Webber, please." Sheriff Ramsey pleaded as he started, squirming in his chair.

"Ramsey, I don't like repeating myself." He squeezed his shoulders harder. The silence in the room was excruciating. Kate and Simon sat in disbelief. Anthony was no longer smiling.

Webber squeezed the shoulders again. This time it seemed, with a little more force. Sheriff Ramsey wriggled in his chair, put his head down, and muttered a low "woof."

"Thank you. As for you, this bank is as close to the million dollars you will ever get. I want you to remember this night for the rest of your life. I want you to remember you weren't just raped once; You were raped twice for even thinking to question the Webber name."

"Simon," she pleaded.

"You think he's going to help you? Add another chapter to your lesson tonight. This savior of yours is also fucking you as we speak. Why do you think he has been with you every day since the incident?"

"Simon?" She whispered. He was silent, motionless, cold as if a mannequin had replaced him. *This can't be happening,* she thought.

"So, all of you knew he raped me?" She looked at Webber.

"What do you think? My son has quite a collection. Videos of you enjoying my son's dick." Everyone in the room sat silent and motionless.

"You didn't answer my question? Did you know he raped me? Are you too afraid to admit it?" She asked again.

"Yes, we all knew you were raped, but don't play the victim; you're the one who chose money in exchange for some rough sex, Sheriff Ramsey, isn't that prostitution? A million dollars doesn't change the fact that you're nothing but an expensive whore."

Ramsey stayed silent.

"These signed documents and the countless videos of you fucking my son will be shown on every screen across America if you dare to jeopardize my son's future."

"Just your son's future or yours too? Your IPO comes out next week?"

He looked at her and finally smiled.

"Yeah, Simon told me you're smart. Yes, that is more important than Joshua's future. Is that what you want to hear? Joshua knows it too. The only people who do not know that are the morons who buy our IPO. And yes, a slut like you will never understand the power that comes with money."

"I need to leave." She stood up.

"You go when I say you go."

"I'm not going to stand here listening to your insults. You have what you want. I'm leaving, and if you want to shoot me or arrest me, do it and add that to the list of the problems you already have to deal with."

She turned and started walking to the exit. She was almost sure she would hear a gunshot, but she made it outside. She exhaled when she finally felt the cold winter breeze. She picked up the pace and started to run. She didn't want to take any chances. Too scared to look behind, Kate kept running till she couldn't breathe anymore.

A 7-eleven sign caught her eye. She needed water, and she needed to breathe. She walked in, grabbed a bottle of water, and finished it in a gulp. She took out her headphones, connected them to her phone, and clicked on an audio file from the recordings folder. It showed 37 minutes. She pressed play.

"Yes, we all knew you were raped but don't play the victim. You wanted money—" It was Webber's voice on the recording. She had him by the balls.

She picked up another water bottle, paid for it, and called a cab.

She scrolled through her messages while in the cab. The last seven texts were from Maya; they all said the same thing: *Record everything!* She was happy she'd read Maya's text when she was at the bank.

Kate had the recording but had no idea what to do with it. The one thing it did for her was to make her feel secure. She now held the cards that could change the game. She kept looking behind to check if anyone was following her. No one was. She paid for the cab and walked to her room, continuously checking if someone was behind her.

Kate was a wreck when she walked into the room.

"You want to tell me what's happening? Why are you ignoring my fucking calls?" Maya jumped up.

"OK, first of all, you need to stop cursing." Kate looked up at her, still trembling.

Maya hugged her.

"I missed you so much," Kate hugged Maya, "I needed that hug."

Instead of giving Maya all the details, she played the recording for her.

"Who's that?" Maya asked.

"Webber, Josh's father," Kate whispered, too scared to say it loudly.

"Woah! We need to talk to someone. You can't do this alone!"

"I have to. Especially after Simon, I can't trust anyone. They can get to anyone," Kate said.

"I knew there was something slimy about Simon. I have a sixth sense about these things."

"Wait before you say anything. I have more." She clicked on another recording. She had recorded the entire conversation with Joshua and Simon at the library.

"You finally took my advice."

"Yes, you gave me the idea when I wasn't thinking straight. If it weren't for you, I would still be—"

"Well, at least you're no longer a sitting duck. Let's screw them," Maya cursed again, "I had a feeling you were meeting Joshua when you didn't pick up. I had no idea you were meeting his father, and as for evidence, this is gold."

"Evidence we can't use; we can't go to the cops. We can't go to the media. So there is nothing we can do with this."

"But Kate, we can't let them get away with this."

"I won't let them. The things his father said to me, I felt like dying. Feels like today his father raped me."

"You should weigh your options carefully, Kate," Maya said after a pause, "You can't mess with these people."

"I know one thing. I can't sit back and do nothing. They have my videos, the signed documents, witnesses. I know I'll be afraid to get up every day, thinking, is this the day I'm splashed across the internet?"

They were both silent, thinking about what to do next.

"My life is over now. I have two choices: kill myself or do something about it. I need a third option."

"There has to be a way out, Kate, and killing yourself is not even an option. You've been through so much already. You'll get through this too."

"I'm not killing myself today if that's what you want to hear. I should, but I'm too angry to do it."

"What about your degree? Don't let them take that away from you."

"Fuck the degree! Do you think I care about it now? I can't face anyone in the college because sooner or later, people will know about it. Joshua is going to ensure that. And after what I did, it's not safe to stay here. I just want to get out of this fucking town."

"New York! The city the world escapes to." Maya was excited.

"Where will I go. I don't know anyone in New York," Kate said.

"Remember that guy from Manhattan who helped you with your media plan? He's your best bet if you want to disappear in New York."

"I have a better idea." Kate felt the excitement building in her.

She looked at her phone; she was running out of time. She started typing.

Hi, remember me? She texted Mark.

Glad you texted. I was thinking about you. The reply came within seconds. Maya moved closer to read the texts with Kate.

Just to be clear, I'm not looking for a relationship. I needed some help.

Just to be clear, I'm almost seventy and about to retire. I'm excited, hoping to get the million-dollar business you promised me!

Kate looked at Maya, waiting for her advice. Maya shrugged, letting her know she was out of ideas. "Enjoy the journey," she reminded herself, turned toward Maya, and dialed Mark's number.

"Hi! I have a plan," Kate whispered in excitement, "But we need to get this out tomorrow."

"Get what out?" Mark said.

"The campaign," Kate replied.

"Hey, hold on, I'm not sure if you know how the business works."

"So you're not sure if you can do this?" Kate dared him, "Because I was told you're the best. Let me know if I'm talking to the wrong person."

"It can happen, but it'll be expensive, and we won't be able to get all the media I recommended."

"I know a million dollars can solve a lot of problems. I'll transfer the million in the morning."

"Morning?" He sounded reluctant, "then you can see your campaign the day after."

It was tomorrow or never, Kate thought. She needed time to think. She had to play her cards, well, at least one of them.

"OK, you'll have a million dollars by the close of business day today. Send me your account number."

Maya was shocked, scolding her with gestures.

"Sending you the account number as we speak. If the money reaches me today, I can guarantee that everyone will be talking about your campaign tomorrow morning, well, at least in North America." Mark chuckled.

"So, are we good now?" Kate asked.

"Yes, as long as the money is deposited. I haven't seen the campaign; let me know what the plan is?"

"You'll know when you see it." Kate disconnected the phone.

The plan was simple. To set herself on fire and everything around her. The Phoenix inside her was wide awake.

"What are you doing?" Maya asked.

"I'm playing my cards," Kate replied. She dialed Simons's number. Predictably, he didn't pick up. She tried a few more times and then decided to text him.

Check your email! She attached the recording that had Joshua's voice, added Mark's account number, and sent him the email.

He called back within seconds.

"What the fuck are you up to? Do you want to get us killed?" Simon sounded scared.

"I want a million dollars sent to the account number in the email."

"Firstly, no bank will be open, and secondly—"

"Listen, you fucking coward; there is no secondly. I want you to listen to my tone and figure out if what I'm about to say next is bullshit or not." She paused for a second.

"I'm listening," Simon said after a pause.

"I'm not afraid of dying. You and your masters have already

killed me. Joshua's family owns a bank and are one of the most powerful families in the world. Find a fucking way to send the money, or this goes public in the morning, and they can kiss the IPO goodbye. You know it as well as I do; I won't survive another day with what I have." She took a deep breath.

"Where are you? Let's talk about it."

"I've left the city. Tell your fucking master if he comes after me, this goes public. I have nothing to lose. On the other hand, Webb Pharmaceuticals is the Titanic heading toward the iceberg." She disconnected the phone with trembling hands and looked at Maya.

Kate turned off her cell phone, picked up her laptop, and hugged Maya.

"Where are you going?" Maya asked.

"I'll tell you in the morning."

Kate kissed her on the cheek and sprinted out.

Chapter 13

Intel Inside!

(Intel, 1991)

Kate walked into the St. Bernadette church, struggling to keep her mind from exploding. The church had become her sanctuary, not just to stay safe but to calm her scathing thoughts. It was the perfect place to wash her doubts as her life was now dependent on several variables.

Would the Webbers send the money? Would Mark release the campaign or disappear with a million dollars? She didn't know him and would have no receipt to prove that she sent him the money. Was she good enough to create the campaign? Her life depended on it.

Kate decided to work on the only variable she could control and started creating the campaign. She looked up and scanned the church. A few people were standing in line outside the confessional. She was sitting far away from them. The gentle pace at which individuals were confessing their sins meant they were here for a few hours.

Ironically, she had been to church in the last few days more times than she had been in her entire life. The scented candles and stained glass generated a transcendent ambiance, calming her senses and her soul. She was happy she chose to come here. She knew this would be the last place Webber and company would expect her to be. Even if they managed to find her, they wouldn't dare to harm her at the church.

She had around 12 hours to kill. Time, she thought, was like a spoilt brat; when you want it to pass quickly, it lingers on, and when you want it to slow down, it sprints. She could almost hear the seconds ticking even though no clocks were around. She started work on her campaign, hoping no one would ask her to leave. The church was big enough for her to go unnoticed. The confessions ended, and the people trickled out.

Kate was halfway done with her campaign when she saw the priest leaving the confessional, smiling and nodding at her. She smiled back. She thought about her future, and all the possibilities seemed grim, including the possibility of her plan working out. Only a miracle would make all the pieces she had scattered fall into place. Of course, there was no better place than a church to try for a miracle.

A few hours later, she finished her campaign. She had done a million revisions and she was getting tired of her indecisiveness. She took a few seconds to press the send button.

Fifteen minutes passed by, and there was no reply. She desperately wanted to call Mark but decided not to. She knew the moment she turned on her phone, the Webbers would find her.

There was pitch darkness outside and complete silence in the church. She picked up a pamphlet. It was for the Sunday mass. Her eyes sparkled when she read the headline on the front page, "For nothing will be impossible with God." She smiled; *now that's a sign I was looking for*, she thought.

She read the entire pamphlet, including the ads on the back page. She learned how much a plumber would charge for unclogging a drain and who to call for a designer coffin. She felt drowsy and tilted her head on the back support. She was asleep in a few minutes.

Kate woke up with a start. No one was around; the early morning sunlight broke through the stained glass, illuminating the extravagant alter. She looked around to figure out the time and turned on her laptop.

Nothing, no messages from Mark, and it was too early for the campaign to break. Kate tucked the laptop under the pew and stood up. She wanted to see the newspapers, still unsure whether Mark had gotten the money, released the campaign, or had disappeared with a million dollars.

Kate stepped out in the wintry, golden light of the early morning sun and looked toward the grotto. She took a deep breath knowing this was her Hail Mary. She started her day with a run, stopping to find if the newspapers were out. But, it was too early for the news.

An old couple across the street lifted the shutters and opened up their bakery. She hoped they had fresh coffee and walked in. Luckily, they were getting ready to serve the early morning delivery workers and offered more than coffee and fresh bread.

Kate felt famished and ordered a hearty breakfast. She had eggs, sausage patties, pancakes, fresh orange juice, two cups of coffee, and still had more time to kill. It was almost as if she believed this was her last meal.

Finally, she looked up at the small TV over the counter, splashing the *Breaking News* sign. She asked the waitress to turn up the volume. The recording of Joshua's screaming in the library was playing on a loop. Seconds later, she smiled, turned on her phone, and texted Maya.

It begins!

Her phone buzzed. It wasn't Maya. There was an incoming call from an unknown number.

"Hello."

"This is Webber." Kate recognized the voice. She composed herself, ready to face the tirade.

"Yes, I know. I was expecting your call." Kate felt confident. She was now in control.

"I want you to enjoy the money as fast as possible."

"Wait, before you say anything more that you'll regret, I want you to know I want to meet you."

There was a pause. "What do you want?" He asked.

"I have a peace offering!" Kate replied.

"There is nothing that you can offer."

"Oh, but there is." Kate was trying hard to hide the fear in her voice.

There was another pause.

"Come over to—" Before he could finish his sentence, she interrupted him.

"Don't worry, I'll find you. I just wanted to be certain if you were willing to meet." She ended the call. Kate took the last sip from her orange juice and walked out of the bakery smiling. It felt great being in control

The cold, dreary morning had turned bright and sunny like any other morning in Greenwich. Except it wasn't. Kate had set the world on fire. She could see around the street people reading the newspaper, their eyes focused on her advertising campaign. She called a cab, and at 8:55 am, she was standing outside the Webber Pharmaceuticals head office.

The address was easy to find, and she remembered Joshua telling her that his father was at the office at 9 am sharp. She took a deep breath and prayed for the first time in two decades. After the first meeting with Webber, she needed all the help she could gather.

Kate was walking into a perfect storm, knowing what had transpired in the morning would make Webber ruthless. She kept repeating in her head what she was going to say. Finally, a black Mercedes pulled in to the entrance. With trembling hands and a pounding heart, she was ready to welcome her new life.

Kate walked to the car and the door opened. Webber was staring at her like a vampire thirsting for blood. She got in, and Webber asked the driver to get out.

"You've got some nerve coming here after what you've done." He threw the newspaper at her face. She looked down to see her final campaign on the front page.

The full-page advertisement in a red tone with white lettering was unmissable. Her picture was centered with a single caption screaming, **"RAPED BY JOSHUA WEBBER!"** The ad had a transcript of Joshua's tirade and a link to the audio recording.

She ignored his insolence and replied, "In case you're not aware, the ad campaign is nationwide and soon will become the headline news across the country."

Thanks to Mark and cash payments on premium rates, the campaign was released nationwide. It was on print, TV, Radio, Digital, and Billboards. Almost all the leading newspapers had a full-page ad. The TV version was running on prime time. The news was already being discussed on social media platforms.

Kate knew this was also the end of her advertising career even before it had begun. She would never be able to graduate, and no agency would hire her. She was bowing out in spectacular flames, just like the Phoenix.

"I'm going to destroy you," Webber told her calmly.

She knew the consequences, and she was happy to embrace them all. "No, you won't if you're smart. My fight was with Joshua, not with you. The campaign was intended to punish Joshua."

"So, why the fuck are you here?"

She took out her phone and played the recording with Webber's voice. He listened to the first few seconds without reacting. Kate switched the recording off.

"You want more money?"

"No, I want a truce."

"After the stunt you pulled off? You drew the first blood and want me to sit back?" he scoffed.

"I didn't draw the first blood. Your son did. He brought this on himself, and if you want to pay the price for his sins, that's your call."

"What the fuck do you want? More money?"

"No. If you back off, I'll back off. I will disappear from the city and your lives." She played her final card, "My suggestion is you come out and say that you're a good father, and he deserves the punishment. I'm sure your stockholders will love you for it."

"And if I don't?"

"If anything happens to me, the next campaign will be bigger, bolder, better. Unfortunately, I didn't have enough time to make this one more creative." She smiled. Webber stared at her.

"They were right. You're a smart bitch."

"No, I'm just desperate. I want both of us to act like adults. Thanks to your son, I've destroyed whatever was left of my life." She felt great, not afraid of Webber anymore, "Joshua's life is ruined after this, but you still have yours. The audio recording will hurt you, your IPO plans, and any future venture you get into, and I think you're a smarter bitch than I'm. You shouldn't be paying the price for the crimes of your son."

"What's the guarantee you won't get adventurous in the future?"

"The same guarantee you gave when you said you had my videos." She paused. "This ends today from my side, and it will only happen again if you push me."

Webber stared at her. She prayed for him to agree and end the trauma.

"I don't want to see your face in this town again," he said.

"I can't stay in this town, and your son made sure of it. Do you want the recording?"

"No, I'm sure you've made more copies," he leaned forward and opened the door, "I just want you to be scared that I will survive the hit if the recording ever comes out. You will not!"

"I'm done being scared; check the leading newspapers and TV channels this week if you don't believe me." She lied.

"I want the campaign stopped immediately."

"I'll stop if you agree. I want the answer right now." After a few seconds Webber nodded. Kate smiled and stepped out of the car.

Kate dreaded going back to college. Joshua's cult, the entire college, would tear her to pieces. They would judge her and mock her and pierce holes in her truth. The campaign was spreading like wildfire. She entered the campus with her head down and picked up the pace to shorten her walk of shame.

She noticed the looks, the pointing fingers, and the whispers. *Keep walking,* she told herself. She crossed the library and heard someone shout at her. She recognized her name but not what they were saying. Then she heard the clapping and the cheers that started, and the words began to make sense.

"Way to go, Kate!" "You go, girl!" "You're the man!" The applause got louder and louder, the stares turned into nods, and by the time she got to her dorm, she was smiling and feeling she had almost accomplished something. Maya was eagerly waiting for her as she walked in. She jumped up and gave her a hug.

"Simon is in the hospital. Apparently, someone mugged him last night. At least that's what the cops are saying. He is fighting for his life," Maya said.

"I have an idea who mugged him," Kate replied.

She gave Maya all the details and told her where she spent her night.

"So, it's over?" Maya asked her as Kate logged in to check her emails. Kate nodded as she saw emails from Ogilvy & Mather and Bates in her inbox. Both had similar content, *"Regretfully"* informing her that she was not selected for the internship. She knew it wasn't a coincidence, and they must have seen the campaign. No one in Manhattan is going to touch her with a ten-foot pole. She clicked on an email from the college.

"Are we good now?" Maya asked again.

"Well, I got Webber back in the lamp, and in other news, I've been expelled." She smiled at Maya.

"Oh shit! We can fight this."

"I don't want to. I want to get out of this city as soon as I can. I have a few thousand left from the campaign. I'll be OK."

"What about your career in advertising?"

"I had one. I created the most trending ad campaign of the year. Creative directors rarely generate this much hype in their entire career. I did it in one day." Kate smiled, "Now back to reality." Her phone buzzed. Kate didn't recognize the number.

"Hi, I'm Traci, calling from Sun advertising. Am I talking to Kate?"

"Yes, this is Kate."

"I'm sorry, I just wanted you to know you weren't selected for the internship."

"Shocker!" Kate rolled her eyes.

"But would you be interested in a junior copywriter position?"

Kate was speechless. "Kate?"

"When is the interview?" It felt too good to be true.

"There is no interview. Mr. Ryan, our creative director, saw your campaign today. He has asked me to make you an offer for $75,000 per year plus benefits. We are aware you've applied to other agencies as well, so we want to move fast."

Kate was silent.

"He has also told me to let you know that the company will cover your apartment rent as an additional perk."

"Kate?" The voice at the other end became louder, "Kate, you there?"

"Yes." She smiled, "Tell Mr. Ryan I'll be happy to join him."

Chapter 14

Impossible is nothing

(Adidas, 1974)

Spring in Head Lion was like an Impressionist landscape brimming with colors and creatures from around the world. It seemed someone gave instructions to the artist: make it look like a painting by Monet. Nothing less could be expected from the most luxurious community in the country.

The main building was strategically located at the top of a hill giving the residents a spectacular view. Artistically scattered villas surrounded the building and were individually occupied by the rich, the famous, and the forgotten.

A maze of Italian marbled walkways connected the villas to the main building, like arteries connected to the heart. A 150-acre golf course, tennis courts, a five-star casino, a mall housing top brands, and 24x7 nurses and doctors were just some of the amenities ready to serve the VIP residents.

A light blue, crystal-clear lake with a fountain crowned the bottom of the hill. Symmetrically placed white benches installed with Wi-Fi, charging ports, and a help alarm tempted visitors to stay longer after their visits were over. Even though the children, grandchildren, and the shareholders rarely visited the dusted and forgotten mavens.

Kate admired the view from the glass wall in the Head Lion boardroom. It was her first meeting with them in six months. She had delayed meeting Sun's lowest billing client for a long time and was out of excuses.

The door opened, and the marketing team led by the marketing director walked in.

"Hi, I'm Emma, the marketing director at Head Lion."

Kate admired her pinkish dress with matching stilettos as Emma introduced the executives and the interns. Kate hoped she wouldn't bring up why Kate avoided coming to Head Lion for over six months.

"I'm Kate, the new creative director. Really excited to be here."

"New? I thought you joined six months ago." Kate expected the cold welcome as she watched Emma plugging in her displeasure. "Well, I'm glad you're finally here, especially since you're wearing the brand colors; hope it was intentional."

Kate was glad she'd worn red and black that day, although she had no idea about their brand colors. Gina had given her an overview docket, but she didn't have the time to go through the file. She regretted her decision.

"Yes, it was. It's such a privilege to work on Head Lion. I've heard you've won an award every year for the past five years."

"Seven!" Emma corrected Kate, "But it was because of Ryan. The brand is his baby."

"Well, it's my baby now." Kate could sense the tension building up. "And I'll make sure you win more than just awards, like more business."

"I hope that is why it took you six months to visit us. You must have come up with a brilliant strategy by now." Kate could sense the hostility was no longer subtle.

"Yes, we will be making a presentation by the end of the month." The standard spiel she gave whenever the work got delayed.

"End of the month? Ryan would brainstorm with us, and we would decide the direction in one meeting."

"I'm not Ryan. I don't work on hunches. I study data; I do research." Another favorite spiel. "Nevertheless, I'm here and will try not to break traditions."

"We have a brief presentation as an overview." An executive seemed excited that the meeting would not be a waste of time. Kate breathed a sigh of relief. The presentation by the marketing team lasted ten minutes. The brainstorming lasted for over an hour. Kate came up with some great ideas and salvaged the meeting and some respect from Emma.

"I'm sorry I was a little harsh earlier. We miss Ryan so much." Emma apologized.

"Oh! That's fine. It comes with the turf." Kate stood up. "We all miss Ryan. There are so many rumors. I even heard he passed away."

"Oh God forbid no!" Emma replied.

"No one knows where he is." Kate shrugged.

"I do." Emma smiled.

"You know where Ryan is?" Kate asked in disbelief.

"So do you!"

"What do you mean?" Kate looked at her and waited for an answer. Emma got up and walked to the window. She nudged her head, telling Kate to look outside the window. Kate stood up and stared down the hill toward the lake.

"He is the one sitting alone, staring at the lake." Kate looked out the window.

Unrecognizable from a distance, the man sat in a wheelchair staring at nothing. *That can't be him,* she thought; *it's impossible.*

"I need to speak to him," Kate whispered.

"I'm sorry you can't. Ryan has forbidden all visitors, specifically from his agency."

"Why?" Kate asked.

"My assumption is he does not want people to see the state he is in."

"What state?" Kate dreaded the answer she was expecting to hear.

"His left side is paralyzed. He doesn't talk. He can't function without help. I'm sure you can understand his reluctance to see people."

"No one visits him?" Kate was surprised.

"No one cares. Very few people know that he is here, and he wants it that way. When Mr. Maxwell found out what happened to him, he brought him here. Mr. Maxwell loves him; we all do, even the residents. He is Head Lion's youngest and most loved resident."

"How did he get here?" Kate was getting desperate to meet him.

"He was in the hospital for almost a month. He had no insurance, no family, no way to pay the bills. And then Mr. Maxwell got a call from someone to help Ryan."

"Who called?" Kate asked.

"We don't know. The person never called again."

"No one knows Ryan is here?" Kate asked in disbelief.

"No one cares," Emma replied.

Kate was certain that they would not let her meet Ryan. She decided not to ask again. She also decided not meeting Ryan was not an option and cursed herself for not coming to Head Lion earlier. He was her first boss, her first mentor, and her first crush.

She had left the agency a few months after joining Sun. She never got a chance to thank Ryan when she resigned. She had her reasons, and the reasons were making her eager to meet him. Her heart was racing with excitement, and she wanted to meet him as quickly as possible.

She wrapped up the meeting with Emma, promising she would

personally conduct qualitative research for the brand. Focus groups with the residents were mandatory.

"Can I get a universal access pass? I want the research to be unbiased, so no one from your side should be involved." Kate was meeting Ryan one way or the other.

Emma seemed excited about the research. She asked her executive to get Kate the universal access pass, then left, seeming pleased. A couple of interns escorted Kate to the main reception area.

"Can I take a look around just to better grasp the facilities?" She asked one of the executives.

"Sure, you have universal access now." He handed her the freshly laminated pass.

Kate waited for them to leave. She was meeting Ryan after years. She knew him as an attractive man who had a vivacious thirst for life, and the same man was now sitting in a wheelchair, unable to talk or move without assistance.

Kate stepped out and walked to him, missing a heartbeat with every step she took. The butterflies in her stomach reminded her that her crush was still alive. He was the only man she could imagine spending the rest of her life with after Joshua, even though he was almost twice her age. Kate finally reached the frail man staring at the lake. There was a sadness in his eyes that was making her feel uncomfortable.

"Hi stranger, remember me?"

There was no reaction.

She couldn't recognize the disheveled man who was always laughing, impeccably dressed in designer clothes. A scruffy salt and pepper beard hid the softness in his face. It almost seemed that he was trying hard to give up. This wasn't the Ryan she knew.

"Ryan, do you recognize me? I was your copywriter, well, junior copywriter technically, a long time ago."

Please say you remember me. No reaction. Kate felt like she was talking to the white wooden bench he sat on.

"We worked on the Pepsi pitch together." She sat down next to him, hoping to perform a miracle. She kept talking to him, having a one-way conversation that lasted for hours. She ignored her meetings and refused to turn on her phone.

No reaction. Kate told him how he saved her life by offering her a job. Ryan had placed her on a pedestal when no one from the advertising industry wanted to be near her. She would probably be dead by now without him.

"I was possibly the only girl at Sun you didn't sleep with." She tried to make him laugh. No reaction. "And I always wondered why, because I know I'm your type, you know: good looking!" She smiled.

Still no reaction.

The sun was setting, and the long shadows from the soft evening light reminded her that she was just a visitor there. An orderly interrupted her one-way conversation. It was time for Ryan's bath and dinner. She kissed him on the cheek and decided she couldn't let Ryan stare at a lake for the rest of his life. He saved her life, and she would save his.

"I'm leaving now, but I'll be back tomorrow, and with all the agency gossip." She tried to get one last reaction from him. There was none. Kate decided to leave. She wrapped her arms around him and gave him a warm hug.

"Oh! I think I didn't tell you my name, did I?" she pushed her hand forward, "I'm Kate."

Kate finally saw a reaction as he turned his head and looked at her. It was the first one she'd seen after spending hours with him. She turned back and walked away, knowing he was looking at her.

. . .

The next day she called the office and told them she had a meeting with a potential client. No one at the office would have questioned her, but she had to lay some groundwork because she knew the visits would not end anytime soon.

Kate had been up all night thinking about Ryan. She was happy about his response when she told him her name. It meant a breakthrough. She woke up early and took an hour to decide what to wear. She finally settled on a more casual look, regretting her choice the moment she walked out.

She stopped on the way and bought something Ryan would like. Fresh sashimi and California roll from his favorite sushi joint, crispy fried bacon and a double cheeseburger from his favorite restaurant, Lindt white center filled chocolates, and a slice of fresh coffee cake from Starbucks. An executive saw her walk into the reception, happy to see her.

"Are you starting your research?" The young executive asked.

"Yes, I can't start working till I finish the research," Kate replied.

"Let me know if you need any help."

"Yes, I was talking to this resident. I think his name was Ryan. How can I find him? I didn't quite finish my interview with him."

"Oh, that's the only resident we can't help you with. I can get you in touch with others. I'm sure many would be happy to talk to you."

"Bummer. I'll just talk to someone randomly. I don't want the residents to know this is for research."

Kate looked around to find a glimpse of Ryan. She recognized many faces—an old movie star, a famous musician from the 50s, a few forgotten billionaires.

She looked out the window and saw no one in a wheelchair. Instead, an older man in a suit sat on the bench near the fountain. She stood out like a neon billboard on a dark highway and felt the residents staring at her. She was drawing unwanted attention. She quickly stepped out and started walking to the lake.

The older man, probably in his 80s, was reading *The New York Times* and had a bunch of other newspapers stacked like a sandwich ready to be devoured. He seemed oblivious to the world around him. He changed his posture, letting Kate know he didn't want to be disturbed.

"Hi, I am trying to find a friend of mine." Kate smiled as he continued to ignore her, "His name is Ryan."

The man looked at her, "When you enter the main building, a huge sign says Information," he said, "The people sitting there are paid to get disturbed."

"They could care less," Kate said. "For an overpriced place, Head Lion has terrible customer service."

The man put the newspaper down. "It's a very millennial thing to say the place is overpriced."

"Nah! I low-key enjoy the place. The people are terrible. The staff needs to be canceled."

"I gather you're going to cancel the food here, too." He stared at the food she was holding.

She laughed. "No, no, this is for my friend, some of his favorite things. They're probably serving some tasteless broth here. No wonder he is depressed."

"And yet you don't know where your best friend is?" He studied her. "Has it occurred to you that maybe Ryan doesn't want to see you?"

"How do you know Ryan?" Kate asked.

"I know everyone here except you. Who are you? How did you get in?"

"I'm Kate." She said it as if that would answer everything. "I'm here to make Head Lion better."

"Hm! I thought that was my job. I am Maxwell William." She

turned red, realizing she was talking to the owner of the retirement community.

"I'm sorry, I didn't realize—" She was dumbfounded and dazed, unsure whether to run or drown herself in the lake.

He picked up another newspaper. "You're not here for Head Lion," Max said without looking at her.

"You're right. I'm here for Ryan." She sat down next to him.

"We all are," he said, engrossed in the newspaper.

"I can bring him back to life," she pleaded.

"I hope not with a kiss. You're telling me you can outperform the top doctors in the world?"

"Yes," she said firmly. Max put his paper down. She finally got his attention, "I'm the only one who cares."

Max stared at her for a while. Kate could tell he was trying to gauge if she was telling the truth. He looked like a man who was never wrong about judging people. His knack for separating the wheat from the chaff was legendary in the industry.

"I care, too. Ryan is like a son to me." He finally smiled, "I hate to watch such a talented man fade away. Although, I'm curious to know what you can do that the doctors have missed."

"I owe my life to him." She briefly told him about her past, leaving out critical details.

"Were you ever intimate with him?" Max asked.

"You mean did we have sex? No, although I still wonder why he didn't try."

"That's astonishing indeed." Max smiled.

"To be honest, we weren't even close. I was just one of the many disciples who worshipped Ryan at the agency. He taught me everything about advertising."

Max stared at her and slowly got up.

"Ryan has given up on life. I think you're exactly what he needs."

He started to walk away. Kate hesitated, thinking he was leaving.

Max looked back and wobbled his head. "Well, do you want to see Ryan or not?"

She sprinted forward to join him as he walked away. "I know I can do this."

"He is my responsibility." He looked at her, "I don't have much time, but I'm not going anywhere till I see him standing on his feet."

"I wish he could talk. He was such a great company." Kate was beginning to like Max.

"He can; he doesn't want to. Physically, he's not as bad as he looks, but emotionally he is in bad shape."

They walked for another five minutes and finally reached a newly constructed residence roughly half a mile away from the main building.

"I'm not going to mess it up." She looked at him.

"I know you won't." He paused before knocking on the door. "I won't let you."

"It's me, Ryan!" He entered the security code and walked in with Kate.

The residence seemed bigger from the inside. Kate felt she had walked into a seven-star luxury hotel suite. It also felt as cold as a hotel room. The furniture seemed luxurious, the paintings expensive, but it was devoid of life. It looked like a movie set.

A Spanish woman dusting the walls moved faster when she saw Max walking in. All the lights were off, and all the curtains were drawn. The only light was coming from a window the size of a wall. Across the window was the backyard. She saw Ryan sitting in his wheelchair on the deck, staring at his hands. It made her sad, and it made her angry.

"Ryan, there is someone here to see you." Max told him, "I know what you're thinking and what you will say, but do this for me." He paused. "I'm going to Europe for a bit and will talk to you when I get back, but till then, be kind to this one." Max waited for an answer.

There was none. Max grunted and left, leaving Kate and Ryan in awkward silence.

Why isn't he listening to music? Why isn't the TV on? He used to love reading.

"Hi," she said. Ryan was staring at a visiting card in his hand. "I know you're angry. I just don't know why."

Not flinching, not blinking, Ryan kept staring at the card. Kate decided to distract him with other topics. She tried politics, advertising, nostalgia, movies, but there was no reaction.

By late evening Kate was tired, her feet hurt, and nothing seemed to be working. She cursed herself for assuming she could do better than the doctors. She switched on her phone and saw the barrage of panic texts, emails, and voice mails from the office. It's a lost cause, Kate thought.

Maybe a weekly visit was a better idea than coming every day. She picked up her bag and realized the sad reality that there was nothing more important than her career. She turned around to say goodbye and noticed something. Ryan had turned his wheelchair, his right cheek was now toward her. *He wants me to kiss him,* she thought. Kate smiled. I need to make this work, she told herself.

"I'll be back tomorrow." She kissed him on the right cheek and left.

Chapter 15

Think small

(Volkswagen Beatle, 1959)

Ryan looked at the card one more time. Someone had dropped off the envelope outside his door in the morning. A gold embossed bust of an ancient pharaoh made the company look opulent and more valuable. It had the name of the CEO embossed in gold: Nour Walid.

The stark oversized red envelope triggered the questions nagging his brain for the past six months. How he got to Head Lion? Why Todd wanted him dead? How to get revenge? And now, who sent him the red envelope? The only thing Ryan was certain of was that he did not want an ordinary revenge.

An eye for an eye was not enough for him. Ryan wanted more. He wanted to take a bow after the revenge and the world to give him a standing ovation. Ryan savored the fantasies every day, not knowing where to begin until today. He had a feeling that the red envelope was the key to his final creative.

The card made Ryan wonder: why now? He had nothing to offer. His career was over, along with the life he had. Yet, someone had made an effort to trigger his craving for revenge. He wanted to throw away the card, but its arrival was the only eventful thing that had happened to him in months.

Ryan had no reason to live. He was too scared to kill himself but hurting himself made him feel better. He searched for new and novel ways to inflict pain upon himself. His last episode almost killed him and got one of the nurses fired. Pain felt good. Pain was his new best friend. Pain was the only thing keeping him alive.

Today he felt different. The intrigue worked like CPR. Ryan felt alive. Getting the red envelope was exciting. He'd spent the last six months using his creative energy thinking up ideas on how to punish himself. Now he could focus his energy on getting even with Todd and Kate.

He wanted to know who Nour Walid was. Suddenly he heard Max's voice. "Ryan, there is someone here to see you. I know what you're thinking and what you'll say, but do this for me."

Ryan saw Kate standing with Max. *She's back*, he thought. He remembered she had come yesterday and rambled on. He was certain after his cold treatment of her, she would not return.

"I'm going to Europe for a bit and will talk to you when I get back, but till then, be kind to this one."

Max left. He heard the door being shut. He couldn't stand Kate. He despised her more than the state he was in. Kate finally spoke, breaking the awkward silence. He kept staring at the visiting card.

"Hi, I know you're angry. I just don't know why."

You know exactly why! Ryan mocked her in his thoughts. She was the reason for his destruction. She was the one who forced him out of Sun, forced him out of advertising, forced him to become someone who had no reason to live. Thanks to her, he would have done it if only he had the strength to kill himself. But instead, his only respite was his vanishing. He had disappeared for a reason. He didn't want anyone to see him like this. Helpless, insecure, crippled physically, emotionally, financially—not the way he wanted to meet the woman who stole his life.

Ryan only knew Kate as his rival. He had forgotten he had hired Kate a decade ago until she reminded him. Ironically, he had nurtured the snake that bit him. He vaguely remembered the girl who did the unusual campaign about being allegedly assaulted. He loved the boldness and strategy and hired her before any other agency could. He knew she would go places. She did. She disappeared when he returned from a conference in Tokyo. Kate joined Ogilvy & Mather. *Ungrateful bitch,* he thought.

Ryan's biggest rival looked different now. She had transformed from a nerdy girl to an attractive woman. At first, her presence annoyed him, but her constant rambling about Sun piqued his interest. He hoped she would reveal more.

Except for Max, Ryan never had visitors, let alone an attractive woman. Ryan soon discovered the fall hadn't hurt his hormones. Sparks surged in his body whenever she came closer. Her scent was awakening his senses. His body craved her to come closer within hours, even though his mind cursed his sudden desires.

She's not going to last for long, he thought. What if she never comes again? The possibility bothered him, and the more time she spent with him, the more intensely it disturbed him. Even though he hated her, he looked forward to her ramblings. A fierce battle erupted in his head as he grappled with accepting her as someone who stabbed him in the back or as someone trying to revive him.

Yesterday, her kiss on his cheek felt like a band-aid on a wound. It didn't make sense; she was the enemy, and he craved her kiss. He cursed himself, surrendering to her mesmerizing scent as she came closer. He couldn't help but turn his wheelchair, craving her kiss on the side that still had some sensation left.

He loved the kiss and hated her more than ever before. She had made him blush for the first time in decades. The moment Kate left,

Ryan steered his wheelchair to his study table. He desperately needed a distraction. He turned on the lamp and took out Nour's visiting card from the red envelope. Ryan had finally found something better to do than stare at the lake. He had a feeling it could answer the many questions that kept him up all night.

Ryan wanted revenge as much as a junkie craved drugs. He wanted the vengeance to be creative, delicious, sensual– all the wrong words were popping into his mind. He had given up on life because he had no idea how to get even. His soul had sulked like an athlete falling before the finish line. His body parts had surrendered too.

Now Ryan wanted to get better to get even. He tried to feel his arms, and they felt disconnected. His toes felt numb, as if they had been asleep for a million years. The only parts that he used were his right hand, which helped him steer his motorized wheelchair, and a head that moved and communicated the two most valuable words in the English language: Yes and No.

He applied pressure on his right toe; nothing happened. He repeated for almost an hour, deciding not to sleep until he saw a sign of recovery. He eventually saw his right toe move, his greatest achievement in the last six months. He was excited, nervous, and hopeful. Finally, he reached out and pressed the help button with his right hand.

"Are you OK, Mr. Ryan?"

"I nneed mmmy lapttttop."

A few days later, Max was back. He seemed excited to see Ryan's progress. "Was it Kate? I'm surprised she lasted more than a day." He laughed as they sipped the cognac he bought for Ryan from France.

"She lasted fffourteen days to be exact. No, It wasnn't her." Ryan frowned, "I can't stand her. I'm only ppputtting up with her because of you."

"I don't care what the reason is, as long as you're getting better," Max said.

"Now you ccan die peacefully." Ryan smiled.

"If you put your mind to it, you can fix both sides."

"Do you rreally want me fixed?"

"Of course."

"I nnneed yyour help."

"What can I do? I'll do anything for you if it helps you get better."

"Do you bbelieve in rrrevenge?" Ryan asked.

"Absolutely. Behind every successful man is a knife that he hides."

"Then help me qquench the fire inside me. Hhelp me take the rrevenge that kkarma owes me."

"Revenge from whom?"

"Yyou know, Max."

"Todd?" Max was no longer smiling. "I hate saying this, but if that's what it takes to help you get on your feet, I know people who can take care of him."

"No. Tthat's the eeasy way out. He is already living on borrowed time."

"Then what do you want? Tell me, what will make you live?"

"I don't wwant an ordinnary revenge. I wwant a beautiful revenge."

"What an odd way to describe it, Ryan." Max poured more cognac. "I never knew revenge could be beautiful," Max said.

"It's going to be epic." Ryan smiled and raised his glass in a mock toast, "Worthy of its place in ppoetry books and art galleries."

"And how do you intend to do it?"

"I was the ggreatest creative director in Mmanhattan and this will be my swan song. Scorched earth for Todd."

"You still are Ryan." Max smiled, "How can I help?"

"I nneed your help with something that's holding me back," Ryan told Max about the file and the manager's death.

"Do you tthink less of me now?"

"No, but even if it wasn't an accident, which I think it was, every self-made billionaire has a closet no one is allowed to see."

"Can you help?"

"I can't promise anything. I'll try to pull some strings, but it'll take some time."

Ryan passed on the red envelope to Max, "Meanwhile you can helpp mme with this."

"What's this?" Max took out Nour's visiting card.

"I ccalled her office. They ssaid the last time she came to the offfice was a decade ago."

Max smiled, staring at the visiting card.

"What if I find her for you?" Max said.

"I will ppole-dance for you if you ffind her."

"And if I get her to have drinks with you?"

"I'll be nnaked while ppole-dancing."

Max laughed. "Nour, she is an Egyptian. Very rich, very intelligent, and very, very interesting."

"Where can I fffind her?"

"Not too far away!" Max finished his drink and stood up, "She lives in Head Lion."

Two weeks went by, and the only thing that kept her going was the one sign that Ryan was alive. He changed his posture every night for her kiss. She stayed there the entire day and went home to sleep. She was getting behind on her work, and Todd had started to notice it. One afternoon her phone buzzed. It was Todd. She turned on the speaker.

"Hey, where's my favorite creative director? I hope you haven't joined one of our fucking competitors."

"Not at all. I'm working remote on a pitch." She panicked.

"A pitch that I don't know about?"

"I'm developing it, boss. A friend of mine is a brand manager at Pepsi."

There was a pause.

"Great because some dickhead spotted you at Head Lion."

"I work here because it's calm and quiet." She tried to justify. "Plus, the routine work is sent to me here."

"Awesome. If you get tired of working at Sun, let me know first before you make any decision. I don't like being fucked in the ass." He hung up.

Kate hated Todd's crude language, but that was a pill she was willing to swallow with her half a million in annual salary. How did he know she was at Head Lion? Kate wondered. She did not want anyone at Sun to know she was with Ryan.

Kate started bringing her work to Ryan's place and would find time in-between to work on her campaigns. She would share her work with Ryan for feedback hoping to get some reaction. The Ryan she knew would go out of his way to stop a lousy campaign from going live. Instead, Ryan sat there like a zombie. It almost felt as if he was waiting for her to leave.

Sun was pitching for a big client, Sphinx Mobile, a telecom giant part of the Pharaoh Group of Companies. Sphinx was a big deal, especially since she had been out of the office for a long time. Random texts from Jeff kept pouring in. It was like a scornful stare piercing through the texts.

The harsh rain outside made it even more challenging for her to think. The county had issued a flood warning. The scolding thunder outside was telling her to stay inside. She hated the rain. It reminded her of Josh.

After her experience with Joshua, she had vowed never to have a long-term relationship with anyone. Three months was the sweet spot if the company was fun and the sex was great, and then she would move on. Ryan was the only exception. He was also the reason she left Sun and joined Ogilvy & Mather. She didn't want to fall in love then; now it was too late, she thought.

Ryan was worth more than three decades, and that scared her. Even with all his flaws, she was willing to spend the rest of her life with him. She wanted to be for him what falling raindrops were to barren land.

The dim, warm light spreading through the lamp and the song playing in the background was pushing her to get up and wrap her arms around Ryan. She glanced at him and caught his gaze; he was light-years away. The crackling thunder pulled her back to reality.

"I need your help, Guru." She pushed Ryan's wheelchair to the dining table layered with artworks, notes, and printouts. She turned her laptop in front of him to see the presentation. His scent had mesmerized her since the day she met him. She came closer to him to open the file and inhaled his scent.

"It's a new campaign I'm working on."

His gaze moved up to the banal painting hanging on the wall. A landscape typically found in model homes.

"It's the biggest pitch for me since I've joined." She tried to get his interest going. "I heard top agencies are pitching for this account." She opened the presentation, "I'm going to share my ideas with you. Blink once if you like them. Blink twice if you hate them."

Ryan was as still as a mannequin at Macy's.

"Guru, your point of view can change the course of this pitch," her voice lowered as she flipped through the presentation for him, waiting for him to react. She finally gave up, leaving her last idea on the screen.

"Tthis is ggood," He finally spoke.

Kate jumped up from her chair, hovering around him in a dance of happiness. She wanted to hug him but restrained herself.

"So you can talk?"

He looked at her and blinked once. She laughed like she had found gold.

Ryan was enjoying the charade. The Sphinx logo caught his attention. It also gave his brain the ignition it needed. He knew it was not a coincidence. If only Kate knew that the reason he tolerated her was for the opportunity to get back at her. He had no intention of harming her physically but destroying her career would be poetic justice.

"Should I make the presentation to you?" Kate felt as excited as a disciple seeking the approval of her guru. Ryan nodded.

"Great, let me fix this mess."

"You know I've always thought you're better than Ogilvy, Bernbach, and Leo Burnett combined. You're a great copywriter, you have a good sense of design, you know how to work strategy, you can sway social media in any direction."

Ryan hated praise, but he could read she was saying how she felt. He wanted her to stop talking and begin. He wanted to see the presentation. Excited, Kate stood up as if she was making an actual presentation.

Ryan had looked at Kate before, but this was the first time he saw her. The silver ring pierced in Kate's nose, the urbanized bohemian look mesmerized Ryan. The golden light above the dining table glowed her subtle nude makeup. Only her red toenails weren't subtle.

Her signature dark blue jeans hugged her long, slender legs, and her white button-down shirt accentuated her breasts. Her husky voice was like the ocean waves hitting the seashore: calming, jarring, intoxicating.

As she clicked on her laptop, her supple breasts grazed his arm. They felt young and firm. He inhaled her scent as much as he could, holding it in and savoring the spring freshness. She moved forward, and her breasts brushed his arms again. He could feel himself getting an erection, or was it his imagination? It had been a lifetime ago since he was sexually aroused. He was trying to control his gaze, and for a split second, Kate caught his stare. His eyes panicked, wishing Kate hadn't noticed.

Ryan wanted to use his immobility like a trojan horse. It was too early for people to know that he was getting better. Ryan looked at her again. She was moving about like a ballerina in slow motion. He suddenly craved to kiss her. Hungry to taste the lips of his enemy, his mind and his heart battled the dilemma.

A glance in the mirror reminded him of what Kate had done. Even if he somehow got over his hatred for her, would she ever consider kissing someone who would spend most of his life in a fucking wheelchair? Girls like Kate didn't waste time with people who had nothing to offer. Sex, love, intimacy, friendship were all transactions, and Ryan had nothing to give and everything to take.

So why was she still here? She could have anyone she wanted, and she probably did, he thought. She must have slept with someone at the top of the Miamart food chain to get rid of Ryan. She may have even slept with Todd. She was a manipulating slut, and she was here for a reason, he convinced himself.

Kate started the presentation by recapping the brief. She then presented research and data that was exclusive to Sun. Thousands of dollars were burnt getting research, intelligence, or any dirt to help Sun win the pitch. Unknowingly Kate had spilled the entire strategy. Ryan was impressed. The presentation was brilliant, and the style was very much his. It seemed the work of a younger, trendier Ryan.

She knows her stuff, Ryan thought, *She is almost as good as me, almost.*

"Do you like the work?" She smiled, "Everyone is telling me to take the safe route, even Todd because the client wants to play it safe."

If you don't like taking risks, you shouldn't be in advertising, thought Ryan; *it's like playing chess with just the pawns.* Ryan stayed silent, sparingly using his words as if he would run out of them.

"Todd wants to see the work before we present. He made this condition a dealbreaker when I joined. Can you believe that?"

Never bow down on your best idea; that's the first thing I taught you, Kate. Don't announce where you're hitting your punch. Ryan looked at the laptop one more time. The last idea was bland, leaving a gaping hole in the strategy. She was fixated on the part of the brief that stated what should be done, ignoring the piece that defined what shouldn't. Creative directors had ADHD and were generally too arrogant to admit it. They rarely went through the entire brief. The ideas were great, but Kate contradicted a crucial part of the brief.

"Are you sure I should work on this idea?"

Ryan nodded.

"Hmm, I trust your judgment over mine." She smiled and started packing her stuff. It was still raining outside. Ryan could sense she was scared, and as much as he hated her, he didn't want her dying in a car accident. That was the easy way out.

"Sstay," he whispered.

Kate looked up at him. She looked like a child craving love. He felt cold and tired of being lonely. She walked slowly to him.

"I have no idea what I'd do without you. You've given me something I never knew was missing from my life." Kate's hair gently caressed his face as she moved forward. Her scent tasted like summer rain.

"I'm so happy Gina found you that morning. We could've lost you forever," Kate whispered.

Staying overnight would make them cross the line from where there was no return possible. The night felt like it was the first time they had met. Everything between them was just a mess. She leaned back and started packing her stuff. She was ready to leave, and Ryan didn't like it.

Ryan was pensive. He could hear Kate's words playing on a loop in his mind. How could Gina have found him in the morning? He distinctly remembered being at Todd's house at night. Gina was never allowed in Todd's house. Where was he the entire night? Maybe the paralysis affected his memory. His mind felt like a maelstrom as he grappled with answers.

Ryan heard the door being shut as Kate left. He looked at the time and called the one person who could have the answers.

"Guru, is that you?" Gina picked up the phone.

"Yyyes, it's me. How're you?"

"Good. It's great to hear your voice, Guru."

"Gggina, I need your help."

"Sure, anything for you."

"Wwho ffound me?"

"What do you mean?"

"The llast night when I ggot to the hhospittal, who ffound me?"

"Not night, Guru. Morning. I did."

"I wwant the ddetails. Ddon't leave anything out."

"Is everything OK?"

"Yes, I jjust nneed to understand what hhappened to me."

"Remember that evening after the Miamart pitch at Harvey's? I wanted to see you for some personal advice."

"Sso tell me now, why did you wwant to see me?"

"I was resigning. You told me to come to your place in the morning. I knocked, no one answered. I had your code, so I entered and saw you. I tried to wake you up. I panicked. Called 911, and that's it." She paused. "The doctor said we should've gotten you to the hospital a few hours earlier. I curse myself every day for letting this happen to you."

"You fffound me on the bed in the mmorning?"

"Yes."

"I fainted at Todd's ppplace. Someone moved me."

"So, what are you saying?"

"I think Todd wwwanted me to die."

There was a pause.

"That's impossible. Todd told everyone you met him but at the office in the evening. You wanted to retire and move away from New York."

"Gina, wwhat do you think?"

"You seemed depressed. Most of us are still in a state of shock." She took a breath, "The only thing I am certain about is I found you at your apartment."

Ryan was quiet. He could not get his head around why he was at the apartment rather than the hospital.

"Guru, when will I see you?"

"Ssoon."

The poison was his remedy. Finally, instead of imploding with guilt and regret, Ryan had someone else to blame. Hate was good. It was giving him a reason to stand up and live. One thing was clear: Todd and Kate were writing the third chapter of his life.

Ryan could hear himself breathing in anger. His anger was less about destroying the authors and more about his helplessness: sitting in a wheelchair, fading away till no one remembered him. Only he should write how his final chapter ends. He reminded himself of his mantra, *"Get out of your way!"*

He looked at the computer screen and saw the last visual for the campaign Kate had created. He knew he could do a lot better. His mind was suddenly exploding with ideas. His life had a purpose again, and sitting in the wheelchair was not in it. He finally realized why he'd gotten the red envelope. It was time to meet Nour.

Chapter 16

I want you

(Uncle Sam, 1916)

Ryan was circling the drain as he decided what to wear. He had lost weight, and nothing fit him. He couldn't remember the last time he was this nervous. It was also the first time he was dressing up in more than six months. He was happy to find Terre d'Hermes, his favorite perfume, and sprayed it on his neck. He felt like his old self, barring immobility. He was working hard to recover. His right side was better. His speech had become coherent. The staff left after helping Ryan dress up.

Moments later, there was a knock on the door. Max entered and smiled when he saw Ryan rebooted, clean shaved, and smelling nice. Ryan had finally settled on wearing a salmon-colored, slim-fitted shirt that had now become a regular fit. His navy-blue trousers held on to him through a tightly wound leather belt. Max fixed his collars.

"After a long time, I see the Ryan I used to know."

"I'm wwwearing my wwatch after a year." Ryan showed him the Patek Philippe Max had given him.

"I don't think it's running correctly because we are already ten minutes late."

They stepped out as Max took control of the wheelchair.

"Just a caveat; she is a fiery woman. She can be extremely blunt, and that's what makes her interesting."

"I'm ggeting the feeling you have a ccrush on her."

Max turned red. "She's going to push your buttons. So don't flinch."

Nour's villa was not far. They took a shortcut through the main building, passing through the power lounge. Ryan could see the other residents smiling and nodding at him. He recognized many. They were people who once upon a time were at the top of their game. Entrepreneurs, movie stars, singers, sportspeople; many were billionaires or were close to becoming one. Ryan kept saying hi to everyone. It was the first time he had spoken to anyone since his arrival at Head Lion. He was surprised that they all recognized him and met him warmly.

"Remember one thing, Ryan; there are two keys to a successful meeting. First is knowing what you want," Max spoke to him as they came closer to Nour's residence.

"Wwhat's the second?"

"Letting the other person assume they have the power."

Ryan knew what he wanted. It was a chance to pitch for the Sphinx account. Max knocked on the door.

"Max, I can smell your cheap perfume from inside. Come." A voice with a foreign accent answered.

Ryan had done his homework. Nour was a self-made woman; at least, that's what she wanted the world to know. Everyone agreed that she was one of the most attractive women in her heydays. She had graced the cover of almost all the top glossy magazines in America. She was also known for her fiery temper and no-nonsense attitude.

Nour had married three times, and rumors about her numerous affairs lasted till the day she disappeared from the business scene. She was nineteen when she got married to an Egyptian tycoon twice her age. A few years later, he died of a heart attack, leaving everything to her, including his family's perfume empire.

After realizing how difficult it was for a young widow to survive in a world that embraced ancient traditions, she left Egypt. She came to America, and in the first year, she established her first perfume brand. Also, the same year, she married the guy who was her competition, merged the two companies, and became the most significant player in the business.

Nour's brains and beauty soon became the talk of every block in New York's financial district. Ryan felt like a dwarf as his wheelchair moved inside.

"Max, you look younger every time I see you." Nour moved toward Max and air-kissed him on his cheeks. Her strong floral perfume engulfed the entire lounge. She wore a long red dress that made Ryan feel miserably underdressed.

"Ah! You were always known for generosity. As I mentioned earlier." Max smiled, "This is Ryan, the most creative man in New York. Ryan, this is Nour, the most beautiful woman in New York."

"New York? Come, come, now, Max. You can do better."

"Nour, it's a pppleasure." Ryan kissed her hand. "You're mmore beautiful than—"

"Ryan." Nour interrupted him and lit up a cigarette, "You can do better too."

Ryan recognized the pungent smell of premium marijuana as she exhaled.

"Hope the marijuana doesn't bother you? I know you're into snorting stronger stuff. I've heard that can kill you."

"I quit. The only ttthing I am into these days is kkkilling time."

"Dahling, we all have very little time left, and no one should understand it's worth more than you."

"Mmmore than me?" Ryan's face was turning red.

"Isn't it obvious? We may be older than you, but we can still move around. You, dahling, will die sooner, not because of your immobility but because you've given up on life. Although your immobility will be the reason you'll quit on life. Ironic, isn't it?"

"Nour, are you going to offer us any drinks?" Max changed the conversation.

"I'm so sorry, gentlemen. I guess dementia is coming earlier than I had hoped." Nour rang the bell, and a maid entered.

Ryan was losing control. This was his one chance at a second life; blowing it was not an option. He remembered what Max had told him: "Everyone wants power; let them have it. Your goal is not power. Your goal is the illusion of surrendering power."

The drinks arrived just in time.

"I've heard you can read minds; indulge me."

"You've done your homework." Ryan smiled.

He took a moment, trying to get back in control. "Well, rrright now you're ttthinking how far you can push me with your obnoxious jabs till I break and say something I'll regret." Ryan smiled and took a sip of the scotch. Her insults were forcing him to speak coherently. His anger was curing his stammer. The poison was becoming his remedy.

She stared at him and then smiled. "You're good."

"Nour, pppermission to be blunt?"

"Oh! I wouldn't like it any other way, dahling." She inhaled one more time.

"I nnneed your help."

"Ryan, let me interrupt you before you start walking that course. Help in my world is like a man who can walk, asking for crutches, metaphorically speaking, of course." She lit up another cigarette, "In my world, there are only transactions, you do something for me, and I do something for you. So wherever you're heading, tread carefully and make sure it doesn't become boring for me."

"OK! Bluntly put. We are all fucked." He moved forward and

took a cigarette from her gold case. He inhaled with a vengeance, enjoying the slight buzz in his head, the confused expressions on Nour's face, and the shock on Max's.

"Not us, Ryan. You are," Nour said.

Ryan had spent enough time with her to read her like a graphic novel. "Erm, I beg to disagree. After throwing you out of the business you created, your families don't want anything to do with you. Your peers feel sorry for you. You live in a retirement community, albeit fancy. The only consolation is that you have money—lots and lots of it. You are literally waiting for the day you die, sipping expensive liquor and smoking fancy weed while you wait. If you don't consider this fucked, madam, respectfully, you're more fucked than I am."

Nour stared at him, took a sip of her wine, and a puff from her cigarette. Max shifted uncomfortably on his sofa. The reading was never wrong. Ryan knew exactly how she would respond.

"I suppose you're going to help us unfuck ourselves?"

Ryan raised his glass, "That madam is the transaction." He took a sip.

"You have my attention," Nour replied.

"Mine as well." Max looked at Ryan.

"Nour, I know how the company you built refuses to acknowledge your existence. They think you're old, senile—"

"They're not wrong, dahling." She smiled.

"I can make you as relevant today as you were thirty years ago."

"And why would I want to do that?"

"Because that's what you've always wanted, especially after the hostile takeover. Remember, I can read minds." Ryan smiled.

She took another puff from her cigarette. "No offense, but I can't believe I am letting one and a half men tell me how to live the rest of my shrinking life."

"And yet before we walk out, that's precisely what you'll agree to do."

The silence lasted for a few seconds before Ryan spoke again.

"What if I told you before the year ends you could be the most sought-after name in the corporate world."

"I can't deny I'm intrigued."

"How do you control the most exclusive brands in the world?" Ryan said.

"I have a feeling you're about to tell me, dahling," Nour said.

"You create the most exclusive advertising agency in the world."

"We both have all the money we need and some more," Nour replied.

"All the money in the world can't get you what power can. Without power, all the money in the world is like being great-looking and having sex alone," Ryan said.

"But isn't that more fun sometimes?" Nour smiled as she took a sip. "Don't answer that. It was rhetorical."

Ryan waited for Nour to respond. He had played all his cards.

"One question, though. Who will give business to a disabled, dissipated creative director, an old man who looks after the retired and a forgotten CEO?" Nour said.

"Head Lion!" Max answered before Ryan could, "That's genius."

"I don't understand," she said. "What business can you get from a waiting lounge at the graveyard?"

"Head Lion is a treasure trove for new business. It's like walking into a vault full of gold, with a sign that says 'all you can take.' It's so easy it should be a crime."

"What motivation will these dying billionaires have? Ryan, as you said, these are dusted and forgotten people," Nour said.

"Their motivation is they are dusted and forgotten people. Lions never lose their desire to hunt for fresh meat."

"We offer them a hunting ground and fresh meat," Max added, looking more excited than Ryan.

"I have to ask the million-dollar question." Nour pulled back and stared at them, "What's in it for Ryan?"

"Money, power, fame, everything," Ryan said.

"None of those things interest you, Ryan. The meeting is over if you can't be honest with me."

There was a pause.

"A beautiful revenge," Max answered before Ryan could.

"How can revenge be beautiful?" Nour said.

"Everyone thinks stars are beautiful. Poets and painters use stars as metaphors for beauty. Yet, they exist in a stable state of nuclear fusion emitting enormous energy, destroying any life near them," Ryan said.

"And you want the world to see that?" Nour seemed surprised.

"I want the world awestruck when I'm done," Ryan said, "I want them to take pictures, laugh, celebrate, nudge others to look at the suffering. I want it to be a spectacle."

"And I presume Todd is the fortunate recipient."

"How do you know?"

"Dahling, everyone at Head Lion knows?" Nour said.

"It's not just Todd, there is one more person. So are you in?"

"Hmm, beautiful revenge sounds interesting." Nour smiled, "Wait. I need something stronger."

Nour stood up. "Max, help me." Max poured scotch for everyone. Finally, she turned around and raised her glass. "The last time I had this much excitement in a night, I came four times. But that was twenty years ago."

They all laughed.

"So where do we begin?" Nour asked.

"I'm still unclear about the plan, but I am sure about one thing. We need power, and our power will come from the strongest agency money can buy." In many ways, Ryan knew more about Head Lion than Max. He built the brand from scratch and crafted the elitist strategy. Head Lion had 135 paid residents, having a net worth of five hundred million dollars or more.

Ryan continued, "I know they want to remind the world who they are. With the right motivation, they will jump for a chance to be relevant again."

"They can hardly walk, Ryan." Nour refilled their glasses with more scotch. "I get what you're offering them, but what are you expecting from them?"

"A nod!"

"What does that mean?"

"Letting us make a pitch, opening the doors for us. They all have enough influence to slide us in front of any brand in the country."

"And you think you will win, presenting while you sit in your wheelchair and ask someone to help you pee." Nour looked at him.

Ryan didn't answer, leaned back, took a sip from his scotch, and glanced at Max.

"He will win," Max said. "If you get him a chance to pitch, he will get the account. That's my guarantee."

"Nour, there are over hundred potential clients here at Head Lion." Ryan took out the brochure and laid it in front, "With an average annual advertising budget of 500 million. So if we get just five, we become the biggest agency in New York with annual billing of almost three billion dollars in the first year. That's unprecedented!"

"And you can choose any position you like," Max added.

"Dahling, you know there is only one position I enjoy; being on top." Nour smiled.

"I guarantee you'll be at the top," Ryan said.

The room turned silent as everyone took a sip. The scotch hit the right spots for everyone as they all contemplated the same thing.

"And who do you propose is the first client we pitch to?" Nour looked at them and asked.

"You!" Max and Ryan answered at the same time.

"Bastards," she chuckled, "why am I not surprised!"

"Can you get us in? Sphinx has called for pitches next week."

"Yes, I can." She raised her glass. "Here's to a beautiful revenge and breaking my number one rule. Never talk business when you're high."

Chapter 17

The happiest place on earth
(Disney, 1955)

There was nothing unusual about the following day. Ryan woke up with a start. He was getting late for work. He despised being late to the office even though he was late every day. He tried to sit up. His body was numb.

The familiar pain woke him up to reality. He stared at the blank ceiling. The blinding light in the room reminded him of last night. Nour was the light at the end of the tunnel. The unusual thing about this morning was he finally smiled.

Today, he felt different. He felt happy, tense, nervous, confident, anxious, bewildered, and alive. It was like a smorgasbord of emotions swirling around in his head. He wondered if Nour would come through or if it had been the weed talking. His phone buzzed. It was a text from Nour.

You're in. Pitch on Friday. New agency announcement on Monday.

The reality suddenly struck him. His stomach churned. He felt like he was going to throw up. He knew it was a mere formality if

Sphinx was squeezing Ryan in at the last minute. He would have to present something out of this world to change their minds.

A win would be monumental. A big piece that would fit in the 'beautiful revenge' puzzle. A lesson Todd and Kate would never forget. It was the reason why he wanted to fight when he could barely stand. And, in some twisted, morbid way, it was the reason for him to live now. Ryan looked at the message again. The most important and urgent task was getting a team to deliver a pitch-winning campaign in 48 hours.

After almost a decade at Sun, the only experts he could trust were the ones on his team. The dilemma was they must have worked on the same pitch with Kate. He needed to get rid of Kate and invite the team over to Head Lion. He sent a message to Kate, letting her know that he was traveling out of town with Max to get some tests done. He then sent a text to Gina.

Can you get the squad to come over and meet me —today at 7 pm?

The reply was almost instantaneous.

Anything for you, Guru! Hugs.

Ryan smiled.

The churn in his stomach had stopped, and now he wanted some coffee the same way he wanted his Wi-Fi signals: strong. At 7 pm, there was a knock at the door. Ryan's former team group hugged him. Andy opened a bottle of Patrón, Ryan's favorite tequila. Gina pushed Ryan's wheelchair and moved the party to the balcony with a breathtaking view of the lake. Fish did the honors as he rolled up a joint, proudly telling everyone that the weed was from Pakistan. Ryan declined but let them have it. He wanted them to relax before dropping the bomb. Fish finally asked the most important question of the evening.

"Why are we here, Guru?"

"You missed us?" Gina smiled.

"You need help?" Fish looked at Andy.

"Yes, I need your help."

"Anything for you, Guru." They all chimed in.

"What do you need?" Gina asked.

Ryan paused for a bit, "I'm pitching."

"Who's the client?" Gina sounded surprised.

"Sphinx!" Ryan said after a brief pause.

They all looked at each other. The room went silent. The only sound they could hear was the crackling of the crickets outside. Fish took the last drag from the joint and turned to Ryan.

"You're aware that we pitched to them today?"

"Yes, I am."

"But how can they let you pitch? It's a huge account. You can offer them nothing," Fish asked in a condescending tone.

"The better question is, how can you even think you can compete with the big boys?" Gina stopped drinking.

"Yeah, and your competition has offices nationwide, an infrastructure, history; they have contacts?" Fish was getting angry.

"I have what it takes." Ryan poured himself a drink.

"Do you have any idea who you're competing with?" Andy asked.

"I don't compete with others. I compete with myself. I want to be better than I was yesterday. The day my previous work seems better is the day I hang my gloves."

"They are announcing the agency on Monday, and it's most likely Sun." Fish smirked.

"I won't let that happen," Ryan replied.

"Yeah right! Even if I believe that absurdity for a second, you're asking us to help you destroy our livelihood." Fish did not seem amused.

"So let me get this straight. It took us a month to make a decent campaign. You want us to make something monumental in 24 hours while backstabbing Todd?" Andy said.

"Yes!" Ryan said.

"Sorry Guru, but he didn't fire me," Fish said, "I wasn't the one snorting coke during lunch hour." Fish stood up and picked up his jacket.

"Guru, I love you, but I'm out." Fish was wearing his jacket. "Even if I get comfortable backstabbing the hand that feeds me, there is no way you can win this pitch." Fish looked at Andy as if waiting for a response.

"You're underestimating Kate. She made a pitch-wining presentation." Andy stood up and looked toward Laura and Allen.

"I know Gina will stay, but you guys need to pick your ass up and start moving. You can't afford to lose your jobs," Fish said to Laura and Allen. Reluctantly, they both stood up.

"Guru, it's better we leave now. I don't want to know more about your plans." Andy looked away from Ryan.

"You can't win this!" Fish looked him in the eye, "Your days are over. The sooner you realize that, the better."

Alone, Gina and Ryan stared at the moon disappearing behind the clouds. The light was dying down, and so was Ryan's spirit.

"So are we doing this, Guru, or are you going to sulk like a 13-year-old girl getting her first period?" Gina said.

"Do you think we can do this?"

"Do we have a choice? We can do this. We've done it before."

"I owe you big time," Ryan said.

Ryan felt the blood starting to flow again, like an engine restarting after losing power. There was a knock at the door. Gina went to the door. Ryan could hear people laughing. It was Laura and Allen.

"I low-key wanted to be a part of a coup ever since I left college," Laura said.

"You could lose your jobs over this?" Ryan looked at them.

"Guru, you hired us for peanuts, and we're still getting the same salary. Just promise us you'll make us rich if you win." Allen smiled and finally spoke. It was the second time Ryan heard him say something.

"I'll win, and I'll make you rich," Ryan said.

"First things first, do you have anything to eat, and do you have extra toothbrushes?" Laura asked.

Ryan laughed, "Anything you want. You can have a lobster for breakfast."

Laura set the alcohol aside, got on the phone, and ordered food for everyone.

"What's the big idea?" Gina asked.

Ryan took out his laptop. He shared with them the work he had done. Thanks to Nour, Ryan had exclusive research no one had access to and finally laid down three ideas. He was leading with the one idea from Kate, fixing the gap she overlooked. Everyone stared at the laptop, seemingly mesmerized by his work. He looked at them, waiting for someone to say something.

"Well, do you think we have a chance?" he asked.

"Respek Guru, I'm glad I came back. You still have it," Allen said.

"I'm surprised Kate missed such a crucial detail," Gina said.

"Hashtag blessed. I'm so glad I stayed back," Laura said.

Ryan could read them. His creativity spellbound everyone in the room and reminded them why everyone called him Guru.

Everyone made themselves comfortable, found small work islands, and worked nonstop after breakfast until the sunlight broke through the curtains. Allen ordered breakfast which included a lobster thermidor. Finally, Gina finished and took over the presentation from Ryan. Ryan was tired, his spine was hurting, and he was famished. She turned him over and gave him a back massage. He was snoring in five minutes.

Ryan woke up with a start. It was 7 pm. The sun was setting, and his team was sitting around him, drinking coffee. Everyone looked like they were survivors of a shipwreck.

"Is it done?"

They all smiled and nodded in unison.

He stared at them after seeing the presentation. "It's perfect!"

Ryan knew how to win a pitch in two simple steps. Step one, surprise the client by presenting what the clients think is right. Step two, shock them by showing how wrong step one is.

"Guru, we all know what happens if you lose." Allen looked at Ryan, "But what happens if you win?"

"Honestly, I don't know. We'll cross that bridge when we get to it." Ryan had not thought about it because, even though his heart was telling him he would win, his brain told him otherwise.

"Can we come with you tomorrow?" Laura asked Ryan.

Allen jumped in, "Yeah, you'll need people with you. You can't go alone."

"No," Gina replied before Ryan could. "All of us will get fired if the word gets out."

"Yes, Gina is right. You've already taken enough risks."

They all left, wishing him good luck. Ryan desperately needed a bath and called for help as he thought about what Laura had said. He realized going alone would make the wrong statement. He needed a team sitting beside him. Great ideas alone don't win you an account. The client will never trust half a man with their multi-million dollars account.

There was a knock on the door. It was the Head Lion staff, a man and a woman. Ryan realized he had never spoken to the two of them before. It was the first time he looked at them. Both seemed in their late twenties, attractive and well-spoken—tall, dark, and good-looking, just what the doctor ordered.

"I'm sorry, but I don't know your names," Ryan said.

"I thought you knew," the man replied.

"I thought you couldn't speak." The woman smiled. "I'm Maria, and this is Lucas."

They both looked like olive-toned Salsa dancers. Perfect for the big, bad world of advertising. A Greek god holding a lightning rod on Lucas's arm was more than a tattoo. It was a sign for Ryan. Maria had long, straight hair tied in a bun. Her body was lean, with curves seemingly carved with precision tools. They brought Ryan to the bathroom and started undressing him gently. Ryan had opened up a floodgate. Maria was talking nonstop. She told him about her life and migrating from Venezuela to chase her American dream. Her firm breasts brushed his elbow as she and Lucas helped Ryan into the tub. Ryan shut his eyes and cursed his newly-awakened, hyperactive hormones. By the time the two placed Ryan in the tub, he had an erection. Ryan ignored it. Maria's eyes were glued to it. She was making no effort to hide her fascination.

"How much do you guys earn in a month?" Ryan tried to divert everyone's attention.

"Erm, about $4000." Lucas looked at Maria, and she shrugged.

"How would you like to earn $4000 for a few hours of work?" Ryan asked.

"I'm sorry Mr. Ryan, if you want to ahem, you know, if you need help with that?" Lucas pointed to his penis. He seemed nervous.

"No, no, no." Ryan was embarrassed, "I didn't mean that."

"I always liked you. You're different. You never treated me like your servant." Maria paused, "I can help you with this, but no sex."

"Guys, you're getting the wrong impression." Ryan covered his penis, protruding like a periscope. "I need you guys to come with me for a presentation."

They looked confused.

"You'll pay us four thousand dollars just to go with you? No work?" Maria finally stopped smiling.

"I want to show a client that I am not alone."

After a pause, Maria said, "We'll go with you, and you don't have to pay us."

"Yes, don't worry about it. I'll come along too." Lucas smiled as he massaged Ryan's hair with shampoo.

"If you agree, I'll give you two thousand now and two thousand tomorrow."

Lucas and Maria stopped and stared at each other.

"Are you sure? What if something goes wrong?" Maria looked at him.

"You'll have four thousand dollars, no matter what happens."

"And there is no catch?" Lucas looked at Ryan, who shook his head.

"Well, I guess in that case, you need a good night's sleep before your big presentation." Maria poured some soap into her hand and started stroking his penis.

Chapter 18

Obey your thirst

(Sprite, 1993)

The Sphinx headquarters was in Long Island, about two hours from Scarsdale. Ryan was nervous. It seemed like a lifetime since he last gave a presentation. Max had sent Ryan his personal Rolls Royce Cullinan with a bouquet and an envelope that said, *"Memento Vivere (Remember to live)."* The envelope contained proof that Ryan's police record was wiped clean. Ryan smiled. This was the energy supplement he needed for the pitch.

Both Maria and Lucas looked like seasoned executives in their formal clothes and brimming confidence.

"What's in the briefcase?" Ryan asked.

"A sandwich." Lucas smiled nervously.

Lucas was wearing a navy-blue suit with a grey flannel shirt and a light blue tie. Maria looked like a typical Manhattan account manager in a black skirt and an off-white top. Her stilettos made her look taller, and her glasses made her look more intelligent.

Ryan knew both had the right people skills needed for the

account management team. Their training began as soon as they sat in the car. Ryan would consume the thirty minutes allotted for the meeting, leaving no time for the Sphinx team to grill Maria and Lucas.

The car pulled up in front of a towering building. Ryan had never seen a cleaner, blacker road than the Sphinx's driveway. The building was shiny, too. Gold-tinted reflecting glass enveloped the structure. There was hardly any concrete visible. The Sphinx logo was etched across the glass from the top to the entrance. The exterior was gaudy and trying hard to make a statement. Lucas took control of the wheelchair as they walked in.

The Sphinx atrium stretched endlessly up to the ceiling. A large reception area facing a well-lit lobby reminded him of fancy hotels. Two young blondes manned the reception desk; they wore traditional Egyptian gowns.

On the left of the reception was a casual dining area filled with uncomfortable designer furniture, giant TV screens, and oozing with the scent of fresh coffee. It was bustling with activity and noise, executives multitasking, pouring coffee, looking at their phones, and talking to their peers, all at the same time. The building felt even bigger from the inside. A young girl, possibly an intern, guided them to the elevator.

The ride up to the 37th floor gave Ryan a daunting view of the challenges ahead. The elevator walls were made of glass as Ryan scanned the atrium while going up. Before the elevator dinged, Ryan saw a familiar face coming out of an office. It was Todd, Jeff and a tall gentleman seeing them off. They were laughing as they shook hands. A chill went through Ryan's spine as Lucas steered his wheelchair out of the elevator. Ryan could sense the camaraderie. He knew what Todd must have said while exiting. It was surreal watching Todd after six months.

The elevator dinged, and one of the receptionists came running to them. "Mr. Ryan! Are you Mr. Ryan?" She smiled like an air hostess about to make a public announcement.

"Depends. Who's asking?"

"Sorry, I forgot. Someone left an envelope for you in the morning?"

"For me?" Ryan was surprised.

She nodded and gave the package to Ryan. It was a red envelope. The red envelope was the last distraction Ryan needed. He shoved the envelope into his laptop bag.

Ryan was expecting a large boardroom splattered with gold ornaments. He was wrong. The intern led them into a small meeting room, and there was hardly any decor, a table, and a few scattered chairs. It was probably a spare room for small vendors and junior executives. He started to feel uneasy.

The size of the meeting room was a clear statement of what Sphinx thought of him. His biggest fear came true when the interns reappeared with two young men in their early 30s. They walked in with an arrogance Ryan was not expecting. They wore off-the-rack suits and introduced themselves as assistant brand managers. Ryan realized this was game over. He wanted to walk out but knew he couldn't.

There was an awkward silence in the room as the Sphinx team waited for him to start. He didn't. He sat there, saying nothing, adding to the awkwardness of the meeting. Lucas and Maria shifted uncomfortably in their chairs. The silence continued as Ryan thought about his next move with his eyes fixated on the table.

"Mr. Ryan," the intern interrupted his thoughts. "I'm sure you're a busy man...."

Her voice became a blur as Ryan noticed the red envelope sticking out from the pocket of his laptop bag. The girl was still talking from across the table as he took the envelope out and opened it. Ryan ignored everyone and stared at the visiting card.

Mustafa Saeed
Vice President Marketing
Sphinx
Extension: 4351

Ryan googled Mustafa Saeed, least interested in the growing awkwardness taking over the meeting room. He glanced through the article that described Mustafa's pompous traits and lavish lifestyle. A picture of Mustafa on his luxury yacht gave away the gist of the story. The sender had sent him his next move. His attention drifted from who sent the envelope to why.

"Mr. Ryan, did you hear what I just said?"

The frustration in the Sphinx team was now visible in her tone.

Ryan finally spoke, "Please don't take this the wrong way. Presenting to you is as useless as a diet coke with a Big Mac."

He picked up the phone in the middle of the table and dialed extension 4351. It was his Hail Mary.

"Hello," said a booming voice with a thick accent.

"Good morning. My name is Ryan. I'm here for only one reason, so I can help you become successful." He paused to catch some air as he felt his shoulders tightening. The Sphinx team looked at each other, panic visible in their eyes.

Ryan continued, "I have spent three sleepless nights to get thirty minutes from you so I can present something to the second smartest man in this building today. I'm sorry, but I'll not be leaving your building until I present my ideas to you. I can wait. I have ample time on my hands."

He put the phone down and smiled at everyone. The brand team took out their phones and started texting in unison like robots on an assembly line. Five minutes went by, and the only sound came from the incoming and outgoing texts.

Ryan was still smiling, trying hard not to show them that he was now almost certain he had blown his only shot. His poker skills were getting rusty. He felt his mouth drying up and reached for the water bottle on the table. The team seemed to wait for some instructions, some guidance, some divine intervention.

The glass door suddenly opened, and a tall man walked in. He didn't seem happy. Ryan recognized the man. It was Mustafa Saeed, the same man who was laughing with Todd and Jeff. The man was well over six feet, but it wasn't his height that overshadowed the room. It was his demeanor. His expensive suit and the shiny gold Rolex also contributed to his intense presence. His trimmed white hair topped his whitish square face. He had a French beard, but there was nothing European about him.

"Mr. Ryan, my name is Mustafa Saeed," he said in a thick Middle Eastern accent as he pulled a chair and sat in front of him. "You have thirty minutes to convince me before I help you exit the building."

"Thirty minutes is all I need to convince you that hearing me out was the smartest decision you made this year." Ryan smiled.

"If you convince me, I'll personally drive the car and drop you off. Shall we begin?" Mustafa refused to smile.

This was it. This is what Ryan wanted. He took a deep breath and began. Part one of his presentation was based on the smartest advertising strategy for Sphinx. Part two was why they shouldn't do it.

Ryan didn't feel guilty stealing from Kate's presentation and proving her ideas wrong. He knew it was wrong, but it felt good, like stealing towels from your hotel. He felt stronger and less sinful with every sentence he spoke.

The Sphinx team moved uncomfortably, whispering to each other. They seemed shocked to see Ryan knew the exact strategy they had decided to take. Ryan was unable to read Mustafa as he focused on his presentation. Finally, Ryan showed them the big idea that would deliver results.

Ryan looked at the timer on his laptop; thirty minutes gone. Lucas unrolled a life-size banner of their advertising campaign and placed it right in front of the Sphinx team. Ryan shut down his laptop and pretended to wrap up when the young executive interrupted his movements.

"I have one question for your team." An executive finally spoke to Maria and Lucas, "How did you decide to work with Mr. Ryan? Especially considering the future right now is very vague for him."

"Ladies and gentlemen," Ryan said, "you have no idea how eager we are to answer your questions. But, sadly, our allotted thirty minutes are over," Ryan said. "We can schedule another meeting to answer your questions, provided, of course, you sign us up."

Ryan shook their hands, thanked them for the opportunity, and signaled Lucas to help him move out. He didn't look back, leaving the team staring at the banner in the middle of the room. Ryan felt the sweat pouring down his armpits, his hair rising on the back of his neck. He soothed his doubts that it was the right card to play and the only one.

In a pitch, it is not the ideas that need to be memorable. It's the one presenting the ideas. That's why agencies don't email their presentations; they come and present. Everything was a presentation from the moment Ryan walked in until he left the building.

The snapshot of Mustafa's life triggered a perfect strategic move. The one way to counter Mustafa was to match his arrogance. The messenger with the red envelope had saved him one more time. The plan was to get back to Head Lion and wait for the phone call. There was nothing more Ryan could do. His stomach rumbled as

Lucas helped him in the car. His phone buzzed. It was a text from Laura.

Hi Guru, Sorry to ruin your day. Todd just walked in. He announced Sun had won Sphinx.

Thanks for letting me know. Ryan replied, sulking back in his seat. He didn't expect the game to be over this soon. He was feeling hungry. He craved a burger. He decided to text Max with the bad news when his phone rang.

"Mr. Ryan, are you still here?" said a familiar voice on the other side. It was the same executive from the small meeting room. His tone was nicer this time.

"Yes." Ryan finally smiled, knowing he had penetrated the wall.

"Mr. Saeed would like to see you before you leave."

"Sure."

"Mr. Saeed says you can send your team home; he'll drop you off."

It didn't take him long to get to Mustafa's office. Ryan told Lucas to go back and strolled into the room in his wheelchair. There was no one there. The office was predictably huge, glamorous, and garishly pompous. Mustafa's framed pictures with politicians and presidents adorned the walls. Finally, the door opened, and Mustafa walked in like a giant grizzly bear about to attack him.

"Ryan, Ryan, Ryan." he surprised Ryan with an awkward hug and a kiss on the cheek. Mustafa walked over to the liquor cabinet and poured a drink from a Waterford decanter.

"I heard you can read minds. Tell me what I'm thinking right now."

"You're thinking I desperately need a drink," Ryan joked. He knew Mustafa was not ready to hear the truth. Mustafa laughed.

"By the way, I like my scotch like my women – aged."

Ryan smiled, relieved he didn't say underaged.

"I'm assuming we're celebrating something." Ryan took a sip and threw a bait.

"Not so soon, Ryan. I loved the presentation; that's pretty obvious. But I have a few doubts about you being the agency for Sphinx, like literally you being the agency."

"I have the best team money can buy." Ryan started thinking about who to hire, and Gina's name was at the top of the list. "All the agencies you've met have creatives trained by me. I can hire any of them."

"How will you afford them? You haven't even started as yet."

"I have investors fighting over me. I have seven pitches lined up, including one to your biggest rival." He lied.

"Hold on. Are you pitching to Totem?" Mustafa was no longer smiling as he made another drink. Totem was the one competitor Sphinx feared, and Ryan knew that.

"Depends on the answer we get from you."

"Who do you know there?" Mustafa probed.

"I know Alyson and James, the Marketing Head. I worked with them for three years at Ogilvy & Mather." That wasn't a lie. However, the truth was that both Alyson and James hated Ryan.

Mustafa finally stopped strolling around the room and sat down on his chair. "Let's cut to the chase. Here is what I'm thinking. Join us as a consultant. Name your price, and you can pick the agency of your choice for Sphinx."

"Mustafa, the offer is tempting. However, my ask is simple: all or nothing."

Mustafa took another sip, "What can you offer us, Ryan, that all the other seasoned agencies in New York can't?"

"Money-back guarantee. Moving you to number two in one year." Ryan paused, "If we are not hired, ensuring the brand ceases to exist in one year. Also guaranteed." Mustafa chuckled. It was an uneasy laugh. Ryan could read he was scared.

"Let's talk on the way back. I promised I'll drop you if you managed to convince me that you're good at what you do."

"I believe you're already convinced."

"Keep in mind," Mustafa said, "you've convinced me that you're the best but not that your agency can handle a big account like Sphinx."

"I have an hour to do that since you're dropping me home." Ryan smiled. Mustafa stared at him and then laughed. He called his driver to get the car. The car outside was predictable. a Mercedes-Benz Maybach Exelero painted in gold. The driver helped Ryan get in the car. Mustafa took a few seconds to make himself comfortable in the driver's seat.

"Ryan, I like you because you're over-confident. A good trait to have in our line of work."

Ryan was getting the feeling he was stalling. Finally, he decided it was time to play his trump card. "Mustafa, if you want to win, hire us. I can even help you with the IPO next month."

"How the fuck do you know these things? Nobody outside the organization knows about the IPO."

Except for Nour, Ryan thought.

"I might tell you after signing the contract." Ryan smiled and kept the tango going.

"I haven't even seen your financial proposal. It wasn't with the pitch."

"1.5 per year with a three-year contract."

"1.5 what?"

"1.5 million dollars per year, Mustafa. No commissions, just a flat retainer."

Mustafa's knee-jerk reaction was bursting into a nervous chuckle. "You must be out of your mind. That's more than what all the others were asking, and they have offices worldwide, hundreds working for them." Ryan could see the droplets forming on Mustafa's forehead. He lowered the temperature in the car.

"They didn't ask because they can't give what I can."

Mustafa was taking his time. Then, he turned to Ryan. "I'll give you a half a mil per year, join Sphinx as a consultant. You choose the days you work, how you want to work."

"Mustafa, no one joins advertising for money."

"So why do they join?" Mustafa laughed.

"There is only one reason, to stand in the company of immortals."

"You make it sound like an epic Greek tragedy." Mustafa chuckled.

"Oh, but it is," Ryan said, "Only the people in the ad world can relate. We want to see brands rise to the top and then hear someone tell us it was because of us."

There was an uneasy pause as they got closer to Head Lion. Time was running out. It was now or never.

"Give me time to think. You'll know the final decision by Monday."

"Todd has announced to his agency that they won." Ryan played his final card.

"They did, but then you showed up and fucked up my plans."

"Will you be able to handle Todd? No agency has walked out on him. Once you're in, there is no getting out."

"You think I am scared of the old weasel?" Mustafa chuckled.

"You should be. Todd doesn't like losing," Ryan said.

"Fuck him! I've dealt with rats like him all my life."

They finally reached Head Lion. Lucas was waiting outside.

"So, where do we stand?" Ryan could read Mustafa was in turmoil. He needed a nudge.

"I like you, but it seems too risky. Here's my cell number if you change your mind." Mustafa gave him his card.

"I won't, but you will. After I sway your biggest rival my way."

Lucas helped Ryan get out of the car. Ryan steered past Mustafa and heard the faint buzzing of the car window going down.

"How about a million per year as a retainer?"

Ryan resisted the desperate urge to smile, turned around, and said calmly, "Welcome to the best ad agency in New York!"

Chapter 19

Just do it
(Nike, 1998)

Ryan was ready to jump up and dance in his wheelchair as he entered his room. He poured himself a drink. He wanted to call everyone Nour, Max, Lucas, Maria, but Gina deserved to be the first to know. Her phone was off.

The familiar ping from his laptop interrupted his next move. The email was from Mustafa to the heads of all the five agencies that pitched. Ryan skimmed the first two paragraphs, landing on the last.

> "...All agencies presented ideas and strategies focused on the core promise and were brilliant, but one stood out. Based on the knowledge of the category and understanding us as partners, I'm pleased to appoint Ryan Walker and his team as our new advertising agency."

Ryan smiled. *This is happiness*, he thought. This is the reason why millions of people love the advertising world. This is better than sex, drugs and rock 'n' roll.

Moments later, his phone started buzzing with text messages and calls from known and unknown numbers. He scrolled through the messages from Laura and Allen, interview requests from *Adage*, *Adweek*, and *The New York Times*. A few vendors that worked with him before, a few who hadn't but wanted to work now. There was no message from Gina.

Ryan was now desperate to tell her about the meeting with Mustafa and the drama he created at the pitch. He wanted to talk about the future. He wanted to discuss where to land the office, the interior, and all the fun stuff. Gina was inaccessible. Instead, he texted Nour and Max about the big news. They agreed to meet at seven. He dialed Gina's number one more time. She finally picked up.

"Hey! Where are you?"

"Congrats, you won!"

"We won." He corrected her, "Drop everything, come over tonight."

"I can't, Guru."

"You can't?"

"I have to go to LA for a shoot."

"Shoot? I thought Kate took care of that?"

"I've been promoted. Accounts were redistributed today, so I couldn't call." Gina sounded low.

"Fuck that. You're coming with me as a partner," Ryan said.

"Guru, Kate was sidelined today. Todd was extremely upset about losing the Sphinx account. Someone saw our Sphinx presentation before it was presented, and he blames Kate."

"Gina, Fuck Sun. Sphinx was just the beginning. We're going to sweep New York."

"Guru, do you really believe you can fight with Todd? Don't you know him? You have a good thing going, don't make this ugly."

"It's already ugly."

"You can't win, Guru. Sphinx was a fluke."

"Who is going to stop me."

"I will."

" I don't want you to stand in the way."

"Oh! But I'm standing." She paused. "Sun was blindsided. No one expected Mustafa to actually handover Sphinx to you, including me."

"I did, and I'm coming for the whole nine yards now."

"You stab my back. I'll stab yours." Gina was getting louder.

"You think you can beat me," Ryan said.

"I will. I know how you operate, and you have no idea how I work. I know all your tactics and the people you'll call to help you."

Ryan became silent. This was unexpected and not what he wanted.

"There is no team in 'I' if you know what I mean."

"We are more than a team. We're a family, Gina. We stick together."

"Family?" Gina scoffed, "Was I your family when you tried to rape me? I forgave, but I never forgot."

"Rape you? I tried to kiss you and backed out when you said no. It was a mistake that happened once."

"That's the version that plays in your head, especially when you're high on coke. What do you think the interns go through when you fuck them? Do you think they have a choice to say yes or no?"

"Bullshit. I've never taken advantage of anyone."

"That's how all men justify when they abuse power. Keep on believing that just like you believe no one knows about your coke addiction."

The pause that followed was uncomfortable. Finally, Ryan decided it was time to wrap up the conversation and the relationship.

"You're right. I don't know what I was thinking."

"Guru, we had a good run together. I can't deny that you were great; you were the best. But your time is up now." She waited. "It's my time. Todd has offered me partnership. I owe everything to Todd, and I'll do whatever it takes to protect him."

Ryan knew why Todd had offered Gina partnership. Without Gina on his team, he'd lost the battle even before it began.

"Guru, I know you." She was driving the nail in the coffin, "It's time to hang those gloves. You're tired, alone, and old."

"Gina, you're forgetting one thing," he said.

There was silence on the other side.

"I don't stop dancing till the song ends." He disconnected the phone.

Gina's call was like the monsoon. It was expected, and it was harsh. Fortunately, her discouraging monologues added the fuel he needed. The fire Gina lit, not even monsoon rain could drown. He had an hour to kill before he met Nour and Max and decided to do the second most exciting thing he could do in an hour—build a team.

Laura and Allen were fired by Gina an hour ago. They were the first ones he hired as creative directors. They were excited to join Ryan's new venture and happy they were no longer jobless, but what shocked them the most was the offer. Ryan matched their salary with the salaries of creative directors at Sun. Their salaries jumped from $55,000 annually to $200,000. He also told them to hire the rest of the creative team.

Ryan still had twenty minutes to hire the Account Management team. He called Lucas and Maria and made them an offer. He could hear them screaming in excitement even before he told them they would be earning twice their Head Lion salary. The core team was complete. It was time to meet Max and Nour and ask for the investment they had promised.

The loud ambulance siren was not an anomaly at Head Lion. Most residents were over seventy. A day without an ambulance arriving was as rare as a blank billboard on Times Square. Even then, the hair on the back of Ryan's neck stood up when he saw the commotion around the lounge. Ryan steered his wheelchair to the power lounge as he saw the frightened staff running past him.

There was something wrong with this picture. Audible whispers and the growing crowd were stifling the usual calmness inside Head Lion. He saw Nour standing near the concierge desk on her phone. She waved at him, and he steered his wheelchair toward her. Maria and Lucas mingled with their colleagues to discover what was happening.

"It was Max," Nour whispered, staring at the commotion. "He had a heart attack and was rushed to the hospital."

"Is he—?" Ryan didn't want to finish the sentence.

"Not sure." She smiled at him and took control of his wheelchair. "I think he was just waiting for you to reboot. This seems like a good reason to have a drink. Let's go to my place."

By the time they reached Nour's residence, they had discovered that Max was still alive but in critical condition. The night was crucial.

Nour raised her glass, "Here's to your win!" and gulped the 18-year-old scotch before Ryan could blink. She poured herself another drink as Ryan nurtured his. His mind was whirling with thoughts, not settling on one. The man responsible for resurrecting him was now fighting for his life, and he had just created the biggest upset in the ad industry.

"Are you sniffing the scotch? I'm on my third now. Tell me what happened at the pitch. Distract me from thinking about Max." Nour interrupted his thoughts.

They finished a couple of more drinks before Ryan finished telling her about the day's events.

"You deserve this win, Ryan. I never doubted you!"

"Liar! You doubted me from the moment I walked in." Ryan laughed. He was enjoying the buzz.

"Why are you doing this, Ryan?" She lit up a joint. "Why are you obsessing over a beautiful revenge? There are more beautiful things to go after."

"I need to do this to stay alive." Ryan poured another drink.

"It will scorch whatever remaining life you have," Nour said.

"Revenge!" Ryan raised his glass, "Just like Scotch, it burns in the beginning, but soothes in the end."

"The hatred will consume you. Be done with Todd and move on. He's on the verge of dying anyway,"

"He can't die before I'm done with him."

"I mean, if you're that angry, why not get that poor guy beaten up? Isn't this obsession more about ego than about revenge."

"Yes, it is. I have nothing left but my ego. It's the only thing I care about."

"What about the girl who comes to see you?"

"I want to destroy her too. She is the real reason my life is fucked up."

"So it's her and Todd? Who do you hate more?"

"Kate, because you expect a snake to be poisonous."

Telling Nour about Kate was the first time he talked about his hatred for her. It was like opening the cage and setting the monsters free. His hatred was now making more sense to him.

"Ryan, sometimes the healing is more painful than the wound." She took another sip, "But that's what you need."

"You think she's my healing?"

"She sounds like every other man." Nour smiled, "You would've done the same thing if you were in her place. In fact, you have. It only bothers you because she's a woman."

"You think she didn't destroy my life?"

"Todd bears the main responsibility," She inhaled, "You're forgetting one more person. You!" She looked at him as if trying to wake him up with her eyes.

"You won't understand because you haven't been through it."

"Oh really! I can teach you a thing or two about revenge."

"And why would you do that?" Ryan asked.

"Because LinkedIn does not offer a course on backstabbing." Nour smiled.

"I have no idea about your backstabbing skills."

"No one does. That's lesson number one. Never confess. When the shareholders pushed me out, I kept thinking of ways to get back at them. Only to find out it was my son who played everyone to gain control."

"Your son sounds like a moron."

"Yes, but he was kind enough to drop me here. Let me rephrase that, his driver dropped me off here."

"So you lost everything?"

"I lost power!" She paused, "I still have a billion dollars."

"How is it my fault, Nour?"

"Because you're harboring hatred as if you're raising a child. I believe you have the power to be your hell or your heaven, and you chose hell."

"Even God loves revenge," Ryan replied, "The thought of destroying them is the only thing that keeps me alive." He poured himself another drink.

"No, it's killing you. You know what made me like you?" Nour sat up, "Your love for advertising, your desire to be in the company of immortals. And now, if your only goal in life is to destroy one ad agency, you've lost even before you began, Ryan."

"Nothing feels stronger than my hatred for them. I could lie, but I won't. And if that means you're pulling out your support—"

"Grow up, dahling. I'm with you through thick and thin. But to be honest, a lie for a lie doesn't excite me." She smiled at him.

"Do you have an idea where Max stands on this?"

"Max loves you. He doesn't need another reason. The kind of money you need, is peanuts for us. You keep driving ahead; don't worry about the fuel."

Ryan should've felt better, but he didn't. It felt like charity, even though he didn't doubt Nour's motivation for a moment. His fingers caressed the rim of the cold glass. His eyes were on Nour, but his mind was wandering elsewhere. He was calculating if he could survive without their money.

The retainer from Sphinx would cover the salaries, but he would need basic infrastructure, a decent office, equipment, utilities, and some money for unexpected expenses. The only sane option was selling his apartment.

There was no word on Max when Ryan left Nour's residence. Within ten minutes, he was in bed and woke up with the sun hitting his face. He sat up swiftly, feeling the painful blood rush to his head. *This is new*, he thought. It usually took him minutes to sit up. It also felt good knowing where he was after waking up. The pressure on his spine was unbearable. He slowly moved his legs to the edge of the bed and tried to stand. It took him an hour of agonizing pain to finally stand up.

He skipped breakfast and decided to go where the grapevine was. The news traveled fast in the Head Lion power lounge. It was a cheerful area that led to various boardrooms. It had an urban vibe mixed with a cigar lounge setting. Residents would have coffee in the morning and drinks after seven pm. Fresh newspapers and financial magazines were neatly scattered around the area.

The mavens meeting brokers, analysts, journalists, and lobbyists usually crowded the lounge. There were large TVs on the walls, displaying live news and stock markets from around the world. Today, there was a little less noise than usual. Most were whispering and talking softly. Ryan stood out like a stork in a petting zoo. His younger, colorful, and vibrant personality defied the traditional, elderly residents.

Ryan was surrounded by his idols, and he felt like a giddy fan among them. He particularly admired a few because they were from his world. He was always too nervous to talk to them. Sophie Lavigne, the famous French artist, was there, and so was Marco Ricci, the Italian film director who had won two Oscars for a foreign language film. Next to Marco, Mark Garcia, the media tycoon, a numbers genius. Isabelle Miller and Clifford Davis were at a separate table; they smiled and nodded at Ryan. Isabelle was a well-known writer and poet who started her career as a copywriter and won three Clios. Clifford was a marketing genius who launched some of the world's top brands.

It was apparent everyone was talking about Max. A few asked Ryan about Max as he steered his wheelchair through the maze of leather sofas. Ryan knew Max had told the Head Lion mavens his story. He could feel the friendly stares and nods.

Ironically, the large crowd in the lounge was perfect for solitude. All the residents were engrossed in their silos. Ryan finally found a spot to be alone and asked for coffee and the newspaper. He wanted to see if there was any news about Sphinx. A hand on his shoulder broke his solitude. He looked up and saw a man smiling at him.

"Hi, I'm Marquis Thomas. I have some good news for you."

Chapter 20

Snap! Crackle! Pop!
(Kellogg's Rice Krispies, 1932)

"You must be the guru Max kept talking about." Marquis smiled. "Any news of Max?"

The wrinkles on his black skin told the story of a life well-lived. His symmetrically chiseled beard and a deep voice made him seem refined and well educated. Marquis sat down and lit up a cigar.

"Nothing new," Ryan replied, wondering what the good news was.

"Max spoke highly of you. He considered you his protégé and the son he never had." His demeanor was commanding but not dominating, "So everyone here is praying for the day they see you walk."

"I'll take all the prayers I can get." Ryan smiled.

"I heard you're getting better," Marquis said.

"Well, mentally, I am better than I ever was." Ryan smiled, "Physically, I'm taking baby steps to recovery."

"Mentally is what matters. By the way, congrats on the Sphinx win."

"Word travels fast here." Ryan was intrigued.

"Nour mentioned. She was here in the morning. She said you did an amazing job for her, and that's why I'm here. The good news is I have some more business for you."

"I'm not sure if I'm equipped to help you at this moment." Ryan's heart started beating faster.

"You'll love to get involved. The best part is there is no pitch. You have the account if you accept it."

The aroma of fresh business coming his way was tempting, but with Gina walking away, he wondered if he could handle more business. Sphinx would expect extraordinary attention and would watch Ryan under a microscope.

"How can I help you, Mr. Thomas?"

"Well, my wife is an idiot." Marquis paused and started puffing his cigar. "Don't get me wrong, I love her, but she is young, inexperienced, and this new project is extremely sensitive. It's my swan song."

"Mr. Marquis, I need more information before agreeing that your wife is an idiot." He waited.

"Forget my wife. You'll never meet her." He smiled. "Three years ago, there was a hostile takeover. I was pushed out from the company I created. A business with over three hundred million in revenue."

Marquis paused as Ryan tried to read him. "My dream project triggered the takeover. It was risqué, extravagant, and like the board said, lavishly indecent. They rejected it. I didn't stop, and I was thrown out. Since then, the stock price has gone down faster than a sailor on his wedding night. Now, I want to relaunch my dream project. That's where you come in."

"And I am assuming they don't know your wife is running the show?"

"No, no one knows, but that's a story that warrants scotch and a long evening."

"And what's the product?" Ryan was curious.

"Ah! I'm glad you asked. I own the second-largest real estate on the East Coast, but that's not the interesting part."

"No, it isn't," Ryan smiled.

"The part that's interesting for you is that I own Elysium." Marquis puffed his cigar.

"You are Thomas and Thomas?" Ryan suddenly realized he was sitting across from one of the Big Five, one of Sun's most lucrative clients. Ryan had never worked on Thomas and Thomas. Everyone assumed that the exorbitant monthly retainer was because of Todd's decade-long friendship with this company.

"Yes, but before you get too excited, I won't be moving the account from Sun." He smiled.

"Then why are we sitting here?"

"I can't afford the project to fail. The product is great, but the response has been below par, and the advertising has been atrocious. So, I want you to help my wife market this project."

"Why don't you ask Sun to help you?" Ryan wanted to know about the peculiar relationship of Sun with the Big Five.

"I can't. It's complicated and not why I'm here."

"What happens when Sun finds out?"

"That's my problem."

"It's my problem too if Todd puts legal pressure and forces you to fire me."

"I will pay you the full retainer in advance."

"What if I run away with your money?"

"With those legs? I'll catch up."

"Sorry, Marquis, but I have to ask, how can you trust me like that?"

"Ryan, I don't trust you. I trust my judgment."

"It's a huge responsibility and a privilege. I'm not ready." Losing

Sphinx was not an option. Ryan had no team, no infrastructure, not even an office. This was too fast.

"Fair enough. I'm disappointed but not surprised." His phone rang as he stood up. Ryan felt the buzz on his phone almost instantly. Within seconds the lounge was silent, except for phones buzzing. Ryan could sense the tension growing around him. He knew what was happening before he read Nour's message.

"Max is no more!"

The only thing Ryan loved more than the sound of the rain was the scent of water mingling with the soil. It was his favorite therapy. Some of his best memories had rain in the backdrop. Today was different. Maria held the umbrella over him as Lucas pushed the wheelchair. The drizzle found his face and the inside of his shoes. He despised the rain today. The splatter covered the tears of many at the funeral. It also hid the indifference of many.

A long queue of black limousines lined up the road, leading up to the cemetery despite the rain. The large crowd with designer umbrellas and expensive suits kept growing at the funeral. The New York elite, including three former Presidents, numerous CEOs, celebrities, and other VIPs, were pouring in as harshly as the rain.

Ryan felt awkward as almost everyone consoled him like he had lost his father. He felt nothing except the guilt for being blasé. The pain that everyone expected him to feel was not there. He was trying hard to feel sad, but his mind wandered around planning his next steps. As the priest gave the sermon and told everyone to repent before it was too late, his biggest concern was that with Max gone, Nour might back out too.

As people eulogized, Ryan was budgeting a scenario without Nour. Ryan conservatively calculated his dues from Sun and savings to be around $2 million. His apartment would be another two after pay off. He could last a year with his dues, apartment sale, and the Sphinx retainer.

The funeral was over, and the haut monde was doing what it did best—networking. Ryan felt better after the calculations. His thoughts were interrupted by a hand on his shoulder. It was Todd, surrounded by his usual minions. Gina held him by his arm, his official crutch, as she helped a frail Todd from falling.

"Fuck, this was terrible news. I'm sorry for your loss," Todd said to Ryan.

"I'm sorry for your loss too, Todd."

"Oh, no loss of mine. Guess you haven't heard the good news!" Todd smiled wickedly and looked at his watch, "I don't like getting fucked in the ass, Ryan, you know that, right? I love pain but not for myself."

The alarm bells started ringing. Gina looked away, avoiding eye contact.

"Let me know if you need any help. I do a lot of charity, but you fucking know that already." He lovingly tapped Ryan's cheek and pushed Gina to start walking like a carriage driver nudging a horse.

Todd stopped and turned back. "Congratulations on your recent win. I sent a present for you. I hope you fucking enjoy it." He whispered, "It seemed inappropriate to bring it here."

Ryan was sure Todd brought Gina to spite him. He looked around and scanned the attendees. He didn't want to be blindsided again. The guests were gradually dispersing and so was the rain. The sun had set to a soft, warm tone that made the cemetery look surreal and serene. He could hear the pulse beating in his ears as he pictured all the possible scenarios.

Ryan had read Gina. He immediately regretted not making the contract formal by signing it. The deal was verbal and his reading showed Gina holding the winning hand. His neck hurt as he thought about losing the Sphinx account. He told Lucas to get him out and dialed Mustafa's number. There was no reply. He tried 17 times before he reached Nour's car.

"Everything OK?" She asked as Ryan got inside. He pressed the side window down to catch some air. The sky had cleared up. The soothing sound of the trees swaying with the gentle breeze calmed the desolate cemetery. But Ryan was far from being calm. He was drenched in a mixture of rain and sweat.

"Yes, everything is fine." He wiped his forehead and ran his fingers through his hair. "Can we go now? I'm exhausted."

The limo moved silently through the picturesque roads as the cool breeze caressed their faces. Both were silent, lost in their thoughts, staring at nothingness. Ryan was tense, almost certain Sphinx had slipped from their hands.

Knowing Todd, he knew this wasn't just a possibility. It was a certainty. He should have asked for the contract. He called again, and Mustafa didn't pick up. Nour asked the driver to drive slow as they settled in her luxurious limo. The Bentley Mulsanne would've impressed any car enthusiast, but Ryan's mind was elsewhere.

"You know, once Bentley offered me a job, on the condition I move to England," she said.

"Mustafa fucked us!" Ryan didn't let her finish.

"I found out an hour ago." She grasped his hand gently. "My source told me Mustafa was very impressed with your work."

Ryan smirked. "And he fired me because I'm good?"

"Apparently, it was his dick that got you fired." She shrugged her shoulders. "I asked my source why and his reply was he couldn't keep his dick in his pants. Whatever that means."

Kate, Ryan thought. She must have done it to save her job. Gina had mentioned that Todd was angry with her. Ryan was blindsided again. He should've preempted Todd's response.

Kate had disappeared in the last few days. It was not a

coincidence that she had suddenly stopped coming after the pitch. Not even to Max's funeral. He dialed Mustafa's number. Still no answer.

"I heard Mustafa is on his yacht," Nour said. "I tried calling him too."

Ryan turned and faced the side window to avoid further conversation. He was losing control and didn't want Nour to see him surrendering. He stared at the tall buildings as the car crawled through the traffic jam. His mind wandered like a homeless gypsy. Kate didn't even call to offer condolence. The world knew he was dead. It was on every fucking news network. She was probably fucking Mustafa on his yacht.

Finally, the car came to a sudden stop. There was another car blocking his pathway.

Nour hugged him and whispered, "You're not alone. Let me know when to jump, so I can ask how high?" Her words felt genuine, but he had been wrong about people before. Ryan thanked Nour as Lucas helped him get out.

"Ryan, there is no point in diffusing a bomb after it has exploded. Move on, find another battle." She threw him a flying kiss and drove away.

Ryan recognized the red Maserati Ghibli and Jeff's unmissable "AD-MAN1" plate. The car blocking his doorway added fuel to his burning anger. The door was ajar. Jeff was sitting comfortably in his club chair, drinking scotch. He had the same devious smile plastered on his face. The first thought that crossed Ryan's mind was: *How did he get in?*

"Well, look who is walking in–sorry, *wheeling* in," he smiled.

"Why are you here?" Ryan asked.

"I missed you." He laughed. "And also to deliver a present from Todd."

"You owe me a fucking apology for breaking into my apartment." Ryan knew Jeff was enjoying the scowl on his face.

"I didn't break in, Ryan. I was given the code."

Kate! Ryan thought. "She deserves a special place in hell."

"Jeff, get it over with before I do something that'll make me eligible for capital punishment."

Jeff walked over to Ryan and stood inches away from his wheelchair. Lucas and Maria watched Jeff like hawks ready to pounce.

"You know Todd loves you! He wanted to send a present for your recent win."

It was a long black box tied with a gold ribbon. It had a few words emblazoned in gold on a black box; *"Get out of your way."*

Ryan opened the box. The shiny black walking cane inside was adorned with a lion handle carved in gold. The one he admired the last time he was at Todd's place. The chiseled details on the handcrafted lion bust were impeccable.

"You're not here just to deliver this Jeff?"

"Why so impatient? This is an hors d'oeuvre, not the main entrée."

Ryan read the bomb Jeff was about to drop. Ryan desperately needed the money Sun owed him, and they were planning to pull the plug.

"I'm here to clear your dues that the agency owes you." He took out a check from his pocket. "You gave us a decade, and the work you produced —no one can put a price tag on it." Jeff gave Ryan the check. "But I can!"

Three hundred and twenty-seven dollars.

"Is this a joke?" He could feel the anger burning inside him, erupting like an inferno.

"Wait, wait, I have to record this. Todd is going to love this." He took out his phone and started recording.

"Two million. That's the minimum the agency owes me." Ryan was trying hard to hide his anger from the camera.

"Actually, three million, plus change, but the deductions led to this."

"What deductions?" His breathing got heavier.

"Oh, this is good!" Jeff kept recording. "Well, you know the contract you signed, the standard requirements you agreed to, like working full-time, forty hours a week blah blah."

"I worked more than that, and you know it." Ryan lashed out.

"Not according to the company records. You never signed in or out. Remember I kept telling you to mark your attendance, and your reply always was 'fuck off!'"

Ryan had never signed his attendance. He and most senior executives enjoyed this unspoken perk but never imagined it would have legal repercussions.

"According to HR, you owe us money because you were off every day, but you know Todd has always been generous. He told me to forgive what you owe Sun." He took out a file and gave the contract to Ryan. Jeff had highlighted the line mentioning the employee must provide proof of attendance and Ryan's initials next to it.

"I'll sue your ass." Ryan ignored the papers.

"Oh, I insist." Jeff was beaming with joy. "Sue us because the five expensive lawyers on our retainers sit on their asses and do nothing."

Ryan could hear the frustration inside his head. He tightened the grip on his wheelchair, his nail piercing the leather on the handles.

"Get out!" Ryan whispered.

"What, so soon? But there is more." He came closer to Ryan and whispered. "Remember that nice apartment with a million-dollar view? Guess who lives there now?"

"No, you can't."

"Oh yes, we can. Turn to page number three, section seven." Jeff started reading from the contract, "If the agency finds the ground to terminate your services, the agency reserves the right to take ownership of the apartment."

Ryan was cursing himself for not getting the contract vetted by a lawyer. He had signed everything without reading anything. Jeff leaned closer, inches away from his face. "I can bet Kate pitches to a new client every night on your bed."

Ryan could not take it anymore. He pushed himself up and managed to stand. His body was jolting with hatred. He clenched his fist fiercely and ferociously swung his arm with every inch of his body behind the force. Jeff moved back. Ryan fell, smacking his jaw on the wooden floor.

Ryan didn't have the strength, nor did his ego allow him to look up. He didn't want to see Jeff's smile. His body gave up on the cold comfort of the floor as he lay there, hoping the shame would fade away. Everyone in the room froze as they looked at Ryan. Maria tried to move forward, and Lucas stopped her. Ryan stared at the banal painting on the wall.

Finally, the sound of shattering bones broke the sinister silence. Ryan saw Jeff's face falling right in front of his. A broken nose dripping with blood had replaced the permanent smile on Jeff's face. Ryan looked up and saw Lucas massaging his bruised knuckle.

"Sorry, I couldn't help it, Guru." Lucas looked at Ryan.

Jeff was in shock, no longer smiling, wiping the blood on his face. "How dare you hit me? I'm going to sue you for assault."

"Please do," Maria said. "You can finally put your lawyers to good use. Now get the fuck out."

Jeff saw Lucas walking toward him, picked up his phone, and walked out. Lucas slammed the door behind him.

Ryan stood up slowly, unsure whether to scold Lucas or thank him. "Give me one reason to live because I can't think of any."

"I will give you two," Maria smiled, "First, you need to fuck these people up."

"And the second?" Ryan said.

"You stood up." Maria looked at Lucas.

"Yes! You were standing on your own fucking feet without any help. You know what that means, Guru?"

"What?"

"It means your hatred is your fuel."

"Sure," Ryan said sarcastically. "Will try harder starting tomorrow." He slowly took a few painful steps to his seat and sat down.

Maria smiled. "Tomorrow? You might wake up in a good mood tomorrow. We're going to try today."

Ryan didn't have the energy to resist. His body was with Maria and Lucas. His mind was hovering around ways to evict the new resident from his most prized possession. He wanted to curse and swear at her. He was uninterested in the exercise but went through the motions.

"Ryan, I have a stupid idea," Maria said.

"I love stupid ideas. All great things happened because someone had a stupid idea." Ryan smiled.

"OK, I don't know whether I should be saying this." She looked at Lucas.

"Woman, just say it," Lucas replied, helping Ryan walk.

She hesitated and looked at Ryan. "If you put in a solid effort for an hour, we'll take you to see Kate."

"Are you crazy?" Lucas said.

"I think it's a good idea that Ryan confronts that woman. Maybe she'll say something that Ryan needs to hear."

"I like the idea," Ryan replied.

Two hours later, Ryan was sweating; Lucas and Maria were smiling. They put on Ryan's favorite song and made Ryan move his hips, sit, and stand. He was screaming in pain but enjoying the new dance move. All of them had forgotten the drama that had unfolded hours ago. Finally, the song died down, and the phone rang. They stopped laughing and stared at Ryan's phone. Maria picked up the phone and gave it to Ryan.

"It's Kate."

Chapter 21

The best a man can get
(Gillette, 1989)

Kate's sleepy voice jolted Ryan.
"Hi!"
He didn't reply.
"Sorry, I missed your calls. Not feeling well. Everything OK?"
Ryan didn't believe a word. He kept it simple. "Where are you?"
"Home. Why?"
"Stay there. Coming to see you."
"Don't," Kate replied instantly," Ryan, please don't—"
Ryan disconnected the phone.
"Where's the house? Do you know the way?" Maria asked Ryan as she helped him get ready.
"Yes, it's very close to where I used to live." He smiled.
Kate was calling him constantly. Ryan switched off his phone. The hour-long drive was silent except for the noise in his head. His mind kept raising questions and then answering them, like a rapid-fire round in a quiz show.
"The building next to the deli, you can park in the alley on the left," Ryan told Lucas.

"Yo! Yo! Yo! Mr. Ryan!" TJ, the doorman, was excited to see Ryan. "I thought you died or something, man."

They laughed and greeted each other with fist bumps. TJ gave him a big bear hug. "It's so good to see you, man."

"I need to surprise someone. Is it OK if I sneak in?"

TJ stared at him for a few seconds and then smiled. "I didn't see you, man. I'm on a smoke break." He winked at Ryan. "Also, I didn't tell you they've installed cameras near the elevators."

TJ stepped aside and lit up a cigarette.

Maria and Ryan hurried through the lobby before anyone else could stop them. The elevator door opened, and the familiar scent of cheap air fresheners hit Ryan's nostrils. He reached his floor and steered his wheelchair slowly to the hallway.

Ryan looked at the familiar view and realized how his life had spiraled downwards in a matter of months. The faded carpet, a few cheap prints of unknown paintings, and bright lights that always bothered him were embracing him tonight. He pushed the joystick forward, realizing it was the first time he was not walking to his home. He reached the door. Maria knocked a few times. No one answered. She looked at Ryan.

"I don't think she's home."

"Kate!" Ryan cried out. "I'm not leaving till you open the door." He waited. "I have nowhere to go. You've ensured that." He shouted again.

A few neighbors opened up their doors to see the commotion. Finally, Ryan heard the latch opening. Kate had no make-up on and looked disheveled. Ryan entered as if it was his own house. He looked around the apartment. It looked the same—everything right where it used to be. Even the scent was the same. Kate looked as if she had been sleeping for days. She wore an oversized T-shirt, her hair spread across her face, and she stood at the door barefoot.

Kate looked at him silently. Ryan got up from the wheelchair, lowering himself slowly onto his favorite loveseat like he was buffering on a weak internet connection. His right leg hurt with all his weight on it. His left leg felt like a lifeless, wooden log.

"Wow! You can speak. You can move. I'm really happy for you, Ryan, but why hide it from me?"

"No! You don't get to ask questions tonight!" He lashed at her.

Maria asked, "Should I stay?"

"Yes." Ryan shouted.

"No," said Kate calmly, "I'll drop him off."

Maria looked at Ryan, who nodded after a few seconds. She left. There was an awkward silence.

"You want a drink?" Kate asked.

"Do you have any idea how much I hate you?" Ryan said.

"I know you hate me, but have no idea why." She passed him the drink. Ryan gulped the scotch. It hit just the right spot. She seemed different today, like a stranger he had never met before.

"Because you're a whore!" Ryan lashed at her.

Kate smiled. "Figuratively speaking or literally?"

"Stop the pretense. All the success you think you have is because you fucked everyone who could help you succeed."

"I didn't fuck you," she whispered. Ryan stared at her like a hawk as she made another drink for Ryan and wiped her tears quickly.

"Because you didn't get the chance." He gulped the drink, making him feel better.

She smiled. "I was possibly the only one in the agency you didn't fuck, and you think I'm the slut."

"I didn't fuck because I wanted to push my career forward."

"And I thought you could read minds." She waited for him to answer. "If I'm a slut, it's because I wanted to be you. All I ever wanted to be was Ryan Walker. You were my mentor, my savior, my everything. I've done nothing to deserve this hate."

"And that's why you fucked Daniel, so you could get me fired and destroy my life?"

"What the fuck are you talking about?" Kate didn't hold back her tears.

He didn't hold back his hatred. "And you're going to pretend you didn't fuck Mustafa to get Sphinx back?"

"Mustafa is gay, you moron, and I've been locked up in the apartment since he announced you as the winner. My career is over, and do you know why it's over? Because you told Mustafa about my pitch. You fucked me, and I'm the bad guy."

"I never told Mustafa it was you."

"Well, Gina got promoted. She is taking over all my accounts. I've been moved to the cemetery to look after the Big Five, which no one wants. So if you think I'm manipulating people to become successful, clearly, I'm pretty bad at it." Her tears dripped steadily.

"Karma is a bitch." Ryan wasn't letting his anger die down. He could read she was not lying. He could read she was in love with him. He could read he was wrong, but he didn't want to believe it.

"Why did Daniel make hiring you a condition for the Miamart account?"

"Bullshit! Who told you that? Daniel loved your work, and he keeps reminding me of that every time I see him. He was very upset with Todd for letting you go."

She was not lying. For the first time in his life, he refused to believe what his mind-reading told him.

"I don't believe you."

"Oh, you don't believe me?" She picked up her phone.

"Who are you calling? It's late, and we're drunk."

"Smile. The worst is yet to come."

Someone picked up. She turned on the speaker.

"Hi, Daniel, I'm so sorry to call you at this hour, but this is important."

"Everything OK?" Daniel replied.

"Yeah, everything's fine. I wanted to know, did you tell Todd that you won't give the account unless he hires me?"

"No, where did you hear that?"

"Did you get Ryan fired?"

"Ryan was the only reason the account stayed with Sun. No offense, I love your work, but no one comes close to Ryan; and I've worked with all the top agencies in New York."

"I hate to say this, but I agree with you. Sorry for calling you at this hour."

"It's fine." Daniel hung up.

"It doesn't make sense. Why would Todd fire me? Why all the drama?"

"You know Todd better than I do. Let me put it this way: I didn't fuck Daniel to get your job." Her tone was bitter.

Ryan felt frustrated. He was losing the one thing that kept him going: his hatred for Kate.

"Do you know why I fucked men and moved on?" She stared at him, "Because I searched for you in all of them. Because I've loved you since the day I walked into that boardroom, and you said 'Welcome home, Kate!'"

He could feel his hatred for Kate slipping away.

"I hate you! You destroyed me," Ryan said. "Look at me, crippled, in every way."

Kate walked over to him, wrapping her arms around his face.

"I hate you," he kept repeating as Kate snuggled Ryan's head in a gentle embrace, hiding his tears.

She wrapped her hands around his face and let her fingers glide through his hair. She lifted his face and kissed him gently.

He whispered one more time, "I hate you," as he realized he was falling in love with her. Her lips finally stopped his whispers. *This is my heaven,* he thought as he kissed her like her lips were the soothing medicine his soul needed. He desperately wanted her naked beside him. He could feel his erection growing. He tried to wrap his right arm around her, unsure whether he could even make love to her. "I don't think I can," Ryan said.

"I don't care. I just want to hold you, taste you, love you." Kate helped his arm embrace her body. "Tomorrow, you might hate me again. I'm not letting this moment slip away."

He looked at her face and smiled. His fingers caressed her cheeks, wiping off her tears. He gently pulled her head to him and kissed her again. The kisses turned ferocious as he tried to put out the fire burning in him for a long time. He felt her her hand slide down and touch his throbbing erection. They stopped kissing. He looked at her, his eyes pleading. "I want you, I don't know if I can?"

She took off her T-shirt and helped take his trousers off. He was trying to hide his nervousness. She looked at him and smiled. "Let it go. I'm not judging you on your performance tonight. Your smile is my orgasm. And I'm seeing it after a lifetime."

He felt his heart missing a beat as she sat astride him, guiding him inside. He tasted the skin on her firm breasts and looked at her one more time. "I think I'm falling in love with you."

"I think I've loved you since the day I was born."

The bright April sun peering through the golden curtains was nudging Ryan to wake up. Ryan looked at the clock, with his eyes half shut. It was 11 am. He yawned and tried to stretch. He was in his bed, in his apartment. He looked around, disoriented. Was he late for work again? he thought. Then, finally, he saw Kate and realized he was not in his apartment. It was now Kate's.

Ryan's anger fizzled out the moment his eyes tasted her sight. There she was, face down on her stomach, sleeping beside him. The white satin sheet barely covered her waist. The sunlight shining on

Kate's back made her glow like the afternoon sun, bouncing off ice cubes soaked in scotch. She was one of those rare creatures who looked more beautiful in the mornings. She lay there in a silent dance of light and shadows.

Ryan had never felt this way before. It was almost surreal. He couldn't resist anymore and nudged her hair on the side. He reached for her, kissing her gently on the neck. Once, twice and then again, he moved down, kissing her, sliding toward the small of her back. Inhaling her scent like oxygen, his lips caressed her skin between the kisses. She turned on her back, smiled, and made him skip a heartbeat.

It wasn't a smile. It was poetry. He reached forward, his lips embracing hers. Slowly her eyes blinked, and she whispered in his mouth, "Now that's a good morning."

"I love your glow," he said.

"It's not my glow. It's you."

"I make you glow?"

"You made me glow three times last night." Kate smiled.

"It would've been six if we had met a year ago."

"I like the Ryan that's with me now. I wouldn't trade him for any other Ryan."

"I would." He stopped smiling.

"Get up." She smiled. "I will make a breakfast you'll never forget. We have a lot to talk about today."

"Talk?" Ryan picked up his phone.

"Yes, ask me whatever is bothering you, and I want you to give me a chance to answer."

"I'd like that, but I need Maria to give me a bath."

"I want to help you with the bath." Kate insisted.

"I'd rather not. I'll feel very awkward. It's not easy."

"Ryan, I want to do this. If I fail, I'll try again and again."

"Why?"

"Because I want to be a part of your life, and I don't just want the easy parts."

Ryan looked at her for a moment. She had her whole life in front of her, and he was a piece of baggage she didn't deserve to carry around.

"On one condition." He unfolded his arm from around her. "And you can say no."

"You're scaring me."

"I don't want you getting closer with any other man. You'll never sleep with anyone else." Ryan was hoping she'd say no.

Her spontaneous laughter was as genuine as her response. "Agreed. I won't. Men or women."

"Just like that? You don't want to argue?" Ryan was surprised by her swift response.

"Ryan, the day I saw you in Head Lion, and you turned your cheek to me to kiss you, I found my purpose. I blocked all previous men in my life. I haven't slept with anyone since then, nor do I plan to."

"For the record, I didn't turn so you could kiss me."

"You did!" She laughed.

"OK, yeah, I did." They laughed together.

She managed to get him out of bed and into the bathtub. Ryan felt like a broken horse, letting his head hang, avoiding her eyes. He could see she was trying to make him comfortable, mentally and physically. The bath was awkward, but she was learning with each passing minute. Being dependent on her was not what he wanted.

They were sipping freshly brewed coffee an hour later and enjoying the Spanish omelet Kate had made.

"What about the office?" Ryan asked.

"I'm staying with you today. If Sun wanted to fire me, they would've done it by now," Kate replied.

"Tell me what happened?"

"Well, when Todd found out that you got the account, he was furious. He called me to the boardroom. I told him I had no idea how you knew. Everyone left; he told Gina to stay back. Moments later, Jeff called me and told me they were shuffling accounts. The ones I had were given to Gina. I got the Big Five."

"Why didn't they fire you?" Ryan was still on the fence.

"They can't. I have an airtight contract, the only smart thing I did in my life, and they can't fire me for the next five years. They can make me resign, and I guess that's what they're trying to do now."

"What? No conditions like incompetency, morality clause? Being good at your—?"

"First of all, I'm great, not good." She smiled. "Todd offered me a job, initially I declined. Todd and Jeff flirted with me for another two months. So I made them an offer they should've refused. They didn't. I assumed they would back off after my ridiculous counteroffer, but then I was invited to Todd's house the day you presented."

"Wait! What time were you there?"

"I think around five or six. Todd seemed desperate. He accepted all my terms, the ridiculously high salary I asked for, joining bonus if I joined in a week, added more terms including the five-year clause, and he agreed."

"And you weren't curious about me?"

"I asked him; he told me you were taking over the European offices and that you named me as your successor." She looked at him and smiled. "I also came to see you that morning to discuss my plans, but you weren't there."

The cigarette butt with the lipstick, he remembered.

Ryan told her his side of the story, all the details except one. He didn't tell her about the red envelope, and he had no idea why. He just wanted to keep that part of the story to himself.

"Ryan, we have to fuck them. We can't let them get away with this."

"We can't do shit. Especially after Sphinx, I feel like a disabled dwarf."

"What about your dues? The way they treated you?"

Ryan didn't let her finish. "I'm not half the man I was. If I speak to Todd, I'm sure he'll give some of my dues back as long as I stay away from his business."

"No, that's not you. You used to say that there is no problem that you can't solve, remember?"

"Yes, but I'm in no condition to fight a giant?"

"You're the greatest creative director in New York. Think of something creative, unique, magnificent."

"Beautiful!" Ryan smiled.

"Beautiful?" Kate asked.

"I've always fantasized about a beautiful revenge."

"Then let's go for it. What do you have in mind?"

"The Mona Lisa of revenge, a getting even story that people tell for the next six generations. Something big or nothing."

"Like what? What's the best outcome of your beautiful revenge?" Kate pushed him.

"Destroy the thing Todd loves the most."

"There is only one thing Todd loves," Kate said.

"Sun." He smiled as if on cue.

"And do you know how the Sun will set?" Kate asked, "Steal the Big Five."

"They will *never* leave Todd. They've been with him for decades. It'll take us years to steal those five even if we're able to," Ryan said.

"Who said a beautiful revenge would be easy. Without the Big Five, Sun goes down. If you pull it off, Ryan, the world will never forget," Kate said.

Ryan stared at Kate, "We'll need a full-time agency if we are stealing the Big Five?"

"Let's get one then."

"The only way I can do this is if we're in it together."

"I'm with you, win or lose. I'll quit tomorrow," Kate replied.

"No, the smart thing is that you keep working at Sun. I hope you know what you're doing. I have nothing to lose; you do."

"Ryan, can you do this?" Kate asked.

Ryan took a deep breath and replied, "Yes!"

Ryan knew that it was almost impossible to breach the Big Five. The Sphinx loss was a huge setback, but Kate on his side covered the loss and made the coup seem possible. He hadn't even scratched the surface of his biggest resource — Head Lion.

However, one element was missing from his team: someone who could close the deals and ensure they did not repeat their mistake with Sphinx. Both Ryan and Kate were not business savvy. He needed someone smart, conniving, and ruthless. He needed Nour.

Chapter 22

Open Happiness

(The Coca Cola Company, 2009)

It was 1 pm when he got to Head Lion. The April sun was kind, shining with just enough intensity to make people step out of their comfort zones. The Head Lion lake was brimming with residents out for a walk enjoying the bright day. Ryan entered his room and saw it lying on the floor, behind the door. It was another red envelope. He tore it open.

Marquis Thomas, CEO
Thomas and Thomas

Every time he received the envelope, his mind erupted in a ferocious battle. Was the sender looking out for him, or was someone using Ryan for their agenda? He knew one thing was true. The messages always worked in his favor. So he decided to meet Marquis. He was also the only lead left for him to pursue. He was also the one Ryan refused. He had to try. A client like Marquis could provide him a backbone to stand up to Todd and look him in the eye.

Ryan had a few hours before he could see Kate. He put on his headphones and decided to kill time by trying to walk. He grabbed the cane Todd gave him. His hatred for Todd was his fuel. It took him ten minutes to step out. Kate didn't deserve a liability in a wheelchair. Ryan wanted to get better for her. Slowly he moved, one leg at a time. His feet felt heavy, like walking on melted tar. He finally looked up and realized he was standing next to the lake.

Ryan decided to do the unthinkable. He prayed. He asked God for one last glimmer of light through the wall of darkness. He felt good that his hatred for God was diminishing. Finally, he felt a hand on his shoulder and took off his headphones.

"Ryan, I'm impressed." It was Marquis Thomas, the Real Estate tycoon. "I've been watching you walk since you stepped out. I wanted to congratulate you."

Ryan smiled and shook his hand warmly. "Mr. Thomas."

"After seeing you walk all the way to the lake, your stock has gone up. You've earned the privilege to call me Marquis." He smiled.

"You make me feel like I've climbed Everest."

"You have Ryan." He sat on the bench next to him.

"I thought about the project Marquis." Ryan didn't want to sound desperate and sat next to him.

"And you have time now?"

"Yes, priorities have changed." Ryan smiled.

"Priorities or Sphinx told you to fuck off?"

Ryan stared at him, toying with the idea of walking away.

Marquis smiled at Ryan. "I have great respect for you; don't ruin it by disrespecting me."

"I wasn't ready before."

"That's not the reason why you're saying yes?"

"Do you want to hear me say I'm desperate for you?" Ryan said.

"Yes, if that's the truth." Marquis took out a cigar and offered Ryan one. "I'm too old and too wise to play games."

"OK, then I want your account. I need it desperately because Sphinx backed out."

"The truth shall get you more business. I don't care what your reasons are as long as you deliver what I want."

"I will."

"And you can assure me your hatred for Sun will not affect my business?"

"It will, but I can guarantee you that my hatred for Sun will make you more money than ever before."

"Max warned me that you're a narcissist." Marquis smiled, "Which is good because if I'm handing over someone the steering to my future, I want him to be as confident as Noah building the ark."

"It's not a coincidence that we are running into each other. I just want to be certain that you can't mess with my business," Marquis said.

"I won't. I have the best creative team in New York." Ryan's heart was pounding with excitement.

"You're aware that it's not the creatives who make an agency successful?"

"I'm aware. I need someone strong on the business side. I'm hoping to convince Nour. She'd be perfect if she says yes."

"Nour is already with you. She told me you lost Sphinx and I need to give you my business. I spoke to her because I wasn't comfortable giving my millions to a bunch of creatives—no offense."

"None taken."

"The only thing I don't want is to piss off Todd."

"Well, you do realize that's the goal, right?"

"I don't care what you do to him." Ryan could read Marquis was scared of Todd. "My name shouldn't come up."

"Agreed. I have a request, too," Ryan said.

"Anything that's within my power."

"I want an office in Elysium."

"I thought we agreed my name would not come up?"

"It won't. We'll be your tenants, just like many others."

"I don't think there is any space available there. I can get you top properties in New York. Elysium will be messy with Todd around."

"It's perfect. It'll be the last place Todd would expect me to be."

"You can't afford the place."

"Marquis, I want Elysium, or I'm out. I don't need a huge space, just a room. You can adjust the rent from my retainer."

"It's all about the ego. Max was right. You're crazy." He started to walk away and then came back to him. "If I get you Elysium, can you guarantee sales?"

"If you get me Elysium, I can guarantee to double your target."

A week later, Ryan was heading toward the third chapter in his life, and this time, he was writing it.

"We're here," the driver announced.

"Yes, we're finally here." Ryan smiled, not just referring to the commute.

The monumental structure of Elysium stared back at him like a face-off between David and Goliath. The gods were waiting for him. They seemed more Herculean than before, as if daring him to begin the fight.

Ryan inhaled the view as the car slowly came to a halt. He picked up the cane Todd had given him and firmly gripped the bust of the lion. He felt the power surge through him as he squeezed the head. It reminded him of his hatred for Todd.

Ryan stepped out and looked up. The evening breeze brushed his forehead as he took a deep breath and stared back at the deities. The streets were silent, a rare breather reserved for a Sunday evening in New York. A few lonely sirens blared somewhere in the background. Someone out there was fighting for survival just like him.

"Welcome home." Kate smiled. It had been a week since the day he began his life with her. She looked divine as the evening sun bounced off her dusky skin. Maria moved closer, gripping his arms tightly as he stepped on the slippery marble stairs. The entrance was still far away.

The aura of Elysium's atrium made Ryan nervous as he entered. The building brought back memories. Some he had forgotten, some he had suppressed, none he wanted to cherish. It seemed like he was giving birth to his new life. And just like any birth, it was painful.

They stepped into the elevator together. Everyone stayed silent as the elevator swiftly moved up, crossing all the floors that mattered. Ryan hoped Marquis hadn't reserved the storage space for him. Although at this stage, he would happily accept that too. Working at Elysium brought many advantages besides access to Sun's clients. For him, the battlefield was as crucial as the battle. He looked at Kate, who had a worried look.

"Well, the size of the office doesn't matter," he said just before the elevator dinged. "We are going to do big things in a small space."

He wanted Kate to feel proud of his achievement. Once he crossed all the main floors, he knew Marquis had taken his suggestion literally and probably reserved a storeroom for him. The elevator door opened.

It was the most exclusive floor in the building; the one Todd was desperate to get. Ryan smiled. A huge reception greeted him. Laura was sitting on the reception chair, smiling. Behind the reception, gold lettering covered the wall:

"GET OUT OF YOUR WAY!"

"Well, you can change it. I know this is one part you enjoy doing." Kate smiled. "We don't have a name, so I thought we could start with what you believe in."

"I love it!" he lied. He also realized Kate was right. They didn't have a name. He moved forward to see his new office. Marquis had given him the entire floor. The office was much more than what he had anticipated. It was the most exquisitely designed floor on top of the building, used by the Elysium management. Marquis had given his office to Ryan. The floor had no walls. Instead, a magnificent 360-degree view of Manhattan behind barely visible infinity glass that needed no additional decor. Ryan could see a helipad and an outdoor garden cafe through it.

Inside, the centerpiece was a large wooden door clashing with the light colors of the floor like a jewel in the crown. They walked toward it as Ryan tried to grasp reality. The garish room probably belonged to Mrs. Marquis. He didn't want to face her today. The doors were as high as the ceiling and made of Bocote wood. An empty placeholder for a nameplate stared back at Ryan.

The door opened, and a young black man in an Armani suit walked out. He took out a gold-plated nameplate and inserted it into the placeholder. It had "Guru" written on it. He smiled and looked at Ryan as if expecting a response. Ryan had no idea how to respond and wondered if this was Marquis' son. The young man looked like a successful model with his square jawbone, chiseled abs, and designer suit.

"Welcome, Ryan. I'm so excited to meet you finally." He almost tripped. "I'm William Thomas but call me Willy."

Marquis was adding his son to the package deal, Ryan thought.

"I wonder what Mrs. Marquis will say," Laura said. "I heard she is a bitch."

"Ryan, can I talk to you alone?" Willy seemed agitated. Ryan didn't want Marquis forcing another person on him. *I can handle Mrs. Marquis, but I don't want to babysit the son,* he thought. He would rather have a small office than a large one with extra baggage. Willy moved forward and shut the door.

"I think you need to call Mrs. Marquis and sort this out before we move in." Ryan's tone was firm.

"I'm Mrs. Marquis." He waved at him.

Ryan was taken aback, trying to grasp what Willy had just said. Marquis had kids and did not fit the stereotype. Willy was scared and restless at the same time. He kept on fidgeting like a 12-year-old in church.

"Then give me a hug because I love the place, and I can't thank you enough, Mrs. Marquis." He finally smiled. Willy moved forward and hugged him.

"Call me Willy," he whispered. "You can't tell anyone about Marquis and me."

"Willy, this place is magnificent, but we can't afford this."

"I can." Willy almost jumped as he raised his arm. Ryan could read a genuine enthusiasm.

"Ryan, you don't have to pay a dime as long as you help us out. Tit for tat." He smiled. "You will be working on the most expensive project we've ever done. The rent for this floor is peanuts compared to what's at stake."

"What do you know about me?"

"I know about your situation with Sun. I can't stand them. I told Marquis this was perfect to fuck them over. The office has a separate entrance, including a separate elevator, so no one will know when you come or go. The floor has the heaviest bandwidth in the building, over 20 iMacs already installed, and all the paraphernalia an ad agency would need." Willy finally took a breath.

"Wait, there is more." Willy was practically beaming with excitement as he led him to a door behind the desk. It looked like the entrance to a private bath. It wasn't. Ryan's eyes widened with amazement. It was a small suite with a bedroom, bathroom, and a kitchen. The entire sidewall was a glass window with a view of the Manhattan skyline. Willy savored his reactions.

"Unbelievable!" Ryan whispered.

"You know we are the number one construction company in America, right?" Willy smiled, "I knew it'll be a struggle for you to come here every day, so why not have the option to sleep here."

Ryan moved toward the large window. For a man who was always impartial to the sights and sounds of New York, he couldn't deny the city looked stunning.

Ryan's phone buzzed. It was Marquis.

"So?"

"I love them both." Ryan smiled.

"Both?" Marquis asked.

"Well, the office is amazing, but equally amazing is Mrs. Marquis,"

"Willy!" Willy enunciated.

"Ryan, please keep this to yourself," Marquis whispered. "Now tell me what's happening?"

Ryan gave him a rundown about his plans and disconnected the phone. He walked out and addressed the team.

"So, where do we go from here?"

"Let's start by conquering the world." Nour beamed as she entered the office. "I have three potential clients from Head Lion waiting for your pitch. Sorry I'm late."

"I'll need more people, a bigger team Nour. We barely have enough workforce to service Marquis," Ryan said.

"There's a reason you made me your business head." She smiled. "You wanted someone to be a part of the solution?"

"I've not forgotten that."

"You forgot one thing." Nour winked.

"What?"

"The goldmine." She started walking to the boardroom. Everyone else followed. The boardroom was bare except for the large windows purveying the glittering skyline. There was no furniture, no art, no decor. The five strangers already in the room made up for the furnishings.

Nour looked at him and smiled. "Ryan, you wanted a beautiful revenge. Meet the beautiful artists who'll help paint your masterpiece."

Ryan felt like a kid who had discovered his hidden Christmas presents. The strangers were the same idols he was too afraid to speak to in Head Lion. They were possibly the most accomplished creative people in New York, and they were standing in front of him, just a few feet away. It was almost as if the immortals had stepped down on earth.

"Bonjour, Monsieur Ryan, I'm Sophie. I heard you were planning the impossible, and I wanted to be a part of it. I can help you with the art department."

Sophie Lavigne was one of the most renowned living artists. Pieces carrying her signature were sold in the million-dollar range. Her long grey hair fell seamlessly on a navy-blue dress. Her erect posture contradicted the reality that she was in her late 70s.

"Hi Ryan, when I heard what you were planning to do, I said ridiculous. The man has gone bonkers. But then Nour told me more about you. I think the only person who can pull this off is you, and I can guarantee the best media and PR deals in the country if you want me on board," Mark Garcia said in a refined British accent. Mark was a legend in the media circles and at one time, owned seven leading publication groups. Having him was like having Rocky on your boxing team.

"Signor Ryan, Nour told me your story and you wanted a, how you say—" He looked around as if asking for help. "—beautiful revenge. I told Nour if getting stabbed in the back was a sport, I'll be a world champion. I'll help you with film, video content for your campaigns." Marco Ricci was a two-time Oscar winner. Top film schools across the country made his films part of their curriculum.

He held an unlit cigar, wearing his traditional shorts and an ill-fitted T-shirt. Despite his loud personality, he was one of the most popular residents in Head Lion.

"Ryan, you can count on me for writing. I'm old but can still teach the younger lot a thing or two about copywriting. When she told me what you were planning to do, I was shocked. I want to join your team just to be a part of the craziness." Isabelle Miller had consistently been on the New York Times bestseller list for two decades. She had started her career as a copywriter and worked at McCann, Chiat, and Ogilvy & Mather. She knew Ogilvy and Jay Chiat personally. Her clothes reflected her bohemian lifestyle, and so did her writing.

"I personally feel it's impossible what you're thinking of doing. Todd is ruthless, and Sun is invincible, but I know that the ride will be unforgettable, and I'm in for that," said Clifford Davis, better known as Cliffy. He was one of the top marketers in the country. He had helped launch some of the most famous brands and recently authored two books on marketing.

"Thank you. I have no idea how I'll pay you back." He was still nervous, trying hard to hold back his tears.

"Well, you can start by giving us a hug." Isabelle moved forward and opened her arms. Ryan hugged her, and all of them joined in a group hug.

"Ryan, forget that you're alone. Head Lion is like a bottomless well of talent," Nour said.

"Don't forget clients. I've also lined up meetings with two potential ones I found in Head Lion," Cliffy said.

"The fun begins today. Find me a workstation, Kate," Mark said.

"Fuck the world. Just when I thought my retirement was going to be peaceful," Marco yelled. They all laughed.

"There is one stipulation, Ryan, before we begin," Sophie said. "More of a request, we've all discussed before we said yes to Nour."

Isabelle stepped forward. "We don't want people to know we are working for an ad agency."

"We want to be anonymous," Mark said.

There was an uncomfortable silence.

Ryan smiled. "You just gave us the name of the most creative agency in New York!" Ryan smiled and looked at Kate.

"Anonymous?" Kate replied.

"It's perfect, and I know exactly how we can turn this into a marketing gimmick." Ryan looked at Nour, "We will create an ad agency like no other. So who's the first client we are going after?"

"Nexus," Nour said. "We have three days."

"Fuck," they all said in unison.

Chapter 23

The choice of a new generation
(Pepsi, 1984)

Ryan and Nour agreed to avoid any confrontation with Sun until Anonymous stood on its feet. Their first fight was against five other agencies, including two from San Fransisco. 'Nexus' was a social media platform that had amassed 500 million followers in just two years. It was the most trending social media platform in the industry.

One of the investors residing in Head Lion had financed the start-up that had turned into a mammoth in just two years. The Nexus team reluctantly agreed to let Anonymous pitch. At the end of the presentation, they said yes and agreed to all the terms laid down by Anonymous, including the condition that they would remain anonymous. Nexus fell in love with the ideas created by a team they would never meet.

The ad campaign became a huge hit garnering over fifty million new followers in a month. It was one of the most expensive campaigns of the year.

The campaign's centerpiece was a video by Marco Ricci that went viral and got over a hundred million views in three days. The slogan by Isabelle became a trend across all social media platforms, and the Nexus hashtag was trending on their rival platforms. The teamwork was as precise as a pair of Russian figure skaters.

The next three months were eventful. Anonymous lapped up four major clients. Ryan and the team had more work than they could handle. More residents from Head Lion joined to help Ryan.

The Anonymous office had become the most happening billionaires club. It was like a renaissance for geniuses. The mavens felt alive and asked for only one thing in return—anonymity. The dream team had managed to remain anonymous for three months. Ryan's plan was simple and ingenious. The clients never discovered the team behind their campaigns.

Only Nour was allowed to be visible. She became the face of the agency. She would present the pitches made by the dream team. The rest of the crew remained behind the Anonymous website. Clients went through a form on their website if they wanted a pitch from them. The millions they were making for their clients became their sales pitch. Their brazen **"Double Your Targets or Money Back"** guarantee pulled many new clients and perturbed their rivals. No other agency could dare to compete with that claim. With dozens of people behind him who didn't care about money, Ryan wasn't scared to fail.

They were no longer running after clients; clients were coming to them. They became busy enough to charge a hundred thousand dollars to deliver a pitch. Clients were willing to call them, intrigued by their anonymity. Their biggest weakness had become their epic strength.

Ryan immersed himself in work and enjoyed every bit of the stress. He felt alive after a long time, and he felt young. He was no longer envious of the people who had goals.

Kate would join Ryan in the evenings after her work at Sun. They worked together on the campaigns in the evenings and made love in the night. Their combination as creative directors became fierce and deadly. They were churning out winning campaigns like an assembly line in Detroit.

Anonymous had managed to skirt around Sun, avoiding any confrontation with Todd. He was making the predictable mistake most leading CEOs make. Todd underestimated the competition. He was too arrogant to believe they were a threat to them.

In a few months, the Anonymous team had strengthened their billing and created a fierce reputation. It was time to challenge Sun. He texted Nour.

Plan our quarterly meeting. This will be our most important meeting ever. Make sure it's unforgettable.

The following weekend a private jet, courtesy of Thomas and Thomas realty, landed at a private airport in Lake Como, Italy. There were eleven people on board, including Ryan. The stay was at a magnificent villa facing Lake Como, owned by Marco Ricci.

The vast property was the Italian royalty's favorite escape from the heat of Milan and northern Italy. The previous owner was a famous Italian politician with a string of scandals, half-buried in tabloids and the other half *allegedly* across the northern Italian landscape. "Not an anomaly in politics here," Marco told them with pride.

Marco fell in love with the property while using it as a locale for his Oscar-winning epic romance, *L'amore non morirà mai!* His affair with the lead actress continued long after the crew had left. The villa became the sanctuary for his clandestine affairs. Every summer for ten years, he fell in and out of love with a new woman here.

Later, when he moved to Head Lion, he used it as a rental for dignitaries, celebrities, and hideaway for rich husbands running away from their wives.

"The place is booked all year round. Even today, I had to cancel bookings to get us in. I'm not the one who gossips, but a famous actress who lived here with me designed the mooring and the cast-iron gate. Let's just say she was the lead in an old Spielberg movie." Marco winked.

The Anonymous team enjoyed Marco's monologue as much as the breathtaking views. The villa overlooked Lake Como like Koh-i-Noor on a Mughal crown. They walked into the grandeur feeling like they were walking into an epic movie set. A dedicated staff welcomed them, including the Villa Manager, butlers, chambermaids, and housekeepers.

Ryan admired his suite. The theme was gold and red. The lavish bedroom had king-sized beds, large Iliana Praline curtain panels, a luxurious bathroom, and wood-burning fireplaces. He had never seen anything like this. It was on the second floor with a balcony that revealed the magnificent view of Lake Como.

Ryan never expected his least eventful chapter to become the most interesting. The third chapter of Ryan's life was off to a promising start.

He was tired, his back hurt, and he craved lying down. He moved toward the bed and noticed the red envelope tucked between the pillows. The struggle and success at Anonymous had made him forget about the red envelopes. He rushed forward and opened it. There was one name inside:

Joseph Brown.

Ryan had no idea who he was. He looked around, realizing that the sender was with them at the villa. The sender was part of the Anonymous team. Even though the sender helped Ryan every step of the way, it still made the hair on the back of his neck rise.

Ryan toyed with the idea of discussing the envelopes with someone. The only two people he could think of were Nour and Kate. He decided to talk to Kate after dinner.

Ryan opened up the curtains that draped the balcony view. The fading golden sun bouncing off the lake and the gentle breeze seeping through the balcony felt like a lullaby, and before long, he was asleep.

"Ryan!" he heard Kate calling him from far away. "It's getting late for the meeting."

Ryan got up with a start. He had slept through the night. He saw Maria and Lucas looking concerned, standing behind Kate.

"Why didn't you wake me up?"

"I came. You were sound asleep. I didn't want to wake you," Kate said.

"Let's get you ready." Maria moved forward. "Today is the most important meeting of your life."

He got up and checked his phone. There were a few missed calls and a text from Willy.

Todd is celebrating Sun's 50th anniversary. The iron is hot. It's now or never.

Anonymous held its first quarterly meeting in the large dining hall of the villa. Ryan left one chair empty as a tribute to Max. The team was already there. Nour and Kate sat next to Ryan, followed by Sophie, Mark, Marco, and Clifford. Maria and Lucas wore matching black suits. Laura and Allen were inseparable, bursting with excitement.

Allen was in his navy-blue suit. It was the first suit he'd purchased. Laura wore a steel grey jacket, and a mauve blouse held together by a matching steel grey skirt. The rest were all dressed as formal as could be expected. Ryan was just glad that no one came in their shorts.

"Welcome to our first quarterly meeting." Ryan finally smiled. "Today is no ordinary day, and this is no ordinary meeting. There will be no presentations or performance charts. We know we've done well. I want to keep it short and focus on two things. You and the reason we started Anonymous." Ryan took a sip of his freshly brewed

Italian coffee. "Firstly, congratulations on joining the company of immortals. I have no doubt Ogilvy and Bernbach would have been envious of your work. We've become legends in our industry and you're the reason why. Secondly, when I spoke about a beautiful revenge, I had no idea it would be the people with me who'd make it beautiful. I wish there was something to show how grateful I am, but there isn't. Most of you refused compensation. So I've made a unilateral decision. I bought Elysium with all the profit we made." Ryan paused.

The silence was so intense he could hear it.

"I wanted something that makes financial sense for you and brings me closer to my goal. Congratulations, you now own one of the hottest properties in New York. Elysium generates around 12 million dollars in profits annually. This means whatever your salary was, you'll get an additional million dollars every year."

Allen fell back on his chair pretending to faint. Everyone smiled.

"Does this include us?" Laura asked nervously.

"Yes, everyone sitting here will be a millionaire by the end of this year."

"Fuccccccckkkkk!" Maria shrieked and grasped Lucas's hand. Lucas started sobbing like a baby.

Ryan smiled. "And to the mavens from Head Lion, you tied my hands by refusing compensation, but I had to do something."

"Don't worry. We can always find ways to spend more," Marco said, and everyone laughed.

"Can I retire now?" Kate smiled.

"No. This brings me to why we're here." Ryan paused. "Revenge is a dish best served cold, but we don't have time. Todd is having his 50th-anniversary celebration and that's our new deadline."

"But why is the 50th-anniversary a deadline?" Nour asked.

"Well, the Big Five don't sign annual contracts. Rumors are the Big Five are pledging a ten year deal on the anniversary. If they do, our revenge is dead. It's literally a deadline we can't miss," Ryan replied.

"I heard it's a huge celebration, around 1000 guests including ex-Presidents, leading businessmen of the country, a few Arab investors, the Mayor, celebrities, and all the leading media has been invited for some special announcement," Nour said.

"The initial goal was to steal the Big Five over a period of time." Ryan paused and looked at everyone in the room. "We do it in the next thirty days."

They all stared at Ryan as if he'd lost his mind.

"Thirty days? That's not possible, Ryan, and you know it," Mark said.

"Wrong! It's impossible if it was any other clients. You're talking about the Big Five. That's worse than impossible. Quick, someone give me a word for that," Nour said. "What's more difficult than impossible?"

"I think you've achieved a lot, we've achieved a lot. It'll make Todd cringe when he finds out," Cliffy said. "It's a good revenge."

The room was silent. Everyone waited for Ryan to respond. Marco's booming voice broke the silence.

"I didn't join Ryan to make Todd cringe. I came because I wanted to make Todd scream. I want the next six generations to hear stories about Ryan's revenge. I don't care if it's impossible. I still want it."

"Yeah! Even I don't want a 'good' revenge. As Ryan said, I want it to be beautiful. The one thing I've learned in the last few months is that anything is possible. The best of the best have come together and we can make anything happen." Kate was excited.

"Revenge is a dish best served with old friends." Isabelle smiled.

"Everyone who matters will be there. It's a perfect time to hammer the final nail in Sun's coffin," Ryan added.

They all looked at each other and nodded in agreement.

"We're in." Nour smiled.

"Five clients in thirty days. What's the strategy?" Isabelle asked.

"That's why we're here. We don't leave until we have a plan," Ryan replied.

Ryan didn't want to leave early. The villa had also presented him with a unique opportunity. The person sending the red envelopes was amongst them. Being isolated at Lake Como was a great chance to discover his identity. He was now getting restless to talk to Kate.

The meeting continued for a few hours. They agreed on a basic plan to tap the Big Five and hit the low-hanging fruits first. They were all hungry, craving Italian food. Nour booked them at La Terraza; a fine dining restaurant considered the custodian of the great Gualtiero Marchesi's legacy.

They sat on the patio against a picturesque view of Lake Como and decided to take one group photo. All were aware the photo would never see the light of day. They all raised their champagnes and smiled as the waiter took their photograph.

Ryan was desperate to talk to Kate. He hadn't been alone with her since they left New York. He waited till they finally returned to the villa. Kate had left the door unlocked. She was in the shower when Ryan entered.

"I was dying to touch you," Kate whispered as Ryan took off his clothes and walked under the steamy water. He wrapped his arms around Kate from behind, grasping her warm breasts and kissing her neck simultaneously. He could feel her nipples responding to his touch. She turned around and kissed him. She held his hand and helped him get inside the bathtub.

Ryan wrapped his arms around her as she settled in front of him in the bathtub. He explored her body as if it was the first time he had touched someone. They both lay there, after making love, savoring the moment.

"Sometimes, you don't go home. Home comes to you," Kate said.

She turned back and kissed him again. Ryan stood up and dried himself. "I need to talk to you about something. I've been waiting all day to get some alone time with you."

"I need a few more minutes. I bought a pack of Cuban cigars for you. They're on the side table." Kate got out of the bathtub and moved into the shower.

Ryan walked into the suite and poured a drink. He found the cigars that Kate had kept for him and decided to enjoy one on the patio. Kate was the missing piece in his life. It was the first relationship where he had complete ownership, and he loved that feeling. She could have any man, but she chose him, a man with nothing to give and a lot to take. He smiled and lit up his cigar.

The matchstick fell, and he bent to pick it up. His eye caught a torn piece of paper. It was red. He knew what it was even before he picked it up. The sudden sweat seeping from under his arms made him uncomfortable, and so did the thoughts swirling in his mind. He went inside, sifting through the cupboards, drawers, and wardrobes.

Ryan saw the bin in the kitchen slightly ajar. He stepped on the lever. The scattered fragments of a red envelope stood out in the empty container. His head started spinning. He felt his legs weaken.

Who was Kate? What was her motive? Was all this a ruse? He wasn't ready to confront her. He had to get out. He had to breathe. Ryan stormed out of the room before Kate came out. In an hour, Ryan was on his way back to New York.

Everyone seemed uncomfortable at the Monday meeting. No one knew why Ryan left early for New York. The frown on Ryan's forehead stood out like a warning sign outside a military base. His communication was short and to the point. Kate and Ryan were not talking to each other, adding to the tension in the air. Willy walked in and broke the silence.

"I got fresh coffee and bagels for everyone." The smile faded as soon as he read the room.

"Who died?"

"Where do we begin?" Isabelle asked while picking up a cup of coffee.

"We begin with the lowest hanging fruit." Nour paused. "Thomas and Thomas realty."

Willy took over as if on cue. "Thank you, Nour, for that intro. Marquis gave Anonymous this opportunity not because he felt charitable but because all the firms we hired to solve our problem came back with one common solution—Ryan."

Willy turned on the projector and started his presentation. The short presentation ended with a dramatic caveat, "If we fail, it will sink the entire group with enough debt to last the next three generations."

"And if that's not enough pressure, it will also be the first direct attack on Sun, and we are expecting repercussions," Nour said.

"How do we handle Sun?" Laura asked.

"We don't. Marquis plans to claim we did this in-house. Your concern should be delivering the best work possible. And to get you pumped up, this will be the most expensive campaign in the real estate industry." Willy smiled. No one else did except Marco.

"I'm getting an erection just thinking about the film we can produce." Marco laughed while eating the bagel. They started walking out. Kate was the last. Ryan grasped Kate's hand as others left the room.

"I'm sorry," Ryan said.

"If you're really sorry, then tell me what happened. It's driving me nuts thinking I did something wrong."

"I can't tell you now."

"Are you over me, Ryan?"

"No. I'm grateful for every second that you're with me, and I hate every second when you're not."

"Grateful? What does that even mean?"

"Well, I keep asking myself, what's a girl like you doing with someone like me?"

"Saving you." She bent forward and held his face. "Stop building that wall around yourself because I'll keep climbing it. Stop underestimating me."

"I never underestimated you, Kate. Do you know why? Because you're great at what you do."

"Better than you?"

"You're like me on steroids."

"Ryan, I've always done what I felt was right. Nothing scares me now. I'm willing to sit in the passenger seat, but you need to tell me what to do."

"Give me some time. Don't ask me why I left."

"OK, I'll give you space. There's too much at stake right now."

"I know. We need to work together without any tension in the air. I can't do it alone."

"I'm with you. What do you want?"

"I want the Thomas and Thomas advertising to break the internet."

Chapter 24

A Diamond is Forever

(De Beers, 1948)

The clock was ticking, and the stakes were high. A successful campaign for Thomas and Thomas would make getting the other four clients easier. A failure would seal their fate. They had thirty days to steal the five biggest clients from the most powerful ad agency in New York.

Marquis had given Anonymous six weeks. Ryan decided to deliver the campaign in ten days. He had no choice. The team chose to work 24x7 to pull off a miracle. The mega-campaign for Marquis included a TV commercial that would have taken months to produce under normal circumstances, but these weren't normal circumstances. This was a Hail Mary for Anonymous.

Marco called in favors and put an entire crew on standby, including a director of photography making waves in the industry. Sophie and Isabelle went to the site and started living in the model apartments. Mark and Clifford worked day and night to get the best digital, print, and electronic media deals. Laura and Allen worked with Ryan and Kate to come up with ideas.

"Ryan, we have some crazy ideas that can go viral." Allen seemed excited as they barged into Ryan's room.

"This will trend like Kim Kardashian's sex tape and get us some unpaid eyeballs," Laura said.

"Please don't waste your time on it. We go the traditional route."

"Ryan, the ad world has changed. It's old school—"

"Guys," Ryan interrupted them, "most young creatives waste energy on misdirected endeavors. The goal should be to make the brand viral, not the ideas. If the work is good, it will trend."

"But the digital world is different," Laura said.

"The medium has changed. Human instinct hasn't. If people see something good, they will talk about it. Period." Ryan smiled.

Ryan spent his days pushing his dream team and his nights staring at the Manhattan lights with Kate in his arms. Kate spent her days at Sun getting paid to do nothing, and she didn't care. Jeff had moved Kate to the Big Five accounts. Freelancers hired by the Big Five directly did most of the creative for them. Yet, the Big Five paid huge retainers to Sun for work no self-respecting creative director wanted to do, like newsletters and direct mailers. It was a win-win scenario for Todd.

Moving an employee to the Big Five account was equivalent to "Cashiering" in the military—a public degradation of disgraced military officers. Gina was now traveling around the world with her team. On the other hand, Kate was amongst a forgotten workforce, pushed to an office area referred to as the cemetery.

The cemetery was a burial ground for the senior staff who were obsolete or redundant to the agency. Firing them would invite payouts and lawsuits. Most pariah staff moved to the cemetery quit within a few days. They chose to stick around because it was almost impossible for them to find a job at their age. The agency kept them at a bare minimum salary, freezing any growth or increments.

Most of them were in their late sixties. The two in their seventies were typographers who had become obsolete thanks to Steve Jobs. The most renowned was 71-year-old Joseph Brown. Joseph was one of the most sought-after typographers in his heydays and the first African American to win an award in typography. However, technology and inflation had forced him to migrate to graphic design. Working on newsletters was a death sentence for any creative person.

The dingy cemetery was a massive hall with depleted frames and outdated ads in desaturated colors framed on cracked walls. The stench of old paper, worn-out ink, and damp carpet filled the room. It was as if the management had forgotten the floor existed. The lighting was terrible in the cemetery, and everything seemed grey.

It worked for Joseph as he preferred hiding in the shadows. His dark skin and short stature made it easier for him to be invisible in the dim lighting. Only five people were visible at their desks during work hours, hardly working. It was as if Kate was walking through ghosts and realized why the floor was called the cemetery.

Her task was to find out about the Big Five, and the frowning typographer was responsible for their newsletters.

"Hi, you're Joseph, right?" She almost stammered, "I worked with you on a project. You did some calligraphy for us."

"Please stop!" He kept staring at his screen, apparently working on something important. Kate moved closer. He was playing Tetris.

"Uhm I jjjusst want—"

"I'm swamped and really don't need this today." He didn't let her finish. "Please don't talk to me, ever!"

She drifted back to her workstation, wondering how to react. Joseph kept playing Tetris. Surprised by the resistance, she decided she would have to be a little more creative. There was no way he was not going to like her.

The next day Kate came early and waited for him. He usually

came around noon and left around 4 pm. She brought Joseph a fresh grilled cheese sandwich from Bessie's and left it on his table. A few hours later, she saw the sandwich in his trash can.

The next day she brought a lobster roll from Red Hook Lobster. New Yorkers loved it. He didn't. She found it in the trash. During the day, she surfed the web, looking for a crack in the door. Except for Miamart, the Big Five had never called for a pitch. Even though they were paying retainers to Sun, they were hardly getting any work done from Sun. Only the newsletters were designed at Sun, and Joseph looked after four of those. She had to break the wall.

Kate tried talking to him again, but he got up and walked away. The only creative solution she could think of was food. She stared at his trash one more time and saw the King Shawarma wrapper she had left for him in the morning. It was a little later than 5 pm. She wanted to be certain. She flinched and grabbed the shawarma wrapper from the grimy bin. The uninhabited wrapper was bare, not even crumbs. She smiled, happy with her success, and turned around. It was Joseph standing in front of her.

"Sue me?" He said, "So I have a thing for Shawarmas."

"I'm glad." Kate smiled and walked away.

"Oy, what do you want?" He shouted.

"Respect." She turned around.

"You're not my boss. I know you're a big shot, but not for me."

"I wouldn't be stuck here if I was a big shot." She came closer to him. "The respect I want is from a colleague who is equal to me."

"You're not going to last long," Joseph said.

"That depends on your definition of long." She smiled.

"Why? Any agency will hire you in a heartbeat."

"I want to destroy Sun." She waited to read his expressions. Kate didn't want to waste time. She thought there had to be a reason that he was bitter, and it had to be Sun.

"What do you want from me?" he whispered.

"I want you to help me destroy Sun," she said.

"What the fuck, lady," he almost jumped and covered her mouth with his palm. He looked around. "Will you stop saying that?"

"I'll stop if you talk to me like a normal person," Kate said.

"OK, jeez." He shrugged and took out a cigarette. He gestured for Kate to come to the exit staircase where he smoked.

"Let's talk. Let's be best friends," he said as he lit up a cigarette. "Let's start with why you're here."

Kate gave Joseph an abridged version of her story. She didn't mention Ryan. Instead, she gave him what the public generally knew and figured he had to be aware of it.

"I don't believe you." Joseph smirked.

"Why?"

"You want me to believe that because of you, Sun initially lost the Sphinx account, and then after firing you, they got it back again."

"Yes."

"If that's how you want to begin talking to me—" he grabbed the door handle, "you'll need a lot more shawarmas."

"Wait. Why don't you believe me?"

"Just because I'm in the cemetery doesn't mean I'm dead. Everyone in the industry knows you. What you did at the college and then at Ogilvy and Mather. Come on, you're not a rookie, and neither am I."

"I have my reasons, and I can't tell you right now."

He started to walk away.

"Isn't this reason enough that I'm good and I'm down here. Surely you can relate to that?"

Joseph stopped. He looked at Kate and lit up another cigarette. He took a few drags before he spoke.

"I know there is more to your story. I also know you don't deserve to be here. No one does. What do you want from me?"

"Tell me about the Big Five."

Chapter 25

Quality Never Goes Out of Style

(Levi's, 1983)

The first week after Italy went by like a fully charged Tesla Roadster. It was day eleven, and it was the day after the release of Marquis' campaign.

A loud knock at the main door turned into banging till Ryan woke up. Kate covered her face with the satin pillows to block the light and the sound. Ryan looked at the watch. It was 8 am. He cursed the person banging at the door. Ryan and Kate had planned to wake up late after working for 48 hours straight and getting the campaign released on time.

They'd gone to sleep around 5 am. Ryan picked up the cane not to support his walk but to hit whoever was there. He was praying the noise would stop, but it got louder. Finally, he opened the door, almost pulling it off the hinges.

It was Willy. He had an iPad in his hand. "Why aren't you picking up your phone?" Willy walked inside.

Seeing Ryan naked, he smiled. "Well, good morning." Willy picked up the throw from the sofa and threw it toward him.

"This better be good." Ryan covered himself and slid onto the sofa.

"The world has gone crazy." He showed Ryan the social feeds. "Ryan, your campaign has rocked America. It's trending on every social platform." Ryan began scrolling. Kate entered the lounge, half-covered in a white bedsheet. Willy pretended not to act surprised.

"Hi, Willy!" She whispered as she snuggled onto Ryan's lap, finding her way between his arms. That was the first time Willy noticed them in an intimate mise en scène.

"You guys are made for each other," he said.

"I feel the same about you and Marquis." Kate smiled.

"So you knew about us?" Willy almost jumped.

"Well, you know about us now." Kate chuckled.

"Girl, the entire world knows about you two," Willy said.

"Ssshhh!" Ryan was going through the chatter on social media. The heavy spending on a real estate advertising campaign shocked the industry. They were on TV, billboards, digital, radio, everywhere. The project was called "Harmony." It was built on the tagline, "Living Together." The idea was based on diversity, people of all kinds living together. An African American sleeping with a cop, a gay couple embracing a priest, a native American carrying a blonde bride through the threshold. It had taken social media by storm, and they were all asking one question: *Who was behind the campaign?*

Willy was bursting with happiness. Ryan wasn't. He was frowning like a priest listening to confessions.

"You don't seem happy," Willy said.

"Nah, I'm happy." Ryan kept going through the feeds. "I think this will win a few Clios."

"Isn't that a good thing? I thought creative directors wanted to win the Oscars of advertising?" Willy asked.

"Sometimes, the wise thing is to do a mediocre job." Kate looked worried too. "Our plan was anonymity. The entire fraternity is now looking for the brains behind the campaign."

"Says who?" Willy said.

"Says the hashtag #WhosAnonymous." Kate walked away to shower.

Ryan muttered, his eyes fixed on the screen. "It's just a matter of time before Todd figures out."

"But that was expected, right?" Willy said.

"Yes, but not so soon. This is not a wake-up call for Todd. It's a battle cry." Ryan finally looked up.

Kate walked in wearing Ryan's oversized Def Leppard T-shirt, with hot coffee for both of them.

"I also have some interesting news that I need to tell." She walked back and poured kombucha for herself. Ryan took a sip from his coffee and admired his favorite view as he looked at Kate in the morning light.

"It's about the Big Five, and I think I've found a way," she said.

"What do you mean?" Ryan was now wide awake. She told them about her stay in the cemetery, Joseph, and what he revealed.

"Sun does no work for the Big Five but gets paid millions of dollars every year," Kate said.

"No, I've seen work being done for them," Ryan said.

"Yes, monthly newsletters. Here's the interesting part: a year ago, Joseph sent them the previous month's newsletter by mistake. He was scared he'd lose his job. Instead, he got a thank you email, the same 'thank you' email he gets every month. Shocked, he tried the same thing again. He kept sending them outdated newsletters that were already published. Guess what?"

"They said thank you?" Willy asked.

"Yes, so Joseph keeps on trying to find out if they would react. They don't. He even changed the name and sent them a newsletter with the wrong name. He got the same thank you email in the evening."

"Why? They're paying huge retainers." Ryan asked.

"Ryan, you're not asking the right question," Kate said.

"What's the right question?"

"Why is Willy not surprised?"

She made sense. Ryan looked at Willy. He was silent.

"Willy?" Ryan said in a stern voice.

"I don't know."

"Willy, if you don't tell me, I'm walking out from your campaign," Ryan said.

"Wait!" Willy said.

"Willy, you do realize how important this is?" Kate said.

"I just know that Sun was off-limits. No one was allowed to talk about them. I asked Marquis many times. Marquis told me not to mess with Todd in any way," Willy finally spoke.

"I have a feeling the response will be the same with the other four. Marquis is the only one who can tell us," Kate said.

"Well, there is one more person who can tell us." Ryan walked away toward his bedroom, leaving Kate and Willy bewildered.

"Who?" Kate said.

"Who?" Willy shouted.

"Andrew Mullen." Ryan shouted back, disappearing into his room.

"Andrew who?" Willy said.

Ryan ignored them as he opened up the closet and took out his bag that had his old belongings. He emptied the entire bag looking for something. He walked back in with the letter from Andrew Mullen, the owner of Miamart.

"Andrew Mullen, the founder of Miamart, left a letter for me. It was given to me when we won the pitch for Miamart. Todd kept asking about it when I last met him. I couldn't figure out why. I had completely forgotten about it till today." Ryan started reading it.

The handwritten letter was succinct.

Dear Ryan,

I am betting my legacy that you will win this pitch. People tell me that no one understands human behavior more than you, and that's why you are the only person I can trust. For decades, my life has been a living hell. I bled every day pierced to the bone by the clutches of evil that held my soul captive. The evil numbed every emotion that I could experience except for pain. You're the first and the last person I'm allowing myself to talk to, not because I want you to do something about it but because the pain of dying without saying a word is unbearable. The life I lived in fear would be in vain if I revealed this to my loved ones. No one should know except a stranger. Only you can understand my predicament: that I did not sign a contract with an ad agency. I signed my death sentence. Whatever secrets are revealed after my death, let my family know that a good man was demolished by an evil one.

Sincerely,
Andrew Mullen.

They were all silent, pensive, trying to come to a conclusion.

Finally, Kate broke the silence. "It's obvious Todd has been blackmailing these men."

"With what?" Ryan said and looked at Willy.

"I know Marquis is petrified of Todd," Willy said.

"Isn't it obvious why?" Kate said, glancing at Willy.

"You mean because he's gay? Oh, come on, girl, this is the 21st century. People who are not even gay claim to be gay just to fit in the emancipation trend."

"Then why is Marquis keeping you a secret?" Kate added.

"Willy, think of the context. This started decades ago, a time when even being friends with a gay person could get you killed," Ryan said. "Marquis can't afford to let his family know, even the shareholders for that matter."

"Only one person can answer all this," Ryan paused. Then, he picked up his phone. "Marquis, where are you?"

"I'm looking at my stocks rise like a twenty-year-old's dick on viagra." He laughed.

"Can you come over for a bit?"

Marquis took a moment to answer, "Sure, I planned to come over. I have lots to talk about."

"So do we," Ryan replied.

Chapter 26

The most interesting man in the world

(Dos Equis, 2006)

In less than an hour, there was a knock at the door. It was Marquis. "It's almost noon. I brought lunch for everyone."

His driver brought the take-out bags inside and left. It seemed enough food for the entire building.

"I'm happy you're here, Willy." Marquis awkwardly shook Willy's hand.

"I'm glad we're all here because I want to make an announcement."

Marquis took off his coat and took out a bottle of champagne from the bag. He paused for a dramatic effect.

"We had a hundred units to sell in ninety days. So the incentive to the team was to sell it in thirty days and get a bonus." Marquis popped the cork and looked at all of them, "Thanks to you, we are sold out in three hours, and as of now, we are accepting advance orders for our next project. The board wants to meet me. " He poured drinks for everyone and raised his glass.

They were all staring at Marquis like mannequins. There was an awkward "Cheers!" by Willy, but it died down almost instantly.

"Marquis, we know what happened in the past." Ryan broke the silence.

"Know what?" Marquis was surprised. "Willy?"

Willy was silent.

"About Todd and what he has been doing to you," Ryan said.

"What has Todd been doing?" Marquis stepped back. He turned pale.

"Marquis, they're on your side. They want to help," Willy said.

"Shut the fuck up, Willy!" Marquis snapped at Willy.

"Marquis, I'm getting Todd one way or the other," Ryan said, "If you help, whatever sensitive information you don't want to reveal stays hidden. Or whatever comes out, you deal with it. You can take this to your grave, or you can help me put an end to this evil."

Marquis' eyes welled up with tears.

"You have to tell us. There is no other way," Ryan said.

Marquis stood there in silence for a while, staring out the window. Finally, he spoke, "I will tell you, but you can't let this come out. It will destroy everything." He wiped his tears. "Promise me; you won't let this come out."

"It won't, Marquis, but it's a new world now. People will accept you if you come out," Kate said.

"You don't get it. It's no longer about coming out. I'm a public figure, an icon in my family and community. It's too late for me to come out now. Every word I utter affects our share price, which will plummet and cost us millions."

"And Todd knows that," Willy said.

"It wasn't just about the blackmail."

Marquis began telling his story. He was one of the few African Americans to become a millionaire in the real estate industry. His initial investment came from his father-in-law, who helped him buy the first building in a tough neighborhood in Brooklyn. But, when he launched the project, no one wanted to buy because no one knew that the building offered state-of-the-art features like hi-tech security, recreation facilities for the family, and a gymnasium.

There was no money left for marketing. He became desperate as time went by, losing thousands of dollars every month. Marquis finally found Todd at a printing press, hoping he could advertise on credit. Todd told Marquis to stay back so he could sort out the paperwork.

It wasn't rape since Marquis didn't resist.

It wasn't easy admitting you were gay back in those days, especially if you were a black man. The next day Todd told him that he wanted a part of the profits and, if Marquis refused, he would make their secretly recorded sex film public. Marquis initially refused, but after realizing how bad things were, he gave in. The advertising worked, and Todd asked him to hire Sun as the ad agency. By that time, Marquis' family had grown. He had a daughter, and another was on its way. He was recognized as a great African American success story. He couldn't afford any scandal, so he complied, and since that day, he has been paying a monthly "retainer" to Todd.

It was a lot for everyone to take in. Even though they had an idea, they were all shocked to hear the details from Marquis. Ryan knew Todd had a dark side, but he never could've imagined it would be this evil.

"Well, the Big Five is finally making sense," Ryan finally spoke.

"What do you mean?" Marquis said.

"The Big Five are five companies Sun relies on to exist and maintain all its worldwide offices. Although they pay exorbitant fees, they hardly get any work done in return." Kate explained.

"If he loses one of these accounts, Sun is in trouble. If he loses all five, Sun shuts down in a day," Ryan said. "You're one of them, Marquis."

"So you think the other four are also—?"

"I have no doubt!" Ryan said.

Marquis paused and then pleaded, "Listen, Ryan, I know how badly you want this, but I can't do this."

"I understand, but there is a way you can help us." Ryan looked straight at him. "Get us the other four."

"Ryan, please don't involve me in this. I'll help you in any other way. I'll help you get clients—" Marquis said.

"I think I have a lead," Willy spoke almost as if he was talking to himself. "An old roommate of mine keeps telling everyone that he is a Sun employee, even though he has never set foot in the building. He is in the—" As he looked away from Marquis, Willy stammered, "Well, mildly put escort business."

"Why do people believe he's a Sun employee?" Kate asked.

"He is listed as an employee and gets a monthly check from Sun. But here is the interesting part: a few weeks ago, he was beaten up badly, hospitalized because of a 'work-related injury,' if you know what I mean. Some rich Arab guy beat him up pretty hard during sex. That guy was a client of Sun."

"A client?" Ryan asked.

"Well, he was a new client, and my friend was," Willy made air quotes, "a gift."

"Why didn't he go to the cops?" Kate said.

"Todd paid him a hundred thousand dollars to sign an NDA. This was on top of the ten thousand for him to record the sex tape. My friend is actually happy this happened."

"Did this happen on a yacht?" Ryan asked.

"Yes, how did you know?" Willy was surprised.

"I think we can get back the Sphinx account." Ryan looked at Kate. "Willy, I need to speak to your friend."

"Ryan, why stir up the hornet's nest? You have enough clients under your belt to last you for a decade," Marquis tried to pacify him.

"How long do you think we have before Todd finds out?" Ryan asked Marquis.

"Your campaign is all over the news. Don't you think Todd will wonder where his client got the work done?" Kate asked.

"Knowing him, I can bet he and Jeff are sweeping the media right now trying to connect the dots," Ryan said.

Ryan's phone started to ring again.

"It's Todd!" Ryan silenced everyone in the room. Had Todd found out about them? He wasn't prepared for a revelation this soon. He looked at Kate.

"Pick it up." Her lips moved without making a sound.

"Boss!" He picked up the phone and turned on the speaker.

"Ryan, my boy, how are you doing?"

"Alive, how are you doing?" Ryan tried to match Todd's breeziness.

"Not good. I need to see you. Can you come over to the office?"

Ryan was taken aback. Every nerve in his body was telling him he shouldn't meet Todd.

"Sure." He stared at everyone in the room, hoping for some affirmation. No one responded, "I'll come over in the evening, but I prefer your home."

There was an uncomfortable pause at the other end.

"See you later then," Todd replied. He didn't give Ryan a chance to say bye and disconnected the phone. Ryan looked up. They were all silent.

"Are you insane?" Kate shouted, "You remember what happened to you the last time you went to his house?"

"He's more open when he is drinking. I know how to handle Todd."

"So he knows about Anonymous?" Willy asked.

"I don't think he knows," Marquis replied before Ryan could, "I've been getting calls since morning. No one knows about it."

"No, this is too much of a coincidence," Kate finally spoke, "Todd has an ego bigger than the billboards on Times Square. He will not stand by seeing someone else get all the accolades for his client."

"Well, there is only one way to find out." Ryan shrugged.

Ryan decided to leave from his apartment instead of Elysium. The evenings were riskier. He didn't want Todd or anyone from Sun to see him walk out of Elysium. He didn't want to go to Head Lion as it was a long drive. Revisiting his apartment alone was not a bad idea, he thought.

Walking into his old apartment felt strange. It felt different from when Kate was there with him. It didn't feel like the place he was forced to leave. Ryan caressed his hands against the walls and felt the mahogany wooden floor under his feet. This was his happy place.

He figured going into the bedroom would trigger more pain. Instead, he moved toward his favorite spot. The balcony was where he did coke. A gentle golden sun reminded him of the evenings he spent there, most of them with naked women. He enjoyed the view of the Manhattan skyline and the lights that would synchronously turn on with the fading sun.

Ryan pulled a broken tile from the wall, revealing a niche. He pulled out a piece of old cloth covering an object that reminded him of his morbid past. It was the knife that put a scar on his back. He still remembered the pain. It was less painful than the backstabbing at Sun.

Ryan had not forgotten about the red envelope. He had just set the confrontation aside, especially since Kate was the one giving him a reason to live. Now, the thought of the red envelope started nagging him again. He resisted the urge to scour her apartment, but it wasn't her apartment. It was his. The truth was beckoning him. He needed to get to the bottom of this. What if Kate was not someone she pretended to be? What if she was working for Todd? His mind was playing tricks and his stomach was churning.

Finally, Ryan got up and walked inside. He looked in the trash cans. Most were empty. He felt sick toying with the idea of searching the apartment. He knew every nook and corner of the apartment. Two places were made for clandestine belongings besides the obvious safe in the bedroom. A niche in the bookshelf was hidden by books and locked with a numbered code. The other was an open nook in the bedroom hidden by a painting.

He tried the nook first and found a few uninteresting files and documents. Then, he went to the bookshelf. He tried a few random numbers. Just when he was about to give up, he pushed the apartment code that Kate had given him to get inside. It was her grandfather's birthday. A gentle click sound made his heart beat faster. The lock opened.

Ryan hesitated for a moment, wondering what he would find inside. A single black binder tied with a thick string and a VHS tape stared at him. He picked up the binder and slowly untied the string. Was this it? The end of his relationship with Kate? He brushed the thoughts aside as an old, faded, over-exposed, colored photograph caught his eye.

It was a little girl sitting on the lap of an elderly white man. A plump African American maid stood behind them. No one was smiling. The house in the photograph looked opulent. Ryan moved his attention toward the press clippings under the photograph.

"Millionaire Jumps from Skyscraper."

The faded picture in the newspaper cutting was of the same man in the photograph. He quickly scanned the article. Next was an old contract that made him realize the invasion of privacy was worthwhile. He immediately recognized Todd's signature; the other signatory was Henry Raymond.

The surname sounded familiar, he thought. *Kate Raymond,* he whispered in his head. An envelope slipped out from the contract and fell on the floor. Ryan picked it up. The black and white pictures were mainly out of focus and taken from an angle that showed very little, except for one. Out of the two men having sex, he recognized one. It was a younger Todd. The dots finally began to connect.

Henry was Kate's grandfather, a Sun client whom Todd was blackmailing. Henry Raymond killed himself, and the granddaughter sought revenge. It made sense. That's why Kate had sent him the red envelopes. He wasn't sure if he was angry or not. He understood Kate's anger and her desire for revenge. The only thing that bothered him was whether Kate's feelings for him were real.

He looked at the time. He was getting late for his meeting with Todd. He called Lucas to pick him up. The new information ensured one thing. The meeting with Todd would be a lot more interesting now.

Ryan liked the fresh breeze hitting his face and kept the windows down once he got out of the traffic jams. The car slowed down. The sound of the gravel moving underneath the wheels reminded him he was there. The last time he heard the gravel rumbling was the worst day of his life. The faint, feminine, and subtly sweet smell of moonflowers brought back memories he wanted to forget. The many cars parked outside the house bothered him, too. It meant a party was happening, and his cotton pants and hoodie would stand out like a TV commercial during the Super Bowl.

The faint noise of people laughing, dishes clattering, and 70s music was distracting. But, perhaps what bothered him the most was hearing his heart beating faster than usual. Todd always made him nervous, and he never figured out why. Ryan knew Todd had a knack for sensing fear, and Ryan didn't want Todd to see his.

"Do you want me to come with you?" Lucas looked in the rearview mirror.

"Nah, I'll be fine."

Ryan gripped his cane. "This is all I need," he said to Lucas. He lifted the cane Todd had given him and showed it to Lucas. Ryan got out, gripping the top of the cane. The lion's bust made Ryan feel stronger even as he limped toward the door. The front door opened before he could reach for the bell. It was Jeff.

"Hi Jeff, congrats on the promotion. You're the official doorman now."

"I'm glad being crippled hasn't taken away your sense of humor. Boss wants you upstairs. Lots of old clients inside. You know how it is."

"Of course, I know. Most of them are here because of me." Ryan smiled as he turned toward the foyer.

Ryan kept walking. He pulled his hoodie over his face so no one could recognize him. He quickly made his way to the stairs and saw someone familiar walking into the main entrance.

It was Nour wearing a red gown and glittering with jewelry. His heartbeat jumped up, his legs felt weak. Ryan grabbed the door as he tried to recover from the shock. What was Nour doing here?

Ryan reached Todd's study, and a cold shiver ran down his spine, thinking about the last time he was there. Knowing the mind games Todd liked to play, Ryan knew it would be at least thirty minutes before Todd showed up.

The thirty minutes gave Ryan time to think over the strategy. He poured some scotch from the bar. He would deny his involvement with Marquis. He would deny he worked on the campaign. Todd would be pissed off, and he would use Todd's anger to his advantage. Thirty minutes were up as he saw Todd entering the study with a glass of scotch in his hand. *How predictable!* Ryan thought.

Chapter 27

Whassup?!

(Budweiser, 1999)

Todd walked in with a glass in one hand, the other hand stretched out warmly. Ryan shook his hand. Todd embraced him.

"Long fucking time. So good to see you, Ryan."

Ryan hated the way his body reacted when Todd was around. Even before his 'accident,' Todd made him nervous. He never knew why his heartbeat jumped when he was there. His mouth was drying up. As much as he hated this man, Todd overawed him with his presence. His nerves would go numb in Todd's presence as if he were a mortal standing in the presence of a god.

"Ditto, boss. Good to see you, albeit secretly. Jeff was scared I'll steal away your clients." Ryan smiled.

"Firstly, that's impossible. Secondly, don't be a fucking pussy. You're from the fucking industry. It shouldn't trigger you." Todd sounded cheerful.

"It doesn't. You know I hate crowds, especially from advertising," he said.

Ryan was waiting for Todd to pounce on him about

Anonymous. Instead, he seemed extremely calm for a confrontation. There was movement behind Todd. Jeff and Gina joined them. The 'group therapy' seemed planned. Todd was coming at him with guns blazing.

"Hi, Guru!" Gina smiled.

"Hi Gina, congrats. I've heard you're the guru now."

"Nah, I'm just me."

"Give it time. Some day you might become one." The sarcasm was obvious.

"Well, you seem fucking angry. That's understandable." Todd interrupted them, "Let's not acknowledge the fucking elephant in the room. Fate has fucked you in the ass, and no one can change that, Ryan. The least I can do is to stop you from getting fucked again. I want to press the reset button between us. In fact, this cunt here," Todd glanced at Jeff, "pushed me that we need to take care of you."

Not the welcome Ryan expected. *They don't know about Anonymous*. Well, this would be fun. He felt better as his heartbeat settled down, and he felt his grip tightening on the conversation.

"And you thought I didn't like you, Ryan." Jeff chuckled.

"Whether you like me is not important. I don't like you. Hope you understand the difference." Ryan smiled. He was finally in control.

"If it makes you feel any better, I don't like this dickhead either." Todd laughed. Jeff kept the same composure with his perpetual smile fixed on his face. It didn't budge a millimeter.

"Boss, we need to hurry. The mayor will be here in ten minutes." Jeff got closer to Todd and whispered loudly.

"Ryan, I'll get straight to the point. I feel for you. You've given us some good years," Todd said.

"I hope by good years you mean 27 Clios, about a hundred other awards, winning new clients," Ryan said.

"The awards were NOT just your work," Gina snapped.

"Nor were the clients," Jeff said.

"Shut the fuck up." Todd lit up a cigar, "I agree with Ryan; he gave a lot to Sun, and in return, we fucking cared for him, looked after him, wouldn't you say, Ryan?"

"Boss, I'm just waiting to hear how you're planning to save me." Ryan was getting impatient. *What was Todd up to now?*

"Permission to be blunt, Guru. No one will hire you in your fucked up condition and age except us. We want to hire you back." Gina broke the suspense. "We all think you deserve better, and you shouldn't be living on handouts from Head Lion."

The offer took Ryan by surprise. He was not prepared for this.

"But I was fired," Ryan said.

"Well, technically, it's not for the same job." Gina smiled.

"You'll be reporting to Gina as a copywriter," Jeff said.

"We want you for the Big Five, Ryan," Gina said.

"You mean the cemetery?"

Ryan didn't feel insulted. He was relieved. He was persistently reading Gina and Jeff. The offer was genuine, and they were desperate to hire him. They wanted to protect the Big Five accounts, and they needed his name to pacify them. Gina seemed the most uncomfortable. She was scared of Ryan's ability to read people, trying hard to hide behind a facade of aggressiveness. He could read that they had no idea about his connection with Anonymous.

"But why the sudden love?" Ryan decided to play along.

"Ryan, I'll be honest with you. I can smell blood. One of our Big Five clients fucked us in the ass this weekend. I want to stop the leak," Todd said.

"Thomas and Thomas?" Ryan was having fun.

"Yes. The estimated spend so far is around five million. That's just one fucking weekend," Todd said.

"Estimated? Isn't Thomas and Thomas a Sun client?" Ryan acted surprised.

"We fucking knew about the release. We had no idea it would be big." Todd glared at Jeff, "Their GM requested a one-time exception, and this cunt here gave them an official go-ahead."

Jeff kept smiling sheepishly.

"Their GM gave the impression it was a small campaign, our team was busy, so I made a judgment call," Jeff said.

"You fucked it up like most of the things you do," Todd said. "Anyway, I'll make sure Marquis pays us for spreading our legs. I'll recover our commission plus damages on this." He paused and took a sip from his drink. "The rumors are a new ad agency was behind it—Anonymous."

"Anonymous?" Ryan was sure he should win an Oscar for his performance. "Is it new? The work looks seasoned."

"I agree," Jeff said. "It seems too polished to be done by a bunch of youngsters. I'm almost positive it's a big agency behind the campaign."

"No. It's modern, probably some kids out of college. The creative is cutting edge, the strategy is refreshing, and the media is data-driven. It's a millennial brain behind the campaign, a creative director who is young, ambitious, and knows what he is doing. Probably AKQA," Gina said.

"So you think a seasoned creative director can't create that work?" Ryan smiled.

"Nope. Your league is too self-engrossed, and you've been hanging on to the old formulas for a long time. I would suggest you study the campaign done by Anonymous before you join, so you know what kind of work is trending." Gina smirked.

"I think this new agency, Anonymous, is a trendsetter, and that's why we need to shut the motherfuckers down as soon as possible," Todd said.

"And the good news, Ryan, the person who stole your role, we are getting rid of her. She'll regret ever messing with us," Jeff said.

"In a few weeks, we will fix everyone by fucking everyone." Todd rarely looked at anyone. It was almost as if he was talking to himself.

"A few weeks?" Ryan asked.

"It's our 50th anniversary Ryan!" Jeff was still smiling.

"I'm returning in two weeks," Todd said, "and I plan to make a few announcements at the anniversary party."

"Including that you're joining us," Jeff said.

"We can't let the Big Five slip away. I think you can make the announcement yourself at the party. You're still a star, and we'll have the press there. Return of the fucking Guru," Todd said. "When I get back, the Big Five will extend their contracts for another ten years."

"How can you be sure? Like Thomas and Thomas, what if they resist?" Ryan knew the answer.

"Ryan, let's just say the fucking owner will give me a blowjob and beg me to let him sign the contract."

"Leave that to us." Jeff interrupted Todd. "You be there for your part of the announcement."

"Ya, I forgot about the anniversary."

"You can fucking read minds, and I'm telling you, my mind is clear. The best place for you right now is Sun," Todd said. The script seemed too synchronized for Ryan, as if they all had rehearsed their parts.

"Provided you accept the generous offer." Gina smiled. Ryan was wondering how everyone was talking as if nothing had happened. As if no one had fired him. As if no one had tried to kill him. They all seemed nonchalant about it. Ryan kept smiling as he imagined cracking their skulls with Todd's golf club.

"Gina will give you the details. It's a generous offer, and I want your ass back in the office." He looked at Ryan. "You were always my favorite."

Gina broke the awkward silence after a few uncomfortable seconds.

"Do you want to hear about the offer?"

"Offer?" Ryan said

"I mean, it's not just the money. You need to get out of that hell hole you call Head Lion. I never liked the name," Gina said.

"I'm listening." Ryan was amused.

"You'll be the level two copywriter on the Big Five accounts. You'll be reporting to me. It's a six-month contract with a chance for extension based on your performance."

"So let me get this straight—" Ryan put the glass down and stood up. "You want a multi-award-winning creative director, as level two copywriter, on a six-month contract, working on clients that no one wants in the agency. Is that about right?"

"An old, disabled, outdated creative director," Gina said. "It's better than getting high on pills every day, waiting to die."

"Let's face it, no one will hire you at this age," Jeff said. "Things have changed."

"Look at the latest Thomas and Thomas campaign. It's making waves because it negates all your rules. That's the difference between your world and our world." Gina added. "Your way of 'advertising' is passé. It's outdated. You need to learn new skills, and I will happily help you learn."

"Now, I have to see that campaign." Ryan was enjoying this. The more they insulted him, the more in control he felt. Finally, he decided to end their agony. "It's a yes from my side. You're right. No one will give me work given my condition and age. So thank you. I just have one stipulation. I'll join on the day of the anniversary as I have to tie up a few loose ends."

"Sure, any fucking thing you want. You'll be the fucking star on the anniversary. I'll make sure everyone knows that my prodigal son is back with us." Todd seemed genuinely happy. "And the cane looks good on you. You're my lion." He walked away as if he had won a poker game. Gina seemed surprised, probably because she didn't expect him to say yes, Ryan thought.

"I'll send you all the files. Come prepared on your first day, and guess what?" Gina smiled. "All the clubbing, coming late and disappearing for hours—that's no longer in fashion."

"Great, being miserable is another perk I look forward to these days." Ryan smiled and walked out.

He had a few more days to destroy Sun. Revenge can be so delicious, he smiled.

Ryan stood at his window, staring at the city. The bright moon gleamed its blue vignette on Manhattan skyscrapers like a spotlight on dancers in a musical. The buildings looked majestic, proud, and narcissistic.

The city looked lonely. He could never understand why New York exuded a feeling of loneliness at night. After the sunset, the bright lights and the scattered apartments awakened millions to how alone they were. And the loneliness was beautiful, like a tragic love story that was alluring and sad at the same time. The city looked ravishing, adorning half-lit monumental buildings like jewelry. But it wasn't the view of the city that Ryan was admiring, it was his favorite sight—Kate.

Wearing just his white oversized T-shirt, drinking wine, standing beside him, she felt like oxygen to a drowning man. Springsteen's 'Secret Garden' played softly in the background. He still hadn't confronted her about the red envelopes. He wanted to find out the truth as long as the truth was that it wasn't Kate sending him the envelopes.

"You have to resign tomorrow," he said to her.

"Yes, thank God!" Kate kept looking at the city lights.

"Todd usually comes to the office at around eleven. Leave the resignation with Patricia and walk out."

"Stop worrying about me. I'll be fine" She turned around and stole Ryan's breath away one more time. His stomach still churned. He felt like a teenager flirting with his crush.

"I still can't believe you said yes to that insulting offer," she said.

"I needed more time," Ryan said as he sipped his Scotch. "They're planning to bury the Big Five in thirty days. Everything ends on the anniversary. Till then, I don't want them to worry about me."

They came back to bed. Kate lay her head on Ryan's chest. He savored the sweet fragrance and the soft texture of her hair. *The moment is too precious for a confrontation,* he thought. Kate was the only real thing left in his life. It was not a good time to ask her about the red envelopes.

"Ryan, can I ask you something without you getting angry?"

"Sure."

"You know I love you, right? I'm with you no matter what you say. I just want you to be truthful."

"I hate circular conversations. Get to the point, Kate."

She waited, and seemed nervous. "Are you the person sending me the red envelopes?"

Ryan sat up, shocked. *Is she playing me?*

"So it was you?" Kate asked again.

"No. What made you think it was me?"

"Well, I saw a red envelope in Head Lion, in your room, and then a few weeks ago I received another one, and I got suspicious, and I saw one in Italy, and then you left for New York. This can't be a coincidence. Even now, you didn't ask me about the red envelopes."

"Because I've been getting them too. What was in the last one you received?" Ryan asked her.

"It's always a name—Joseph Brown. The guy I met in the cemetery, the one who told me about the Big Five."

"When did it start?"

"The first one was before I joined Sun. It had Todd's name. Your turn now."

"I found one torn up in your room and was about to ask you."

"When did you start getting it?" Kate asked.

"The first one was when we pitched for Miamart. It saved the pitch. They all gave names and helped me." Ryan paused,

"It also destroyed you," Kate said.

"I disagree. I think all the envelopes led me to a win."

"Same here. Which means whoever is doing this is not the enemy."

"What matters most is that we have a few days before Todd finds out about Anonymous. Whatever help we get, I'm OK with it."

Kate hugged him. "I'm so relieved it wasn't you."

"Me too."

"Only fourteen days left, Ryan? We have no inroads. The Big Five seem impossible. What can we do?"

"Sink Sun. There is no plan b."

The bright sun woke Ryan up early. He had again forgotten to draw the blinds. Kate was still sleeping beside him. He decided to take a shower. *It's a great feeling to know where you are when you wake up.* The shower was like an ignition button for his mind. His brain went into overdrive.

He knew the Big Five also needed a savior. They just didn't know about it. He spent an hour on the treadmill. He remembered seeing Nour at Todd's party. What was Nour doing there? It was almost 8 in the morning. He decided to call her. He called her three times before she finally picked up.

"Please tell me there is a zombie apocalypse happening right now," Nour said, groaning.

"I need to see you soon." Ryan wanted to read her, and confronting her on the phone would not get him anything.

"I was planning to come over after lunch," she replied.

"Now would be a good time."

"I hate you, Ryan." Nour disconnected the phone.

Ryan scrolled through the newsfeed on his timeline as Kate got ready. *"Anonymous is Making Waves in Advertising,"* read the headline in *Adage*. They were still trending on Twitter. This wasn't good, but Ryan was enjoying the accolades.

"You've still got it, Guru!" Kate smiled. She put on her signature white button-down shirt.

"Wish me luck." She kissed him, wiping off the remnants of her lipstick from his lips, and left. Five minutes later, the bell rang. It was Nour. She stormed in.

"I hope you're aware that I'm not your fucking employee." Nour seemed angry.

"I'm aware," Ryan said.

"You better have a good reason to call me over like this."

"I have." Ryan stared at her. "Why did you not tell me that you were going to Todd's party?"

There was a sudden silence. Ryan could feel Nour's anger subsiding.

"If you're reading my mind, tell me what it says," Nour snapped.

"Let's not play games, Nour."

"Read my fucking mind, Ryan."

Ryan kept staring into her eyes.

"I can read you're looking out for me," Ryan lied. She was betraying him, and it was eating her alive.

"Great! Then, you might want to sit down for this." Nour smiled

Ryan sat down. He wanted Nour to drop her guard. He could read she was hiding something big, and it wasn't good.

"I've found two owners from the Big Five, and they're willing to meet you tomorrow."

Ryan pulled back; his eyes widened, his anger dissipating. This was the best news since Nexus. "How?" He finally reacted.

"We have two weeks to do the impossible. I had to do something crazy. I called Sphinx to get an invite for Todd's party." She paused, lit up a cigarette, and inhaled. "But you still didn't ask me the million-dollar question."

Ryan took the pack from her and lit one for himself as they walked toward the balcony. Ryan could read she was sharpening her knives and getting ready to stab him in the back. There was no point confronting her now.

"What's the million-dollar question?"

"Fuck the question. The answer is Head Lion."

"The two are in Head Lion?"

"Not two." She smiled. "Three."

"Three?"

"Two are willing to meet you. The third one refused."

"Which ones?"

"Red Bridge Hotels and American Motors."

"American Motors; they're huge." Ryan was excited now. Time to put the confrontation on the back burner. He desperately needed this.

"Perfect timing." Nour winked. "They're launching their Electric Vehicles lineup, and the team got really excited when I told them about Anonymous."

"Yes, they've been desperate to break into the electric vehicles market."

"They're unable to make progress because they can't work with any other agency but Sun. I told them we have a way around it."

"Which means you've told the same thing to Red Bridge Hotels?"

She nodded, "So now, do you love me?"

"I love you, but I've been burnt too often to trust you."

"I get that, and for the record, I trust you, but I don't love you." Nour smiled.

"When are we meeting these guys?" Ryan asked.

"Three weeks from today." Nour waited for a response.

If a betrayal were in the offing, he would need some chaos to counter it. "Tomorrow. I want to meet them tomorrow." It wasn't a question. It was a decision.

"Are you insane? How can you prepare a presentation in a day?"

"Two."

"What do you mean two?"

"Two presentations. I want to present to both of them at the same time—tomorrow."

"That is beyond insane. Two clients will not agree on short notice, and even if they miraculously agree, how can you present to both of them at the same time?"

"You said you trust me. Both clients are desperate. Make it happen," Ryan said.

"Ryan, no one can make this happen," Nour said.

"One person can. You. Think of it as your loyalty test."

Chapter 28

We can do it!

(Westinghouse, 1943)

It was 6:59 pm the next day. The crackling sound of the rain on glass windows and the orange hue of the evening sun seeped into the Anonymous boardroom. The eerie silence inside was deafening.

The boardroom was minimalistic by design and brightly lit. The centerpiece was a round, dark brown, oakwood table etched with a lion's head in the middle. Ryan had insisted on a round table to dispel the hierarchy and make clients realize that everyone was equal. It was unique and made a statement about the agency.

There was nothing else in the room except green planters scattered around aesthetically. The dark brown oakwood floor matched the table and spelled an air of experience and expertise. The only intrusive object were two easels placed strategically for a 180-degree view. Both were covered.

Kate stood up. "Thank you, ladies and gentlemen, for trusting us and being here on such short notice."

Against all odds, Nour had managed to get both the companies to attend the meeting simultaneously. Ryan was ecstatic. He'd sent the rest of the team home. They were horrified. The team let Ryan know they thought he was making a big mistake.

Ryan and Kate woke up at four in the morning and finished the presentation by six in the evening. Ryan decided that staying hidden and anonymous for the Big Five was not a good strategy. He would get one shot, and it had to be a face-to-face meeting.

Besides Kate and Ryan, there were seven people in the boardroom. None of them were from Anonymous. On Ryan's left was Red Bridge Hotels. The Marketing Director, a blonde in her late thirties dressed in an indigo suit, looked bored. It seemed she hated being there, and her superiors probably had forced her to attend.

A tall, grey-haired CEO seemed interested but was typing constantly on his mobile phone. His tan looked artificial, and he reminded Ryan of an older George Hamilton. The owner was next to him, pushing his chair away from the table. He was old, disheveled, and drooping. Wrinkles and freckles made a seamless pattern on his aged face, almost like a Jackson Pollock painting. His piercing eyes never blinked, and he kept staring at the rain outside the window. The only noticeable thing he wore was a shiny golden Rolex that lit up the room. Ryan could read he was sending a message that the meeting was a waste of his precious time.

American Motors sat on the other side. There were four, and all seemed young except for the owner. He was old but sat like a hawk, erect and proud. He wore an Armani suit with a red tie and a checkered scarf tucked into his pocket. He kept smoking a cigar without seeming to care how others would react. Perhaps he was waiting for someone to object. No one did. His charisma came from his arrogance.

"We are aware that this is an extremely unusual request to have you all here at the same time," Kate said. "But we can assure you that in the next sixty minutes, you will be happy that you decided to join us here."

The blonde marketing director from the Red Bridge Hotel scoffed. Her boss gave her a stern look.

"We are aware that simultaneously presenting solutions to two clients is not normal, but let me assure you today is not a normal day. You will know why we did this by the end of the presentation," Kate said.

"What exactly is the objective of this meeting?" The Red Bridge Hotel boss asked. He admired the arrogance of this newborn agency that imagined getting Red Bridge's multimillion business.

"Well, the objective is simple," Kate answered. "You fire Sun and give Anonymous your entire business."

The eerie silence was broken by sneers and mocking whispers. The room suddenly became animated. That was all part of Ryan's mind games. He wanted these people to feel the confidence Anonymous had.

"Even if we resign from Sun, what makes you so sure we'll hire you?" The young CEO from American Motors smirked at Kate.

"We are pretty sure! We've done our homework," Ryan interrupted and stood up. The cane with the golden lion that Todd gave him supported his erect stance and provided the surge he needed. "Since we have exactly 47 minutes left, let's not kid ourselves. All of us have thoroughly done our due diligence. We know each other inside out, and that's why we are not wasting time on introductions. I don't want to know your name and what you do. I can get that from LinkedIn. What I want is your signature on this contract that we will share with you at the end of the session."

"And you really think I'm going to waste another 47 minutes on this arrogance?" The Red Bridge CEO stood up.

"Yes," said Ryan, "because we know Sun has got you by the balls, and we can cut off their hands to let your balls breathe."

The CEO stopped moving and stared at Ryan.

"All we are asking is forty-five more minutes. You are already here. Your time will be wasted if you walk away. We know their contract locks you up for ten years. We know the contract is up for renewal in about ten days. And we know you'll have to sign it unless we help." Ryan paused. "Yes, we've done our due diligence."

The Red Bridge CEO looked around and decided to sit down. So did Ryan.

Kate continued. "Here's what we intend to do. We will give fifteen minutes presentation to each of you. We will present a single big idea. We will then offer you a contract for our creative services for one year. We will not tie in any of our clients for a long-term contract."

"What if we don't like the work you present?" The blonde marketing director asked.

"We will still get you out of the contract. You don't have to sign with us. We don't want to be another Sun for you. You have to like us to hire us. It has to be a win-win scenario."

The two presentations were timed precisely like a trapeze act in a European circus. Kate made the presentation to Red Bridge Hotels. She started with research and showed them why they have been at number nine in their category for the last two decades. Kate then presented them with a strategy to be in the top three in the next five years. Her strategy rested on a nugget she'd discovered that the trust for Airbnb amongst millennials had dropped 63%. This was an audience that the hotel industry was ignoring for various reasons and for many years.

Her campaign was based on "Red." Her concept cards showed different scenarios that stressed millennials. Finally, the campaign offered a solution that had one thing in common.

From "Red Eye" to "Red Alert," all pointed the audience toward one solution, Red Bridge Hotels.

The blonde no longer looked bored. The CEO had turned off his phone halfway through the presentation, and Ryan could tell Kate had them by the balls.

"I have a question," said the marketing director, slightly raising her hand.

"You can ask questions, but we will only answer once you sign us up. Right now, we have about fifteen minutes for American Motors." Ryan continued with his mind games.

It was an open secret that American Motors was desperate to establish a foothold in the EV market. It was the fastest-growing segment in the automotive industry. The sales of hybrid vehicles were at an all-time low, which had scared them to enter the EV market. They knew that with the market inundated with newer electric vehicle brands, they would fail if they didn't have a decent advertising strategy. They had no choice.

They needed to hear Ryan out. Unlike other creative directors, Ryan reversed the order of the presentation. He started his presentation with the solution and followed up with research, strategy, and the implementation plan. It was a great way to grab the client's attention right from the start.

"In a few years, the EV market is expected to reach over 230 million units. Currently, the EV market has eleven main players, fighting for almost the same high-priced target audience. It's out of the reach of the middle class who actually need this the most and should be the priority audience. Unfortunately, they have made electric cars so complicated that they have forgotten the basic promise EV brings simplicity. Our solution is simple." Ryan revealed the concept card on the easel: "Change the positioning. Make it easy."

His concept card was simple, and so was his big idea. The visual was a learner's permit of a high school student. The name for the new car was "EZ," and the caption was simple: "Make Life Easy."

He then described all the proposed executions and how "easy" would be the central part of the creatives. Next, he talked about the audience and the pricing. His strategy rested on dropping the price for a higher volume. Finally, he presented numbers that justified how the price drop would increase the revenue. He closed with the Anonymous guarantee: Number one in three years or they get their money back. After fifteen minutes, Ryan stopped, turned toward the CEO, and waited for a reaction.

The CEO responded, "Where do we sign?"

"Now wait a minute," the owner in the fancy clothes interrupted. "We are not signing anything today. Your time is up. Thank you for the work you did. We will be in touch." He started to walk away. His team stood up and started to follow him.

"I need a minute," Ryan said, "with only the owners."

"You've had your time, and we've been more than accommodating mainly because of Nour," said the older man. It was time for Ryan to play his last card.

"I can help you end what Todd has been doing to you for the last few decades." The old man looked at him. "Paul, I know." Ryan looked the older man straight in the eye. A sudden silence engulfed the room, like a mist taking over a winter street. Time seemed to stop at that moment, and everyone could feel the tension building.

The owner of Red Bridge Hotels spoke for the first time, "I want to hear what you have to say." Kate walked out with everyone. The two owners stayed behind with Ryan.

Chapter 29

Real Beauty

(Dove, 2004)

It was past midnight. Ryan and Kate were going through the final execution for the Red Bridge campaign. They had been working non-stop for over a week.

Ryan had a few days left before the Sun event. He was running against time. His multitasking was now affecting his temper even though he was happy with what the entire team had achieved.

What wasn't possible a few weeks ago was now beginning to look probable. He had wrapped up three out of the Big Five, one was still a mystery, and the fifth was the prize catch. It was Miamart.

Miamart didn't fit the traditional pattern. It was the only Big Five account that had become extremely active after a long hiatus. It was also because it had a new CEO Daniel Stewart, the no-nonsense bean counter. Mullen was no longer there. This meant the emotional advantage that came with Todd's blackmailing was futile now. Only numbers, logic, and data would convince Daniel to move the account to Anonymous.

Getting a meeting with him was not a challenge. They knew Daniel admired them both and agreed to meet the next day. The only problem was that Daniel was in Montercy, California, for a conference. Ryan could not wait for him to return. He asked Kate to go to Monterey, and she reluctantly agreed. Kate and Ryan argued about the strategy to convince Daniel. She wanted to persuade Daniel with facts. Tell him about the agency's success, the names behind the big clients they had won, and reveal the Anonymous team.

Ryan disagreed. He didn't want to break his promise and expose the team. He was sure Daniel was aware of their capabilities, which should be enough. They had their first heated dispute, which ended with Ryan reminding Kate that he was the boss. She was furious and walked out of the creative department.

Kate managed to catch a red-eye flight out of New York to Monterey. The connecting flight took Kate through four airports and twelve hours of torture. She could never sleep on flights even though the first-class seats were comfortable, and the service was acceptable. She hated her first fight with Ryan. She was tired even before she landed. She was eager to get back to Ryan with some good news and hug him. She landed at the Monterey airport at around one in the afternoon. Her meeting was at three. She turned on the phone, hoping for a text from Ryan. Instead, the phone buzzed once. It was Daniel.

Stuck at the conference, let's meet at 7 pm.

That was cutting things too close. Kate had to be at the airport at 9 pm for her return flight. She toyed with the idea of calling Ryan, then decided not to. *Ryan had no right to be rude to her in front of the team.* She called a cab and checked into a hotel to eat and sleep. She woke up at 6 pm.

Her Uber dropped her off at a beautiful boardwalk near Carmel Beach. She had twenty minutes, so she walked to the beach. She felt cold, wondering if it was the sea breeze or Ryan. The sight of the sun kissing the shores reminded her how close they had become to each other. Nothing could tear them apart now. Then she looked up and saw Daniel arriving.

Daniel was already seated in a hidden gem of Monterey. The restaurant was famous for its wine collection. The exterior was subtle, almost camouflaged. Almost trying to convince the world it did not exist. It had a waterfall outside and a place to sit near it without getting wet. Few locals knew about it. No tourists had heard about it. Daniel picked the place because it was perfect for a discreet meeting.

"I like being early to meetings. It gives me time to recuperate from the madness." Daniel said with a smile. The place was loud with the waterfall behind them and would've muffled what they were saying if they were an inch further from each other.

"So good to see you. Where is Ryan?" Daniel asked.

"It's hard for him to get around." Kate smiled.

"Is he OK? Physically?"

"He is getting better every day."

"I'm glad you guys got together. Surely burying the hatchet has led to greater things."

"It has, and that's why I'm here." Kate didn't want to waste more time.

Daniel ordered wine. "So tell me, why fly a thousand miles to meet me? What can't wait? I know you're here to sell me something."

"Well, there is only one thing we can sell you," Kate said. "You love our work, and we can do wonders for Miamart."

"Define wonders; humor me," Daniel said.

"Your current market share is 17%, and you're not a leader in the category." Kate was glad she had done her homework. "The e-commerce strategy that Ryan pitched is being run by your team like it was 1949. Just a little juice in distribution could—"

"OK fine. You know your work. I never doubted that!" Daniel interrupted her, "What I doubt is the stability. As much as I hate Todd, I respect the stability that comes with Sun. You guys are great creative directors, but you could be disastrous as entrepreneurs. Business is a whole different ball game."

There was an awkward silence. Daniel wasn't wrong, she thought.

"The group has over five hundred million invested in advertising. Surely you don't expect me to risk all that with an agency that doesn't even have an office." Daniel paused. "I would gladly hire you, even Ryan, to work for me. You choose the title, the salary, the work hours, whatever you want."

Kate knew he wasn't naive. She could sense he was waiting for the big revelation to negotiate.

"What if I told you that we have entrepreneurial experience," Kate said.

Daniel waited, "Go ahead. I'm listening."

"I can't tell you the details, but we have an office, we have a team, we have clients, and we've been working as an agency for the past few weeks."

"You can't be serious. Where is it? How come I haven't heard about it?"

"As I said, I can't."

"Then I can't either. Tell me you understand my dilemma. I can't tell the board that we are allocating five hundred million dollars to an agency that feels too shy to reveal its name."

"Daniel, we've done some great work for some very big names. The biggest campaign in the media right now is done by us."

Daniel stared at her for a while, then smiled, "You guys did the Harmony campaign?"

Kate shrugged. She didn't want to answer.

"Of course! You guys did the Harmony campaign. You're

Anonymous. I should've known. That was some brilliant stuff, and it had Ryan written all over it."

"We can do better stuff for you."

"But who's the team?" Daniel wasn't letting go.

"I can't reveal the team. That's the whole point of Anonymous." Kate was getting uneasy.

"It's a no from my side if I don't know who's working on my brands."

Kate had a return flight in less than an hour. She finally gave in. She couldn't leave without getting the account. Reluctantly, she told Daniel about the help from Head Lion, expecting him to react negatively. But instead, he got even more excited. They discussed the roles and the transition. Daniel even agreed to sign a higher retainer than Sun.

"It's a dream team," he said. "Miamart is yours."

"Just like that? Are you sure?" She didn't believe him.

"Yes. Absolutely."

Kate realized it was getting late, ended the meeting, and rushed to the hotel. She got in an Uber and deleted a million lines she typed to send Ryan before she finally texted. *IT'S DONE!*

Her return flight was from San José. The traffic was moving at a snail's pace. Kate looked at her phone one more time, hoping to see Ryan's reply. There was none. She looked at the time on the phone. She had missed the flight. Suddenly her phone buzzed with a text. It wasn't Ryan. It was Daniel. *Hoping you've missed the flight, if yes, let's have a drink.*

She looked up at the driver and told him to turn around.

Ryan heard Maria waking him up. It was almost five in the morning when they finished and decided to crash at the office. They had to brief Nour about the changes in the campaign. Only she was going to meet the Red Bridge team. Ryan wanted to keep it that way. For him, nothing was more important than keeping the promise with his mavens from Head Lion.

"Here, I got you some coffee." Lucas looked nervous.

"What's the time? Can someone charge my phone, please?" Ryan was desperate to see if Kate had messaged him. He waited impatiently for the phone to turn on.

"It's 8 am, Guru," Maria said.

"What's wrong?" Ryan looked at Maria and Lucas, "You guys look spooked." The phone buzzed. He picked up the phone.

IT'S DONE!

There was one message from Kate, cold and calculated. *She's still mad at me,* he thought. He was missing her now, so he decided to call her, but her phone was switched off.

Maria gave Ryan her iPad. "You need to see this."

It was the *Adage* website. The lead story was **"Anonymous - no longer anonymous."** He switched to other websites. **"Disabled ex creative director slave drives retirees from the old home."**

Anonymous was trending almost everywhere, but it wasn't for the right reasons. The media had revealed all their names along with their photographs. There was a barrage of nasty comments on Twitter. Ryan's eyes widened as he frantically flipped through websites.

"We can fix this." Maria grabbed his trembling hand.

Ryan shook his head. "Call the team. Everyone at Head Lion."

"I called everyone. No one is answering," Maria said.

"Call them again." They started calling again.

"Red Bridge canceled the meeting." Lucas read the email from his phone.

"How did the media know?" Laura was almost in tears.

"The question is, how do they know so much?" Maria gave up

and put her phone down. "It has to be an insider. Things even I didn't know have been published."

Ryan called Kate again. Her phone was still off. He was getting an uneasy feeling. His fingers turned red as he clenched his cellphone as hard as possible. He called her again, pressing hard on the dial button as if the force would somehow switch her phone on. It didn't. He knew how the leak happened but didn't want to believe it. He screamed as he heard his blood running through his veins.

WATCH THE BUSINESS NEWS! Lucas received a message from Willy. It was the lead news on CNBC. The anchor was making fun of the team from Head Lion. Ryan threw the phone at the large TV, smashing the screen.

"Guys, I want you to go," he whispered.

"Are you sure?" Lucas asked.

"Just leave!"

Maria picked up her stuff and told everyone to leave. "We can fix this." She waited for him to respond. "Call me if you need anything." She walked out.

Ryan picked up his cane and walked toward the window. He started calculating the repercussions. *Would he be able to resurrect Anonymous? It had to be Kate.* She wanted to tell Daniel everything. It was a lost battle if Kate was involved. The end came earlier than expected. He should've never started to work again. He should've died. He felt old, feeble, disabled, and loathed his existence. His mind went on a punching rampage, hitting him with negative thoughts. The sound of footsteps awakened him. He turned around, hoping it was Kate with a simple explanation of what had happened. It wasn't Kate.

"Hello Guru." It was Todd, with Gina and Jeff.

"We came to congratulate you on your new business. And also to see your new office," Gina said.

"Very impressive!" Jeff was smiling his wicked permanent smile as he looked around the floor.

"Yes, it is. Pity you have to move out," Gina said. "Todd, I want this room when we move in. I always wanted a large window overlooking the city."

"Surprised to see me?" Todd sat down. "You look like you got fucked by a dinosaur. I'm disappointed, Ryan. I thought you knew me better, especially with all that mind-reading mumbo jumbo."

Ryan felt that same fear gripping him. He wanted to say something, but his mouth felt as if it was plastered with vinyl tape. He felt the pain in his spine creeping up. He tried to sit down but couldn't.

Todd seemed as excited as a kid on a Christmas morning. "You thought this fucker is old. He'll never find out. Well, Guru, I wanted to teach you one last tip of the trade, never teach your father how to fuck."

"I don't think he's paying attention to these golden nuggets. He is zoning out," Gina said.

"Reminds me of the last time I fucking shared my wisdom with him." Todd looked at Gina. "It was fun. He was trembling and screaming like a pussy. I had to give him a little nudge from the first floor to teach him a fucking lesson. Thank Jeff. If it weren't for this cunt, you'd be dead."

The truth was finally setting him free. He didn't fall. It wasn't a stroke. Todd had pushed him. It was all because of the letter by Miamart. Finally, it made sense why Todd wanted him out. Gina and Jeff looked at Todd. Even they seemed shocked, as if not believing what Todd was saying.

"Imagine your fucking existence. You were more useful dead than alive."

Ryan was panicking. It was the same feeling of suffocation the last time he was at Todd's place. He couldn't feel his body from the waist below. His legs felt like jelly. He was trying hard not to fall on the floor.

"Go ahead, fucking fall. I'm sure you won't survive this time." Todd looked at Jeff. "Because I'll kill this cunt before he tries to save you this time."

Ryan was struggling to breathe. Gina and Jeff seemed scared and looked at each other as if wondering what to do.

"All the clients you stole are returning to Sun. The Big Five are staying with their daddy." Todd stood up and started to walk away.

"How did you know?" Ryan wanted to know who betrayed him more than he wanted to save the agency.

"Ah, I almost forgot. I'm glad you asked." Todd turned around and took out an envelope from his jacket. "That bitch is better than you in one way, Ryan, she knows what she fucking wants, and unlike you, she'll fucking get it." He threw the envelope on the table, forcing a few pictures to slide out.

Ryan lowered his eyes and looked at the pictures as Todd, Gina and Jeff walked out. His eyes moved slowly as his focus on the photograph cleared like a picture developing in the darkroom. It was Kate, tied to a bed and a man going down on her. He recognized the pleasure in her eyes and the familiar expressions on her face.

His eyes glanced through the pictures, trying to identify the man. The face was hidden between her legs. The photographs became more graphic, and he finally came to one where he could see the man's face—it was Daniel. It was the reason why she wasn't picking up her phone.

Ryan could feel his body crumbling as he realized he was about to have another stroke. He had a few more seconds before he blacked out. He looked for his phone. It was next to the window, the screen cracked, but it was on. He fell to the floor and reached for the phone. Before his thumb touched the dial button, darkness embraced him like a warm blanket on a cold December night.

Chapter 30

Be all you can be

(United States Army, 1980)

The Newark airport was as busy as a Catholic Church on a Sunday morning in the Vatican city. Middle-aged men in ill-fitted suits gathering for the annual insurance convention had swarmed the airport. They were oblivious to the passengers around them.

One particular passenger was trying her best to get out of the airport she hated the most. Kate had no choice. She had missed her flight. She felt her lungs easing up the moment she stepped out, breathing a sigh of relief, loving the putrid smell of the city. It was better than the stink of sweat she endured throughout the flight.

It was a hot afternoon for this time of the year. Kate took off her jacket and took out her phone. No calls from Ryan. She was in a hurry and dialed for an Uber Black. Two minutes away, and it felt like a lifetime. She didn't want to prolong the tug of war with Ryan and decided to give in. She was ready to hug Ryan, apologize, grovel, do anything to make him happy.

The sun was grilling New York City with its heat as she stepped out of her Uber. She looked up, walked by the giant deities, and entered the building. She picked up the pace, hoping to see Ryan moping and missing her. The elevator bell dinged, and she reached the office.

The first thing Kate noticed was the eerie silence. The office seemed empty as she walked toward the creative department. She knew something was wrong even before seeing the lion bust of Ryan's cane on the floor. Kate looked up, shocked to see the office in shambles as if a tornado had erupted from inside: shattered glass everywhere, printouts scattered, tables overturned.

Kate started trembling, wondering if someone was still there. She took out her phone and dialed Ryan's number. She heard the familiar buzz. She looked around, trying desperately to search for the source of the sound. A piece of paper covering the phone was trembling periodically, just like her. She moved forward and picked up the phone.

The screen was shattered. Kate called everyone frantically. No one picked up. Then she saw the pieces of photographs on the table. She picked them up one by one, putting them together, trying to get a sense of who it was. She started to get a hazy picture of what had happened. Eventually, she found one that was not torn. *No! Please God, No!*

Her phone rang, and it almost slipped from her hand. It was Maria.

"Thank God you called. What the hell is going on?"

"Kate, it's over. Someone leaked all the names and how we operate. It's all over the news. The clients are pissed off, and the team from Head Lion is angry as hell. No one is picking up their phones."

Kate scanned the web and was shocked to see what Maria was talking about. "Oh my God, this seems like an inside job."

"You think?" Maria waited. "Did you do it, Kate?"

"What? No. How could you even think that?" Kate said.

"Well, Ryan tried calling you, and your phone was off," Maria said.

"I missed my flight and have constantly been traveling to get here."

"You could've messaged."

"I couldn't. Where is Ryan?"

"No one knows. He is not picking up his phone."

"Did you check Head Lion?"

"He's not there. I went to Head Lion, and they're not letting me in."

"Did anyone call 911? Maybe he's not well." Kate was panicking.

"He is angry, Kate. You need to give him space." Maria sounded like she had already given up.

"Space? We have less than two days to pull this off."

"It's over. Just let it go."

"I won't let it go." Kate cried, "I need to see you. Where are you?"

There was a pause at the other end.

"I'm in my room." Maria disconnected her phone.

Kate hurried toward Maria's room. She was packing. Maria's room was bare. Her photographs and paintings were no longer on the wall. Two cartons on her desk were filled to the brim. There was also a half-empty bottle of vodka on her table. She was sipping some when Kate walked in.

"Vodka? It's the middle of the fucking day."

"I'm no longer employed. I don't have anywhere to go. Do you? Unless you're meeting Daniel later."

"Oh, shut the fuck up. I'm going to fix this."

"You can't. The sooner you realize it; the sooner vodka will make sense to you." Maria offered Kate the bottle.

"Listen. This is Todd, not Daniel." Kate ignored her offer.

"Did you tell Daniel about the team?"

"Well, yes, but—"

"You fucking idiot." Maria was furious, "He's a bean counter. He will go where he gets a better deal. Even if Todd leaked the information, Daniel must've told Todd. You're probably in with him if you can't see that."

"Can you stop saying that? I love Ryan more than anything in the world. We need to find him before he does something stupid."

They tried calling everyone again. Ryan was nowhere to be found.

"We can't keep running in circles," Kate said.

"We need to fix this before we find Ryan." Maria stood up.

"How?" Kate asked.

"We start at Head Lion." It was Willy standing behind them. "We get Marquis on board. He can get you inside Head Lion."

They reached Head Lion in less than an hour.

"Let me handle this," Willy said and walked in while they stayed behind in the car. After a few minutes, he returned with Marquis alongside.

Marquis spoke before anyone else could say a thing. "Listen, it's over. No one is willing to have any discussion with you guys."

"Marquis, Ryan is missing."

"Good. It's better if he stays missing." Marquis sounded annoyed.

"I'm scared he might do something to hurt himself," Kate pleaded.

"I'm sure he'll turn up in a motel," Marquis said.

"What if he doesn't? What if it's too late?"

Tears rolled down her eyes. It was the first time they saw the vulnerable side of Kate. Marquis moved forward and hugged her.

"I'll give you one chance to talk to everyone. If you can't convince them, I'm afraid I can't do anything then." Kate nodded.

They entered the gigantic glass doors of Head Lion one more time. Kate thought Head Lion without Ryan felt different as she passed by the power lounge, noticing the mavens glaring at her. The news had spread like wild fire. It seemed like a long time since she was here. She entered the lounge and saw the Anonymous team sitting on couches, scrolling on their tablets and phones.

Marco was the first to notice Kate walking in. "What the fuck, Marquis! I thought we all agreed, man."

"Marquis, have you seen the latest blog on *Adage*?" Isabelle flipped her iPad so Marquis could see the *Adage* masthead.

"She did this." Mark stood up.

"I can't take this shit anymore." Cliffy and the others started to walk away.

"Guys, give her a few minutes to make her case. If she doesn't, you won't hear from her again."

"I don't need three minutes," Kate said. "You didn't do any favors for Ryan. You think you saved Ryan. He saved you. He gave you guys a reason to live, to get excited about something good that you can do, instead of checking how high or low your stock or blood pressure is. He needs you now more than ever. This is when you save him." She paused, "If you know the Ryan I know, you'll know he'll die. He'll die if you don't help him finish what he started."

"We didn't stop helping him. You did. You told Daniel about us," Isabelle said.

"Yes, and I would do that again. I did it for Ryan and the agency. He was never going to come on board without—" Kate was interrupted by Marco.

"So you fucked us up. And I thought you'd deny everything." Marco was shaking his head in disappointment. Kate felt like a wounded lion surrounded by hyenas.

"Someone told me that Daniel fucked you when you joined Sun. Is that true?" Isabelle asked.

"We fucked each other, yes, but what does that have to do with any of this?"

"Slut!" Isabelle muttered and walked away.

"I'm glad this never worked out." Mark also stood up.

"Who I fuck is nobody's business," Kate said.

"It is, Kate." Marco walked toward her, "Especially if you fucking leads us *getting fucked in the ass.*"

"Why would I backstab the one I love?" Kate asked.

"You only backstab the people you care about. That's the only stabbing that hurts. Only a fool is surprised when an enemy stabs," Sophie finally spoke.

"How would Todd find out? It has to be Daniel," Marco said.

"The only thing you deserve is an Oscar for your performance, pretending you love Ryan while fucking Daniel," Isabelle said.

"Where were you when Ryan was trying to call you?" Marquis asked.

"I missed my flight. It took me 12 hours to get back. I was continuously traveling, trying hard to get back quickly. Check my fucking boarding passes." She threw her boarding cards on the table.

"What about the photographs?" Marquis didn't have to tell her which ones. They've all seen the pictures, she realized. She finally understood the reason for their hostility.

"Is that you?" Isabelle asked again.

"That's me in the photograph," Kate said.

"I knew it," Marco said.

"Yes, I fucked Daniel. It happened once, months ago, before I even met Ryan. I don't feel guilty about it. You know why? Because I was never in love. And then I met Ryan. There has been no one since then because I just wanted to be owned by him."

"So those photographs are not recent?" Isabelle asked again.

"No. Daniel is a prick, but he didn't tell Todd. I received the signed contract from Miamart today." She showed them Daniel's email on her phone. "News flash, he is not signing up Sun. Why would he destroy an agency and then sign them on for a two-year contract?"

"We have Miamart on board? Is this true?" Mark was getting excited.

"Yes!" Kate exclaimed. They all stared at each other.

"I believe her." Marquis finally broke the silence.

"I do too!" Sophie and Isabelle said simultaneously.

"You know that Ryan is certain you betrayed him?" Marquis said.

"I don't want to lose Ryan. I can't. I'm trying to make things right. I've loved no one the way I love him," Kate said.

Marquis walked over toward the large window and looked outside toward the lake.

"Why don't you tell him yourself?"

"He's here? How?" Kate asked.

"Willy. He never left the building that day." Marquis smiled.

Kate ran toward the window. She looked outside toward the lake. She scanned the garden, the walking path, the fountain area, finally stopping her gaze at the one familiar place. She recognized the man sitting on the bench. It was Ryan. She found the exit and ran toward him.

She wanted to embrace him and kiss him and taste him and inhale his scent, all at the same time. She stopped. He sat there like a mannequin staring at the lake.

"Hi!" She waited for him to say something. He'd didn't. She finally sat next to him, "The pictures you saw are old when you weren't in my life. It happened once, six months ago. It never happened again." She paused, waiting for him to respond.

He didn't.

"I didn't pick up your phone because I missed the flight trying to convince Daniel to give us the account. No, I didn't sleep with him. No, I didn't betray you. But yes, I told him about the team because I made a judgment call and felt he would not give us the account unless I told him." She waited for him to respond. He didn't.

"I got the contract." She waved the phone at him.

Ryan sat there staring at the lake.

"We need to do this, Ryan. We can still fight Todd. We can still get our beautiful revenge." She paused.

"I'm not leaving you till you talk to me. I don't care how long it takes; I'm not going anywhere. You're the reason why I've never had a stable relationship. I've loved you all my life. From the day I met you, I wanted to be yours." She waited for him to react. "I don't want to own you. I just want to be owned. My thoughts, my breath, my scent, my soul are yours. I want to hear you say it, Ryan. Say that I am yours."

Ryan looked at her for the first time. She was not lying. He could read.

"You're mine." He said, "You belong to me, no one else." It was not a statement. It was a decree.

"Yes!" She hugged him as if her life depended on it. Sobbing and laughing at the same time, kissing and talking at the same time, whispering words in his mouth. Ryan held her face in his palms and kissed her, devouring her lips as if he would starve if he let her lips go.

"I'm sick and tired of thinking whether I'm good enough for you. This is it. Let me know now. I want to own you, every single breath that you take."

"I want to be owned, Ryan. Yes, I'm yours. Every single part of me. Every single breath."

"And you will never be with another man."

"Man or woman, I promise." She laughed and wiped her tears.

He kissed her one more time before being interrupted by Marco.

"So, where do we go from here?"

"Back to Elysium," Ryan replied.

. . .

The Anonymous team was back in the boardroom the next morning. Only Nour was missing.

"So, where do we stand?" Ryan began.

"We still have a day left to wrap this up," Kate said.

"No one from the Big Five is picking up their phones," Maria said.

"Where is Nour?" Ryan asked, knowing the answer.

"She is not in Head Lion and not picking up her phone."

"There is no way we can reach the Big Five without Nour," Kate said.

"We have two from the Big Five; Miamart, and Marquis."

"That's still not enough to bring Todd down. It'll be a bad blow but not devastating. We need Red Bridge and American Motors," Kate added.

"So if we get four, isn't that enough?" Laura asked.

"It's enough but not beautiful," Ryan said. "We need B and R bank to sink Sun. If we don't get B and R, the plan is fucked." Ryan looked at everyone for approval. They all nodded.

"I've found a lead there. The marketing head at B and R is from Greenwich. Maybe Kate knows her or plays the alumni card?" Mark looked at Kate.

"What's his name?" Kate was curious.

"Her! Maya Hamid. She's from Pakistan."

"Yes, I'm sure I can get an appointment." Kate smiled, excited to meet her best friend after a lifetime. The last time Maya contacted her was right after Kate moved to New York. Maya needed Kate's help with a project, and then she disappeared. Kate was ecstatic that she had finally found her.

"Great! We still have one full day. Stop all work. Let's start with the low-hanging fruits. Get me Red Bridge and American Motors."

The day went by like a Ferrari on steroids. They were all running into roadblocks. Ryan could feel the pressure building up in his neck. By evening his pain had spread to his spine and legs. He was on his phone, working on campaigns for the existing clients, praying that a miracle would happen before Todd's party.

The thought of Nour's disappearance kept popping up like a nagging migraine. He brushed it away. His biggest worry was getting through to the two major clients before the party. He knew time was no longer his ally because if this didn't happen tomorrow, it never would. He looked at his phone. It was almost 10 pm, and the office lights were being turned off one by one. There was a knock on his door. It was Willy and Maria.

"Guru, we are leaving. Do you need anything?"

"No thanks. I'll see you tomorrow."

"Get some rest," Maria said and left. He poured himself a drink and decided to press pause. He turned on his playlist and heard knocking on his door when the song stopped. He turned around and saw Jeff smiling.

"I'm glad I caught you here. I heard you disappeared or something, but knowing you, I was almost certain I'd find you here."

"Get it over with." Ryan sat down. "Go ahead, give me a reason to kill the messenger."

"On the contrary, Ryan, you've always underestimated me. I'm here to deliver you the invitation for the anniversary. Todd thinks your disabled ass is back at Head Lion. I knew I wouldn't find you there."

"And you want me to come?"

"I don't, but Todd does. He insisted I convince you to be there tomorrow."

"No convincing needed. I'm not going to miss it for the world," Ryan took the cards from Jeff. "Who is the second one for?"

"Kate, Todd wants her to be there too."

"Why am I not surprised. And if I want to bring more guests?" Ryan asked.

"More? You want more people to see your humiliation?"

"Wouldn't Todd enjoy that?"

Jeff came closer and whispered in his ear, "Depends on who. You know it's very exclusive. You're lucky Todd wants you there."

Ryan could smell the stench of alcohol on him. His uncoordinated movements suggested he drank a little more than he could handle.

"Well, I was thinking of inviting my team. Maybe Todd can hire them later."

"Oh, I doubt that, but he still wants you to join Sun."

"After all the drama, he still expects me to join?"

Ryan knew why.

"Well, let's just say he has reasons. He can't be an idiot to get where he is today." Jeff paused as if groping for words.

"So Todd said you saved my life?"

"I had no idea Todd pushed you. As much as I hate you, I had no idea Todd could be this sinister."

"For some reason, I don't believe you," Ryan said, even though he could read that Jeff was telling the truth.

"I don't care what you believe. I know you survived because I was there." Jeff snapped at him as he took out a few more invitations from his leather laptop bag. He was clumsy, and a few more documents slipped out. A bunch of red envelopes caught Ryan's attention. They both paused and looked at each other.

Ryan waited for him to say something. His continued silence was jarring. Finally, Jeff closed his eyes and started to sway gently. It almost felt like he was falling asleep.

"There is one more thing I have for you, Ryan!" He opened his eyes which seemed redder than before. He took out a red envelope and threw it on Ryan's table. Ryan knew what it was before it hit the surface.

"What's this?" Jeff asked.

"Go ahead, open it." Ryan opened the envelope and took out the visiting card. It had one name on it: ***Jeff Barr***.

"Yours truly. Yes, I'm the anonymous sender. I've been trying to nudge you in the right direction, but you were dumber than I thought."

"Why?" Ryan asked, shocked.

"I'm surprised you're even asking that. We have more things in common than you think. I hate Todd just like you do, maybe a bit more. He tried to kill you once, Ryan. It happens with me every day." Jeff was slurring. Ryan could read Jeff like an open book. The hatred for Todd seemed genuine.

"Do you think being mean to you is the same as what he did to me?"

"It's worse. Todd has humiliated me every day from the day I joined. He destroyed my self-esteem and a lot more. There are things I don't want to talk about."

"Why didn't you leave him?"

"Do you think it's easy? I've left everything for him. If it weren't for him, I would still be married, sitting home with my beautiful wife and kids."

Ryan felt something he thought was impossible to feel for Jeff: empathy. He could relate to what he was saying. Ryan had seen Todd treat him worse than an animal. Ryan felt guilty because he'd enjoyed Jeff's humiliation.

"I'm sorry I relished those moments. I hated you back then," Ryan said.

"I know you did, but I admired you. I thought you had something till you created this disaster."

"What disaster?" Ryan asked. Jeff moved closer to his face; the stench of alcohol consumed Ryan.

"I handed you everything on a fucking platter, man, everything. The leads I gave you, all you had to was follow the light, and we would've been fine."

"We?"

"Yes, we. It was a win-win scenario for both of us till you fucked up."

"How was it a win for you?" Ryan was curious.

"If Todd loses over 50% of the revenue, the board hands over the company reins to me. If he dies, I get a full partnership, and I run the company. He is not going to fucking die, and he is not losing any of his business. Thanks to you, he might be getting more clients."

"Did you know about the Big Five and the sex tapes?" Ryan asked.

"I had a suspicion. I confronted him once. I knew within weeks that five clients were paying a lot more for a lot less. He said I have something that the clients don't want the world to see. Five tapes of each client. He showed me his vault where he kept them!" Jeff said.

"Do you have access? Get me the tapes. We can still do it." Ryan asked.

"You really are stupid. Do you think Todd will let me have access to those? It's in his vault," Jeff said.

"Why didn't you go to the cops?"

"Not my circus, not my monkeys. Why would I care? Sun runs on the Big Five retainers. The sportscar I drive, the apartment you had. Where do you think the money was coming from?"

"He has something on you?" He could read him easily now.

Jeff stayed quiet.

"And that's why you sent the red envelopes."

"It doesn't matter now. You fucked up." Jeff started to walk away, "My last tip; don't come tomorrow."

"Wait, I need to know one more thing," Ryan shouted.

"Yes, it was Nour, not Kate. She told me about Lake Como. She got you Red Bridge and American Motors because she thought you'll never be able to win two pitches in one day. She set you up to fail."

"But why?" Ryan asked.

"She felt sidelined with Kate in the driving seat. She was upset with you because you spent all the profits without asking her." He stopped and turned around. "And no! I don't want to see you ever again. I hope you rot in the customized hell you've built for yourself."

There was a knock on the door.

"Ryan, are you OK?" It was Mark. Willy and Kate came to the door as Mark walked in.

"He's fine. We are done," Jeff said and then walked away.

"I need to talk to you guys. We've been invited to the biggest party in New York." Ryan looked at his team. "Sun goes down tomorrow night."

Chapter 31

Connecting People

(Nokia, 1992)

They gathered around Ryan.

"I need a drink," Mark said and poured himself one.

"So, what are we missing?" Kate said.

"We're thinking about the obvious," Ryan began. "Let's switch our perspective. Think of this problem as an advertising brief. We have a communication problem. The target audience, in this case, is Red Bridge and American Motors. The desired outcome is we get in touch with them. The one thing I've learned in advertising is that the right communication will solve any issue. Now, with all the advertising geniuses in this room, tell me how to solve this."

"The party is just hours away. Let's face reality. Getting three clients to quit Sun and sign us up is impossible." Willys sat down across from Ryan.

"Four, not three," Ryan said. " We will also get Sphinx."

"That's impossible," Kate said.

"I have a stupid idea," Mark said.

"I love stupid ideas. All great things happened because someone had a stupid idea." Ryan smiled.

"There is a way to make them call us," Mark said. "It can also backfire and destroy what we did."

"I love it already," Ryan said.

"We never addressed the scandal that destroyed us. It's a one-way story constantly being run by Todd on every media channel. What if we made a public announcement in response to the scandal. Rather than being defensive, we own it. We are not making old people work; instead, we position Anonymous as the most star-studded ad agency that offers years of experience," Mark said.

"But how would that help contact the two clients?" Kate asked.

"Name-dropping! We come out identifying who Anonymous is and name our clients. We've got celebrities on both sides. Why not use their names as an endorsement?" Mark said."

"But wouldn't Todd immediately react and block the Big Five?" Willy asked.

"That's the beauty of it. The idea is to have a press release precisely targeting the Big Five. Only the people from Big Five see it, no one else. LinkedIn gives you that option," Mark said.

"It also has the option to exclude an audience." Ryan was getting excited.

"We announce Red Bridge and American Motors have moved to Anonymous. Best case scenario, it will confuse them. Worst case, it will piss them off. Either way, who do they call?" Mark smiled.

"Crazy but clever, two mandatory ingredients for a solution," Ryan said.

"This could seriously backfire," Willy said.

"It can't get any worse," Mark said.

"I agree. Let's first get out of our way." Ryan was thrilled.

"We literally have nothing to lose," Kate said.

"I'll schedule the press release. The first thing they'll see in the morning is that they've moved their advertising to Anonymous." Mark said.

Kate and Mark walked out. Willy was about to leave, but Ryan stopped him. He asked Willy to call his friend, the one who made the video for Todd. Willy seemed a bit surprised but dialed his number. Ryan took the phone from Willy.

"Willy told me you kept a copy of the video that Todd asked you to make, the one with the Arab on the yacht."

"I have no idea what you're talking about, honey."

"Listen, you're always a decision away from a different life, so I want you to pay attention to what I say next." Ryan didn't want to waste any time. "Because it can change your life. Do I have your attention?"

"Yes," said a reluctant voice.

"I'll give you a million dollars, transferred to your bank account in the next thirty minutes, and then I'll provide a private jet to take you anywhere in Europe."

"You have my attention," said the voice on the other side.

"In return, I want the film."

There was another pause.

"I don't know what you're talking about. There is no film."

"Fine, your loss. Adios amigo."

"Waitttt." There was silence at the other end, except for heavy breathing. Ryan knew he had taken the bait.

"You know I'll get whacked if I accept your offer," the voice finally said.

"You can hire ten butlers to wipe your tears while lying on a King-sized bed in Paris. You'll be able to forget all your worries for the rest of your life." Ryan gave the final push.

"What do you want me to do, assuming I have the, umm, film?"

"I want you to pack, go to the airport and, on the way, upload the video onto Twitter." Ryan paused. "Willy will give you the details." Ryan gave the phone back to Willy. He listened to some bantering and screaming from the other side.

"Yes, he's good for it." Willy finally managed to say something to the person on the other end. He disconnected the phone and looked at Ryan,

"I sincerely hope you know what you're doing."

"I never do, and that's what makes it fun." Ryan smiled.

"You know you'll be ruining a man's life."

"Whose life?" Ryan asked.

"The guy in the film! I thought we were the good guys."

"We don't have time to be the good guys." Ryan ended the conversation.

Ryan couldn't sleep the entire night. It was 4 am. Kate was still sleeping. He kissed her on the forehead and walked out. He was dying to check LinkedIn. He had a few cups of coffee waiting to check his timeline. Finally, at 6 am, the press release was up.

Anonymous No Longer anonymous. Wins Record Business From Red Bridge Hotels and American Motors.

The text revealed the names with a picture of the Anonymous team, the one they took at Lake Como. They all looked classy, happy, and like a team ready to devour the ad industry, unlike their current state. Ryan decided to call the team early as he got ready for the office. They were already there. Everyone could feel a new burst of energy flowing through them. It felt like Anonymous was about to go to war.

"Any news? Or is it too early to ask?" Ryan asked Mark. Suddenly the office went silent. All the noise faded on cue. They all stared at Mark.

"Half the job is done," Mark said.

They all smiled.

"No, no. It's too early to celebrate. The only thing the press release accomplished was getting a call. Ryan still has to pull off a miracle. They are really pissed off. They took your number, Ryan. Let's see if your pitching skills are as good as everyone says." Mark seemed excited. "Red Bridge will call you in an hour."

Before Ryan could reply, his phone buzzed. It was an unknown number. He picked up the call, walked to his room, and closed the door behind him.

"What stunt are you pulling off?" Ryan recognized the owner's voice from Red Bridge at the other end.

"Stunt?" Ryan turned on the speaker.

"We never signed," he said in a barely audible voice.

"But you agreed. You shook hands; you said it's yours," Ryan said. "You can't blame us for assuming you've become our clients."

"Ryan, please don't underestimate my intelligence."

There was an awkward silence.

"We have the films," Ryan said.

"Films?"

"The ones Todd used against you. I know he has been blackmailing you. I can stop that," Ryan said.

There was a long uncomfortable pause.

"You have the tapes?"

"Yes," Ryan said.

"All of them?"

"Yes."

"How many do you have?"

Ryan knew he was trying to verify its existence.

"Five." Ryan remembered what Jeff had told him. There was another pause. Ryan could hear the sound of heavy breathing.

"How did you get them?"

"Is that important?"

"So, what do you want?" The voice asked, "You want money for the films?"

"No. I don't want anything. I'll give you the films so you can destroy them with your own hands," Ryan said.

"I sense a 'but' coming."

"I'm not Todd. I'd be happy if you signed us on as your agency, but that's not conditional."

There was a pause. The sound of heavy breathing continued.

"When can I have the tapes?" The voice asked.

"The tapes are secure, and you can send someone after Todd's party tonight," Ryan said.

There was a pause.

"I'll get it picked up tomorrow. I'll wait one more day."

The door opened. Mark and Kate walked in, followed by Willy.

"Well?" Mark asked.

"He didn't say no," Ryan replied.

"What does that mean?"

"Well, I'm not sure." Ryan's phone buzzed. There was a text from the same "Unknown" number.

YOU DESERVE MORE THAN OUR SIGNED CONTRACT

Does this mean we are getting the Red Bridge contract? Ryan swiftly typed.

You'll have it in an hour, he replied.

Ryan looked up and smiled. "It worked." He looked at Mark. "We have Red Bridge."

They all jumped up and hugged each other.

"There is one more thing, Mark," Ryan said. "How soon can we make the press release public?"

"It's ready to release. Will spread in seconds, with the right budget behind it," Mark said.

"What if we fail?" Willy asked.

"If we fail, we don't release. But if we succeed, I want the news to spread as fast and wide as possible. I want Anonymous to trend on every social media in five minutes."

"It'll be expensive."

"I don't care what the cost is. Can you make it happen?"

"Absolutely," Mark replied.

Ryan closed the door, blocking the noise of excitement behind him. He looked out his window and stared at the New York skyline one more time. Ryan knew the Red Bridge account was big, but it was not enough. He had around six hours to pull off his beautiful revenge.

He checked Twitter to see if there were any reactions to their press release on LinkedIn. There were none. He checked the trends. They were the usual; #POTUS, #TomHanks, #OscarBuzz, #Sphinx. He clicked on Sphinx. The chatter was around a hidden-cam video of Mustafa Saeed, the marketing director of Sphinx. It had gone viral with over 100,000 retweets, and screen grabs were turning into memes.

Ryan wanted to feel sorry for Mustafa but didn't. He had forgotten about it, and now his plan was in motion. He could gain a thirty-million dollar account and a chance to relish Todd's suffering. And, especially Gina. This was her baby. He called Mustafa a few times. There was no answer. He decided to text him.

I know what Todd did. I can help. He impatiently waited for a few minutes. The phone rang. It was Mustafa.

"I'm sure you're enjoying my destruction on social media."

Ryan could sense Mustafa wanted to dominate the conversation. He said, "If you want to act like a baby, there is no use having this conversation."

"What the fuck do you mean?"

"I'm no longer pitching to you, and I don't have time to be nice. I'll be blunt, so let me know if you can handle it." There was a short pause at the other end before Mustafa spoke in a much calmer voice.

"I'm listening!"

"You're fucked in every sense possible. I can unfuck you—"

"If?" Mustafa interrupted him.

Ryan knew Mustafa believed life was about transactions. You give something to gain something.

"If you give us the Sphinx account, I'll help you retain your position and make this disappear."

"And how do you propose doing that?" Mustafa asked.

"Nour Walid has a seat on the board," Ryan replied.

"My community wants my head on a platter." Mustafa lashed out at Ryan, "She can't do it alone."

"Do you have a choice? She's smart."

"You mean manipulative?"

"Do you want Todd to get away with what he did to you today?" Ryan ignored his question.

"How do you know it's Todd?" Mustafa asked.

"I'm sure you do, too," Ryan said.

"You know I had signed the Sphinx account to you."

"I know."

"I can give you the account provided you get me back at Sphinx."

"I will."

"I want to fuck Todd for what he has done to me. I want to cut off his balls and feed them to my dog!" Mustafa shouted.

"Leave the ball-chopping to me. Nothing will piss Todd off more when he finds out you gave me the account. Remember, it can only happen before they ask you to step down," Ryan said.

"You will have the signed contract before Todd's party tonight," Mustafa said. "I want to see his face when I tell him."

The line went dead. Ryan breathed a sigh of relief. It was another win that he desperately needed before time ran out. His phone dinged. It was an email from Red Bridge with the signed contract. Ryan rushed out and called everyone into the boardroom. There was excitement in the air as they gathered around Ryan. The team could sense that they were inches away from their goal, yet it felt like miles.

"We now have three of the Big Five and Sphinx." He paused as the team burst into shouts of joy. "And even though we are almost there, it does not bring down Sun."

He paused again, "It's not over. We are four hours and two clients away from sinking Sun. So if you think you can't do this, you need to get out of your way because this can be done and will be done before the party tonight."

"What do you want us to do?" Laura asked.

"Find me, Nour," Ryan replied.

"Doesn't she still have the company phone? We can trace her location," Laura said.

"Laura, you're a genius." Ryan hugged her.

"She is in Central Park." Mark was staring at his phone.

"I know where in Central Park." Ryan rushed to his room.

"Laura," he said as he turned back, "use the company card to buy everyone the best outfits for tonight's party. I want all of you at Todd's party no matter what happens. If we go down in flames or rise from the ashes, I want all of us looking great." Ryan walked back into his room, followed by Kate, shutting the door behind him.

"I don't think you can convince her," Kate said as Ryan picked up his cane.

"You're the last person on earth I would've expected to underestimate me." Ryan smiled as he texted Nour:

MEET ME IN CENTRAL PARK. I'LL BE THERE AT 2.

He kissed Kate and walked out of the office. He called for a cab as he stepped out of the elevator. He looked at his phone. He had approximately three hours to wrap up the third chapter of his life.

Ryan knew Nour hated being the sidekick. She needed an emotional nudge. He found an empty bench near the fountain. He sat down and realized he had walked the park without his cane.

There were the usual updates from Mark. Willy had sent him pics of the team trying out clothes at designer outlets. Someone had convinced Isabelle to forget her virtues and buy a designer dress.

"You've always been stubborn." It was Nour. "But I'm not here to apologize."

"On the contrary, I want to apologize. Before making all those big decisions, I should've taken you on board. I should've asked you before buying Elysium."

Nour looked at him for a few seconds, came forward, and sat next to him. "What do you want, Ryan?"

"I want you," Ryan replied.

"You're too old for me, dahling." Nour smiled. "It's over. You lost. Todd will have all the contracts today."

"I still want you on my team," Ryan said.

"What team? No one is with you," Nour said.

"Well, in that case, I need you even more. All this started because of you, and now I need you to help me end this."

"It has already ended."

"It hasn't. I still have a few hours."

"You need a shrink, not me. There is no Anonymous. The team has refused to even talk to you. How can you even think you can poach five of the biggest clients in a few hours?"

Ryan paused for a moment. He could read she wanted him to give her a reason. His emotional bait had done its job.

"What if I told you I have four?" Ryan said as Nour stared at him.

"You're joking, right?" Nour seemed surprised.

"I want you to help me bring one last client home," Ryan said.

"Which one?" Nour was curious.

Ryan looked at her, trying hard to read her. "American Motors."

"What about B and R?"

"Kate said she will take care of B and R."

"And you trust her to get a million-million account."

"We have Sphinx, and we don't have any other choice."

"What about the team? What about Anonymous?"

"They are with me." Ryan showed Nour the pics on her phone. "All are back, except the one who can run our business."

"Who?"

"You Nour, you. We can't do this without you. So will you do it?"

She looked at him for a brief moment. "Yes! Here's some more good news for you. American Autos already signed the contract, I just didn't forward it to you. That's why they didn't react to your LinkedIn post."

"You knew?" Ryan asked.

Nour took a deep breath, looked at him, and said, "Yes." She looked at the fountain. "For the record, I hate you."

"For the record, I love you." Ryan smiled.

"Is this your way of saying thank you?" Nour smiled back.

"No, this is." Ryan reached out and hugged her, smiling. "I hope you're bringing your life jacket tonight."

"Why?" Nour seemed surprised.

"We are sinking the Titanic."

At 8:30 pm, they gathered outside Elysium. Ryan was the last to arrive. He was sitting in his car in the underground parking lot, thinking about the past year. Even though Ryan had lived a lifetime in a few months, he felt no sense of achievement. He was trying hard to feel happy, excited, satisfied, anything. But instead, he felt nothing, not even sad.

He still didn't have B and R bank. He had enough to make tonight the most memorable night for Todd but not enough to sink him. His phone buzzed. Kate texted that everyone was waiting for him. The team wanted to take a group photograph.

Ryan took a deep breath, grasped the lion's head on his cane, and stepped out. He walked toward the facade of Elysium and saw the blinding lights dazzling the dark October night. Unblinded by the moving floodlights, the paparazzi snapping the celebrities, fireworks, and the headlights of the limos arriving, Ryan walked toward Elysium.

The Greek gods stared back at him, their piercing eyes beckoning him to step inside. He suddenly felt something. It was an undefinable emotion that felt like pride but wasn't pride, that felt like happiness, but it wasn't happiness. The only thing he was certain of was that the gods made him feel good. Kate waved as she saw him staring at the statues.

The team started whistling as they saw Ryan for the first time in a tux. He anxiously tugged at his bow. Kate had picked up a Tom Ford for him and forced him to dress up for tonight. He was blushing as he tugged uncomfortably at his bow one more time. He walked toward his team. They looked like stars on an Oscar night, wearing designer clothes and shiny jewelry.

Kate was wearing a backless black gown; the deep slits on the sides revealed her slender legs. Willy wore a black velvet Armani suit and looked like a model straight from a Milan fashion show. Marco chose to wear a white Ralph Lauren tux with a maroon bow. Even Isabelle wore a dress that didn't look like she had bought it from a thrift store. The lights flickered on her red satin gown.

Kate fixed Ryan's bow and nudged him toward the center. He could tell that everyone felt nervous and excited, like the feeling you get just before getting on a scary ride. The Anonymous team knew, one way or the other, this would be the most memorable night of their lives.

Ryan looked up at the 40th floor. The light was on in the corner office. It was Todd's room. He imagined Todd sitting there with his top clients, offering them gossip and 'specialties' inaccessible to people beyond his room. Kate wrapped herself around his arms.

"I have a surprise for you," she whispered.

Before he could ask her about the surprise, Mark and Willy walked toward him. Mark was holding a file and took out a few envelopes.

"Well, Guru, all the contracts and the eviction letter are here. I've checked with the lawyers. Sun has never paid rent. Todd won't appeal, because after tonight, he won't be able to afford living here."

Ryan told everyone to wait for him in the lobby. He held Kate's hand. He kissed her after the team left.

"What was that for?" She blushed.

"For saving me." He smiled. "And for the contract you're about to give me."

"How did you—" She sounded surprised. "Never mind." She opened up her purse and took out an envelope.

"It's the final nail," she said and gave it to him. It was a contract from the fifth in the Big Five—B and R bank.

"It was the easiest pitch I ever made, thanks to Maya."

"Who's Maya?" Ryan asked.

"One of the few memories I cherish. Do you have a memory you cherish?"

"I'm going to make one when we sink Sun tonight."

She held his arm as they walked toward the atrium. He glanced back and looked at the gods one last time.

Chapter 32

Here's to The Crazy Ones!

(Apple, 1997)

Sun's event management company transformed the Sun office into a perfect replica of Studio 54. It allowed Todd to showcase his other companies for business. The event team had done a meticulous job. The only untouched area was Todd's office. The designers had turned the rest of the floor into a 70s-themed disco.

The deafening music was intentional because Todd wanted the conversation between the guests to be minimal. Todd's room was the only audible place where the guests who mattered were allowed. Besides the music, the only other sound the guests could hear was the blasts of the fireworks. The elaborate fireworks exploded from the surrounding areas every thirty minutes, lighting the bare windows with a million colors.

New York's mayor was part of the elite guest list, who also took care of the permissions for the fireworks. The guests included the crème de la crème of the country. It was a rare gathering of stars from all fields except advertising, from movie stars to models, singers to entrepreneurs, journalists to artists.

The only people invited from the advertising industry were the senior employees of Sun. No one from other agencies was allowed inside the building and Ryan knew why. Todd was insecure and didn't want hunters poaching on his trophies. Ryan knew most guests came reluctantly because not being seen here was a fatal career move. Todd had invited Ryan for a reason, and he needed to figure that out soon.

The designers had transformed the smaller rooms into mini discos for private gatherings. Alcohol abundantly flowed in the bigger areas, drugs in the smaller. The drugs were as diverse as the guests and included cocaine, ecstasy, and marijuana. The consumption depended on the age and where one stood in the food chain. Young models looking for an early start in their careers were paid to be there. Many were not even paid but were ready to 'serve' for the free booze, drugs, and a chance to get ahead in their careers.

Ryan saw Gina was the first to notice their entrance. He felt proud of his dream team. They all looked like an ensemble cast from a Guy Ritchie movie, and he could tell many were surprised to see another agency arriving. Led by Ryan, the team walked through the stares toward the center. Ryan could feel the tension building up in the room. Gina seemed surprised as she moved forward and greeted Ryan.

"Wow, the boomers are here. You must feel right at home in Studio 54," she said to Ryan as she kissed him on the cheek. "Todd must really love you since no other agency got an invitation, but I guess that's OK since you're a *former* agency."

"We wouldn't have missed this for the world." Kate smiled.

"Well, since you were so desperate to come, enjoy the free drinks." Gina smiled and walked away.

"I hate her." Laura was the first one to comment.

"It's a good sign, dahling, if you're pissing someone off at a party." Nour hugged Laura.

"I'm taking her offer and enjoying the free drinks," Marco said and picked up two drinks from the waitress serving the crowd.

"Have fun like there is no tomorrow because there might not be one for Anonymous after tonight," Willy said, also picking up two glasses.

"Drink as much as you can handle. Todd is unpredictable. We have to exit together without an incident," Nour said.

"By the way, I don't see Todd," Sophie said.

"Todd right now is sitting in his room surrounded by a bunch of powerful white men. As we speak, he is humiliating Jeff, standing behind him, pouring everyone drinks. Jeff is serving a Dalmore 62 and is lighting up King of Denmark cigars, which Todd saves for these events."

"Can you see them?" Isabelle looked around.

"No, but I know Todd." Ryan took a deep breath and looked at Mark. "Is the press release ready?"

"Yes," Mark replied.

"Run it."

"Now? Are you sure?" Mark asked.

"Yes, now!" Ryan turned toward Kate. "Are you ready?"

"Like never before." She smiled.

Ryan gripped her trembling hand and walked toward Todd's office. He grasped the door handle to Todd's room and looked at Kate. She was still trembling and gasping for air. Ryan gently pressed her hand. She took a deep breath and nodded. He turned the handle and opened the door. Kate walked in first, followed by Ryan.

The contrast of the room against the rest of the office was jarring. It was the only room without the music blasting and the one place that resembled an office. The only outside sound was the muffled fireworks exploding behind Todd's window. Todd was laughing, sitting at his desk with Jeff standing behind him, pouring a drink from a bottle of a Dalmore 62. Smoke and the stench of tobacco filled the room. Around five men were facing Todd, all around mid-sixties smoking King of Denmark cigars, all white. All seemed powerful.

"Hey guys, you can't come in here." Jeff shouted.

The obnoxious laughter died down, and the room gradually turned silent as if someone had lowered the volume on a TV. The men turned around and looked at Kate and Ryan. It was apparent their presence had taken everyone by surprise.

"Shut up, Jeff, they're family." Todd smiled and leaned back in his chair. "Gentlemen, these are my protégés. They worked for Sun in the past and will soon be working again."

Ryan could feel Todd's dominating demeanor overpowering him. He was at a loss for words. His palms started sweating, and he feared his voice would crackle if he spoke. He could hear his heart beating at breakneck speed. *This is a mistake,* he thought. The silence was becoming awkward.

"Thank you for inviting us, Todd," Kate almost whispered. Her voice trembled more than her hands.

"I didn't invite you." Todd sounded genuinely surprised. Kate and Ryan looked at Jeff. His smile got wider.

"Good evening, I'm Kate." She seemed intimidated and tried to cover her nervousness with a smile.

"Yes, Kate came from a leading agency to Sun. She's an award-winning creative director, extremely talented." Ryan could tell Todd was trying hard to be charming, perturbed at their presence. "Too bad she couldn't handle our difficult clients, and we had to fire her."

"Not fire, Todd." Kate smiled, quick to interrupt. "You demoted me, gave me clients no one wanted."

"Nothing personal, Kate." Todd's smile was shrinking, "I'm a stickler for quality, and your work was just not at par with our standards." His smile disappeared. The only person smiling in the room was Jeff.

"And Ryan here, I'm sure you've heard about him. Was good while he lasted, then he thought he could fly and landed on his back. Couldn't walk, couldn't stand, couldn't even speak. I felt sorry for him, so I offered him a job as a copywriter."

Ryan felt his legs weakening. He wanted to sit down just to get back in control. This was a bad idea. *Think, think, think,* he scolded himself three more times.

"He wasn't good," Kate said, sensing Ryan was losing control. "He was great. He helped Sun rise to the top."

"No one got Sun where it stands today except me." Todd lashed out, "People like you are like books I check out from the library. I can return them any time. If the book is kept a little longer, like Ryan, I can always pay a late fee." He was fuming in rage, saliva dripping down from the side of his mouth. A few men started to get up and leave.

"Sit!" he said, and looked at them. "This meeting is over. Enjoy your free drinks and fuck off!"

Jeff moved forward, the smile still plastered on his face.

"Ryan," Kate whispered and looked at Ryan.

Ryan couldn't move. His feet were stuck to the ground. His mouth felt dry. *Come on, get a grip,* he whispered in his head, afraid someone would hear his thoughts.

"Ryan is mentally fucked," Todd said. "He was always the weak link, carried by his juniors like Gina. He can't speak for himself and wants a woman to speak for him."

"He is still ten times the man you'll ever be," Kate said.

"Funny coming from a slut who slept around with a hundred men to make her career. Her illustrious career started when she got drunk, got fucked by three boys, and then advertised the whole scenario," Todd said.

The guests were getting restless, looking for a way to leave the room.

Jeff finally spoke, "The audacity to compare Ryan with Todd. Todd has the most successful ad agency, hundreds of employees willing to give their life for him, millions in revenue. Ryan has nothing."

"I have the tapes!" Ryan felt a rush of energy as he spoke in a loud whisper.

"What? Speak up. Stand up for yourself, do you need a fucking cane?" Todd mocked in a booming voice.

"I have the tapes." Ryan lied and decided to play his bluff. Pitches were like poker games; it was the confidence that wins you the bluff. He straightened his spine, corrected his posture and gathered his strength. He stepped forward, feeling the strength building up in his legs.

"You know the same tapes you used to blackmail your clients to get their business." He finally managed to look Todd straight in the eyes.

He was interrupted by Gina walking in. She had an iPad in her hand and took it straight to Todd. His face turned pale as he looked at the screen.

"Out! everyone, leave the room!" He shouted.

The men looked at each other, got up, and walked out.

"Oh, we're not finished yet." Ryan was in control. He knew the press release had done its job.

"What the fuck is this?" Todd turned the iPad toward them.

"That is the Sun going down." Kate smiled.

Jeff was frantically scrolling through the iPad.

"It's a fucking lie." Todd shouted, "Call David and check!" He looked at Jeff.

"I tried. No one is picking up," Gina said nervously.

"Call again!" Todd yelled and started calling himself. Finally, he threw his phone at Jeff. "You fucking idiot, stop this. I don't care how." Todd yelled at Ryan. "I'm going to destroy you. I'll get the best lawyers in town, and I'll fuck your next ten generations."

Ryan moved forward and poured himself a drink. "I'll take your free drink offer now. Even though it's not free, my clients are paying for it."

Ryan gulped the drink and felt his voice breaking the chains holding him back, "After I'm done with you, it's unlikely, but if you're ever able to sue me, I'll be happy to send a reply to your new office in Brooklyn."

"What the fuck are you talking about?"

"I also have the eviction notice from your new landlord."

Ryan threw the papers on Todd's desk. Jeff picked it up and scrolled through the documents.

"That's impossible. It says you own Elysium?"

"Yes, I do, along with your balls. Gina showed you the tip of the iceberg on your iPad." Ryan handed him the contracts. "These are the Big Five contracts. All five have signed up Anonymous as their agency and have sent termination letters to you."

"What do you want?" Todd could barely speak as he looked at the signatures on the contracts.

"I want to see you suffer. I want you to prepare for what's coming. I want you never to poke a wounded lion again." Ryan gulped his drink. The wall that blocked Ryan from reading Todd was disappearing. He could sense the panic exploding inside Todd's head. "And if you do, the evil you did will be trending on every social media tomorrow."

Todd held on to the contracts and stared at Ryan. The outside noise was dropping along with Todd's shoulders. The excruciating silence continued.

"We can work this out, Ryan." Todd was no longer screaming. "You've made your point. You've won. Now let's find a way where everybody wins. Global creative director? Partnership? Money? Name your price."

Ryan moved closer to Todd. For the first time in his life, he could read Todd clearly. The wavering eyes, the twitching fingers, the shifty hands, the itching forehead, and the sweat appearing on his face, his body and demeanor were singing like a canary. Ryan could read Todd was now thinking about his escape plan. Todd was groveling. His anger had subsided. He was no longer the dominating emperor of the advertising world. Instead, he suddenly looked like an old man holding his hand out for spare change.

"There is one thing you can do."

"What? Ask for anything, and it's yours." Todd wiped his sweat off his face.

"You walk out tonight and never return to Sun."

"So, you want to take over the one thing I sacrificed everything for. I built this fucking company with my blood, sweat, and tears." Todd no longer appeared to be in control. He was looking for a lifeline, one of the rare occasions when he was cornered and had no idea how to get out.

"Not with your blood, sweat, and tears, Todd. The blood, sweat, and tears came from people like Kate's grandfather. I don't want Sun. I want you to realize what you did was wrong. I want you to suffer. I want you to die of shame and regret."

"Who's Kate's grandfather?" Todd asked.

"Henry Raymond. He jumped from the 50th floor because of you," Kate said.

"Yeah, I remember him. Your grandfather didn't jump. He wanted to fly. I just nudged him in the right direction," Todd whispered. Ryan could tell Todd had given up. He knew he had lost.

"And that's why the world has to know about the tapes," Ryan said.

"You're bluffing. You don't have those tapes." Todd was trying to claw his way out, grasping at straws.

"Let's just say there is a reason I don't want Sun. I want you to hand over the reins to Jeff."

Todd looked at Jeff. "You fucking moron, I knew you were useless, but I never knew you would stab me in the back. Is he bluffing? Say something. Open your fucking mouth," Todd roared.

Jeff looked at Ryan. They all saw Jeff's smile disappear for the first time. "Yes, they have the tapes."

"You bastard." Todd threw his glass at Jeff.

"I also told Ryan that you pushed him. You wanted him dead." Jeff's smile was back.

"Yes, I fucking pushed him." Todd looked at Ryan. "You should've died that night. You deserve to die like a dog, and I'll make sure you do, along with this bitch."

"So what was on the tapes, Todd? What made my grandfather kill himself?" Kate said.

"Oh, you would've enjoyed the tapes. Your grandfather loved getting fucked by me. And not just him, many powerful men in New York too. The clients you think you've won, they will come crawling back to me because of those tapes. As I said earlier, your grandfather didn't jump. I pushed him."

"Stop talking, Todd!" Gina rushed forward. "Everything you're saying is streaming live on the internet."

Todd pulled Gina's phone. Ryan was surprised. This was not part of the plan. He opened up his Facebook account. A video was streaming on his timeline. They were live, with the camera focused on Todd. The constantly climbing viewership was in the thousands. The account streaming the live video belonged to Kate. Ryan looked at her. She was no longer smiling.

Todd was trembling in anger. His hand firmly gripped the table, his nails digging into the mahogany wood.

"Stop this, right now!" his barely audible words came out.

"This wasn't part of the plan, but I'm not sorry it happened," Ryan said. "This is perhaps my shortest meeting with you, boss, but this has been the most enjoyable one."

The sound of fireworks once again shattered the cold and savage silence and lit up the quiet room with loud booms.

"I have something for you too, Gina." Ryan took out the last envelope. "This is the Sphinx contract." He handed it over to Gina. "By the way, the campaigns you were raving about and wanted me to learn from, guess who was behind those?"

Gina was silent, tears slowly dripping down her eyes.

"Get out." Todd's voice was like a kid shrieking in pain, "Everyone, get out! I don't want anyone here."

Gina wiped her tears as she rushed out before anyone else could.

"One last thing, Todd." Ryan lofted the cane Todd gave him toward Jeff. "I don't need this anymore."

Ryan exhaled the moment he stepped out and heard the door being shut behind him. The Anonymous team swiftly gathered around them, looking eagerly at Ryan and Kate to announce the verdict.

"How was it?" Nour asked.

Ryan looked at Kate and smiled. "It was beautiful, worthy of its place in poetry books and art galleries."

The team rushed forward to embrace them. Ryan noticed the guests at the party staring at them, holding their phones, whispering to each other. It seemed they had watched Kate's live stream.

They started walking toward the exit. Ryan saw Jeff standing at the bar, having a drink alone. Jeff raised the glass to him and nodded. Ryan smiled and nodded back as they exited the hall. The team was dying to hear what happened, and they wanted details. Ryan saw a well-dressed man in his mid-fifties approach Nour.

"Are you Anonymous?"

Nour nodded.

"I just read the press release. Here is my card. Call me."

"Which company?" Nour yelled as he walked away in the deafening music.

"Pepsi," he shouted back.

Ryan felt an uneasiness creeping up his spine. *Everything seemed too easy,* he thought. The final read before exiting the room was that Todd had decided to do something terrible. He was used to having the last word. The problem was Ryan couldn't read Todd's next move. The only thing he was certain of was that it was something sinister. They had to get out of the building fast. They split for the elevators. Ryan told Kate to hold on to the details until everyone was safely outside.

The Anonymous team converged outside Elysium. Marco Isabelle and Sophie were excited to swipe a bottle of Dom Pérignon and glasses from the bar.

"We need a selfie. We have to immortalize this moment." Laura shouted, the exploding fireworks drowning her excited voice.

"Laura wants a photograph," Marco screamed and finally got everyone's attention.

"No matter what happens tomorrow, this will be one photo we will never forget for the rest of our lives," Kate said.

They gathered around Laura, embracing each other, trying to fit in the frame. Ryan moved his arms around Kate and pulled her closer. With the other arm, he pulled Willy closer to him. A photographer walked over to them and offered to help.

Another photographer joined in a few seconds later. "Are you guys from Anonymous?"

"Hey, that's the team from Anonymous!" Another photographer said loudly.

"It's them!" someone shouted.

Everyone had seen the press release and wanted to know more

about Anonymous. Within no time, photographers and journalists swarmed them. They were shouting questions Ryan could hardly hear. The only audible sounds were coming from the fireworks and the clicking of the cameras as the flashes blinded the Anonymous team. The crowd of photographers and journalists kept on growing till there was hardly any space to fit in more.

Suddenly the fireworks stopped along with the shuttering of the cameras. A sudden silence engulfed the Elysium entrance for a few seconds. A huge thud shattered the void. Kate felt a splash of warm liquid splattering her face. Everyone tried to grapple with the sound wondering where the thud came from.

A shrieking scream brought chills down their spine. The cry gained momentum as others joined in. Ryan stared at the red splatter on his white shirt and wiped off the warm wetness on his face with his arm. He looked toward a group of people moving away from the source of the thud. A naked body of a man covered in blood was lying face down on the sidewalk.

More people gathered around the shattered body, the terror on their faces telling the story. Ryan slowly moved forward, praying his reading was wrong. He bent down and turned the face toward himself. It was barely recognizable except for the scar on the forehead. His worst nightmare came true as he jumped back.

Ryan looked around for answers and saw faces in shock staring at Todd's body. He looked at the stunned faces of his team and felt Kate's hand grasping his. She tugged him to walk away from the startled public. Ryan's lifeless body followed her lead. He looked back one last time at the crowd trying to make sense of it all. He could see their faces silently screaming as he drifted further away.

He turned and finally looked at Kate. She was smiling as if it was the most tranquil sound she had heard in decades.

About the Author

Neil Peter Christy has two chapters in his life. He dropped out of engineering college to pursue his career in advertising. Within a year, he moved to Ogilvy as a copywriter. Ten years later, he started his advertising agency called Head Lion.

A few awards and ten years later, he began his second chapter. He moved to America, leaving behind a successful life in Karachi. Neil worked as a communication specialist, drove Uber, completed two degrees, including his Master's degree in communication from George Mason University, and wrote his first novel.

Neil lives in the Washington DC Metro area with his beautiful wife, four talented children, and a loving mother. He is currently writing the third chapter of his life.

To follow everything current, join Neil's newsletter. You can also become a beta reader for his next novel.

Email: neil@headliongroup.com | Web: neilpeterchristy.com

Instagram: neilpeterchristy

Acknowledgments

To Kodie Van Dusen and Big Cheese Books for chiseling, polishing, and making the diamond shine. Thank you for your editorial support and commitment to championing self-published authors. My goal was to get Ryan in bookstores. Your contribution ensures his revenge earns its place *"...in poetry books and art galleries."*

To my Kapellmeisters, my beta readers.

Dr. Catherine Wright, O Captain! My Captain! The suggestions you gave have genuinely made the book stronger.

Debbie Joy, the first critic. Thank you for making me look better.

Irfan Malik, the first believer, the one who said to keep walking.

To Laraib Rabbani, the Guru of the digital world.

———

To Tin Tin, the one who stood with me through thick and thin and passed the test of time with flying colors.

To the best-looking nephews and nieces, Joshua, Zack, Sascha, Ivana, Sinead, and Seth, and the source of those genes, Patrick and Shahid. To Derick, who has always been there for us.

And lastly, to everyone at Head Lion, the ones who believed in me and the few morons who didn't, there is a part of you scattered across this book.

Afterword

I hope you enjoyed Head Lion. This is my first book, and I can't thank you enough for supporting me by reading it. I'm genuinely grateful for the time and effort you gave.

Your reviews allow me to get the validation I need to keep going as an author. My promise to you is to continuously improve as a writer and ensure that my next book is always better than the previous one. I love making new friends. Drop me an email and I will reply.

Yours, Neil Peter Christy

P.S. If, for some reason, you didn't like this book or found typos or other errors, please let me know personally. I do my best to read and respond to every email at neil@headliongroup.com

Made in the USA
Middletown, DE
20 September 2022